TRUTH

ON THE

BRINK

TRUTH ON THE BRINK

a novel

W. D. McCOMB

TreaShore
PRESS

TRUTH ON THE BRINK

wdmccomb.com

All rights reserved. Published by TreaShore Press.

ISBN 979-8-9903578-2-2 (hardcover)
ISBN: 979-8-9903578-1-5 (paperback)
ISBN: 979-8-9903578-0-8 (ebook)
First edition.

Printed in the United States of America

ACKNOWLEDGEMENTS

Thank you to my wife and children for inspiring me on the front end of my writing projects and putting up with me during them. I know I get preoccupied, but I could not do it without your support. You mean everything to me.

Huge thanks to my mom for always being my first reader, most reluctant critic, and biggest fan. To my dad, aka Coach, for his inspiration and impact. And to my sister, an avid reader who is always willing to move my books to the top of her queue and give me feedback.

The best stories should evoke a sense of place, and I hope Amberton and its characters accomplish that. They are born of the Mississippi places I call home and the people I call friends within them. Thank you all for having me.

The **CASE FOR TRUTH** Series
W. D. McComb

THE RECRUIT *– a short story*

Novels
Book 1 - THE TRUTH THAT LIES BETWEEN
Book 2 - ANATOMY OF THE TRUTH
Book 3 - TRUTH ON THE BRINK

PART ONE

We walked to the brink
and we looked it in the face.
—John Foster Dulles

ONE

Friday, October 26, 2018

PLUMES of vapor erupted around the bars of the players' face masks with each exhalation, dissipating quickly into the cold November night while their shoulder pads rose and fell with their gasping heaves. I hoped my guys in Amberton scarlet and gray recognized the burn in their chests as an asset, a thing that had tortured them during hot summer two-a-day practices but spurred them now, *drove* them, because they knew they were prepared to push through the pain and find a way to win.

My name is Case Reynolds, and I am a football coach. My job is to motivate, to teach impressionable teenagers how to exceed what they believe to be possible. To hate failure more than they love success, and, to that end, to never quit, never give up, no matter how insurmountable the obstacle seems to be.

Still, it would be a lie to say doubts had never plagued my thoughts as an abysmal season for my Amberton Cougars had worn on. Murphy's Law had prevailed for much of it, and here we were with the game on the line in its waning seconds against the Haughton County Mustangs. Coming up short in similar situations had been the rule rather than the exception for much of the season, but in Mississippi on fall Friday nights, especially against your cross-county archrival in the last game of the season, the only rule that matters is that of the victor.

And at that moment, as my team lined up across the football

from their enemy in white and blue, I believed we would find a way. And the look in the eyes of my players said they still believed too.

"One more play!" Devlin James, my senior defensive captain, urged his teammates on as he lined them up for the next play. *One more play.* I had made them recite the words a hundred times before, just for moments like this, when they were on the brink of exhaustion after three hours of battle on the football field. Give maximum effort just once more and then ask for a breather.

Of course, my leaders like Devlin never asked for a breather. He pounded his chest once with the thumb side of his fist and stared across the line of scrimmage at his archrivals—not just fellow players from the other side of the county, but real bona fide enemies, as far as he was concerned. His speech in the huddle during the timeout had been compelling to say the least. *This* was the reason he endured the pain of practice. *This* was what he lived for—a Friday night with the game on the line, the crowd in a frenzy, and the difference between winning and losing now hinging on their sheer will more than pure talent.

"Rocky! Rocky! Rocky!" Coach Kinkade, my defensive coordinator, shouted the coverage call as Haughton's receivers across from him trotted into their positions.

Devlin echoed the call for his teammates and pointed at the outside receiver on the opposite side. "J-rock, watch 82 on the fade! Watch the fade!"

Devlin's warning had merit. Even though number 82 had not done much damage so far other than blocking like a fiend and talking a lot of trash to Devlin in particular, he was tall and thick and athletic, and our scouting report was that he could be dangerous.

I was more worried about number 22, though, a kid who had terrorized my Amberton defense all night, his efforts accounting for much of the reason Devlin and my other defensive backs could barely breathe. They must have run at least five miles chasing him up and down the field. No matter what happened now, they wouldn't have to chase much longer.

It was the fourth quarter, only 27 seconds left on the clock, and to win the game my team needed only to prevent Haughton from scoring on fourth down and goal to go. *One more play.* "One more play!" I shouted for the last time of the season.

At the snap, the Haughton quarterback faked a handoff to the running back to his left and rolled right. Number 22 and the inside receiver surged forward and pivoted, angling toward the middle of the field, their movements synchronized as if each were a shadow of the other. Just as he had been coached, Devlin stayed with 22 and let the safety take the inside guy. Suddenly, 22 planted his right foot and cut toward to the corner of the end zone, and my heart sank even though Devlin had swiveled a split second earlier as if he had guessed the route.

Even with the head start, Devlin was a step behind. His legs churned, straining to make up any modicum of the distance separating him from Haughton's star. Still, in that instant I had no doubt we were going to find a way to win the game. No doubt, that is, until I saw the ball arc upward with a graceful tilt, spiral to its apex, then nose down precisely toward its target. A heat-seeking missile homing in on the hottest player on the field, running behind my gutsy—but much slower—defensive captain. Devlin's effort was valiant, but it would not be enough.

But that's the beauty of sports, isn't it? The foundation of the miracle that more coaches don't keel over and die in the middle of the field. The reason that players play. The fuel that spectators crave like air and water. That yo-yo of emotions from despair to confidence to sudden dejection to absolute elation within a matter of seconds.

At the last second, Devlin leaped like I had never seen before, straining to stretch his five-foot-nine frame beyond its natural capabilities. It could not have been more than a fingernail, only a few millimeters of keratin interjected between the ball and the fingertips of the sure-handed receiver. But somehow Devlin managed to break up the pass and send the ball careening harmlessly out of the end zone.

Either the throw wasn't as perfect as I had first thought, their player faltered just a bit, or one extra gasser in some forgotten practice had helped Devlin summon one final burst of speed. Or perhaps a brief gust of wind on an otherwise still night slowed the flight of the ball. Whatever it was, Devlin somehow made up a step and saved the game.

Number 22 stopped, motionless, his hands frozen in position for the ball that was never going to settle within them. Devlin landed in a heap with arms and legs flailing wildly in celebration even as he was colliding with the ground. Coach Kinkade practically tackled me as chaos erupted, with players darting and jumping and screaming in every direction in a blur of scarlet and gray, the bulk of which was streaming like a Halley's comet toward the corner of the end zone where Devlin had risen to begin a triumphant race to the sideline for high fives and chest bumps.

I pointed toward the clock with urgent jabs, reminding my frenzied team that our offense still had to run one more play to run out the clock. "Offense, offense!" I screamed, grabbing my quarterback by his face mask to tell him how to run the final play as my coaches ushered the remainder of the celebrating players off the field.

Then suddenly something changed. A hush of the crowd followed by a collective gasp. Then shouting again—a different kind of shout, the timbre of which told me before I even looked that this victory would somehow be bittersweet.

Both sidelines suddenly cleared in a swarm of scarlet and gray and white and blue. I ran onto the field myself, yelling at my players to get back without knowing the source of their motivation. Then I saw it: Number 82 for Haughton straddling one of my boys, on the ground near the ten-yard line, punching him mercilessly. My first instinct was to rescue my player, but his teammates beat me to it. Number 82 was promptly taken out by the lowered shoulder of Luke Wiseman, one of my linebackers, who was immediately engulfed by two other Haughton jerseys, and the melee was on.

A Haughton player swung his royal blue helmet and slammed it into the lower back of one of mine, who howled in pain before turning to rock his attacker with a vicious forearm to the jaw. One player took another in a headlock, pounding him relentlessly despite a teammate of his victim trying futilely to dissuade him with halfhearted punches of his own. My backup kicker, the smallest player on my team, jumped around amid the fray swinging at anyone and everyone in a white jersey until one of them sent him to his knees with a fist to the gut. A giant Haughton lineman marched confidently through the chaos, slinging some of my players around like last Christmas's discarded toys.

I scanned for a law enforcement officer but found none. Jack Masterson, one of my two best friends and the deputy sheriff who provided security for our games, was out of town, and I didn't have time to wonder why he didn't have a replacement.

Both the Amberton and Haughton coaching staffs struggled for ten minutes to separate the two teams.

Like trying to control sharks in a feeding frenzy, the effort seemed futile at first. No sooner could I grab a player and sling him toward the sideline than he would race ten yards down the field and enter the fracas again, fists swinging and blood in his eyes. "Get off the field, NOW!" I screamed at a trio of my players lingering at the periphery and pretending they wanted to join in but obviously thinking better of it. "I'm not gonna tell you again," I yelled in every ear I could find, "or I'll have you expelled!"

The ferocity of our yells, the loss of willpower as adrenalin became depleted and some realized they weren't even sure why they were fighting, and those threats of expulsions—even though I didn't have the authority to enforce them if I'd wanted to—seemed to turn the tide.

"Coach Reynolds!" I turned to see what Coach Kincade wanted. "Look!" He pointed to where it all had begun. "I think it's Devlin."

The fighting had stopped, and a small cohort of players from both teams were beginning to take a knee around a player lying motionless on the ground. The crowd, seemingly near a boiling point only seconds before, almost instantly cooled to a low rumble as they collectively realized the fighting had stopped and someone might even be seriously injured. "Get Dr. Townsend out there!" I said to everyone in earshot, "and don't move from your spot if you want to live to see tomorrow!"

Dr. Gracie Townsend was already on her knees at Devlin James's side by the time I got to him. She pulled a misplaced strand of auburn hair back over an ear and leaned over, face-to-face with him. One hand moved up and down the back of his neck while the other held his chin. One of the players kneeling nearby held his helmet. "Should've known I'd beat you out here, Coach," she said without looking up. "Always do." Before I had a chance to respond she spoke again. "Okay, Devlin, so you're telling me you have absolutely no pain when I press back here on your neck?"

I realized Devlin was awake; he just wasn't moving. "I'm here, Devlin." I dropped to a knee beside him, across from the doctor. "You're gonna be okay."

"He knows, Coach," Gracie said, hands still in position on his neck and chin. "No pain here?"

"No, ma'am." Devlin gave a weak shake of his head.

"Hang on, don't move your head yet," Gracie cautioned. "Now I need to know if you can wiggle your toes." His left foot moved, then his right, up and down, then side to side.

I sighed in relief but held my next breath while she continued her examination. "Okay, what about your hands?" Devlin promptly moved the fingers of both hands, then flexed his wrists and elbows. "Great!" she said with a reassuring smile.

"What happened?" Devlin asked, glazed eyes searching back and forth between Gracie and me.

"We'll get to that later," Gracie said. "Got to get you checked out first." She performed a few other maneuvers on his neck then gingerly examined his face with her fingers. "Not bad considering you were out cold like you were. Thought your face might be caved in from the way that guy was punching you. You may not even have a bad bruise."

"Punching me?" Devlin said. "Who?"

"Number 82," I said. "I know numbers, not names."

Devlin's eyes widened in surprise. "It can't be," he said. "I'll kill him!"

"You know him?" Gracie asked.

"I'll kill that sucker!" He tried to sit up.

I held him down with a firm hand to his shoulder pad. "Dev, settle down now. You know the guy?"

"Know him? He's my best friend."

TWO

GRACIE stepped into the emergency department exam room and crossed her legs as she sat in one of the two vinyl chairs against the wall. Her name and credentials were neatly monogrammed above the pocket of her long white coat: *Gracie T. Townsend, MD, Family Medicine.* She wasn't officially on duty and certainly didn't have to dress up for us, but Gracie was old school in some ways. If a person was going to perform as a doctor, then they should most certainly dress like one.

"What do you think, Doc?" Devlin's voice was much stronger now than it had been earlier on the field. "Can I go home?"

Devlin's mother patted his arm in a soft scold. "We're not worried about going home. We're worried about you being healthy." She brought her hands together and wrung them nervously as her eyes darted back and forth between Devlin and the vital signs displayed on the monitor above his bed. Tammy James was a few years younger than me, so we had never been close, but I had known her since we were kids. She had always struck me as a bit high-strung, but in an endearing way more than an unpleasant one. She was a good mother as far as I knew, and I hoped Gracie was about to allay her fears.

"He's going to be fine," Gracie said. "The CT scan was negative. No bleed, no facial fractures." She stood and walked to Devlin's side then gently leaned over him to examine his face and head as she spoke. "You'll be fine, Devlin. In fact, I might not even have done the CT if you hadn't been knocked out. Looks like you may have a black eye there, but generally, you came out pretty good considering how that guy was pounding on you."

"He came of nowhere." Devlin smiled and flexed a bicep. "But I'm a man o' steel, so it's alright. I did save the game, you know." He proceeded to replay the last play of the game in intricate detail, sharing his thoughts as the play ensued, embellishing his performance where he could, right up to the climactic pass breakup that did, in fact, save the game.

"I hear ya, big boy." I grabbed his foot and shook it playfully. "Number 82 must have had some kryptonite in his fists, then. What'd you say his name was?"

"Ronny Shane." Tammy James had a note of disgust in her tone. "Used to be like a son to me."

"Used to be?" Gracie stepped back and crossed her arms. "I heard Devlin say they're best friends."

"It's … complicated," Devlin mumbled, looking at his mother.

"*Were* best friends," Tammy said. "Were. Ronny and Devlin grew up together. Same church, preschool, kindergarten, same school through sixth grade. Then Ronny started going to Haughton. I think he and Devlin stayed pretty close though, playing summer baseball together, stuff like that. But the last year or so things changed."

"Changed?" I said.

Devlin shrugged and shook his head.

"Changed, as in Ronny started doing drugs." Tammy's voice dripped with contempt now.

"You don't know that!" Devlin glared at his mother, his voice suddenly decibels stronger. "Can you just leave it alone?"

Tammy clenched her jaw and turned her head abruptly away from Devlin. "His brother Buster got outta prison. I hear he's a meth head or something. Devlin won't say so, but I know for a fact he and Ronny had some kind of falling out. And Ronny looks like he's lost weight to me."

Devlin gave an eye roll and shook his head as he took an exasperated breath then blinked heavily, a look that said he wanted to drop the conversation but intended to take it back up vigorously with his mother later. I didn't know if Ronny Shane was on drugs or not, and frankly I didn't really care unless it was going to lead to more violence between him and Devlin, or any other student at my school, for that matter.

"Okay," I said. "Drugs or no drugs—Devlin, why do you think Ronny did what he did? Were y'all talking trash during the game or something?"

He shrugged. "Yeah, we did some talking. He blindsided me, but I'll get him."

"I suggest you leave well enough alone," Gracie said. "But the good news is that you're fine. I know you wanted the football season to go a bit longer, but I'm looking forward to seeing you for one more season on the basketball court." She held up a finger and pointed it at Devlin. "But—but—you do have a concussion. So, you can't go full speed in practice yet. I'll send your coaches my concussion protocol and have the school trainer keep an eye on you."

"Alright, Dev, you have your orders," I said. "Now on another subject, you know what *I'm* looking forward to?"

Devlin frowned, trying to decide whether I was serious or not. "What?" he said.

"I'm looking forward to telling Jack about what happened and seeing the look on his face." Devlin grimaced as I smiled and continued. "He'll have you taking jiujitsu lessons or something."

Devlin's reply was interrupted by a loud knock at the door as it swung open.

"Speak of the devil," Gracie said.

Jack Masterson was my oldest friend in the world. We had shared many good times over the years but had also found more ways to get in trouble than I cared to remember. I thought of the description of Devlin and Ronny growing up together, how familiar their childhood relationship sounded to me. And how that made whatever happened between them even more tragic.

"About time you got here." I walked to Jack and patted him on the shoulder as I sized him up. Flannel shirt, green-and-brown-stained jeans, muddy work boots that made him look two inches taller than me instead of just one. "You been mud wrestling river bottom hogs instead of doing your civic duty and watching your man play?"

Jack had a fondness for hog hunting that I never shared, but I knew he had been out of town for work. In addition to being a part-time deputy for the sheriff's department, he owned a landscaping company. He liked the former better, but the latter paid the bills.

Jack shoved me away and accepted a side hug from Tammy. "Very funny. Wish I coulda been there tonight. Sounds like you needed me. Had to work this contract, though, before rain hits again. Laying sod for a Pizza King down in Yazoo and just rolled back in." He nodded at Devlin. "How are you, boy?"

Jack and Tammy had been dating for the better part of the past three years. They had met at church. He was a twice-divorced man disgusted with the idea of romance and struggling to keep up with Janie, his wild, teenage niece he had adopted after her parents died. Tammy was a former addict with depression constantly nipping at her heels, looking for hope and some positive influences for Devlin, her middle school son. Sunday school acquaintances had become weekend friends and, eventually, more than that. I had long since given up wondering whether they would get married, and I certainly didn't push it.

Whatever the eventual outcome of Jack and Tammy's relationship, he had been good for Devlin, who as best I could tell had been a bit lost until Jack came into the picture. Devlin's father had run off when he was just a toddler, and because Jack had lost his father in similar tragic fashion as a baby and then his stepfather when he was fourteen, Jack had a soft spot for Devlin right from the start. In many ways they were perfect for each other.

Gracie patted Devlin on the leg. "He's fine," she said. "A little concussion but nothing major. I was about to go fill out his discharge paperwork. He'll be home before bedtime."

Jack crossed his arms over his chest and eyed Devlin with a serious look. "So Ronny worked you over pretty good?" I knew where this was going. Jack wasn't a violent person by any stretch of the imagination, but he was tough and expected toughness from those he cared about. I had thought many times over the years how I never wanted to fight him, and thankfully none of our countless disagreements had ever come to blows.

"Naw, Jack." I winked at Devlin. "Shane caught him by surprise, but Devlin gave him all he wanted. That boy is probably in an ER somewhere himself. What you really missed was Devlin saving the game. Made one heck of a play. He'll have to tell you about it." I smiled at Devlin. "And I'm quite certain he will. He's already given us the play-by-play several times."

Gracie waved a goodbye, mentioned that she had some

charting to do, and headed toward the door. Jack grabbed her by the arm as she passed. "Hey girl, not gonna speak?"

Gracie smiled. "Sorry, Jack, been a long day." She patted him on the cheek. "You may be ignored but will never be forgotten."

"Where's your old man?" Jack said. "Putting in a robotic heart or something somewhere?"

Gracie curled her top lip and feigned a frown at Jack. "You know good and well Jet's not putting in a heart, silly. That's cardiovascular surgeons, not cardiologists. And to answer your question, he is in the cath lab. Heart attack came in a while ago."

Gracie's husband, Jet Townsend, was my second oldest friend. They had met in medical school and hit it off, and somehow Jet had convinced her to settle back in his hometown. Jet was known for two things: his name being something of an oxymoron (his initials were J.E.T, and he was anything but fast), and his superior intellect. I personally thought Jet should be running Harvard's medical school or something, but he never considered anything other than coming back home. I could relate to that part myself.

All three of us had left for a time but had been drawn back home for reasons none could adequately explain. I speculated I had written so much about Amberton that I couldn't function anywhere else. Jet had described the reason as "indelible connections to our parent town like ornithological imprints," which required considerable contemplation on my part and led to nary an attempt to understand by Jack, who succinctly nailed it by saying he moved back home because "it just felt right."

Still, there was some reason for surprise, as it wasn't like every moment had been idyllic. Quite the contrary, in fact. Jack would forever battle the demons of abuse from his stepfather

Stone and the events surrounding the man's death. Jet had never fully recovered—physically or mentally—from the automobile attack by our childhood nemesis VJ MacIntosh. Who knew if the fact that VJ had been dead for nearly twenty years made it any better? And I had nearly been killed in this very town a time or two myself.

The fact was, we could empathize with one another like few friends could. Whatever the magnet that brought us back to Amberton, perhaps that was the glue that now held us here.

Jack returned Gracie's fake frown with a huge smile. "Well, if I don't see Jet before we leave, tell him again I said he married up."

Gracie rolled her eyes and grabbed the door handle. "Y'all should be out of here in about ten minutes. Just got to sign a few forms, and the nurse will come check him out."

"Thank you, Gracie," Tammy said. She glared at her son and cocked her head. "Devlin?"

"Thanks, Doc," Devlin said. "My first dunk this year is for you."

Gracie raised one eyebrow. "Can you really dunk a basketball? I know you knocked down that pass, but I didn't see you as a Michael Jordan type."

Devlin grinned roguishly. "Jordan is history. I'm more of a Lebron. But no, I haven't unleashed my dunking fury yet. That's what will make the first one all the more special."

Gracie burst out laughing and turned to leave, but the laugh faltered as she almost bumped into a girl standing in the doorway. I wondered how long she had been standing there. "Excuse me," Gracie said as she stepped around her.

The girl stepped into the room, silent, her eyes locked on Devlin. She was petite, barely more than five feet tall with straight, blonde, shoulder-length hair supporting an oversized blue-and-white bow. A round button of a nose and thin lips matched her small stature. Her eyes were striking though, not in their dull brown color nor generous size, but in their intensity—she eyed Devlin with a focus that was both captivating and disconcerting. A Haughton Mustangs sweatshirt caught my attention almost as quickly as her eyes, and I realized the reason for the big bow: She must be a cheerleader.

"Hey Lena," Devlin said softly as he sat up on the edge of the bed. "Guess you saw what happened."

"Sort of." The girl named Lena eased closer to him and examined his bruises, not unlike the way Gracie had. "It was over before I knew what was going on. I just can't believe it."

"Son, are you going to introduce your friend?" Tammy asked.

I shot Jack a look and got a shrug in return. He didn't know who she was, either.

"I can tell you who she is," a different voice answered instead.

I turned to see Luke Wiseman standing at the door. Luke was one of my linebackers and was as tough as a bodock fence post. From what I could tell, he and Devlin were tight. They usually sat together on the bus on road trips and had been punished with gator crawls on at least one occasion for showing up late together for practice. From the scowl on Luke's face, I gathered that perhaps he and his friend had differing opinions of Lena, whoever she was.

"Luke, it's okay," Devlin said. "She's just checking on me."

Devlin's mother huffed and walked around the bed, extending her hand to Lena. "I'm Tammy James," she said. "You are Lena..."

The girl nodded. "Cole. I've heard a lot about you. It's nice to finally meet you."

Tammy gave a stiff smile and introduced Jack and me. "And I take it you know Luke?"

"Mom," Devlin said.

Luke huffed. "Let me tell you who she is."

"Leave it alone, Luke," Devlin said.

"I won't leave it alone. I'll tell y'all who Lena is. She's Ronny Shane's girlfriend. And she can go tell him I'm coming for him."

THREE

Saturday, October 27, 2018

FLIP *them when they bubble in the middle.* Armed with a spatula, I hovered over the pancake-filled skillet, replaying my wife's instructions. The mixing of the batter had not intimidated me—after all, following instructions on the Bisquick box was simple enough—but cooking the devilishly good delicacies just the way she usually did, buttery crisp edges and fluffy with no goo in the middle, was a whole different proposition.

Typically, on Saturday mornings after a football game, I would meet the other coaches at the field house by seven so we could get done with the uniform washing and cleanup in time to catch the first college game on television. But since our season was over, Abi had informed me it was her turn to go catch up on some work at the office. Which meant I was in charge of the Saturday morning pancake ritual.

I yawned and peeked out the window. The newspaper was still there at the end of the driveway, like I knew it would be. It used to bother me that Abi didn't retrieve the paper when she came to the kitchen before me, that she loved to say how getting the paper, along with taking out the trash, was wholly a man's job. We'd even had a shouting match or two about it, once upon a time. But this morning I just smiled and shook my head. It wasn't important. Especially since she was mostly perfect in all the other ways that mattered.

I would go pick it up later. I had missed all the local game highlights on television the night before while we were at the hospital—and I really hadn't been in the mood to see all the commentary about our game-ending brawl just yet—but curiosity wouldn't let me ignore the newspaper for long. I would have to see all the other games' scores. Still, I didn't look forward to reading words like "probation" and "fines" in reference to my team. My thoughts drifted back to Devlin and whether he had suffered any new concussion symptoms during the night. And what in the world that Shane boy had been thinking. I considered whether to call Haughton's coach later to get his thoughts but decided against it. We weren't the best of friends.

"Dad, you're gonna burn the pancakes."

I jumped at the sound of my daughter's voice and turned to see her words were true. Smoke was rising from the skillet, and even I knew that was a bad sign. The spatula was out of my hand before I could react, and my fourteen-year-old had taken over my job.

I kissed the top of Kellen's head and grinned at the knotted, bedhead tangles in her cocoa-colored hair. "Sorry, baby. I can't cook."

She grunted. "Can't never could do nothin'. Isn't that what you always tell us?"

"Yep, you have a point. Let me rephrase. At this juncture, I'm not as proficient at cooking pancakes as I'm sure I can be, but with practice I'm confident I can learn to excel at it."

Kellen laughed out loud and plated the first batch of our breakfast, each pancake browner than usual on one side but still perfectly edible. "You're so goofy, Dad."

"Where's your brother? Do I need to hit him with the spray

starch to wake him up?" I simulated spraying an aerosol can near her ear.

Kellen covered her ears and winced before breaking into a smile. "No, Dad, I hate when you do that! Remember, he's camping with Gabe."

Of course. How could I forget? Kyle and his mother had argued about whether him spending so much time with a kid two years older than him was a good idea. And even if it was, she wasn't at all sure that Gabriel Liston was the right one for the job.

I thought even if he was quiet and didn't play football, Gabe seemed to keep his nose clean at school. And yes, he was sixteen, but Kyle was just as big, and you couldn't tell their age difference by looking at them. Their love for all things outdoors had brought them together, and I figured if they were spending time in the woods or in a boat it would keep them out of other, more nefarious, activities.

I had gone quiet when Abi reminded me of the trouble my friends and I had found ourselves in at the same age, but she knew I considered that a different set of circumstances. The odds of Kyle and Gabe finding a body and being drawn into a murder conspiracy were less than negligible.

Eventually, Abi had relented. She made it clear she didn't like it, though.

"What do you think of Gabe?"

Kellen shrugged. "He's okay, I guess. Don't know him very well. He's quiet."

A loud knock at the door stopped me before I could inquire further, but I didn't have to move to find out who it was. Jack barged in like he owned the place, just like he always did. I noticed he was in uniform: brown pants, khaki shirt, sidearm strapped to his belt He flashed a wide smile. "What's with the smoke? Kellen, did you leave your dad unsupervised in the kitchen again?"

She wrinkled her nose and scowled. "Hey, Uncle Jack! Don't worry, I rescued them before he could burn more than one." Kellen grabbed a pancake off the plate and prepared to toss it frisbee-style to Jack but stopped when she was saw he had paused in the doorway and was looking back over his shoulder.

"Come on, slowpoke," Jack said. "Look who's here."

Two blue eyes peeked around the door frame for a split second before their blonde, pigtailed owner tiptoed in, one hand holding Jack's and the other clutching a doll almost as big as she was.

"Lily!" Kellen chirped. "Who you got there? Is that a Baby Best Friend?"

Lily dropped Jack's hand and held the doll out at arm's length for Kellen to inspect. It was one of the most realistic dolls I'd ever seen—all except the lavender eyes, though they did perfectly match her T-shirt that read, My Best Friend Is Lily.

"Lily, why don't you sit down and let Kellen get you some syrup for a pancake?" Jack winked at Kellen and then grabbed my attention with a jerk of his head toward the door.

"I'm going outside to talk to Jack a minute. You got Lily?"

Kellen nodded and picked up the child and planted her on a barstool, and Lily begin telling her the baby's name and what costume she had picked out for Halloween in one jumbled sentence as the door closed behind us.

I lowered the garage door to break the chill from the morning breeze. "Being Grandpa fits you well, Jack."

Jack rolled his eyes but didn't smile like I expected him to. The seemingly easy smile he'd shown earlier had disappeared, reminding me how good he'd always been at manipulating a situation as necessary. "Janie had to work today, so Lily and I are making a day of it."

I loved to tease and called him Grandpa—it made me feel younger—but Lily was actually his great-niece, biologically speaking. Her mother, Janie, had been with Jack ever since she was five, after Jack's sister had died of cancer much too young and her husband was killed in a car wreck a few years later. Jack had adopted Janie without hesitation.

Janie had been a good kid and was a good mother, but she had questionable taste in men. She never brought up Lily's father and had never told Jack his name. Maybe she didn't even know it. All she ever said was that he was gone. The truth of it was, Jack had told me many times that he didn't care who the guy was and was glad he didn't know. A man sorry enough to neglect his responsibility was a man better off out of the lives of his girls. I suspected Jack had contemplated many times what might happen to the fellow if he ever decided to show up. He'd been around enough to have some ideas about good places to hide bodies.

Yes, Jack was overprotective, but he was gentle with it and doted in all the right ways over Lily so that Janie never seemed to mind. To see him with the child was usually to see his face beam like a sunrise over Lake McKinley. But today there were clouds in the way. "I'll cut right to it," he said. "Ronny Shane is dead." My friend began pacing, weaving back and forth through the space that should have been occupied by a vehicle but was instead filled with the baseball, softball, and soccer equipment required to support year-round tournament team participation for my twins.

I stepped back and sat heavily onto a bucket full of baseballs.

"What are you talking about?" I replayed the events from the night before in my head once more, trying to remember whether anyone had hit Ronny with a helmet or anything that could have caused his death hours later. But nothing came to me. "Car wreck?"

Jack shook his head and sighed. "I got called out before Janie went to work. Found dead at the bottom of Logan's Bluff early this morning. No idea what happened."

My heart sank. Poor kid, playing his last football game one night, does something mindless and doesn't live to see the morning. How devastated must his family be?

Suddenly, Devlin's words on the field gut-punched me. *I'll kill him.* Then Luke Wiseman at the hospital, threatening to avenge his friend. *I'm coming for him.*

I shook my head, trying to process what Jack was telling me. Logan's Bluff had once been the location of a popular campground high above the Timtullah River. I remembered pitching tents there with the Boy Scouts a few times as a kid, playing Capture the Flag in the dark and being warned by our Scoutmaster not to stray too close to the edge and risk tumbling the hundred feet or so into the river below.

A few years back, the Corps of Engineers had shut down the campsite for reasons I couldn't recall. But I had heard my football players talk of kids driving around the barricade and sneaking up there to do what teenagers do. And despite the purported danger of the place, I had never heard of anyone actually falling off the edge.

"He was found at the bottom? Like he fell off? Tell me it wasn't one of my boys."

"I told you I don't know. But if you think about it, it's not a good look. Player attacks former best friend right under the

Friday night lights for everyone in the county to see, friend is dead before morning."

The optics of it were terrible indeed. But anyone who knew Logan's Bluff—and those who did not would surely be informed very soon—knew it could be a dangerous place to be in the dark. And I hated to assume, but that was especially true if alcohol was involved. "Well, I know people love a conspiracy, but I don't care. The truth is the truth. You've spoken to Devlin?"

Jack shook his head. "No, he's at Tammy's, but I will shortly. He needs to know there will be questions." He lifted an eyebrow. "Accident or not, there might be a book in there, eh?"

I shook my head violently. "No way, Jack. I'm done with all that. Don't have the energy or the want-to for another. Two times is enough."

Jack laughed. "I get it. And if you thought sticking your nose in police business was bad when your daddy was sheriff, I can't imagine what it'd be like with Abi."

I returned his laugh. "Yeah, not good." Abi had worked in the Mississippi Crime Lab for a time after college, but that didn't last long before she decided she wanted to go to law school. Now she was County Attorney. I had no intention of mixing myself up in her business, now or ever.

Jack held up an index finger. "Seriously, though. One thing. If you don't mind, keep it to yourself about where he was found. Officially, he was found dead at Logan's Bluff State Park." He made air quotes with his fingers. "No other details available at this time."

Just as I nodded understanding, Kellen flung open the kitchen door. "Dad."

I waved her off with scarcely a glance. "Not now. Tend to Lily. Jack and I are talking."

Kellen was ashen and saucer eyed. She held up her phone. "Dad, you…" She put her hand over her mouth. "You've got to see this. It's bad."

She had found out about Ronny Shane. I missed the days when it was possible to share information with my kids on an as-needed basis—both in content and timing. But those days were long gone. Somehow the shoes had switched feet; instead of being the purveyor of information, I had become the last one to find out more times than I preferred. My friend Jack was old school as well, thus the reason he showed up at my door to tell me face to face. But in the time it had taken for him to tell me what he knew, I had no doubt Kellen had already found out more than either of us. I hated social media.

"What is it, baby?" I asked. "I take it you heard about the Haughton player who got killed?"

Kellen's bottom lip twisted in a guilty confession. "Yessir, my phone started blowing up as soon as you two walked out the door. I figured that's what Mr. Jack was here for."

I held my hand up. "We'll talk about it later. Let us finish talking here."

She shook her head and held her phone up again. "But Dad, that's not it. There's something else. Both of you need to look at this."

I sighed and nodded, agreeing to look to placate her, but fully expecting her to show me one of those memes or GIFs or whatever they were called—something done in poor taste without proper respect for a teenager who had tragically lost his life.

Jack peered over my shoulder as Kellen tapped the screen.

I literally felt a rush of air past my ear when Jack gasped.

FOUR

"YOU don't know that it means anything."

"Maybe not, but I don't know that it don't."

Jack punched the gas and sped out of my driveway. He reached out his hand, palm up, and snapped his fingers. "Give me your phone."

"My phone?" I raised an eyebrow and nodded toward his cell phone resting on the seat between us.

"If it ever comes up, this call can't have come from mine."

I understood. Jack was officially off duty, but his uniform suggested otherwise. Given what was surely about to happen, the less it appeared he was impeding an investigation, the better.

Jack rattled off the number and grabbed the phone from my hand before I even got a chance to listen for a ring. "Devlin. It's Jack. Yes, I know. Get dressed, you're going fishing … I don't care about the concussion. From what I hear you weren't too worried about it after you got home. Grab a fishing pole and tackle box and get down to Sipsey Bend … Right now … I don't have time to tell you … Right now! And Dev, don't tell your momma. Case and I will meet you there. Hurry."

Jack tossed the phone back to me, and while we rolled toward the Amberton city limits I considered the implications of what we had seen on Kellen's phone: a video of Devlin, leaving his home at 12:32 a.m., then clips of him driving the two or three miles to the Amberton Lock and Dam before finally turning off the main road in the direction of Logan's Bluff. Granted, whoever had followed Devlin, if indeed it was him, had been at a distance too far back to see much more than the outline of a vehicle resembling his gray Tacoma, too far back to identify the markings on the license plate. But the apparent continuity of the footage certainly made it appear to be the same truck that had left Devlin's driveway.

Kellen wasn't sure of the origin of the video. One of her friends had gotten it from another friend, and so on. Jack figured it could eventually be traced back to the originator. Eventually. But now wasn't the time for that. We also considered it might have been taken on a different day, but the odds of that were minuscule, under the circumstances.

"What are you planning to do?" I asked.

"He's going to tell me what's going on."

"What about Tammy? Can't she shed some light on this?"

Jack hit the blinker, spun the steering wheel counterclockwise, and took a hard left turn, off the highway onto a county road. As he straightened the wheel, he pivoted his head back toward me and cut his eyes in a way that gave me his answer before he spoke it. "She was at my house. We both fell asleep on the couch watching TV. When I called her this morning to tell her about Ronny, she said she left about midnight."

"And Devlin was home when she got there?"

Jack shrugged. "I assume so. Didn't know to ask that question when I called her earlier."

"And so now we're going fishing?"

Jack gave a half-hearted chuckle. "Ha ha. No, we both know that once that video hits the right person's phone, Devlin and Tammy will have blue lights in their driveway, taking him in for questioning. I'd like to think they'll call me first out of courtesy, but I don't think our goofball Police Chief Percy likes me too much, so I doubt it. Hopefully Devlin is hitting the road in the next five minutes, before anyone shows up." Jack winked at me. "And I'll just happen to know where he most likely snuck off to fish in peace this fine morning. His favorite honey hole."

"Doesn't seem likely a kid who'd just been responsible for the death of another the night before would just go off fishing, huh?"

Jack nodded. "Now you're getting me." He navigated through a sharp bend in the road and punched it again on a straightaway. "And I'd rather take him in instead of the city guys."

I had never heard of it, but according to Jack, Sipsey Bend was just what it sounded like—a bend in the Sipsey River— which itself was really just an average-sized creek for most of the year. Except the bend wasn't exactly in the river anymore. Some years before, the flow of water had carved out a shortcut and left behind a narrow, but deep, L-shaped oxbow. It was easy enough to access from a public, though seldom-used gravel road, but hardly anyone did. Jack, who could find a productive fishing hole in the Sahara, had brought Devlin to the spot a few years before, taught him how to fish it, and to hear the two of them talk, helped him pull out enough crappie to fill up an ocean tanker.

Jack coasted to a stop on the shoulder of the road behind Devlin's truck and nodded at the narrow foot trail meandering through knee-high grass toward a nearby tree line. "Down there." He was out of the truck and on the trail before I got my door open, and I had to hurry to catch up. The ground was soft beneath our feet, and water pooled in Jack's tracks behind him. The clusters of bulrushes along the trail edges told me the moisture was nothing new.

Devlin wasn't hard to find, leaning against a cypress tree at the oxbow's edge, tossing acorns methodically into the coffee-brown water. I was surprised at first that he had beaten us there, thinking he must have gotten dressed and out of the house as abruptly as a drunk man's hiccup, driven like a *Fast and Furious* movie stuntman, or both. Yes, he had begun a few miles closer than us, but except for the fact the fishing pole Jack had told him to bring was lying at his side with the bait still hooked to one of the casting guides, Devlin managed to look like he'd been hanging out all day. He didn't move or look up when we approached him from behind, and he spoke before we could even see his face. "I guess you know about Ronny."

I stood off to the side, out of the way. As Devlin's coach, this was much less my business than Jack's as mentor and possible future stepfather. Jack moved past Devlin and leaned on the next closest tree in silence for a few seconds, then reconsidered, picked up Devlin's fishing pole, and casted a chartreuse jig nonchalantly into the oxbow. I imagined he had stood in that very spot and cast in similar fashion hundreds of times over the years. It was comfortable. "Yeah, I got the call this morning, early. What do you know about it?"

Devlin shrugged. "I guess you saw the video too."

Jack pulled the bait from the water and reeled it up to the end of the pole. He turned to face Devlin, whose gaze seemed locked on the leaf-strewn ground between their boots. "Tell me."

Devlin rubbed his eyes with the back of his hand, turned to catch my eye but couldn't hold it. His eyes spoke of a deeper aching, possessed a pleading in them that I didn't yet know how to assuage. I noticed for the first time that he had been crying. "Talk to us, Dev. We're here to help."

The boy shook his head. "I can't say anything." His voice broke, and he swallowed hard. "Except I didn't do that to Ronny."

"Do what?" Jack stepped closer to him.

Devlin's eyes flashed a new emotion. The anger was subdued but lurking there nonetheless. "Come on, Jack. I'm not stupid. You didn't have me race down here because the fish are biting. I wasn't sure what was up, but I saw it on my feed a few minutes ago. That video is all over social media, people saying I killed Ronny." He paused and gnawed his lower lip, as if trying on for size what he would say next before wearing it in public. "You're just here to beat the crowd, be the hero."

Jack surprised me again. Rather than getting angry himself, he smiled somberly. "You know that's not it. But you're right, unless you can clear things up, there'll be questions. A boy is dead, and the person who had the most motive to hurt him was driving to the crime scene at about the same time it probably happened. Tell me what happened." He put the fishing pole on the ground and shoved his hands in his jeans pockets, eyes locked on the teenager.

"I didn't do it. I don't know how or why Ronny fell, but I didn't do it. I ain't saying nothing else."

Jack caught my eye and gave a head jerk, just a flinch but enough for me to know what he wanted.

I felt a twinge of nausea about where this seemed to be heading and had no idea how to stop it, no desire to inject myself into the mess the way Jack wanted. I sighed and spoke anyway. "Devlin, come on, we all know you wouldn't intentionally hurt Ronny or anyone else. But you've got to give us something."

Devlin shook his head. "I'm done."

I shrugged and spread my hands, incredulous and growing frustrated. I moved to confront my player—or former player, as of about twelve hours prior—chest to chest. It was time for some tough love. "Done? I'm sorry, Dev, but that's not gonna cut it." I put an index finger in his chest. The gesture was forceful in meaning, if not physicality. "It's time to put your big boy pants on and clear this mess up, before you find yourself in a load of trouble. Trouble that Jack doesn't need or want. And your momma certainly doesn't need it."

"Leave Momma out of it. She's been good lately."

I crossed my arms and stepped back, fearing thin ice beneath future dialogue on the subject. Former coach or not, tough love or not, I had no intention of touching Tammy James's mental health issues with a ten-foot pole, fishing pole, or anything else, for that matter.

Jack picked up the fishing gear, clearly frustrated. "If you're not gonna talk, then I'll have to take you in. I know you didn't do it. I'll call your mom, we'll sit down at the station and all figure out together what happened. But we're gonna have to go in, like it or not. Last thing I need is to be accused of nihilism on this thing and lose my job. Won't help people believe you, neither."

"Nepotism."

Jack frowned at me. "What?"

"It's nepotism. When you give special treatment to family."

Jack frowned again. "That's what I said."

I patted Devlin on the chest with the back of my hand and smiled, trying to lighten the mood. "Nobody butchers words quite like my old friend, you know?"

Devlin didn't smile. Instead, he pressed the keys to his

Tacoma into my palm and began walking toward Jack's truck. "Guess you'll have to drive mine, Coach. Truth is, I guess you could say maybe I did kill Ronny."

39

FIVE

EVLIN'S revelation, that he had killed Ronny Shane after all, had left Jack stunned. He had stood beside the Sipsey oxbow for several seconds, unmoving, unblinking, holding the fishing gear. I had opened my mouth, either in shock or possibly to say something to him, but I left whatever it was hanging there and turned to catch up to Devlin.

Catching up had done me no good. Devlin refused to say another word. I implored him to tell me exactly what he'd meant, but he just shook his head. I ignored my coaching instinct to get in his face again and insist he talk to me, both because I knew it wouldn't do any good and because I thought it was now Jack's place, if anyone's.

So, I had waited patiently at Devlin's vehicle, and Devlin waited at Jack's. In what was probably several seconds but seemed like minutes, Jack had emerged from the soggy trail and climbed in his GMC without saying a word. I followed them to the sheriff's department, replaying the morning's events and the questions that came with them while I drove.

Jack's shock had changed to anger by the time we got there. I could see it in his eyes. He marched ahead of Devlin into the single-story brick building and through clenched jaw asked me to sit with the boy so he could "sort some things out." So, we sat on a bench just inside the entrance and waited. Jack stomped in and out of an office, on and off the phone while a clerk whispered something into her phone and pretended not to be cutting eyes in our direction every few seconds.

I patted Devlin on the shoulder, but he didn't move or acknowledge me. I felt sorry for the kid. His jaw was set, and he eyed the wall across the room as if he could see through it. I had seen the look many times on the football practice field, when the requirements of a coach's assignment exceeded his execution—though seldom, if ever, his effort—and he found himself enduring a severe tongue lashing.

No one wanted to succeed—to win—more than Devlin, but he could go into an emotional lockdown like few kids I had encountered. But no matter what he let the world see on the outside, nothing about Devlin James was truly nonchalant. He would fight a grizzly to win a game or protect a friend. He loved fast cars, high water towers, and the occasional fistfight. To hear other kids tell, he also loved hard and lost even harder. I figured it was the losses that shaped his reaction to the world around him. He put up a wall when he faced something he couldn't change, like the loss of a father or the screaming of a coach, but I'd seen him release torrents of passion when he saw an opportunity to effect a change.

Which was why this was so odd. An old friend had died—or been killed—and he was directly linked to it. The Devlin who I knew would be shouting his innocence from the rooftops. But he had gone mute. Did that mean he was guilty and resigned to his fate? Was he protecting someone? Luke Wiseman, perhaps? If I was a betting man, I would have put my money on the latter. But then again, I couldn't imagine Luke intentionally hurting someone, either. Maybe the explanation was a terrible accident and nothing more.

Jack emerged from a room toward the back and motioned for us to rise and meet him. I patted Devlin again, but it felt more forced this time.

The more I thought about the whole situation, the more puzzled I became. If it was possible to feel a sense of purpose and awkwardness simultaneously, I was feeling it. As Devlin's coach, Jack's friend, and the son of the former sheriff, I believed I had something positive to bring to the moment.

But then again, I was just a football coach, had very little firsthand knowledge of Devlin's personal life, and had been chastised in the past on more than one occasion for "wishing I was a cop," or something to that effect. And while, by my estimation, more positive than negative had come out of those events, I had no intention of going down that road again.

Jack stopped Devlin with a hand to his chest as we approached. He dropped his chin and spoke in a hushed tone, just above a whisper. "Okay, Dev, listen to me, now. I can't exactly remember what you may or may not have said back there at the fishing hole, okay? If you don't want to say nothing, don't say nothing. But don't say *that*."

Devlin didn't move or speak.

"Tell him, Coach."

I cocked my head in a forward tilt. Wanting to agree, but not really wanting to acknowledge that I'd heard his confession, either. To do so within the confines of the sheriff's office seemed like lying in church, or something like that. "Son, you need to listen to Jack. Now's the time to talk to get yourself out of trouble, not *in* it. The world will be hard enough on you without you adding to it."

Jack grabbed his shoulder and shook it, only once but enough to show he meant it. "Look at me, boy!"

Devlin obliged, but his expression remained flat.

"If you care about your mother, you keep your mouth shut.

Ya hear me? Do you love your mother? Or you want to make her life a living hell?"

The boy answered with a nod and a wet glaze across his eyes, but his glance diverted to something behind us.

"That's enough, Jack. Leave the personal out of this."

I recognized the voice before I turned around. Shallow and wispy, like one strained by shouting or never fully developed by the usual surge of testosterone. And I knew the appearance of its purveyor wouldn't match its sound. Sheriff Rappaport was short and borderline rotund, but beefy shoulders and forearms spoke of a man not to be taken lightly, regardless of his height or his voice. His hair had once been a rich caramel, but it was gone, the only remnant a bushy gray mustache and eyebrows to match, with enough feathers of its original color to make one wonder if it was dirty or smoke-stained.

I reached out to shake his hand and forced a smile. "Hello, Rap."

"Case."

The sheriff looked past me, craning his neck back and forth. "I'm a little surprised to see you here. Didn't realize we had football practice."

I ignored the jab. "Just here as a friend, Sheriff." I emphasized the word 'friend,' knowing he would understand the point of it. Friend to Jack, friend to Devlin. Once-upon-a-time friend to a boy a few years older than us whom we called "Rap," back when we played tennis baseball together in a neighborhood vacant lot. A boy who grew up and lost his job when the furniture factory went belly up and who was offered a job as a sheriff's deputy by my father.

But then my father had gotten sick, a mysterious illness with fatigue and aching muscles. He hid it at first, thinking it would "pass," but it didn't. By the time he relented to my urging and went to see Gracie, he had become so weak he couldn't work. By the time she had him better, one deputy named Wayne Rappaport had wormed his way in as interim sheriff and convinced the voters at election time that the current sheriff was over the hill. The truth was, Dad's condition was reversible—something called polymyalgia rheumatica—and resolved within a few months of treatment, but by then it was too late. And I suppose because he felt threatened by the possibility that my father would come back and run against him next election, my friend Rap transferred his ire to me. It didn't help matters that he knew about the other murders my friends and I had solved as civilians.

Sheriff Rappaport grunted. "Guess maybe I'm not surprised. Law enforcement is in your blood. You like to try it on for size, eh?"

I shot Jack a look. *I knew I shouldn't have come.*

"Case was with me when I found Devlin."

"Mmm hmm. Found him, huh? You said he just up and decided to go fishing by himself?" He cocked his head and stared at Devlin sideways for a second.

Devlin mirrored the sheriff's gesture but remained expressionless. "Believe it or not, I can cast and reel all by myself, Sheriff."

Rappaport reached out and lightly grabbed Devlin by the elbow. "You done gone and got yourself in a mess, boy." He looked back at Jack. "I'll take it from here. You need to separate yourself."

"C'mon, Rap—"

"Sheriff."

Jack sighed. "Yeah, sorry. Sheriff. Let me work on this. He

didn't do it, and I can help you figure it out."

The sheriff released his grip on his suspect and folded his arms across his thick chest. "See, that there is the problem. You've already got him innocent."

I wanted to stay out of it, but I couldn't help it. "But he *is* innocent, Rap. Right? Innocent 'til proven guilty? A man with your experience as a law enforcement officer knows that. I don't see how Jack believing that is a problem." Of course, I knew it wasn't as simple as that. It was certainly true that one might not be as objective as he should be if he's already reached a verdict, but as my father had pointed out to me many times, the lens through which a law enforcement officer views a crime and its suspects is not the same as that of a court of law.

But I wanted to believe Devlin was innocent too, and if I could coerce Rap into letting Jack stay close to the investigation, it would surely help the boy's cause.

Jack winked at me, out of view of his boss. I'd seen that look before.

Rappaport narrowed his eyes at me, and the muscles of his jaw rippled as he clenched it, trying to decide if he'd tangled himself in his own words.

"Of course I know that, Case." He turned to face Jack. "You can stay on, at least peripherally. I'm assigning someone else as lead, but I'll keep you in the loop. That's the best I can do."

Jack nodded. "Fair enough. Now what?"

"Now, we get to the bottom of this mess." He glanced at Devlin with a quick tilt of his head. "What's he told you, Jack?"

Jack glared at Devlin with a keep-your-mouth-shut look. "Nothing."

The answer was technically a lie, but for practical purposes, maybe not. Devlin's "confession" was surely just an emotional kid spouting off in the heat of the moment. And since then, nothing was exactly what we'd gotten out of him.

Rappaport looked at me. "Good seeing you, Case. This is where the friending ends and the investigating begins." He reached and grabbed Devlin again. "Now, boy, let's get you to the back for some questions."

Before anyone could move, the door burst open, and Tammy James darted through it, waving her arms. "Wayne, get your hands off my son! I don't know what you think you're doing with Devlin, but you need to leave him alone. I can tell you exactly what happened to Ronny Shane."

SIX

"NICE teeth."

"Teeth?" Gabe Liston rolled his eyes. "That's the dumbest thing I've ever heard. Boobs, butt, eyes, all the possibilities out there, and you're gonna tell me you want nice teeth on a girl more than anything else?"

Kyle Reynolds tilted his camp chair forward and scraped the last vestiges of his scrambled eggs into the sizzling campfire, then watched tiny wisps of black smoke finger their way into the prevailing grays while he gulped the last of a canned Coke. He belched and glanced toward the water as if the sound might have disturbed the fish. "You said physical, right? There's other things I like. Personality stuff. But physical? Yeah, gotta have good teeth."

Gabe laughed. He was about Kyle's height, which was average for his age, two years older. He was overweight but with baby fat that might disappear when he hit a growth spurt, with curly brown hair that would hold tight until about a week past haircut time when it would it explode into a wiry bush. "Whatever floats your boat, man. I like nice, full lips myself."

Kyle watched his friend stoke the fire with a charred hickory stick and wondered if Gabe Liston had ever even kissed a girl. He talked a big talk, but Kyle figured if he was such a ladies' man, he probably wouldn't be camping on a sandbar and running throw lines up and down Miller's Creek with a fourteen-year-old. Either way, Kyle was glad Gabe wanted to hang with him. They understood each other.

While his twin sister Kellen was a straight-A student, a gifted volleyball and softball player, and an outgoing type with throngs of friends, Kyle was an average student, average athlete, and an introvert. None of that bothered him terribly, but he was afraid it bothered his father. A football coach hearing from his son that he's going to stick with baseball (even though he's not even sure he's good enough to make the high school team the next year) couldn't have been a pleasant thing. Nor could an attorney mother seeing only average grades on every report card. And if that wasn't enough, both parents had a way of engaging other people—that "never meet a stranger" ability—that Kyle never could seem to tap into. God had skipped right over him on the day that gene was handed out. His mom had once joked that Kellen must have gotten his portion and forgotten to share. And even though neither parent had ever openly suggested he was a disappointment, he couldn't help but wonder.

What he *was* good at didn't seem to count, at least not according to the world's usual standards. Fishing. Hunting. Growing. Anything involving nature. All of it came natural to him, no pun intended. He could watch a deer search the forest floor for acorns and know which species it was looking for: the big sawtooths in September and Nuttalls along the slough bottoms in December. He could listen to the crows calling from the tips of the tallest pines and distinguish their territorial caws from the ones signaling danger. He could catch the big river flatheads when a slow bite forced other fisherman to eat farm-raised at the local steak-and-fish house, even though the river cats tasted twice as good. He could resurrect his mother's dying peace lilies and spider ivy and grow more tomatoes on three plants than most truck patch farmers could grow on ten.

And if he wasn't outdoors—and often even when he was—he was drawing. He had stacks of notebooks beneath his bed, the pages filled with charcoal and pencil sketches of everything from animals to landscapes to fantasy creatures. Lately, he had become more interested in reproducing images of the animals he encountered on canvas with pencil and watercolor than in bringing them home for eating.

Gabe tossed an armful of deadwood on the fire and looked at his watch as he settled back onto his upturned five-gallon bucket.

Kyle frowned. The November morning air was certainly chilly, maybe more so where they were, exposed on a sandbar with nothing to break the breeze. But there was no reason to keep a fire going now. It was time to go check the lines they had set the night before. Then they would come back, pack up the tent and other gear, and head home. Good firewood was a precious commodity, better to be saved for the next camping trip than to be wasted on this one.

Neither of them had any desire to haul their own wood to the campsite—especially not by boat. Their sandbar was on Miller's Creek about two hundred yards above where it emptied into the Timtullah River, just a quarter mile north of Logan's Bluff. If there was a decent way to get there by land, Kyle didn't know about it. Besides, they didn't know who owned the land along the sandbar's edge, though they'd never run into any issue with gathering some dead limbs there for firewood after dark.

"It's about time to go, dude. Should've saved that wood."

Gabe just shook his head and stared at Kyle intently. Something was on his mind.

"What?"

Gabe looked at his watch again. "You're lucky, you know."

Kyle raised both eyebrows and gestured with both hands, palms up. What was Gabe talking about? He had been acting a bit odd this trip. Preoccupied, maybe—though he'd never seemed like much of a deep thinker.

"Your family. You're lucky with what you've got. Mine don't give no hill of beans about me."

Kyle didn't know much about Gabe's family life. A half-hearted mother, maybe. Never heard mention of his father. Kyle had asked once, but his friend had said he didn't want to talk about it. He didn't press the issue, mostly because it didn't matter. If Gabe wanted to be his friend, that was all he needed to know. Friends who understood each other were hard to come by, so what did it matter where they came from? One was independent of the other. "They're okay, I guess."

Gabe nodded. "At least you got a father."

"Everybody's got a father. Technically."

Gabe rolled his eyes. "Nope. I got a sperm donor is all. You and yours pretty tight?"

"It's complicated."

"Complicated how? Got a momma and a daddy under the same roof. Lawyer, coach. You got it made, man."

Kyle stood and folded his chair. He tossed it into the sand beside their four-person tent and began yanking up the stakes holding down the corners. "You know it ain't that simple, Gabe. I mean, I ain't sayin' I want to trade with you, but you have no idea what it's like."

"Hold your horses, I'm coming." Gabe stood and stoked the fire one last time. "No idea what what is like?"

"Being a disappointment. My social butterfly twin sister is all-everything. Mom's a brainiac. Dad's the former star quarterback, now the football coach." He tugged at a tent pole and nodded at Gabe to work it from the other side. "I'm exactly none of that."

Gabe winced. "When you put it like that, maybe it don't sound so great. But trust me, it could be worse. A lot worse."

Kyle pulled apart the sections of a fiberglass tent pole, stretching the elastic cord running down the center so that he could fold it on it itself. He knew life could be plenty worse. He'd heard enough horror stories from his grandfather's sheriff days, and it didn't take a mental giant to realize he should be infinitely thankful for his family. It wasn't that he didn't like them, or love them, even. He just wished they thought more highly of him.

"Let me ask you this." Gabe began folding the other pole in similar fashion. "Which is worse? To be judged too harshly, or to not be important enough to be judged at all?"

Kyle whistled mockingly and couldn't help but smile. "Wow. Maybe you should be my mother's son. That sounded mighty lawyerly."

Gabe returned the grin. "Came up with that all by myself just now."

"To answer your question, I guess it just depends. If I committed a crime that I'd like to get away with, I believe I'd prefer not to be judged at all. And if you think about it, we're all criminals in one way or another."

Gabe rubbed his chin. "I believe you got me there, Kyle. You have a point." He opened his mouth to speak again but stopped short. He swiveled his head abruptly to peer into the woods to his left.

Kyle's heart leapt in his chest when he saw the reason. A figure was emerging from the morning shadows, and he didn't have the appearance of a man wandering up by happenstance.

He looked to be a man on a mission, with his eyes locked on his targets.

He was coming for them.

SEVEN

TAMMY James could be an attractive woman. There was once a time when that was a constant, but now it depended on one's taste and her style of the week. Her hair ranged from blond to black to deep maroon, occasionally wandering into one of the ROYGBIV rainbow colors, though Jack would usually suggest a return to the salon when that happened. Her green eyes were a constant, though, with a feline quality especially noticeable when her makeup highlighted them. She was about five foot five, slight of frame with narrow hips, but full chested to make gossiping women discuss whether she'd had work done. Her most recent hair color choice was sable with shimmers of violet highlights. Not really my taste, but oddly enough, when she first burst through the door of the sheriff's department, the first thought that crossed my mind was that it was actually a good look for her.

Then she erupted again, and the fire in her tongue burned away all other thoughts. "Get away from my son, Rap, you spineless piece of garbage!"

"Hang on now, Ms. James. Let's all stay calm here." Sheriff Rappaport reached out with a gesture intended to calm her. It did not.

"Don't touch me!" She flailed one hand in his direction and settled the other on her hip. "Jack, you better have a good explanation for this."

Jack cocked his head toward Devlin with a raised eyebrow,

swiveled and caught my gaze in passing, then settled a puzzled look on wildcat-eyed Tammy. "How exactly did you know we were here?"

She locked an unwavering glare on Jack, her tiny nostrils flaring. "Everybody in McKinley County has heard about Ronny and seen the video that's supposed to be Devlin. So, I tracked his phone. Imagine my surprise when I saw he was here!" She dislodged her hand from her hip and crossed her arms over her chest. "I'll ask again. How did he wind up here, Jack? Did *you* arrest him?"

I took a small step forward. "It was my idea, Tammy. There wasn't any other choice, really. Anything less would look like they were trying to cover something up, and we all know that's not true. Jack wasn't really too excited about coming here—he's so protective, you know? But I insisted."

"Coach is telling the truth, Mom."

Tammy's posture and angry glare both softened. She rubbed a hand down her face, and for the first time there was a damp worry in her eyes. She sighed. "Okay, okay. Like I said, y'all know Devlin didn't commit no crime. And it shouldn't take an Einstein to figure out who did."

"Ms. James." Rap's tone was soft and less patronizing than before. "You said you know exactly what happened to Ronny Shane. Perhaps if you elaborate it will help the situation."

"C'mon, sheriff. Do I have to spell it out for you? A last name ain't all that Ronny and Buster share." She grimaced. "*Shared,* I guess now. Anyway, you think the fact Ronny's brother is the biggest drug dealer in the county is a coincidence? And why don't you go question Luke Wiseman, who threatened Ronny in front of a half dozen people last night?"

"Leave Luke out of it, Mom. Good grief."

Rap frowned and looked at Jack. "Is that true?"

Jack nodded. "Yes, but heat of the moment. Luke wouldn't hurt a flea, and Devlin wouldn't either. Like Tammy said, you need to look somewhere else."

The sheriff sighed and fingered his mustache. "I'm not sure what to think right now. It's very early. But I do have a video of a truck like his going to the crime scene last night."

"I'm glad you mentioned that, Sheriff." Jack was studying his phone as if it displayed the script for his next words. "Unless you have a different video than I do, all you have is a truck that looks like Devlin's." He held the phone up to show the screen. "No license plate number, no visual on the driver. And I'm betting Devlin doesn't have the only gray Tacoma around."

"Yet here you are."

"Did I mention," Jack continued, "that Devlin was at home before midnight last night?"

Rap tilted his head back and eyed Jack through narrow slits. "How do you know?"

Tammy James stepped forward and wagged a finger at the sheriff. "'Cause I told him. My boy was home when I got there. About 12:30."

"Mm-hmm. I guess we'll see if that bears out. I'm sure his phone record, as you mentioned, will show where he was."

Tammy's body tensed and her hand came up again, but before she could speak I touched her shoulder and stepped up beside her. "Sheriff, is there anything else? It seems to me that a grainy video of a truck similar to dozens of others in the area, including that of my Devlin here, who just happens to have an alibi, isn't enough to keep him. Can he go? The other option is to call his attorney, which is absolutely going to happen before he utters a word, who will then point out how you have no real evidence and no case, and more time will have been wasted when you could have been finding the actual killer, if there even was one."

"Coach," Devlin said, "what do you mean, if there even was one?"

I held up my hand with a "not-another-word-from-you" look, one that he and my players were quite familiar with. "I'm saying that unless Sheriff can tell us otherwise, maybe they're just assuming Ronny was killed because of the video. Is there any actual evidence of a murder, Sheriff?"

Rap was seething, with jaw set, eyes ablaze, and a bulging vein at his temple. "You think you know something, Reynolds? Daddy was sheriff and you wrote couple of books, so that makes you an expert? If you know so much, then you know I can keep him for forty-eight hours just for the hell of it. Maybe we'll try that, lawyer or not."

"And maybe I'll have Alethia Abbot up here doing a nice feature piece in the *Amberton Advocate* about the sheriff persecuting the hometown football hero without cause. I can see the headline now. 'The Devil Versus Devlin James.'"

Rap blinked hard at the name. Abbot was a decent journalist with a talent for coloring outside the lines of her stories just enough to fit her agenda, one whom you'd rather not notice you at all but wanted on your side if she did. She and I had gotten crossways once before, and I suspected the sheriff knew what that could mean for him.

"I'm sure you'd love that, wouldn't you?" He turned to Jack. "I suggest you get your friend out of here before I lose my temper."

"And Devlin?"

"Take him home for now. We'll be in touch."

I decided I had said enough and that saying more wouldn't do Devlin any favors. Jack either, for that matter. I motioned Devlin and Tammy toward the door, but before any of us took a step it burst open again. A deputy slid in, one whom I had not seen before. He was tall and slender, with a long, easy stride. His uniform hung from his narrow shoulders and hips like it had been draped around him rather than donned intentionally. He gave us a stern but concerned, almost apologetic, nod as he passed. "Sheriff, you need to look at this." The voice was deep and the syllables as long as his frame. His drawl seemed a better fit for a white country singer from the outer rims of the county than for the black man who owned it.

The sheriff motioned for us all to stop, even though we hadn't moved. "What you got, Nash?"

Nash waved a sheet of paper before the sheriff then dug a phone out of his deep pocket and showed something on it to him.

"Let's all go outside," Sheriff Rappaport said. He pointed to the door. "Need to look at something."

Curiosity trumped contentiousness, and no one protested. Instead, we all followed and were soon standing beside Devlin's truck in the parking lot.

"Deputy Nash has a couple of interesting things to share with us. First of all, he has photos of what appears to be tire marks at the scene on Logan's Bluff that perfectly match those of this here Toyota Tacoma. What's the make?" He squatted and peered at the right front tire. "Reisende Road Rockers. Isn't that nice? Made right here in our county."

"Doesn't prove anything, Rap," I said. "Same make as a few hundred others around, I'd reckon."

"True, but it doesn't rule it out, either. And what else do you have for us, Nash?"

"Search warrant for this here pickup truck, sir." The deputy's tone was matter of fact without any of Rappaport's "gotcha" inflections.

Rappaport smiled. "Well, let's get to it."

I glanced at Devlin to get his reaction, but it gave away nothing.

Nash searched the back seat, and Rap rifled through the front. It didn't take them long. The sheriff backed out of the passenger seat of the truck like a miner pulling a gold nugget from a hole in the ground. "What do we have here?" He waved an envelope like a finish flag and then pulled out a wad of cash. He counted out $250, then showed us the other side of the envelope, where two letters were scrawled in red ink.

R. S.

The sheriff stuffed the envelope in a back pocket and nodded at his deputy. "Deputy Nash, as much as my new friends here don't want it to be so, I'm going to ask Mr. Devlin James to spend the night with us. Cuff him, read him his rights, and escort him for a tour of his new accommodations. He is under arrest for the murder of Ronny Shane."

EIGHT

"WHAT'S gonna happen to him?" Tammy's demeanor bordered on hysteria, trembling from head to toe, hands wringing, pacing the parking lot outside the sheriff's department. On the curb, then off it, weaving between cars in no particular pattern. "I need to know, Jack." Her voice cracked.

"First thing is, you have to settle down. It won't do you any good to go back in the hospital with a breakdown."

"I know, I know. But you've gotta do something. Ol' Egghead ain't gonna be able to help him."

Bert Eggleston was the public defender. I didn't know him personally to judge the validity of Tammy's assessment, but I had gathered from Abi in various conversations that he wasn't one to set the world on fire with his legal skills. Most people called him "Egg," but some preferred to add "head" behind his back. Whatever his legal aptitude, it was better than nothing, which was what Tammy said she could afford. So, we had left Devlin with strict instructions not to say another word to anyone until his attorney arrived.

Much to Tammy's dismay, Rap had made us all leave while Devlin was "processed," rather than allowing his mother to stay around until Eggleston arrived.

"We don't have to use Egg. We'll do what we have to do to hire somebody better," Jack said.

Tammy stopped moving long enough to give him a

dismissive wave. "I'm not gonna let you do that. Besides, to figure that out would take time, which we don't have. Devlin needs somebody now."

"I can make some calls," I said. "I know a few people." Abi would be more than happy to recommend someone. As a favor to Jack. As an act of justice for the kid. And especially to make sure they had such good representation that I would stay out of it.

Tammy waved me off just as she had done Jack. "No, Case. Abi needs to stay totally out of this. Conflict of interest. I've been in courtrooms enough to know judges can make that knife slice both ways."

"I really don't think—"

"No, and that's final." She took a deep breath. "We've got to do something. I know Devlin didn't do it."

Jack reached out and embraced Tammy. "I know he didn't. Case knows it too." Jack fixed his gaze on me. "We've just got to prove it."

I gestured like a crossing guard stopping traffic and took a step back. "Oh, no. No sir. There is no *we*. I'm not gettin' in this. My murder solving days are over."

Tammy pushed away from Jack and gave a pleading stare. "C'mon, Case. Help Jack. Please! I don't care whether you find out who killed Ronny. Just prove Devlin didn't." She glared at me. "You know my son would fight an army by himself for you if you needed him."

She wasn't wrong. But I found it odd that Tammy didn't want me to help Devlin find legitimate legal counsel, yet she had no problem asking me—unauthorized and untrained—to help prove his innocence, despite the possibility my wife could be asked to do the opposite, and in an official fashion. But then again, why would I expect anything else? Tammy was about as predictable as a July hailstorm.

"Case, you know I need you." Jack's eyes had not wavered. "Rap has a chip on his shoulder and ain't likely to give a fair look at any of this."

He likely was spot on, too, on both counts. I sighed. "Where do you want to start? And not a word to Abi."

Jack smiled. "You know she'll find out."

"Yeah, but trust me, you don't want to be the one to tell her."

"This is it." Jack steered left off Waterway Road onto a gravel thoroughfare meandering up the hillside. "Ever been up here?"

"It's been awhile." Five or six years, maybe more. Back before they shut it down. Kyle and Kellen and I had tent camped near Logan's Bluff but not at the top near the cliff's edge. Young as they were, I would have been a nervous wreck. Instead, we set up near the other end of the road where the slope softened toward the water's edge at ground level. Kellen had hated it, so we were one and done. "Think they'll let you near the scene?"

"Rap called up and told them to let me look. Maybe there's a heart in that black hole somewhere."

"Did you tell him I was tagging along?"

Jack smiled. "Negative, Ghost Rider."

"You know Goose gets killed in that movie, right?" The question was rhetorical. Jack had *Top Gun* practically memorized.

He winked at me and held up an index finger. "Yes, but that movie was a long time ago."

I hoped that at least made sense in his own mind.

What had once been a manicured gravel road was heavily punctuated with sprouts of broadleaf weeds, crabgrass, and sectioned by dozens of shallow trenches washed out by a thousand rains. Sweet gum and pine saplings lined the edge of the original road like juvenile sentries, encroaching the edges and scraping the truck windows as we bumped along our climb. The road had not been formally maintained, but it had not been left entirely to its own devices, either. Tire tracks upon tire tracks were visible in the bare spots of red clay where most of the gravel had been washed or spun away. I doubted the tracks here would be of very much help, though. Sure, we had a heavy rain the day before, so most of the tracks were fresh, but doubtless this little road had seen traffic like an interstate since the kid's body had been discovered that morning.

As the slope leveled out, the thick growth hovering at the edges relented to allow an open, grassy expanse at the zenith of the hill. There, a row of more statuesque oaks and white ash stood tall at the perimeter, tossing curled brown and red leaves onto the turf below. To our left and at the far side of the meadow the trees at the edge were backed by scores of the same, but to the right only open sky lay beyond. There, those trees hugged the edge of the bluff and dug deep, like wooden nails pinning the soil to the rock lest it slip and fall to the water a hundred feet below.

Jack stopped the truck in the middle of the road just where the edge cover broke into the clearing and killed the engine. "No sense driving up in the middle of the evidence, and no sense letting anybody else, either. You'd think they'd have it taped off or something."

"It's a shame folks can't camp here anymore." I nodded toward the trees to our right. "Used to be a wooden fence there, remind people where the edge was. Shouldn't be too hard to build another."

Jack shrugged. "Might as well leave it as is and open it. People gonna do what people gonna do."

I had expected a posse of people to be there, milling around, investigators investigating, sections taped off, like Jack said. Instead, only a single vehicle from the sheriff's department was pulled off to the left edge at the far end of the clearing some fifty yards away. The site was otherwise pristine. A tree trunk moved near the car, and Nash separated himself from it like an apparition. I wondered if he'd ever considered sniper school. I didn't know if he could shoot, but he sure could hide, intentional or not.

"Hello, men." Nash spoke loud and brusque, much like a high school football coach running into a couple of his players a few years later. He closed the space between us quickly with his long strides. "Sheriff said for me to meet you here. In case you needed anything."

Jack gave a knowing nod. He expected the escort. "Fine. Maybe you can help us. Can you tell us anything? Figured they'd have things marked off."

"We got what we need." Nash adjusted his cap and pointed to the center of the clearing. "Kid's car was parked right there. Blue Maxima, black rims. Looks like he hung out there a bit. Butts from a couple of smokes matched the half pack in his car."

"And the tire tracks you say matched Devlin's?" Jack asked.

Nash pointed to a spot near the first one. "Right there. Pulled up behind the Shane boy's car."

"Anything else?" I asked.

"Condom or two."

Jack raised an eyebrow toward me.

Nash laughed. "Not from last night, and not right here. Been there a minute."

I chuckled, glad we didn't have that to sort out.

Nash's demeanor shifted. He frowned. "What exactly is it you think you'll find that we can't, Coach?" He spread his hands toward the presumed crime scene. "What's your play here?"

Jack moved toward the spot Nash had pointed out, and I instinctively followed. Nash huffed and caught up to move with me. Jack spoke as he walked without looking back. "Nash, I don't mean no offense, because you're a good lawman and you me always been straight." He stopped, pointed at some tire tracks to signal this was where we'd stop and folded his arms. "But I'm gonna ask you this. How many murder cases have you solved? Like, legit, by yourself, or mostly."

Nash huffed again. "Well, now, that's complicated, I—"

"Naw, it ain't complicated. How many?"

Nash held up an index finger. "First was the Stevenson woman from over at Sandy Hollow. Second was that cold case last year we dug up from '07–"

"Guy on death row sent you a letter where to find the body, but okay, we'll count it."

Nash rolled his eyes. "And I helped on that Chavalier feller last month—"

"Okay, three then, if you stretch it." Jack pointed at me. "My bud here has four—five, depending on how you count it—and he's just a football coach. And a kid we both care about very much has his whole life on the line. So, if you'd cut us a little slack here, I'd appreciate it."

Nash eyed me sideways and moved his lips in and out like they might actually churn out his thoughts on the matter. Then the lips turned inward and froze, and he nodded slowly. "Fair enough, Coach. We straight. How you help Jack is his business. But I'm sho' not gonna look the other way if I see something out of line."

I reached out a hand to the deputy. "Fair enough here too. I'm mostly just here for eyes and ears and a sounding board. Won't get in the way."

Nash shook my hand and opened his mouth to speak, but Jack's voice stopped him short.

"Lookee here, what y'all think about this?"

NINE

S the stranger emerged from the trees and strode toward them, his gaze was fixed on Kyle, but a flickering shift of his eyes left no doubt he was also attuned to Gabe's presence a few feet to the side. What first appeared to be a billowing, olive-brown robe was a waxed cotton trench coat that moved in the draft of each deft step of his leather Wellingtons, and his thick mane of smoky gray hair flowed over the back of his head and nearly reached his shoulders.

Kyle froze and calculated his next move. Maybe the man just wanted to talk, but if his intentions were more sinister, what were the options? There was nowhere to run. The creek at their back was too deep to wade and too cold to swim, and the boat couldn't be launched in time. And a break for the trees would be intercepted by this man who looked to cover ground like a phantom. Kyle gathered his tent poles in both hands. Use the bundle as a weapon to strike or throw and hope it's distracting enough to allow escape? If he could get past him, Kyle thought his chances were good. He was no phantom, but he might have a little Tarzan in him. Mowgli, at the very least. Either way, the woods were home to him. But what if there was a gun? From the movies he'd seen, the man in the trench coat always carried a gun.

He suddenly realized that not only was Gabe not running away, but he had a satisfied upturn of the corners of his mouth suggesting the stranger was only a stranger to one of them. Kyle held his ground, relieved but still apprehensive. Why was this person here? How did he know where they were? Maybe he was the landowner, and somehow Gabe had made a connection Kyle didn't know about.

The man stopped at the edge of the campfire and toed the unburned end of an oak stick. "A good fire is a necessity, isn't it, Gabe?"

Gabe smiled and broke from his statuesque posture like an overinflated balloon with its air valve popped open. "Yessir, it is." He pointed at Kyle. "This is—"

"Hello, Kyle." The man stepped around the fire and extended a hand. "Proffit."

Kyle tucked the tent poles under his left arm and returned the handshake. "How do you know my name?"

Proffit smiled. His eyes were almost perfectly round and darker than Kyle expected. Not that he'd thought it out exactly, but they were striking in how they hid in the shadows of his sockets like half-buried coffee beans, contrasting his pale skin like they belonged to someone else. "My friend Gabe has told me all about you. Doesn't like many people, but he likes you. Which makes you my friend too." His eyelids flared to let in some of the morning light.

Kyle was mesmerized by the man's demeanor in the way one might suspect a creature is friendly but dare not look away in case he pounces. "It's umm, nice to meet you, Mr. Proffit. Are you related to the Proffit's Pizza people, you know, the place out by Admiral Lake?"

"Nope. Never tried it but I hear it's good. And can't say that I know them. But could be distant kin, way back." His gaze was locked on Kyle, studying.

"He won't let you call him Mister." Gabe had stepped up

to join them. He nodded at the man, who motioned toward the space around the fire.

"It's just Proffit. Mr. Proffit is my father. Mind if we talk?" He took the chair Kyle had occupied earlier and waited on them to find similar seating.

No one spoke for a moment. Kyle studied the fire and fiddled with a stick in the sand between his feet. What was this all about? Clearly it wasn't a random encounter. The vibe was that the mission was to meet him, but why?

Gabe was never one to be silent for very long. "It's, uhh, good to see you."

Kyle waved a finger between the two figures before him. "How, uh, how do you know each other?"

Proffit pointed upstream, to the wooded area behind them. "I was around the bend of the creek there, checking some fences, figured I'd come over and check on you since Gabe told me you'd be here."

"You live down here?"

Proffit smiled. "Depends on how you define that. We're either living or dying everywhere we go. I prefer to think of it as the former." He motioned toward the water. "Any luck?"

Gabe shook his head. "We didn't catch much last night. Gonna run our lines once more this morning before we go."

"There'll be time." Proffit rubbed his hands together over the fire, even though the morning cool had nearly evaporated. He pointed at the flames. "Kyle, I hear you're quite the outdoorsman. Flint and steel?"

"Always." Kyle shot Gabe a look. He still had no idea what Gabe's connection to this person was, but evidently Gabe had told the fellow some things about him, maybe how he usually insisted on starting their campfires using primitive methods while Gabe stood by chiding him with a butane lighter in one hand and lighter fluid in the other. To Gabe, it was all about getting the flame going.

To Kyle, it was about the process. And preparedness. *Stay hydrated. Stay fueled. Stay warm.* A mantra for wilderness survival, with two of the three requiring fire. That's why Kyle kept a multitool in his pocket. He could start a fire with just that and some grass and cedar shavings if the weather cooperated. Sometimes he would bring along an old Altoids tin containing a sealed plastic bag with char cloth to catch the spark and oakum fiber for tinder, just in case.

"He can start a fire in a thunderstorm," Gabe said.

Not quite, but Kyle appreciated the sentiment. He shrugged.

"Impressive." Proffit said. "Perhaps you should consider a career in pyromania." He held Kyle's gaze with a coal-eyed stare for a moment before breaking into a grin. "No, seriously, what do you see for yourself in the future, Kyle? Somehow, I don't see you as a lawyer or coach."

Kyle fidgeted on his bucket. So Gabe had told him about his parents too. This was all very odd, but the man's interest in him and apparent appreciation for his skills was a welcome change. "Me either. Uhh, I don't know what my options will be. Gotta get through high school first."

"True that. But it's never too late to start thinking about it. I know a professor in the Forestry and Wildlife Department at State who does a hands-on camp for a select few just like you every year. Neck-deep in wilderness with the deer and fish and who knows what. Invitation only." He cocked his head and shrugged palms up, questioning. "I could make a call. He owes me a favor, not that you'd need it once I tell him about you."

Kyle nodded and couldn't help but smile. "Yessir, that

sounds cool." His father had laughed and cuffed him on the arm when Kyle had mentioned a career in forestry or something similar. *Sure, maybe, but I bet you'll grow out of it.*

"It's settled. I'll make a call." Proffit stood from his bucket and brushed the hem of his coat where it had touched the sand. "I'll head on. You boys be safe." He looked at Kyle. "You've got a lot going for you. I could use a kid like you on my team. If you want to earn some extra money, Gabe can put you in touch." He stepped over and extended a hand to shake. He held Kyle's grip firm as he spoke. "I understand not being appreciated. Been there, done that. But there's always a way to live your life and not someone else's."

Someone else's life. Was that what he was trying to live? Did Proffit know how to help him find his way? Kyle was uneasy about finding out. But maybe he was more afraid not to.

TEN

JACK pointed at the ground. "Case, what do you see?"

The tire tracks were obvious, just behind the spot Nash had indicated Ronny's car had been found. "Nash, I assume those are the ones you said match Devlin's truck?"

"That's the ones. Perfect match."

Jack pointed at the ground again, with a jabbing motion this time. "C'mon, you're better than that."

I snorted in protest, spread my stance for stability, and folded my arms over my chest. I'd study it as long as I had to but would not be shown up by Jack seeing something I didn't. The tracks were obvious enough, right there in a bare spot on the ground, with some white residue from a cast that had been made earlier by Nash or some of his colleagues. What else was there? I moved in a rectangle approximating the shape of a vehicle, picking up on the less obvious track from the right side of the vehicle, mostly obscured by grass. But that wasn't where Jack had been pointing. Back at the starting point, it suddenly stood out like a Lilliputian playing linebacker. A thin, jagged depression in a sliver of bare ground about ten inches to the side of and behind the other tire track.

Jack read me like a book. "You see it now, don't you?"

I nodded. "Look there, Nash. What's that?"

Nash moved over and squatted for a closer inspection. "Well, I'll be. That's another track." He peered at it for several more seconds. "Not much there, but sure looks likely identical to the other one."

"Exactly," Jack said. "Did y'all let anybody else park up here this morning?"

"Of course not. I was the one got the call, and I parked down there." The deputy pointed to the road coming into the meadow. "Blocked the road. Wasn't sure who was up here or what they'd do if they were up to no good."

"So it appears that whoever was here must have left and come back," I said. "But why?"

"Ask Devlin," Nash said.

Jack shrugged. "Maybe. Case, what you think?"

I snapped a closeup photo with my cell phone and stood erect. I told Nash we would send him the photo. "Show me where he went over."

Nash was in motion before I finished the sentence. I was surprised by the direction he headed. For whatever reason, I had unconsciously imagined the spot to be immediately perpendicular to the orientation of the car, at the edge of the bluff nearest to where we were standing, at about the halfway point. It's where I would go if I parked and wanted to walk to the edge, to look out over the river below. But instead, Nash was angling toward the far corner of the meadow. Jack peered to our right as we followed, as if his thoughts mirrored mine. But neither of us spoke.

The sun was nearing its November zenith, just south of directly overhead but bright enough to warm our necks after its rise above the trees hugging the edge of Logan's bluff at the eastern edge of the meadow. A breeze rustled the straggler leaves still hanging on, coaxing some of them to disembark, dancing against the bluebird sky as they rode the waves of the sun-warmed currents, indecisive whether to land in the meadow or ride on to the water below. Much too beautiful a day for a teen-ager to die. Especially here, at what should be a peaceful place.

"Down there." Nash stood back from the edge and nodded toward it. Before I could ask, he answered my question. "Afraid of heights. This is as close as I get."

Jack and I moved to the edge of the bluff, peering care-fully at the ground. It was dotted with plumes of brown grass but mostly covered with leaves, a few dry from their recent drop but most moist from rainfall the day before. "Any good impressions?" Jack asked. There were depressions consistent with footprints but nothing I could see of any evidentiary value. No upturned earth or sign of a struggle that either of us could appreciate. I snapped a few pics again to study later.

Nash shook his head. "What you see is all we could see."

We both attempted to peak over the edge to the shore of the bluff below, but the angle was too steep and obscured by vege-tation clinging to the vertical face of the clay. I tried holding on to an oak to gain a few more safe inches of lean, but that didn't give enough clearance either.

Jack grabbed my belt. "Easy, there, Case. Making me nervous."

I pushed back off the oak and brushed some bark shards off my shirt. "Can't see nothing. How'd you find him, Nash?"

The deputy was on the move again, back toward the spot I had imagined Shane fell from, closer to where the car was parked. He stopped after about twenty yards and stepped up onto a small boulder, one of a few scattered around the meadow. It was familiar to me, flat on top and about the size of a bench, unlike the others. I had stood upon it sometime in the past and looked out over the river, but the specifics of the moment were long lost.

Nash pointed. "Right down there."

I joined him on the rock. We were still several feet from the cliff but at what was likely one of the only vantage points where once could see down to the water's edge below. Ribbons of yellow caution tape flickered in the breeze. If the bluff was a hundred feet straight down, and we were sixty feet from the site of the fall, I estimated I was looking at a spot about 120 feet away. It occurred to me that my friend Jet could run the exact Pythagorean calculation in his head in a flash, but it didn't matter. It looked like it was half a mile away. I couldn't imagine what it felt like spotting a kid lying there.

"How'd you get to him?" Jack asked.

"Got the game wardens and went by boat. Ain't no other way."

"Guess we can do the same later."

Nash shrugged. "If you want. Nothing to see that won't turn your stomach, though."

"Yeah, I reckon you're right. Maybe I'll pass."

I studied the edge of the bluff at this spot, snapping pics as they talked. I could sense Jack's eyes following me as I moved, but he didn't say anything. I stopped and gave him a look he understood.

"Let's get going, Case. Looks like Nash has it all covered." Jack turned and moved toward the truck and swatted Nash on the shoulder as he passed. "Not sure what we thought we'd find in Devlin's favor, but we had to look."

"Don't blame you," the deputy said. "I'd do it if he was mine."

"I guess that's part of it," Jack said. "He ain't mine, but maybe he needs to be."

———

"Tell me what you saw." Jack was quizzing me before he even closed the truck door. "I know that look."

"You know how there were footprints but no sign of a struggle or anything above where they found Ronny?"

"Yeah."

"Further down, where Nash was when he spotted him, there was a chunk of clay broken off at the edge." I showed him the pic on my phone. I swiped the photo to the right to bring up another showing some marks in the soft earth where grass was sparse at the same spot. "And look at these."

Jack pointed at the screen. "Footprints?"

"That's my guess."

Jack whistled. "Maybe Nash made those earlier."

"Highly unlikely, unless he was lying about his fear of heights."

"Agoraphobia."

"No, that's fear of public places, or something like that."

Jack shook his head. "You need to study your phobias. Anyway, I was just playing devil's activist. I don't think he was faking. The man's fear looked real."

Jack needed an advocate for his vocabulary, but it had been a lost cause for a long time. "So, what are the odds that Shane fell from that spot, and someone moved the body to where he was found?"

"Doesn't make sense, either. We can go look, but Nash made it sound like it was a gory scene. Plenty of rocks down there."

"Yeah." I shuddered. "Just doesn't make much sense."

"About as much as the double tire tracks. What's next?"

I glanced at my phone. Abi was texting me. "Next is me

getting home so I can stay married."

"Sounds important." Jack slowed at the bottom of the hill as we approached Waterway Road. He looked both ways and began turning the wheel toward town.

Suddenly I had an idea. I pointed the opposite direction. "Go that way. Abi will have to wait just a sec."

Jack smiled. "Dangerous, but I like it." He spun the steering wheel and lurched onto the pavement, toward the Lock and Dam.

ELEVEN

URRY up. Need to talk. What you find?

Jack answered Tammy's text while he waited at a red light. *I'll be done soon.* That's all she needed to know. She had called a half dozen times before that, but he didn't have time to talk. She could ramble on a normal day, and this was no normal day. Maybe it was insensitive of him—he'd been called that before—but if he was going to help Devlin, time was of the essence. If the boy was innocent, and Jack believed unequivocally that he was, that meant the guilty person was running free. And the longer that went on, the more likely he or she was to get away with it. Jack remembered a seminar he'd been to the year before, where they pointed out that somewhere in the neighborhood of one third of cases are solved in two days, two thirds in a month, and only five percent after a year. Time may heal wounds, but it also lets killers get away.

There had been a time—a lifetime ago, it often seemed—when he and Case had solved a cold case as teenagers, the murder of the sheriff, of all things. And that was almost on accident, in the process of searching for the whereabouts of Jack's missing stepfather. But Jack had no intention of letting this case get cold, or solving it by accident, either. He had every intention of getting to the bottom of it quickly, like they had a few years later when their friend Jet had reported a murder and, for his trouble, been accused of being mentally ill and gotten suspended from medical school. Jet's career had hung in the balance of his and Case's ability to find the truth, and quickly. Now Devlin's life might depend on the same thing. As an eighteen-year-old, Devlin would be charged as an adult. A capital murder charge was a real possibility.

And in Mississippi, a capital murder conviction often meant the death penalty.

No matter what happened, it appeared the kid was stuck in jail for the weekend. The judge was out of town and not available for an emergency arraignment. Egg had called Jack and told him Devlin wasn't saying a word, could he or Tammy please convince him to help himself? Jack had feigned frustration about Devlin's silence but was glad, at least for now. Let him and Case work what they could before the waters got muddied. Rap had agreed to let him talk to Devlin again the next day. He hoped the boy would open up and give something useful, maybe even provide some actual clarity.

So many questions, so few answers. Why had Ronny Shane attacked Devlin on the football field? Jack assumed it had something to do with the girl he'd met in the emergency department, Lena Cole. But why did Devlin have that $250 in an envelope with Ronny's initials on it? And if that was him in the video, and it sure did appear to be, what had happened when he went up to Logan's Bluff? And who had shot the video? Jack had to admit, given Devlin's public threat to kill Shane and the video, if there indeed was a motive revolving around Lena Cole, it looked bad. Really bad. It was hard not to doubt.

But he couldn't let himself do that. Not until he had no choice. Recalling Devlin's threat reminded Jack of something else: Luke Wiseman had done the same thing. Jack would have to talk to him too, and soon. Maybe he could drag Case back out later.

Before he quit to go update Tammy and maybe even called it a day, he had one more stop to make. His and Case's trip to the Amberton Lock and Dam had not revealed any information specific to the case, but they hadn't expected it to. What they did get was the names of the men working the night before, who had called after seeing lights up on Logan's Bluff and discovering Ronny Shane's abandoned car up there the next morning at the end of the shift. He could have gotten the information from someone down at the sheriff's department, but he and Case had agreed that the less Rap knew about what they were doing, the better.

Jack really wanted to talk to Boyd Poe, the one who had made the call, but he hadn't answered his phone. So, Greely Grantham was next up. He wished Abi hadn't pulled the wife card and called Case home, because two heads were almost always better than one. Especially, Jack mused, when theirs were the two heads.

Greely Grantham's house was a yellow wooden bungalow in the old part of Amberton, two blocks off of Main Street, behind the old post office. The gray brick columns and steps needed a fresh coat of paint, and the small yard hadn't been topped with the mower since the last green of summer had turned brown, but the place was in good shape otherwise. Some colorful yard art and haphazard clusters of pansies in the flower bed suggested Greely didn't live alone.

Indeed, a woman answered the door. Her face and body were equally round, somewhat akin to a snowman with only two sections, but unlike most happy snowmen, her facial features were gathered like a brooding storm cloud. "Come in," she said, before Jack could even introduce himself. "I know who you are. I'm Tilda. Greely's coming. All this has got his stomach a little upset. Irritable bowel, the doctor says. I sho' nuff agree with that. Makes me irritable, all the running to the bathroom when he gets stressed out. Stinks too."

Jack followed the woman into an open living room with off-white beadboard walls and hardwood floors that flowed into a kitchen area at the back. The whole space reeked of turnip greens, and Jack spotted a pot with steam rising from it in the kitchen. He wondered how she could smell anything else and if that was actually what had Greely's stomach messed up. He wasn't as picky as Case was, but he drew the line at eating greens.

Tilda gestured for Jack to sit at a round table in the corner, and he settled into a wooden chair with a wicker seat. "Ma'am, I'm sorry. Nothing for him to be upset about. Didn't do anything wrong. To be honest, this is probably a wasted trip. Just trying to be thorough."

She moved to the stove and stirred the contents of the pot. "Naw, you need to talk to him. Greely's the one that saw the lights up there, not Poe. Poe's a celebrity hog, is what he is. Greely saw it first. You need to talk to him. Terrible about that boy. Terrible." She knocked the moisture off the spoon into the pot and placed a lid on it with a clang. "Greely! The man from the sheriff department is here! Wipe yourself and get out here!"

Jack cringed. *Irritable, indeed.*

Greely must have done as he was told, because he appeared from behind one of the doors just a few seconds later. He was as slender as his wife was large. His feet bounced when he walked, and his arms matched the rhythm, like a marionette. If she hadn't been in the room, it would not have been difficult not to imagine Tilda as the puppeteer. The man smiled as he approached Jack and gave a quick, deferential bow of his head. "Hello, Mr. …"

"Masterson. But you can call me Jack."

Greely took a chair beside Jack and rested his hands on the table. He didn't look up, as if there was something fascinating going on with his thumbs. His wife stood near her greens and surveyed the scene at the table, arms folded.

"Thanks for talking with me." Jack locked his eyes on the man across from him, hoping to convey his intent to get answers from him, not his wife.

"No problem. Ain't got much to tell, though."

"Yes, you do, Greely. Go on now, tell the man."

Greely held up a hand to Tilda and nodded. "Saw some lights up there on Logan's Bluff, little before midnight."

"Is that unusual? Don't people go up there all the time?"

"No. I mean, yeah. Well, not exactly." Greely shook his head as if trying to dislodge a bug from atop it. "What I'm saying is, it's not unusual. But folks ain't up there all the time."

"Did you call anybody when you saw the lights?"

Greely shook his head.

"Why not?"

"Cuz it ain't unusual, like I said.

"So why did you drive up there the next morning?"

"Protocol. We supposed to go look at the end of the shift if we see something."

Jack waited, studying Greely, hoping the man would open up instead of having to pry every detail from him. But it didn't look promising. He sighed and moved ahead. "And so what did you find? Go ahead and tell me everything."

"A car. Blue Maxima."

Jack waited again, leaning forward as if that might some-how coax another detail from his interrogee. It did not.

"Dang it, Greely." Tilda was at Greely's back now. She

rapped him on side of the head. "That's all you talked about after you got home this morning. Wouldn't even go to sleep. How you was the one who saw the lights and found the car, but Poe got to tell about it. Wouldn't shut up about it. Now's your chance and you act like you talking to Elvis or something."

Jack didn't think he looked like Elvis, but maybe Tilda's lurking was useful after all. Heck, if she'd slap her husband around a little more, no telling what he'd say.

Greely swung a half-hearted elbow in her direction and shifted his chair away a few inches. "There ain't much to tell, Tilda! It was a car. It was empty."

Jack fought back a grin and suppressed his desire to see a brawl break out. "It's okay. You're doing great, Mr. Grantham. So you found the car and called?"

"He yelled out to see if someone was off walking in the woods or something, but no one answered. Pretty brave if you ask me. I hear there's drug deals up there."

"Yes, that was brave," Jack said. "Who says there's drug deals up there? Have you ever seen that, Mr. Grantham?"

Greely shrugged. "That's what Poe says. I dunno. Ain't never seen it myself."

"Okay, let's go back to the lights you saw. One vehicle? Two? More than that?"

Greely rubbed his chin and cocked his eyes upward, like the answer might be on the ceiling. "Hard to tell. You can just see headlights up there through the trees, kinda flickering. And it ain't like we can just stand out there watching all night. We got important work to do in the lock house, ya know. But I'd say there was more than one, yeah."

Jack tried to imagine what the scene might look like. It might not be a bad idea to go there one night and recreate it, although at the moment he couldn't envision what it would add. He knew by the tire track patterns there was more than one vehicle. If Greely couldn't give a definitive number, it didn't add much. "You saw two sets of lights at the same time?"

Greely searched the ceiling again. "No, it was lights at two different times. Maybe."

"And you saw the lights, not Poe?"

Greely shook his head. "Just me."

"Okay. Nash told me they had looked at the security cameras near the lock house, where Waterway Road ends and cars sometimes turn around to go back out. Said no vehicles came through after eleven last night. Did you or Mr. Poe see anything unusual that the camera might not pick up on?"

"Nope. That's it." Greely stood from his chair. "I need to get a nap before I go in tonight. Sorry I couldn't help."

"Yep, sorry he couldn't help, Deputy," Tilda chimed in. She was back in the kitchen now, taking the greens off the eye. "Greely don't miss much. If'n there was somethin', he woulda seen it. Hope you catch that man."

Jack raised an eyebrow. "Who said it was a man?"

Greely laughed. "Just like a woman, huh? Assuming the man did it." He shot a nervous eye toward his wife, like he was glad she had moved several feet away.

Tilda grinned and nodded, not only not offended by Greely's humor but agreeing with it. "Yeah, 'cause men act crazy as bats on crack half the time. You seen that for yourself this morning."

Jack frowned. All Greely had told him about was lights and an abandoned car. He looked back and forth from husband to wife, waiting for some elaboration, but none came. They were both stuck in a musing half-grin, like with an inside joke. "You said *the* man. Is there something you aren't telling me, Mr. Grantham?"

Greely gave a dismissive wave. "Naw, you're busy. Nothing to do with that kid."

"Humor me. Maybe I'll at least get a funny story to tell."

Greely laughed. "Okay. We see crazy stuff all the time. Just this morning a feller came down the river on an upside-down table."

"A table?"

"Yep. I saw it first. Boyd wasn't paying attention, as usual." He shot Tilda a look and puffed his chest out. "But I swear, from afar we thought it was some weird four-masted boat or something, but then up close them masts was just table legs, and what looked like the cabin turned out to be just an old man sitting on it with a life vest and a backpack.

Jack held up a hand to slow Greely down.

The lock operator took the hint and took a breath before continuing. "Feller yanked the pull rope to signal us to lock him through like it was just another Saturday."

"Did you talk to him?"

Greely nodded. "Had to see what he was on and what he was doing. Make sure he was seaworthy. He showed us, had her all sealed up with roof tar, just wanted to see how far he could ride. Said he put in about a hundred miles upriver at Ethelsburg and was going strong."

"Not going anywhere in particular?"

"Nope. Said he goes wherever the notion takes him, and since the river flowed south, that was where he was headed."

"No motor, no paddle?"

"No motor. Had some oars but said he don't really use 'em except to stay in the middle. Said the river had enough power of its own without interfering with her. Or something weird like that. Who said the river is a girl, anyway?"

"Did he say why he was on a table?"

Greely pointed at Jack. "Asked him that very question, I did. Know what he said?"

Jack sighed. "I do not."

"He said because he had one and figured it would float."

Of course he did. "Did you get a name?"

"I ain't real good with names, but I can't forget his. Peregrine."

"Like the falcon?"

Greely pointed at Jack again. "Exactly. I asked the same question, and he said yes. Did you know them things can fly like five hundred miles an hour? Anyway, that was it. And before you ask, he didn't give a first name. It ain't required to be able lock through, neither. You just got to have a Coast Guard approved life jacket."

The story was odd, to say the least. Jack agreed that it was unlikely to have anything to do with Ronny Shane's death. If the cuckoo floating on the kitchen table had something to do with it, would he be coming through a few hours later, like nothing had happened? He couldn't have known the body hadn't already been discovered, in which case he would have been stopped and interrogated. On the other hand, was it possible he had seen something pertinent to the case? He would have passed very near Logan's Bluff coming down the river, although the spot where Ronny was lying dead would have likely been obscured by a bend in the river there. But the timing even for that seemed off too. If the timing of Greely's account was correct—and like it or not, it did match that of the video of Devlin at midnight—the events on the bluff would have been long over by the time Mr. Peregrine passed by.

No, this trip had been a waste, for the most part. Jack had only confirmed, if one could even call it that, information he already knew. Information Nash and Rap already knew as well. The key to everything was Devlin himself. Tomorrow, Jack would get the truth out of him one way or another.

As for the man on the table, as intriguing as the story was, Jack would just have to file the information away to process later. He had more pressing matters at hand now, but he was eager to get Case's thoughts about it. Mr. Peregrine sure did remind him of an equally enigmatic figure from years gone by.

A figure from a time in his life he'd rather forget.

TWELVE

"PLEASE tell me Jack is staying out of this."

I slid onto one of the stools at the center island in my kitchen and gave Abi a silent grimace.

Abi set her briefcase on the computer desk in the corner and leaned against it with her arms folded, eyes locked on me like blue lasers "How, Case? He's too close to it. Has Rap lost his mind?"

"I don't know that Rap is endorsing Jack's involvement, exactly. I think he's just not standing in his way. Or at least trying to make it appear that way."

"Well, that's just dumb."

"Better than losing a good deputy. Jack is hardheaded, you know that. Gonna be involved whether you or me or Rap or anybody else likes it. Would have to lock him up to keep him from it."

Abi shook her head and gave a disgusted sigh but followed it with a playful eye roll that settled on me. "Sounds like someone else I know."

I loved when she gave me that look. Too bad I was going to ruin it. I took a deep breath. "Speaking of that."

Abi's eyes flared and she cocked her head. "No."

"He's my best friend."

"No, Case! Conflict of interest."

"The only interest is proving that Devlin didn't push that kid off Logan's Bluff, if anybody did at all. Anything other than that is a conflict of justice."

"Clever."

"Can't you recuse yourself or something? Jack is your friend too."

"There's only one McKinley County Attorney, so the case is mine until it goes to a grand jury."

"Ask Walton to handle it."

Abi gave an exasperated huff and sat on a stool beside me. "Case, the arraignment has to happen within forty-eight hours of the arrest. That means Monday. The DA's office is swamped as it is; I'm not gonna ask Jim Walton to send one of his assistant DAs in to do my job because my husband wants to play detective."

My face grew hot, and I wasn't sure if it was because she had insulted me or because she was right. Abi took her job very seriously and was darned good at it. Murder cases in McKinley County weren't that common, but more times than not, if a felony landed on her desk with the perpetrator in custody, she had the case wrapped in an airtight package by the time she handed it off to the district attorney's office for the grand jury appearance. If the roles were reversed, I certainly wouldn't want her helping the opposing team and asking me to get someone else to coach mine.

Of course, this wasn't a football game. This was a life. One had already been lost, and neither I nor Jack nor Abi nor anyone else with an ounce of moral fiber wanted another to be unjustly ruined. Of course, none of us wanted Devlin to be guilty as accused, either.

Abi put her hand on my arm. "I'm sorry. That was ugly."

"Never wanted to play detective. In case you didn't notice, I didn't choose to go into law enforcement. I'm a football coach."

"And a good one too. Yet somehow you always find a way to get dragged into the other."

"Always is a strong word, I think. It's been almost twenty years."

Abi slipped on her reading glasses and checked her phone. "Looks like I'm meeting with Bert and Devlin tomorrow."

I nodded but said nothing. Jack would be there, too, but she could find that out on her own. As for my role in all this, I would just have to tell Jack that I was bowing out. I cared about Devlin, both as my player and because of his closeness to Jack, but it wasn't worth a conflict at home. Besides, there would be plenty of competent people on the case to get to the truth of it.

Suddenly our door that Abi had come through minutes before flew open again. This time our son filled the entrance. Kyle had a sleeping bag over one shoulder and a backpack dangling from the other. He looked tired but possessed a smile I had not seen recently.

"Hey, baby," Abi said. "All that stuff goes to your room. Don't drop it here."

"I know, Mom. And I'm not a baby."

Abi laughed. "You'll always be my baby."

"Son, ignore your mom. On the baby part, not the 'don't clutter the kitchen' part. Did y'all catch any fish?"

Kyle shrugged. "A few. Not a good bite this time." His smile returned. "But I did get a job offer."

"Didn't know they were handing those out on the banks of the Timtullah." I was being sarcastic but couldn't imagine what kind of job he was talking about.

"Miller's Creek, actually. But we had a visitor. A friend of Gabe's."

Abi motioned for Kyle to go ahead and set his gear down

on the tiled floor, despite her earlier admonition. The stakes had changed. "What's his name?"

"Mr. Proffit."

"Like Moses?"

Kyle rolled his eyes. "I doubt it, Dad. Like that pizza place we never go to."

"And he just showed up in the boondocks and offered a job?"

Kyle smiled and shook his head. "Don't be so obtuse. He has some land or something near where we camp. I think Gabe told him where we were camping, so he walked over."

"And the job?" Abi asked.

"I guess fixing fences on his land or something." He picked up his sleeping bag and backpack. "But a job's a job."

"Good for you." I could pester him later about details, but no point in ruining the moment. Kyle was excited, and it was good to see. He was not an unhappy kid as far as I could tell, but he had seemed more withdrawn in recent months. Abi said it was just a phase, that he was trying find his place in the world. Whatever the case, if the offer was legitimate, a little hard work would be good for him. But I would have to find out who this Mr. Proffit was. It was odd that this fellow just showed up out of the blue and magically offered Kyle a "job." Wouldn't be the first time a pervert had moved in on a gullible teenager with fake promises. Color me cynical.

My phone buzzed. It was Jack.

Glad u workin it out with Abi. Can't do it without you. There's a development. Call me.

THIRTEEN

JACK cut his truck off but didn't open the door. Aside from a deep breath, he didn't move. The five minutes he would sit in his driveway before going inside were often the most useful of the day. Not the best—he'd take five seconds with Janie and Lily over an eternity any other place—but the most useful. Now he relished the silence. An opportunity to catch his breath, organize his thoughts after talking to Case, and plan his next move.

A cat shifted positions on the hood of Janie's car parked in the carport. It was too dark to tell, but it was probably the gray tabby he'd seen around. He would be sure to mention it to Janie when he went inside. She was a neat freak —certainly not inherited from his genes—and kept her car spotless. Paw prints across her hood might just be enough to distract her away from being mad at him.

Janie had wanted Lily to spend the day with Jack, but it just hadn't worked out. From Lily's perspective, a day with Kellen Reynolds was like a day with a rock star. But Janie wouldn't see it that way. Jack had been working more than usual, and she had thought it would be good for Jack and Lily to spend some quality time together rather than get a babysitter while she worked her shift at the furniture factory. Sure, Janie would understand the extenuating circumstances in principle, but the specifics of them would not engender warm and empathetic feelings.

Janie was not particularly fond of Tammy, especially Tammy in the role of Jack's significant other. Janie wouldn't want Devlin to suffer for something he didn't do, but she would be hard pressed not to believe Tammy had coerced Jack to put his nose where it didn't belong. That might be partially right, but if Tammy dumped him tomorrow, Jack would still feel a bond with Devlin and a desire to fill the void where a father should have been.

Jack sighed and reached back with his right hand to touch Lily's leg. It was their routine, him bumping her lower leg after they stopped, inching his way upward, her giggling and wriggling in her booster seat even before he got to her knee, where he would squeeze her kneecap between thumb and middle finger. "Let me show you how a horse eats corn," he would say, mimicking a chewing motion with his hand, and she would cackle uncontrollably until he stopped a few seconds later. He smiled when she didn't move. Five-minute decompressions in the driveway didn't happen if Lily was awake. It was horsey corn or go inside, but never quiet time.

The cat moved again, but something was different. Then the shape shifted in a way that caused the hairs to stand erect on the back of Jack's neck.

It wasn't a cat.

Jack yanked the door handle and lurched out of his truck. "Hey!"

The cat-shadow suddenly stood erect and darted out of the carport, turning left toward the backyard.

"Hey, get back here!" Jack pulled his Glock 23 and gave chase, stumbling as he rounded the front of his truck but recovering in a flash. "Police! Stop!" He stopped at the corner of the house rather than running carelessly right into a trap. A two-by-four to the forehead had taught him that lesson years before.

He peeked around and pulled back quickly, listening. Nothing happened. Neighbors' wind chimes drowned any chance of hearing something useful. He eased around the corner, gun leading. He scanned the darkness for a glimpse of the intruder, but the darkness between the neighborhood houses was too deep. And the person wasn't dumb enough to venture into the light. They were gone.

Jack's mind raced to comprehend what had just happened. Had he interrupted a break-in when he pulled into the driveway? A quick glance at the house revealed that all doors were closed, and through the yellow glow of the kitchen window he could see Janie moving around inside. Whomever it was had not gone inside, thank God, and the outside, including Janie's car, appeared to be unmolested.

Jack walked to the back of the house again, peering into the still darkness as if the perpetrator might change his mind and reappear. If he had thwarted a break-in by coming home, why hadn't the intruder just crouched out of sight and crawled away undetected? It was almost as if he had chosen to watch Jack sit in his truck. But why?

Or maybe he wanted to be seen.

Lily!

Jack gasped and whirled to race back to his truck. He covered the distance in five gut-twisting steps that hurt like a hundred.

He hurled open the door to the rear passenger seat where Lily had been sitting.

Her booster seat sat empty, suddenly as small through the gaping door of the truck as a lily pad on an endless ocean. A wave of cold hit him but was instantly replaced by a hot dread that blanketed him like a red Sahara storm. There would be a killing before the night was over if he had anything to do with it. "Lily!" He stepped back and pivoted to project the roar to anyone in the zip code. "You'll wish you had never been born!"

A sound stopped him before he could gather himself to do anything else. What was that? Then he heard it again. A tiny whimper, much smaller by contrast than actuality in the wake of the yelling seconds before. Then two words. "Papa Jack?"

The front seat of the truck.

Lily was curled in a ball where Jack had been sitting moments before, when he had been watched by the lurker in the carport. Jack grabbed her up and hugged her close, protecting her with two muscular arms. He spun in a circle to make sure the man had not returned, awash with relief but also feeling silly. How many neighbors had heard him scream out his threat?

Lily pushed back to see Jack face to face. "Why did you yell at me so mean?" Her tiny voice was growing as she awakened.

He kissed her forehead. "I'm sorry, baby. I was being silly. I wasn't yelling at you. I thought someone else had done a bad thing."

"I thought you were gone."

"No, no. I'm right here. Just stay in your seat next time until I get back, okay? It could be dangerous for you to climb up to where Papa Jack drives."

Lily frowned. "I didn't climb over. That man moved me."

"I don't understand. Why would someone do that?"

Jack pointed at the suitcase Janie was packing and shot her a stern look. *Keep packing.* She was as stubborn as her mother had been, and he loved her dearly for it. She was a little taller than

Michelle had been, with a rounder face and darker skin tone, but she had the same tender eyes and mouth that moved with her thoughts and often gave them away.

Janie's lips pursed. "I can actually pack and talk at the same time. Surely you can manage to talk while I pack."

Jack sighed. "Sorry, baby. I don't know. The only thing I can think of is a warning."

"Warning for what?"

"I'm not sure. Maybe stay out of Devlin's case?"

"And you really think Lily and I should leave?"

"Your idea is a good one. It's just for a few days. Until some things blow over. Meg said it was okay?"

"Absolutely. What are old college friends for if not to offer witness protection services?"

Jack gave Janie a one-armed hug and glanced at Lily asleep among the throw pillows on the bed. "It's not like Tupelo is the other side of the world."

She closed the top and pressed on it with two hands to help the zipper function. "Okay. And I appreciate your caution. I still think it was probably one of Devlin's friends being silly. Think about the moronic stuff you did as a teenager."

"I'd rather not." Jack grabbed Janie's suitcase and nodded for her to get Lily. He squared his shoulders to Janie's after she had Lily gathered in both arms. "Don't tell anyone where you are. Don't call or text anyone. I'll have a burner phone in your hands first thing tomorrow so we can communicate."

Janie rolled her eyes and shifted Lily's head to a better position on her shoulder. "Yeah, because the Russian mob might be listening."

"I'm serious." Jack's fixed jaw and stern eyes backed his words. "Not a soul."

"Okay, okay."

Something caught Jack's eye. White, barely protruding, wedged into the waistband of Lily's pants. "What's this?" He reached and pulled out a folded slip of paper, torn from a notepad.

Janie tried but failed to jerk it from Jack's hand, her eyes wide with alarm.

What Jack saw written on the paper sent chills rippling down his spine and burned tears into Janie's eyes.

Stay out of it and let justice be served. Next time I won't give her back.

PART TWO

We stand upon the brink of a precipice.
We peer into the abyss—we grow sick and dizzy.
Our first impulse is to shrink away from the danger.
Unaccountably we remain...
—Edgar Allen Poe

FOURTEEN

Sunday, October 28, 2018

I F anyone needed prayers, it was Devlin. So when Brother Ferrell Martin had called to check on Jack and Tammy and tell them about the special prayer time they would be having for Devlin at church the next morning, Jack understood why the preacher ended the conversation with, "I look forward to seeing you there."

But unless Jack had been misunderstanding things all these years, the Good Lord wouldn't need him to be there to answer the prayers when they were lifted up. He figured he could help more by beating the bushes for a killer than by sitting in a pew with a somber face. Yes, The Bible said the sparrow would be provided food, but God expected the little bird to go find it.

But Tammy wouldn't hear of it. Mentally, she was already barely hanging on, crying and pacing, bordering on frantic at times as she pressed Jack incessantly to prove Devlin's innocence. She had even said she "might break" if that did not happen in the immediate future, which Jack saw as an even better reason to be out searching for answers. But the preacher said they needed to be there for the prayer, and by heavens, she wasn't going to let Jack do anything to jinx it by skipping, no matter the motive.

So, Jack relented and did as Tammy insisted. He put on a button-up shirt, picked up Tammy, and headed to the church.

He dutifully looked at the preacher when he preached, stood for the songs when they sang, and bowed his head when everyone else did. But his mind was elsewhere. At the jail interviewing Devlin, searching the crime scene again, reviewing phone records and statements from friends and classmates and turning over a dozen other stones that had thus far been left undisturbed.

Tammy elbowed him and nodded toward the back of the church when the announcements began after the special prayer. Evidently, God had what he needed, so Jack could go do his thing.

He hoped Rap's offer to let him see Devlin thirty minutes before his one o'clock meeting with Abi still stood. He and Rap had had quite a round the day before. Jack could normally come and go as he pleased to interview detainees, but for some reason the sheriff had insisted he be limited on this one, not just on the time but also on who could be present. "No wannabe detectives in my prison," had been the words he used.

Jack had accused him of having little-man syndrome, which prompted Rap to threaten to ban him from any participation in the case altogether. Rather than make things worse, Jack had just hung up.

Now as he raced his truck to the prison, hoping all the highway patrolmen were sitting on a pew getting a special prayer somewhere themselves, he feared what might happen if Rap had changed his mind and tried to stop him when he got there. It was difficult not to imagine the stocky sheriff as the same kid from high school he used to flatten on the football field. Be cool, he told himself. Be cool. Getting fired wouldn't help a thing. Nor would going to jail himself.

But Rap wasn't there to stop him. Nash met him near the entrance instead. He looked at his watch. "You're late."

"Didn't realize we had a date," Jack said.

Nash chuckled and turned down a short hallway. He stopped at a door and spoke with his hand on the knob. "He's waiting for you. Kid ain't said five words since we got him."

"Good."

The deputy swung open the door and stepped back. "I'll leave you to it."

Devlin was sitting at the small table in the interrogation room. He didn't look up. Jack slid into the chair across from him and studied the boy. The area around his left eye was not as swollen as Dr. Gracie had told him it might be, but it was indeed a deep purple with blood red staining of the white sclera. She had called it a conjunctival hemorrhage and said it might take a couple of weeks to fade away, that he could scare little kids with it for kicks until then.

Jack had never met Devlin's father, but from the photos he'd seen, the man had certainly marked him. Narrow brown eyes with an upturn at the edges and long lashes that softened them, rectangular nose with equal width of the bridge and the tip, a deep center cleft leading down to full lips. Straight brown hair fell to his eyebrows in front and flowed into a slight wave over the collar of his shirt in the back. He was an even-featured, nice-looking kid. Normally boisterous and brimming with confidence. But not today.

"Tough night?" Jack asked.

Devlin shrugged. "Nothing I can't handle."

"Didn't become anyone's girlfriend, did you?"

Devlin looked up for the first time. "Not funny."

"Sorry. They say you aren't talking much."

He shook his head. "Nothing to say. I did it. Told you I did."

Jack nodded. "Okay, fine. So just tell me what happened."

"Shane jumped me. I met him at Logan's. Things went south." He sighed.

Jack watched the kid a moment. Jaw set, stoic, the same determined look he'd have when Jack would give him a pep talk before a big game. Football wasn't about *rah-rah* emotion, it was about being tougher than the guy across from you. And no question, Dev was a tough son of a gun. No father, never given much of a chance. Had to raise himself at times before Tammy's medications got regulated. He had been through some rough spans. And maybe he was the killer. But no way he was a murderer. If Ronny Shane had died at Devlin's hand, it was an accident. But why wouldn't Devlin just say so? An idea was taking shape. And Jack didn't like it.

"So that's all you have to say? You're not gonna help me help you?"

Devlin shrugged.

Okay, then," Jack said. "I'm just gonna walk through it. Stop me if I miss something." Jack lowered his voice to a whisper and covered his mouth with a hand. "Here's the deal. Keep your mouth shut so's not to say something I have to testify to, since we technically ain't family and I am an officer of the law. You can nod yes or no. Deal?"

"Maybe."

Jack hated to even broach his theory, but him just speaking wasn't going to incriminate so long as Devlin didn't admit anything. And he needed answers, fast. "What were you and Ronny fighting about? I'm assuming it was about that girl, Lena. It's always about a girl. Luke said she was Ronny's girlfriend, so for him to attack you means you've been messing with her. Right?"

Devlin gave no reaction.

"So after Ronny cleans your clock on the field, you threaten to kill him, your pal Luke threatens to kill him too, you get released from the ER and go home. Your mother comes to my house for a bit but goes home just before midnight, and you're still there. Good so far?"

Devlin looked up and raised an eyebrow but said nothing.

"Somehow, you sneak out and meet up with Luke. Based on the video—I haven't figured out who shot that yet, but I will—you go pick him up. I'm not sure how you contacted Ronny, but we'll find out from phone records. Anyway, you make plans to meet him at Logan's."

Devlin's eyes narrowed, and one corner of his mouth quivered upward before settling back into a stoic stare.

"Your truck had the envelope labeled R.S. with the cash. My guess is that envelope wasn't yours. I'll bet we find Luke Wiseman's DNA all over it. He came loaded and ready to buy. What's a friend's honor when there is money to be made? How much meth can you buy with two-hundred fifty bucks? I can't imagine Luke having that kind of cash for himself, or doing that much meth, for that matter. My guess is, he had several buyers at school lined up, maybe they even gave him the money ahead of time." Jack leaned back in his chair and folded his arms. "I'm close, aren't I?"

"I ain't no drug dealer, I'll tell you that."

"Exactly." Now they were getting somewhere. "So Ronny gets there first, parks in the middle of that little field at the top of Logan's. You and Luke pull up shortly thereafter. The three of you share a smoke, maybe talk about old times, pretend for a bit that the fight didn't happen."

The boy cocked his head, almost imperceptibly.

"After the smoke you decide to move, maybe check out

the river for kicks. I don't know exactly, but there's no sign of Ronny being dragged. So he walked to the edge."

Devlin had mastered the art of no reaction. "Sounds about right," he said.

"I just can't figure out what happened to make Luke push him over. Maybe the girl came up. You and Ronny argued, and Luke stepped in? Heck, maybe Ronny was high and just walked off the edge by mistake. But if that's the case, why don't you say that?"

The door opened, and Nash stuck his head in. "Time's up. Attorneys are here, Jack."

"Okay, give me one minute. Please."

Nash stepped in halfway and stood tall. He looked from Jack to Devlin and back again, waiting for Jack to proceed with whatever was to occur in the requested minute. Neither of them said a thing, so Nash gave up and retreated. "One minute."

"One more thing. Last night someone was in my driveway, left a note threatening to take Lily. How does that factor into what happened at Logan's?"

Devlin's reaction to this question was an open book for the first time. Both eyes widened. Incredulous, shocked, angry. Confused.

Jack didn't press it. He would have to find answers about that elsewhere. "Okay, I don't know, either." He pushed back from the table and rose to leave. "Hang in there and be smart."

He would ask Abi and Egg if he could stay, but he wasn't going to get his hopes up. If Devlin behaved as expected, they would be sorely disappointed in what new information they gleaned from their visit. That wasn't necessarily a bad thing, though. No point in Devlin saying something to dig his own grave. Egg wasn't the best, but he was better than nothing. And with just a little time, Jack was confident he and Case could sort it all out. But the clock was ticking. The arraignment was the next day.

"Jack?" Devlin's voice stopped him. "Thanks."

"Thanks? For what?"

"For figuring it out."

Jack's heart sank. Surely he hadn't actually figured it out. Or had he?

FIFTEEN

spun the steering wheel and glanced at Jet in the passenger seat. "How did you get dragged into this?"

He shot me a look and rolled his eyes. "You know, Jack has a way of doing that."

"Yeah, he does. Plus, Tammy begged me."

"Tammy? Didn't know she had that kind of effect on you."

I shrugged. Normally she didn't. I wasn't fond of Jack's involvement with her, but that was nothing new for his choice of girlfriends. But Tammy was a mother, and the mother of a kid I cared deeply about at that. The problem I couldn't get out of my head was that this kid had confessed to a murder. What was I getting myself into? The prospects of ruining my reputation trying to protect a killer had planted a lump in my throat that wouldn't go away. But so did the idea of an innocent kid going to jail. It wouldn't be the first time a hormone-driven teenager had said something stupid without understanding the consequences. But if so, what was the reason?

I accelerated past the turn to Logan's Bluff and moved on down Waterway Road to the boat ramp, where Jack would be meeting us. We were heading back to the crime scene again, but this time from a different angle. It was time to look at the spot where Ronny had been found, and there was only one good way to get there.

I was glad Jet was coming with us. In years gone by, his

astute logic and quick thinking had helped us solve more than one murder and had also saved my life. Not only was he the smartest person I had ever met, but he was good company too. I hoped that years of practicing cardiology hadn't dulled his ability to solve crimes. I was rather certain that coaching football had dulled mine.

Having him along also made me feel better about my decision to come. I had been second-guessing myself, thinking maybe I should have bowed out. Doing so would have been good for my marriage. Abi didn't understand why I was involved at all, since it was a potential conflict of interest for her. As the county attorney, she had no choice but to participate. My argument was that I didn't have a choice, either. Jack and I were like brothers, and if he asked for my help, I was obligated to give it. I had already resigned myself to the possibility I might be sleeping on the couch for a time.

"This is no weather to be out on the water." Jet turned up his fleece collar and gave an anticipatory shiver as I slid into our parking spot.

"Ain't that the truth." It wasn't bitterly cold, but a fifteen-MPH breeze on a midforties day was enough to chill the bones. Thank goodness the sun was shining. "Let's make this quick. Nash said there wasn't anything but gore where the body was found. Sounds like he hit the rocks pretty hard."

Jack was ready at the dock. He had already unloaded the boat at the ramp, parked the truck and trailer, and was sitting at the center console with the motor idling. "C'mon slowpokes. Freezing my nuts off waiting on you two."

I stepped onto the deck of the eighteen-foot NauticStar and moved toward the back. "Sounds painful."

Jet loosened the mooring line from the cleat and pushed

the boat away from the dock as he stepped in. "When'd you get this?"

"Wanna buy it? This out-of-town job is killing me."

I laughed. "Jet in a fishing boat? Maybe a cruise ship."

Jet smiled. "You're not wrong." He motioned toward the ruddy face of the bluff looming in the distance. "Now let's go see what we can find."

The wind bit at our cheeks and drew tears from our eyes as Jack navigated away from the dock, through the lagoon, and out toward the main channel. Even though the bluff was visible from the boat ramp, access to its base required a loop out into river and around a four- or five-acre island. Technically it was more a peninsula than an island, since a narrow isthmus connected it, but everyone called it an island anyway. Hog Island, actually. Supposedly a crazy old codger had once raised hogs on it because he thought its location would deter thieves, back before the Army Corps of Engineers had bought everything up. It seemed plausible; everyone loves bacon.

The water was choppy from the wind. Not ocean-choppy but enough for the keel to bounce and give our motion some rhythm as we idled the around the island abutting the river channel.

It was difficult to imagine anyone farming anything but briars on the island now. Once upon a time I remembered it being inhabited with majestic oaks that shaded out much of the undergrowth. Abi had once commented on a boating outing that it would be a nice place for a picnic, and I suspected many had done just that. But most of the trees were just stubs now, perhaps victims of disease or flooding or something else. Maybe a tornado that I didn't remember. With the death of the trees and their canopy, the ground cover had flourished. Thick tangles of every briar species imaginable had taken over. Mother Nature giveth, and she taketh away.

Jack spun the wheel and steered port side, bringing Logan's bluff into full view before us. I had been to its base many times but only to fish when the current was just right and the river eddies swirled, attracting ancient flathead catfish to lurk at the bottom and let the river feed them. No matter how many times I came, it was impossible not to crane my neck and gaze at the vertical, red clay cliff face, always alive with a different expression each time, depending on the angle of the sun's rays against its jagged wall and which tree roots were protruding at that particular moment near the top. It was as if the roots would burst forth, be surprised at the absence of nourishing earth, and attempt to dive back in. And Logan would hold firm, unwavering, a spectator.

What had the old bluff seen yesterday and in days gone by? Had anyone fallen off before? Surely Ronny was not the first person Logan had watched tumble across its face. Maybe a Native American had slipped once upon a time while climbing the wall to prove his bravery. Or perhaps some hapless settler had wandered off in the night, lost and oblivious to the fact the land dropped away without warning. But had anyone been forced off before? And what about Ronny? Had he been forced, or had something else happened?

"About fifty-five miles per hour."

Jet was staring at the top of the bluff, and I knew exactly what he was talking about.

"If you say it's a hundred-foot drop, which is about thirty meters, estimate Ronny's weight at eighty kilograms, it's a pretty easy calculation." He smiled. "Just have to figure the square root of 588 and convert meters per second to miles per hour. That's ballpark, mind you. To be perfectly precise you would also need to estimate resistance, which would require the air density at the time, then a drag coefficient, a cross-sectional area, and a shape coefficient, all of which depend on how his body was positioned during the fall. Et cetera."

Jack gave me a look he and I had shared many times over the years. "English, please."

"He hit the bottom at about fifty-five miles per hour."

"What if he had hit the water first?" I asked. "Survivable?"

"Water is a lot like concrete at that speed. Depends on whether the water was still or not, believe it or not, and especially how he was positioned. Force would be, let's see … 785 newtons, which is tremendous. He would have to go feet first to have a chance. Even then would have to have his hand over his mouth to keep from inhaling. Legs crossed too. A river water enema at that speed could shred the intestines."

"Dang, Jet," Jack grimaced. "Coulda done without that image."

"Thanks for the physics lesson, Professor." I turned my attention to the scene before us. Hitting the water would be terrible, but oh my—hitting here on the rocks?

Yellow caution tape fluttered and strained in the breeze, conspicuous and unnecessary in my opinion, likely drawing the attention of river passersby rather than discouraging nosy intrusions as was intended. It was tied off roughly in a square, stretching from two rocks on one end to two flimsy saplings struggling for purchase on a measly parcel of flat ground along the edge of the bluff at the other. Jack eased the boat to the edge of the rocks, letting it drift the final few feet until the hull scraped them with a gentle nudge. Jet stepped off the bow onto a rock not much larger than his foot, struggling to find a foothold on something more substantial without crossing the tape line.

"Easy there, Grace," Jack said. Our friend was anything but graceful, and Jack loved the irony of calling Jet by his wife's formal name.

Jet grinned and almost fell into the water. "It's not nice to pick on people with disabilities."

I stepped out of the boat and found a patch of dry ground closer to the edge of the bluff. "I'm not sure you can use that. You were disabled before you were disabled."

Jet jabbed me with an elbow. "Then it should count double."

For as long as I could remember, Jet had been a bit on the slow and portly side, never as athletic as Jack and me. Then as a teenager he had been nearly killed in a motor vehicle assault by VJ MacIntosh and had never fully recovered from his injuries. He made light of it at times, and we chided him, too, the way close friends will. But we didn't let anyone else do so if we were around, and there was never any doubt between us as to how much we admired his grit and determination to overcome his physical limitations. The fact that his mental gymnastics were to our cognitive capabilities what a double back flip with three twists is to a jumping jack was his trump card, seldom played but always available if we gave him too much grief.

Jack was still in the boat, rocking with the pulse of the waves lapping against the bank, his eyes locked on the jagged rocks enclosed by the tape cordon.

I followed his gaze but didn't see anything obvious. "What do you see?"

He blinked hard. "Nothing. Just trying to imagine."

"What do you really think happened?" Jet asked. "You talked to Devlin."

"He didn't do it."

"How do you know?"

Jack shook his head. "I just know it. I see it in his eyes. But he didn't tell me anything."

Which was all the more intriguing. Why wasn't Devlin talking? Was he trying to avoid incriminating himself—which, if so, didn't necessarily mean he was guilty—or was it something else? Was he protecting someone? How far would Devlin go to protect a friend like Luke Wiseman, perhaps? Or maybe Lena Cole? It wouldn't be the first time one point of a love triangle had killed another to simplify things. To hear Jack talk about Devlin, he was the type to be loyal to the point of his own destruction. I knew the kid nearly as well and couldn't disagree.

I studied the scene before me while Jet did the same and Jack finally began to make his way out of the boat. Burgundy stains on the rocks within the taped-off area left little doubt where the body had been found. Unless of course it had been moved from somewhere else, which seemed unlikely. Why would someone go to that trouble? If they had, what evidence would they leave behind?

The moist sand between the rocks seeped with the footprints of a half dozen law enforcement personnel and who knows how many others. No clues to glean from that. I hoped they had taken photographs on arrival and would have to ask Jack to look, but I knew if anything as conspicuous as footprints had been present when the body was found, the investigation would be taking a totally different turn right now. "Jack, was Ronny wet or dry?"

Jack frowned. "Huh?"

"Wet or dry?" I pointed to the crime scene before us and then up and down the edge of the bluff. There was this peninsula of dryish ground and a couple of others much further down, but for the most part the vertical face met the water at a right angle, especially to our left, which was directly below the meadow at the top where Ronny—and someone else—had been parked. "It didn't rain last night, so was he wet or dry?"

Jack nodded in understanding. "Dry, from my understanding."

It was a long shot, but Jack and I both had seen evidence that something had disturbed the edge of the bluff further down from where Ronny appeared to have gone over. A shoe-sized chunk of earth was missing. But anything that went over there would have gone straight into the water, where rocks lurking beneath the surface could have caused severe trauma matching what Ronny undoubtedly suffered.

Since the body was dry, though, it seemed highly unlikely Ronny had gone over the edge down there and been dragged to be displayed on the rocks. Ruling that out didn't hurt my feelings, as the theory never did make much sense, anyway.

"He died right here." Jet was crouching over the blood spots.

I balanced on two rocks closer to him. "How do you know?"

He reached out to a two-foot bush an arm's length away. "Look."

I strained to appreciate a maroon hue on the leaves.

Jet snapped a photo with his phone. "See how the blood looks like it came out of a spray bottle? That's expiratory splatter."

"English, please," Jack said.

"Hemoptysis."

Jack signed and shot me an exasperated look.

"He coughed up blood?" I said.

Jet nodded. "That doesn't prove that his injuries occurred here, but he took his last breaths here. And if his clothes were dry, then put two and two together."

I folded my arms and craned my neck again, peering up the face of the bluff above us. Trying to imagine. "You got anything else, Jet?"

He shook his head and looked upward with me. "The answers are up there. If there was anything else to help us here, it's either on a photograph at the station or is long gone. Wouldn't be surprised if it's the latter." He cut his eyes to Jack. "No offense to your peeps."

Jack stepped into the boat. "Truth is truth. Let's go."

Jet was last in the boat and pushed us off. He pointed down the bank. "Let's slide down that way just for kicks."

Jack shrugged and steered the tiller to move us down the bank, along the edge of the bluff. "Nothing down here really. Gets shallow where the bluff quits. Doesn't fish as good as it looks."

About fifty yards further, the vertical face of Logan's Bluff began to give way to a gradual slope up a wooded hillside, and the water did just as Jack had said, shallowing into a narrow cove that struck me as a likely spot to catch bass on the bed when the season was right. But what we were fishing for wasn't going to be here. We were after a killer.

"Told you," Jack said. "Let's go."

"Hang on." Jet stood just as the bow veered left toward the deeper water. He pivoted to point up into the cove. "Look, how the bulrushes right there are different."

Jack gave the tiller a push, and boat lurched back to the right, causing Jet to stagger and nearly tumble over.

"Sheesh, Jack! Take it easy."

I would have laughed under other circumstances, but my eyes were fixated on what Jet had seen: a swath of bulrushes crushed and laid askew amid undisturbed clusters of the coarse, tubular grass filling the shallows along the edge of the cove.

"Jack, how wide is that?" I said, already knowing his answer.

"About as wide as a small boat." Jack raised an eyebrow and cocked his head. "Or a kitchen table."

SIXTEEN

J ACK and I debated about the standard width for a kitchen table versus that of a johnboat until Jet spoke up. "Unless one of you has a tape measure, it's moot. We can't measure the width of disturbance of whatever it was anyway."

Jack patted the starboard gunwale where he sat at the wheel while the boat idled. "Okay, fine, but what I do know is that the width of this beaut is seven-foot-eight."

"It's the beam."

Jack shook his head at Jet with a narrow-eyed shrug. "You're getting' on my nerves now. What?"

Jet pointed with both index fingers at the widest portion of the NauticStar's hull. "The greatest width of a boat. It's called the beam."

Jack shot me a look. "Tell him we don't care about boat anatomy any more than gross anatomy."

I ignored him and leaned out over the bow, spreading my arms before me. "Based on that, we're looking at something about five feet wide. And my guess is that's about right for a table or a boat." Perhaps some expert forensics could distinguish between the two, but even that seemed unlikely given all we had was some turbid water and flattened bulrushes. But there was something else. "Pull up and let me out."

Jack eased us close enough for me to step out onto dry land, a few feet further down. "What you got?"

The crackle of dry leaves mingled with the squish of moist

earth beneath my feet as I made my way along the shore edge to the indention made by the other boat. Or table. Sure enough, I confirmed what had appeared little more than a shadow from my position moments earlier in Jack's boat. "Footprints." I pointed up the hillside, in the direction of Logan's Bluff. "Going that way."

Jet whistled. "The plot thickens."

"Prolly was fishing and had to pee," Jack said.

"Maybe. But I've got to find out."

Jet stood and moved to the bow as if to join me.

I waved him away. "No, you and Jack meet me at the top." Jet was many things, but a woodsman wasn't one of them. I doubted I could follow the footprints very far, as I could see them already fading several feet up the leaf-strewn rise where the ground became dry. But if there was something to see, I could do it better by myself. I had learned from experience trailing wounded deer that nothing was more frustrating than someone fouling up the evidence. Plus, I wanted Jet to give his take on what Jack and I had noted atop Logan's Bluff earlier. Light would be fading soon, and truth has a way of hiding in the dark.

"Don't get lost, Red Riding Hood." Jack shifted the boat in reverse and began backing out into the cove. "The Big Bad Wolf may be hungry."

I glanced down at my jacket and asked myself how I had gotten tangled up so many years prior with a friend so deranged. "It's maroon."

Jet laughed and mouthed, *Red* as they pulled away. Jack shoved the throttle forward and motored on, sending waves from his wake rolling to the shoreline. I watched them make the turn around Hog Island in the distance and disappear.

I glanced down the shoreline, toward the point where Ronny's body had been discovered. If the indentations in the grass were indeed evidence that Peregrine moored here, there were two additional possibilities with strikingly different implications. He left in the dark, in which case he could not have seen the body lying on the rocks, or he left after sunrise, when it would have been impossible not to notice it.

Neither made any sense considering the other circumstances. I scrolled through the possible scenarios in my mind. One, he left in the dark and had nothing to do with Ronny's fall. If so, where did he go between then and the time he locked through in broad daylight? The lock was right around the bend, and it's not like he could have pushed upriver for a time. The lock operators had been very clear that he did not have a motor on the watercraft, if one could call it that.

Two, he was guilty in Ronny's fall. If so, why did he wait to lock through in broad daylight? Did he want to get caught and was surprised when he wasn't? Three, he left in the daylight and had nothing to do with Ronny's fall but saw him lying there as he passed by. If so, why wouldn't he have told someone? It was enough to make my head spin, and I didn't have time for that.

I turned my attention to my task and asked myself whether I was wasting my time. How difficult would it be to make my way up to the top of Logan's from here? And what was it I thought I would find? Twenty steps confirmed what I had feared, that the footprints—which were little more than vague depressions in the earth, with nothing specific about their owner to reveal—disappeared quickly. Maybe Jack was right. Maybe the person had just needed to empty their bladder.

Oh well, it wasn't like I didn't need the exercise. But I didn't like how the shadows were already lengthening. I had underestimated how much more quickly the darkness would come here beneath the trees, in the eastern shadow of the rising earth, than out on the open water.

The brisk breeze from earlier in the afternoon had subsided, and the trees had followed suit by also growing still. The woods were largely silent, save the occasional shrill of a brown thrasher or last-minute rustle in the leaves of a towhee. It was the type of quiet I usually relished when I had nothing but time to spend on a lazy afternoon, in familiar settings, neither of which applied now.

I began my ascent, picking my way carefully to avoid breaking twigs and landing on layers of dry leaves with my steps. I had no real reason to be quiet other than the instinct implanted at a young age by my father, who said it was our duty to respect Mother Nature and melt into her surroundings whenever fortunate enough to be invited.

Who had been here, and why? Somehow, I knew it had to be the man who called himself Peregrine. The questions were, did I know him, and was it a coincidence? My father in his role as sheriff had also taught me that when a crime was involved, believing in coincidences was as useful as planning to marry the tooth fairy. So, in my mind, this Peregrine fellow, whomever he was, was guilty until proven innocent. But how to find him?

My quadriceps burned as I moved up the hillside, my labor made doubly difficult by the fact I covered ground in a zigzag pattern, trying not to miss something. I scoured the ground for anything that might be a clue and begged my lungs to hang in there for the effort. It occurred to me that unless the mystery table-rider was half mountain goat, a leisurely stroll would not have led him up the path I was taking. He would have gone the other way, to the south, where the trek was much easier. Unless he had a particular reason to get to the top of Logan's.

I pushed on, alternating between bending oak and hickory limbs out of my way and using them to pull myself up the steeper parts. I came to a sharp slope about four feet high rising up before me and paused to catch my breath. If there were many more of those ahead, they might have to call a helicopter to get me out of there. I looked side to side for an easier way up but saw none. I aimed for a young sourwood perched at the top of the rise and small enough to grab, dug my toe into the earth where one of its roots gave me a foothold, and jumped.

The root gave way, and the athletic landing I had envisioned for my vault deconstructed into a belly flop. But I made it, no worse for my effort than a little dirty and glad nobody saw it. I stood and brushed leaves and debris from my jeans and jacket while I caught my breath before climbing again.

I realized it was going to be much easier going from that point than anticipated.

I was on a trail.

I peered through the trees to my right and saw that the trail wound its way down the hillside toward the cove where I had begun and up toward Logan's in the other direction. It was a flat ridge about five feet wide, hugging the hillside. Somehow, I had missed it. So much for my woodsman skills. I laughed to myself that I should have brought Jet after all. He would have made sure to find the easy way up if anyone could.

Suddenly the stillness of the woods was interrupted, and it wasn't from my clumsy efforts this time. It was the unmistakable sound of footsteps. On the run and coming my way down the hill. Must be a deer. No doubt they used this trail too. As I had done so often over the years on deer drives, I eased to the edge of the trail and flattened myself against a tree, hoping not to be spotted. Not that I was hunting, but the instinct was always there.

But it was not a deer.

An upright figure appeared above me, slipping and fighting to gain a foothold as it raced down the ridge trail. The size and posture were that of a man, and not Jack or Jet. *Peregrine.* The thought appeared and vanished in the same instant. It could not be him. He had locked through the dam the morning before and was who-knows-how-many miles south by now.

It's the killer, revisiting the crime scene.

I pressed my shoulder hard into the pale-gray bark of the tree, sideways so as to make my profile smaller and obscure the red of my jacket with the trunk of the pine. Had I been clothed in my hunting camo, there was a chance the person might zoom by me unaware. But he would pass within two feet, so a confrontation inevitable. My heart hammered in my chest.

He was on me now, and as I knew he would, he saw me. He whirled, startled and off-balance. Then he squared his shoulders as if to confront me.

And then he reached for his gun.

SEVENTEEN

HALFWAY through my lunge, I recognized him. I didn't have time to contemplate the likelihood of him actually shooting me, but I didn't like my odds considering he was being ambushed by a man behind a tree on a shadowy ridge a few hundred feet away from a murder scene. Were the roles reversed, I would sling lead first and ask questions later. Guilty of murder or not.

I flailed at his right hand with my left, desperate to disrupt the aim of the pistol now firmly in his palm, and lowered my shoulder, intent on burying it in his gut. He grunted something indiscernible as my body slammed into his. I gritted my teeth and closed my eyes, expecting a shot to ring out and hoping against a sear of pain—or worse, a sudden nothingness. But the shot never came.

Suddenly we were airborne, hurtling off the ridge I had so ungracefully crested moments before. The flight came to a crashing end just as it had begun, abruptly and with my shoulder crammed in his belly. The gun rolled harmlessly away, and I scrambled in a frantic crawl to claim it. I grabbed the weapon and turned in case he was lunging upon me but saw there was no chance of that. His eyes were flared wide in white-eyed terror, lips opening and closing in quick, futile guppy breaths.

A flash of worry that he was mortally injured evaporated when he rolled to a prone position and gathered his knees beneath him, gasping to reclaim the air that had left him. I stood and brought the pistol up for inspection, keeping him in my line of sight in case he had another one ready for action. It was a Ruger Standard Model .22 caliber, as common as mosquitoes in this part of the country. I had one just like it in my gun safe. It wasn't ideal for putting a man down instantly, but it was more than powerful enough to kill. I certainly had no intention of feeling its 40-grain slug slip between my ribs, small caliber or not.

"Dang … Coach." Deep breath. "What'd you go … and … do that for?"

I tucked the pistol into my waistband at the back but took a step back as my adversary rose to his feet. "The better question, Luke, is what are you doing racing down the hillside with a gun in your belt?"

"You scared the sh——, sorry, the mess out of me, Coach! About gave me a heart attack."

I suppressed a smile. Luke Wiseman had done more than a few bear crawls over the years for cursing in practice. I guess he thought I might make him bear crawl all the way to the top of Logan's Bluff. "You didn't answer my question. What are you doing?" The notion that Devlin's best friend would enact some revenge on Ronny for attacking his friend on the football field was not some wild idea. After all, he had told us two nights before at the hospital that he would do as much, and the square-jawed linebacker with the military-style buzz cut was known around town as a kid you didn't want to cross.

Then there was Jack's theory that Luke had been buying drugs from Ronny and had dragged Devlin into it. I had disregarded it, but suddenly even that possibility was on my radar. But pushing Ronny off a cliff to his death? I just didn't see it. Not on purpose, anyway. Still, this was suspicious.

Luke looked up the hillside, toward the trail from whence we had tumbled. "I guess I could ask you the same question."

"I'm investigating a murder, knucklehead. Trying to help your friend. If he's innocent."

"Oh, he's innocent, all right. And that's exactly what I'm doing."

"The difference between you and me is that you're a suspect and I'm not."

Luke frowned. "Suspect? Why?"

"A whole crowd of people heard you threaten to get Ronny."

His face contorted in a look of disbelief. "Aw, c'mon, Coach. You know I wouldn't kill nobody! I might kick some ass, but nothin' like that." He winced and brought his fist to his mouth. "Sorry."

I waved it off. "I really need to know what you're up to." I gestured up above us with a head jerk. "Deputy Jack Masterson is at the top there, and if he thinks it needs to happen, you'll be arrested."

Luke turned ashen. "No, Coach. I didn't do nothin'. I was here trying to see if I could figure out what happened. Devlin didn't do it, and I didn't, neither."

"Do you know who did?"

He shook his head. "No sir. But I can tell you that Ronny Shane was up to no good. He was into some bad stuff. Maybe that got him kilt."

"What kind of bad stuff?"

Luke grimaced and bit his bottom lip. "Don't seem right to talk about a dead kid like that."

"Okay, then tell me what was going on with Ronny and Devlin and Lena."

Luke gave a pained expression again before sighing in

resignation. "Lena was messing with both of them. You know, she and Ronny went to school together. I think they hooked up or something. Devlin says she don't mean nothing to Ronny. But Dev loves her."

That raised the specter of Lena's involvement and, if so, explained Devlin's desire to protect her.

"Why were you running down the trail like a jumped jackrabbit?"

He rubbed his face with one hand. "I was up there looking for clues, and somebody drove up. I hid at first, but then I saw one of 'em had a gun, and that was enough for me."

"But you have a gun too."

Luke frowned. "Do I look like I want to be in a gunfight? I play—played—football, and I'm goin' in the army when school's out. But getting in the OK Corral don't make much sense when it's two on one and you can just exit out the back door." He smiled. "That gun was just for emergencies. Didn't know I was gonna be hit by a charging bull before I could get it in my hand good."

I smiled back at him. "See? Told you I knew a little bit about tackling. Too bad you never listened to me."

Luke thumped his chest. "All Division says otherwise."

I liked the kid. I really hoped he was innocent.

But supposedly there's no such thing as coincidences.

I thought I knew every back road and trail in McKinley County. And maybe I had at one time, back in my teenage years when my friends and I explored it with a wanderlust like Lewis and Clark. But somehow, we had either missed this trail, or it was new.

You can exit out the back door. Luke's description of how he had escaped when he saw Jack and Jet baffled me. Where was there a way down from the edge of the bluff? I chose to let him show me rather than try to explain.

The trail eased up the hillside to our right, toward the steep face of the bluff where I knew it would have to turn away. But it didn't turn away like I expected. Much to my surprise, we soon found ourselves on a flat, narrow ridge hugging the cliff. Straight down to our right, straight up to our left. Suddenly the trail angled sharply left and up, and Luke began to climb.

"Luke, stop." At the apex of the switchback the view changed. Where scrub brush and saplings struggling to set root had obscured the view before, it suddenly opened, and I could see the full face of the bluff all the way to its base. All the way to the spot on the rocks at the edge of the water where Ronny had breathed his last. The sight was both magnificent and somber.

I pointed to the rocks below us. "That's where they found him."

Luke slid back down to stand beside me. He peered at the site, eyeballing the distance from top to bottom, but his expression gave away nothing. "That's a long way down," was all he said.

I gestured for him to continue and followed behind, laboring much more than my former player to make the ascent. The trail pressed to the left away from the bluff and meandered up through the woods again before switching back to the right. I knew we must be nearing the crest and finally understood where we were likely to come out, in the corner of the top meadow just where the clearing pulled back away from the edge of the bluff.

Luke pointed ahead to a patch of sunlight among the vegetation and confirmed my suspicion. "That's it."

I nodded and quickened my step, anxious to see what Jack and Jet were doing. Just then I noticed a detour off the main trail, directly toward the cliff. It wasn't much more than a faint depression in the leaves, but it was there. And considering where it was going, it wasn't a deer trail, either. No deer that I had ever hunted was interested in scenic vistas. "What's that?"

"You don't wanna go there, Coach."

I ignored him and ducked under a low-hanging limb to follow the path.

"Gonna get yourself killed."

Luke had never been one to shy away from hyperbole, but I soon saw he might be serious this time. The path ended abruptly on a rocky outcropping, where the hillside peeled away at a right angle to the bluff and a careless step would send one tumbling out of control. But then I saw something even more interesting than that. Across a six-foot gap was another narrow ledge that ran along the face of Logan's bluff for a span of fifteen or twenty feet.

"Don't do it." Luke was beside me now, eyeing the gap between the rock and the ledge. "It's too far."

I laughed. "I'm not crazy. Couldn't have made that jump when I was eighteen, much less forty-eight." I picked up a stick and tossed it across for no reason. "Why would I want to, anyway?"

"You wouldn't. But some kids like to climb up and around to get to it for kicks and giggles." Luke pointed up the hill to our left and made an arc with his finger. "Not me, though. Heights ain't my thing."

"Ahhh." There was a way to bypass the gap by climbing up, around, and over. "How do you do it?"

"They step on those rocks poking out of the ground and

hold on to those little trees to keep from slipping." Luke grabbed my arm. "C'mon, Coach, let's get outta here."

I pulled away and held fast, still studying the situation. I had no interest in teenager dares or whatever was the usual motivation, but I couldn't stop looking at the top of the bluff eight feet or so above us. "Hey Jack! Jet!" I heard no answer, so I called out louder. I waited several seconds and did it again, but again nothing happened. I sighed and said I'd come back later, generating a look of relief from Luke, who turned again to leave.

"You okay, Case?"

It was Jack's voice, above us.

"Jack! I'm fine. Where are you?"

"I'm on top! Where in hell's bells are you?"

"Come to the edge." Soon I caught movement above us and could make out Jack's silhouette, peering out over the edge as far as he dared.

"Go back around, and I'll help you up," he said.

"No need. I'll explain in a minute. I need you to do something first. Go to the spot where we thought Ronny might have slipped."

He agreed and disappeared for a few seconds before emerging again at the edge, only a few feet further down. "What's the deal?"

"Hang on." It was a good question. My suspicion was that Jack and I were on a wild goose chase. The marks on the ground at the edge of the bluff where Jack was now standing probably had nothing to do with Ronny's death. My thought had been that perhaps he had gone over the edge there instead of above where he was found. It wasn't evidence, but it was something the investigators would have missed, so who knows what else there was?

But the blood evidence we had seen below that he had died right where he was found suggested otherwise. Not to mention the fact he was completely dry; with no indication he had fallen into the water and been moved to the rocks. The ledge I was now looking at just seemed to solidify all of that. If Ronny had actually gone over at this spot, he would have landed there. Injured, but not dead.

I glanced up at the path over the gap. I had to get to that ledge, one way or another, if for no other reason than to prove that my eyes weren't playing tricks on me. I nodded toward the hillside arc over the gap. "Right up through there, huh?"

"Naw, Coach, don't do it. I gotta get home."

I frowned and shook my head. Luke sure was intent on keeping me from going out there. Was he hiding something? "Not yet." I stepped up to find a rocky foothold and reached to grab one of the small trees. I would have to remember to make Jack and Jet swear not to tell Abi.

Fear of heights had never been an issue for me, so the thought of climbing across that gap with a near one-hundred-foot gap below me didn't cause a second's hesitation. I was no adrenaline junkie, but if I needed something that involved a climb, no problem.

To be fair, that didn't mean I didn't have issues with some things. The sight of an armadillo would spur irrational visions of leprosy and send chills coursing down my spine. And I would just as soon bathe with water moccasins as to eat one bite of asparagus—I had once vomited at the vile vegetable's asparagine smell lingering in Abi's urine one morning. Yes, armadillos and asparagus (among other things) were my kryptonite. But heights, no problem.

I hesitated at the idea of relying on flimsy trees with shallow root systems to help me as I climbed, but I barely needed a handhold. The footholds were more solid than I anticipated. I traversed the gap in short order and hopped down onto the ledge. I clapped my hands in triumph and to rid them of dirt and debris. "Nothing to it, Luke. Come on over."

The kid waved his hand and shook his head. "Not happening,"

I wouldn't have let him try it, anyway, but now I had ammunition to tease him with. I smiled and gave him a thumbs-up and turned to examine my position. The ledge was slightly wider than it had first appeared, probably four to five feet. Plenty of room to walk, but not much room for error if one jumped or slipped from the top of the bluff above me. I glanced down over the edge and back up to the top. "Jack, you still there?"

"Whoa!" He peaked over just enough for me to see his eyes. "How'd you get there?"

"There's a ledge here. Big enough to stand on."

"Interesting. What you thinking?"

I was thinking we had wasted a lot of time. "Did you guys find anything new up there?"

"Negative."

Great. "Jet with you?"

Jack laughed and nodded behind him. "Sorta. You know him. He's like Nash. Heights ain't his thing."

I sighed and turned back to peer out over the dark waters of the Timtullah below and the main channel of the waterway further out. A barge was moving out of sight, heading north after locking through the dam. I couldn't see the water's edge below but could make out the sound of tiny waves from the barge's wake lapping against Logan's foot. I gathered a thick wad of phlegm in my throat and spat over the edge, an instinctive thing for a guy to do, especially when frustrated. The spittle somersaulted away, disappearing over a rock several feet below me.

And then I saw it. A cigarette butt, lying in a groove of the rock as if sunbathing while catching my loogie flyover. Suddenly I remembered Nash mentioning finding some butts where the cars had been parked. Would they check DNA evidence on those? Surely they would. And would this be a match?

I dropped to one knee, looking for a way to reach the butt. It would take some maneuvering, but I could get to it from my belly without much of a stretch. "Jack, stay where you are. Gotta check something." Luke offered some sort of adamant protest once again, but I ignored it. Between him and Nash and Jet, this fear of heights was darn near an epidemic. Good thing Amberton was a river town and not on the Continental Divide.

If there is a rule of thumb for how much of one's body can hang over a cliff without tipping the scale of balance, I wasn't aware of it. I figured I'd feel it sneaking up on me well before it happened. And I wasn't worried about the earth giving away like it might have done above us on top of the bluff, because the edge here was solid rock.

Without further thought, I snapped on rubber gloves from my pocket and was down in a prone position, inching forward on my belly, reaching down as far as I could. Feeling the solid rock beneath me. Confident in my balance. Glad the gray shroud of dusk was concealing the dizzying depth of the void below me, even if I hated to admit it. I dug my toes in like pickaxes and stretched to my limit, straining to touch the butt taunting me from just beyond my grasp. I could come back with a rope and some type of tongs. It would make so much more sense. But it was only three more inches now—a finger's length—and I'd have it. One more tiny slither.

"Stop, Coach!"

I ignored Luke and inched forward. Almost there. Touching my fingertips.

And then in an instant the rock pressed against my belly was gone, and over the edge I went.

EIGHTEEN

t has been said that a man's whole life flashes before his eyes in the instant he knows he is going to die, but I saw no such thing.

What flashed through my mind in a millisecond was a singular thought of inevitability and nothing else. I was going to die. That was it. Fifty-five miles per hour against an abrupt stop would be my end.

Fortunately, instinct prevailed. Perhaps instead of being preoccupied with the events of my life, the primal will to survive acted without me even knowing it. Instead of hurtling to an impact velocity of a highway speed limit, I suddenly found myself dangling from the cliff, my left hand clutching a two-inch root protruding from the edge. I didn't remember noting its presence, but maybe I had unconsciously. My legs swung like a pendulum, and I almost lost my grip. I kicked wildly to find purchase. Any foothold to buy me time.

Then I found it. A groove in the face of the cliff just large enough for the toes of my left foot to wedge into. It wasn't much, but the slipping eased, and I reasserted my tenuous grip. Still, I knew it wouldn't last long, and I had no idea how sturdy it was. Plus, whatever was under my toes might dislodge just like the rock under my body had. And that would be the end of me.

I struggled to find something for my right foot to rest upon but kicked and scraped the cliff face to no avail. "Jack!" I doubted I could hang on long enough for him to get back around to the trail, up and over the gap onto the ledge to get to me, but he was my only chance. My left arm and leg were both outstretched with no way to gather leverage to improve my position. I couldn't even shift enough to switch hands. I was stuck and couldn't last much longer. Seconds, at most. "Jack!"

There was no use, but I didn't know what else to say. Was I calling for help or saying goodbye? I suppose it was one masquerading as the other. Either way, I would be gone before he could get to me. My fingers burned as the branch slipped through them.

"Case, hang on! My belt!" There, dangling just over my head. A silver buckle with a leather belt looped back through it. Somehow, Jack was there above me, holding the other end with the holes. "Grab it!"

It might as well have been a mile away. Even on my tiptoe I couldn't reach it, and what little jump I might be able to muster would likely come up short and definitely give up what little grip I had left. "Can't get it!" My hand was numb now, and my shoulders and biceps screamed to give up. I was spent. It was over.

"Jack, tell Abi—"

"Shut up and grab it!"

Suddenly the loop was just close enough. Right there by my outstretched hand. I jabbed my right hand through the loop and felt it cinch to my wrist, pinching the skin with a sharp but welcome pain. My left hand slipped away and fell limp to my side. The belt was my only lifeline now. "Pull, Jack!"

"Pull!" It was Jack's voice yelling now. Why was he telling me to pull? And then I realized, he was hanging over the edge, much as I had been earlier. My heart dropped with a fear that he had slipped and was coming over too. "Pull!"

The jagged veins at Jack's temples bulged as he fought to hold me and himself. The whites of his gritted teeth matched the rims of eyes wide with strain, both reflecting what little light remained in stark contrast to the dark red of his shadowed face. I kicked in desperate effort to help and clutched at the root again with my revived left hand.

Slowly, we began to inch upward. Six inches. A foot. A few more. Another voice was yelling now, Jet from the top of Logan's. And Luke somewhere. Jack inched backward and was suddenly on his knees, roaring with one final surge of effort. And like a marionette being pulled from duty mid-performance, I was suddenly jerked back on the ledge, in a heap on top of Jack. Luke was there, too, on his butt, clutching the belt with both hands just where it wrapped around Jack's hand.

I understood now how Jack had pulled me up from his vulnerable position. He hadn't. When Jack couldn't get to me, Luke had extended his reach from behind and then yanked us both up. It was an incredible feat of strength. What I didn't understand was how both of them had gotten there to help me in the first place.

My breaths labored long and deep as I worked to gather my wits. I loosened the belt from my wrist, ignoring the blood where the buckle had dug into my flesh. "Thanks guys. How did—"

"Logan's leap! Mr. Jack did it!"

"Dang, Case, 'bout got us both killed   !" Jack's chest heaved as he fought to catch his breath. He pointed to what was left of my shredded rubber gloves. "What in the hot hell were you doing?"

"I saw something on the rock down there."

"Saw something."

"A cigarette. I think it matched the ones we found up on the bluff."

"Like someone threw it over from the top?" Luke said.

"Or smoked while standing on that ledge."

Jack gave a disgusted snort. "Almost died for a cigarette butt. That's something stupid like I would do but not you."

We shared a stare for a split second, his angry, mine incredulous. Then we both burst into a relieved laugh. "Was kinda stupid. Maybe," I said.

Jack shook his head emphatically. "No maybe."

I frowned for a moment then let it go and nodded. Jack was right on several counts. He was usually the impetuous one. And my risk had been too great under the circumstances. I hoped I hadn't ruined something important, something that could help prove Devlin's innocence.

I turned to Luke, who now had his back pressed into the cliff. "Thanks for the help. What was that you said earlier? Something about a leap?"

"Logan's leap is what they call it." He glanced back over his head to the top of the bluff and then looked at Jack. "That's what Mr. Jack did."

"You jumped off of that?"

Jack shrugged. "What else was I supposed to do? My best friend was hanging a hundred feet up like an orangutan. Same ugly face but without the orange hair and natural ability."

"Luke, so you're saying that's a known thing?"

"Most ain't got the guts to do it, but yeah." He shook his head, wide eyed. "Not me, though. That's nutso stuff."

"Ronny Shane?"

Luke frowned. "No idea. We didn't hang much. But he fits—uhh, fit—the nutso category."

"What about Devlin?"

Luke looked at the ground but didn't say anything. An answer without giving an answer.

"You know, Luke, you also told me you are afraid of heights and wouldn't climb over that." I gestured back toward the gap between the trail and the ledge we were own. "Yet here you are."

He hesitated, like he was searching for an explanation. Then he gave a weak grin. "What can I say? My coach was hanging from a cliff. But I thought you looked more like a chimpanzee."

NINETEEN

GABE Liston's black Jeep Compass fishtailed on loose gravel just enough to make Kyle grab the door handle. Gabe wasn't the best driver, but beggars can't be choosers. Kyle was just glad to have a friend with a driver's license. Not every fourteen-year-old could say that.

Gabe blinkered right and veered onto another dark gravel road. "I know it looks like the boondocks, but it's a cool place."

"I don't know Brock Bolger." Kyle knew him by name alone. McKinley County was small enough for most kids at Amberton to know others from the county schools and vice versa. Brock Bolger, as quarterback for Haughton, was probably known by more kids at Amberton than not, by reputation if nothing else.

"What's that got to do with anything? It's a party, and you're with me."

"Since when do you hang out with the cool crowd?"

"Since I got invited. Brock says everybody is coming."

"And you know Brock Bolger how, again?"

"It's complicated." He glanced at his phone where a British woman's voice was instructing him to stay right at a fork in the road.

"You and Siri come here a lot, do you?" Kyle snickered.

The road eventually sloped upward for a half mile and ended by converting into a narrow drive protected by an arching canopy of oaks and lined with crushed gray slag contrasting the earth-toned river gravel of the road. Open iron gates hung from brick columns on each side.

The oak bower guarding the driveway gave way to open night sky spread wide over a lake. A two-story house rose up in the distance on the other side, casting its glow across the water. Just off the end of a wooden pier, a fountain sprayed luminescent streams in an arcing circle, cycling through a rainbow of colors. When it turned orange it reminded Kyle of the flowers of the wild trumpet vine native to the area. Earlier in the fall while watching hummingbirds he had learned the hard way that trumpet vine flowers were as toxic to the skin as poison oak. He scratched the back of his hand out of recent habit.

"Told you it's a nice place," Gabe said.

"Not bad at all. Who's gonna be here?"

Gabe stopped the truck at the end of a line of cars parked along the driveway and opened his door. He bobbed his head to the indistinct beat of music throbbing in the distance as he got out. "Let's go find out."

The music was coming from a patio situated between the lake and the house. Kyle hesitated at the edge of the yard before following Gabe's lead and trailing him up to the house. A few people milled about, but most were relaxing on outdoor furniture and scattered concrete benches. A small group was huddled around a stone fire pit off to the side. Kyle recognized no one.

"Gabe!" A voice called out from the unfamiliar faces. "Wondered if you were coming." The person who rose to meet them was about three inches taller and looked a year or so older than Gabe. He wore a trucker cap turned backward with a thick lock of dark hair working its way out of the hole over the snapback, a flannel shirt, jeans and square-toed ostrich boots.

"Hey, Brock." Gabe's deferential downward gaze and

awkward hand bury into pockets belied his chirpy tone. "Didn't, uh, want to, uh, miss it."

"Who you got with you?"

"My friend Kyle."

"Y'all make yourself at home. Beer's in the fridge." Brock looked hard at Kyle. "You handle your alcohol?"

"Sure." Kyle's mom had let him try her wine a couple of times because he begged, and he'd once sipped some Jim Beam that Gabe had stolen from the pool bar of a neighbor down the street, but he hadn't liked any of it. He had certainly never had enough to find out what he could handle.

"Okay, well don't get stupid on me. Parents ain't home, but I don't want to have to do no explaining later."

Kyle nodded to the lake. "Any fish in there?"

"Naw, we try to keep 'em poisoned out." Brock was stone faced. Then he broke into a crooked grin and looked at Gabe. "Is that what y'all gonna do tonight? Fish?"

"I was jus—"

"I'm just messin', Kyle. Yeah, we got some trophy bass in there. Caught a nine-pounder about a month ago. Go check out the pier if you want. Just do it before you get plastered so you don't fall in."

Brock wandered off to speak to someone else, and Kyle stood there in silence with his friend wondering what they were doing there. The other attendees looked at them like one would at two new pimples—not exactly welcome but not worth messing with if they disappeared soon enough on their own. "What now?" Kyle finally said.

"I'm gonna sit here a minute. Brock said there's gonna be hot girls here."

"Not sure what that has to do with you, but okay." Kyle

didn't need Brock's forecast to know there were hot girls around. He'd already spotted a few. But they would be out of his league even if they weren't older. Gabe could sit and gawk if he wanted. "I'm walking down to the pier."

The grass down the slope to the pier was perfectly manicured St. Augustine. Kyle had cut enough of it to know. He wondered if Brock had ever mowed a yard or if his daddy—who Gabe had said owned a metal fabrication company—hired someone to do it. It was a stupid question, asking about the fish. But what else could he have said? Coming with Gabe was a dumb idea, and Gabe inviting him was a dumb idea. If you want to try to be cool, don't bring a freshman friend to an "upperclassmen party," as he had called it. Kyle wouldn't tell Gabe that, though. Getting left behind was probably coming soon enough.

Dumb question or not, he sure would like to fish here sometime. The lake was about six or seven acres with a levee on one end and some tree structure in more shallow water on the other. Nine-pound bass for sure in there. Crappie and bream too. Maybe if he offered to mow the lawn for free, they'd let him fish. Dumb idea again. He didn't have a way to get his mower way out here.

He walked to the end of the pier and stood mesmerized by the fountain for a time. Red, orange, yellow, green, blue, indigo, violet, repeat. In one way it ruined an otherwise pristine scene, but then again it was pretty. He turned and headed back toward the house. Time to see if Gabe had his fill of gawking at girls yet. Heck, maybe he'd actually gotten lucky.

There was someone waiting for him on the bank. Just a hooded dark silhouette against the lights of the house, unfamiliar in size or shape. "Hey."

"Hey yourself." It was a female voice.

Kyle quickened his step. She was shorter than him, sweatshirt, narrow face, couldn't tell much else.

"I'm Emma." She pulled back her hood. Freckles, auburn hair? Oval eyes, too dark to see the color.

"Kyle."

"I know."

"How's that?" Kyle had seen her at school but only from a distance across the courtyard and had no idea who she was.

"Saw y'all walk up. Met your friend Gabe. He told me." She smiled. "You looked lonely down here."

Looked lonely? Code for looked like a loser who needed pity. But he didn't say it. "Cool. I came with him. Knows Brock somehow. I don't know anybody here really." Dang it. Didn't mean to say that. *Lonely loser, confirmed.*

"Well, you know somebody now. Aren't you a little young for this party?"

"No. Almost fifteen. You don't look too grown up yourself."

She laughed. "Okay, then I got you by at least a year. Got my license last month."

So she was sixteen. Possibly out of his league by age criteria alone. But he was tall for his age, so there's that. "Got a last name?"

"Harlow. Your dad is the football coach, right? For Amberton?"

"That he is." Kyle shifted his weight and folded his arms across his chest. Might as well get it over with. Full disclosure. No jocks here, if that's what she was hoping. "I'm not much of a football player myself."

She gave a thumbs up. "I can respect that. Brock is my friend, but he's quite full of himself."

A positive development. "You go to Haughton too?" *Play it*

cool. She doesn't have to know you noticed her at school.

She laughed and shook her head. "No, silly. I go to school with you. Sophomore."

Another positive development. Only one grade ahead of him.

She raised an index finger. "But I just moved to Amberton this year. So maybe that's why you haven't seen me before."

"That was bad about Ronny Shane."

She gave a slow nod. "Did you know him?"

Kyle shook his head. "Heard of him. I know Devlin James, though."

"Me, too. Sorta." Emma tucked a loose lock of hair behind one ear and pulled her hood back up. "Chilly out here." She sat on the grass, pulled her knees up to her chest, and patted the ground beside her. "Tell me what you like to do, Kyle Reynolds."

Kyle sat down beside her. He was shivering but not because it was chilly like Emma had said. "I don't know. Just normal stuff, I guess. I like the outdoors." Kyle pointed across the lake. "Listen."

Emma leaned forward and peered in that direction. "I hear it. Some dogs barking."

Kyle shook his head. "Nope. Coyote. It's a different sound. Dogs bark when they're bored or if they hear something. Coyotes bark at night as a warning. Saying, 'This is my territory.'"

"Impressive."

He shrugged. "I wish it was summer. Bet we'd hear some green tree frogs out on the end of the pier. Stalking insects attracted to the light."

"Sounds like a date."

Kyle's heart rate quickened, and the shiver hit him again. He wanted to slide closer to her. What would she do?

A foot pressed to his back ended the moment.

"A date, huh?"

Kyle whirled and stood in defiance. The foot hadn't hurt, but there was little doubt that it wasn't a friendly gesture. "What the heck?"

The foot owner wore leather roper boots, jeans, and a fleece jacket. Kyle had seen him before but didn't know his name. Slender, narrow eyes, bulging Adam's apple. "I can say the same. What the heck are you doing here? Shouldn't you be out pretending to be a cop like your daddy? Trying to get that murderer Devlin James off free as a bird?"

Emma stood shoulder to shoulder with Kyle. "C'mon, Carter. Leave him alone."

"What's it to you, Emma?"

"He's my friend. Leave him be."

"It's okay, Emma," Kyle said. "No trouble. I don't know anything about what happened with Devlin. Not my problem."

Carter poked a finger in Kyle's chest. "It's your daddy, which makes it your problem. And mine, since Ronny was my friend."

"I'm sorry about your friend." Kyle sidestepped to go around Carter and reached out with a light tug on the sleeve of Emma's sweatshirt. "Want to walk back up to the house?"

Carter slapped Kyle's arm down and gave him a shove. "We're not done yet."

The force of the push caught Kyle off guard, and the slope of the hill made it worse. He tumbled backward and rolled, submerging his right arm in the lake. The chill had long since disappeared, and the cold of the water did nothing to bring it back. Instead, an inferno raged in its place. He jumped to his feet and gathered himself to confront his tormenter.

Emma stepped in front of Kyle. "Ignore them."

Ignore? Bull. Wait, what? Them? Brock was there, too, now. It didn't matter. Kyle was many things, but a coward wasn't one of them. He rushed around Emma and charged straight at Carter, intent on taking him down. A fist shot out from Carter's side and met Kyle squarely on the left jaw.

The house and everything around it shimmered like a mirage then went gray. His knees buckled, and the ground rose up to meet him.

TWENTY

CARTER loomed over Kyle, who was on his knees trying to focus and stop the spin. "What you gonna do? Huh? Get up and let's go." He shoved him in the back with his foot, and Kyle fell to all fours. "Or stay down. I don't care."

"Leave him alone!" Emma's voice was close. Kyle felt her hand on his back.

Then Kyle felt a different hand, stronger, grab him by the arm. It was Brock. "Get back, Carter. What are you doing, you moron?" He pulled Kyle to his feet with one hand and shoved Carter back with the other. He held up some fingers. "How many you see?"

"Two. Three."

Brock laughed. "You'll be alright."

Emma moved to face Kyle and touched his lower lip. "You're bleeding."

"He's okay, Emma. Sorry about that. Not sure what's gotten into Carter." Brock turned to face Kyle's assailant. "You told me you wanted to talk to him, not hit him. Go cool off. Or go home. I don't care."

Carter glared at Kyle. "Come at me again, see what happens." He turned and walked away.

"Sorry about that," Brock said. "He's just upset about Ronny. We all are. But the rest of us are smart enough to know it's not your fault." He started walking toward the house and called back over his shoulder. "Come up here and cool off. I'll give you a tour."

Kyle didn't say anything and watched him walk away. He rubbed his aching jaw.

"Been in many fights?" Emma asked.

He gave her a sideways glance. "One. Didn't last long."

She burst into a shoulder-shaking laugh. "Did you always have a sense of humor or is that a frontal lobe concussion thing?"

"Ha ha." He rubbed his jaw again. "I'm a bundle of laughs when not being attacked by a psychopath."

Emma reached out like she might touch his face but pulled back quickly. "Sorry that happened. Everyone's just on edge about Ronny."

"Sounds like they're ready to string Devlin up. But maybe he didn't do it."

Emma grunted. "More like, maybe he did."

Devlin was intrigued. "Why do you say that?"

Emma gave a dismissive wave. "Forget it. What do I know?"

Kyle wanted to know what she knew about that among a thousand other things. But if she didn't want to elaborate, he wouldn't push. With any luck there would be other opportunities. "How do you know these people so well, anyway?"

"My dad works for Brock's family. Logistics. I guess he's good at it. Mr. Bolger says I'm welcome here any time, whether Brock invites me or not."

"That's cool," Kyle said. "Both my parents work for the state. No perks."

"Your mom's a lawyer, huh?"

Kyle hesitated, wondering how she knew so much about him.

Emma didn't wait for an answer. "Wish my mom was around here, but she lives in Memphis now."

"You live with your dad?" Kyle didn't want to pry, but he found himself wanting to know everything about this girl he had only just met.

"Mom got a promotion, had to move from Tupelo to Memphis. I didn't want to live there, so here I am. Living with Dad until we figure things out." Her expression brightened. "I'm seeing her more than I thought, though. Mom says she's working on a special project around here, whatever that means." She nodded toward the house. "Let's go see what's up."

Kyle agreed and moved that direction. He was ready to find Gabe and go home, but meanwhile he might just follow Emma Harlow anywhere.

The patio was empty and the music silent. Kyle glanced down the driveway and saw that most of the cars were gone. Emma went straight to the back door and opened it. Not the first time she'd been there.

Gabe was palming a red Solo cup, sitting alone on a barstool at the kitchen counter. "There's my buddy. Kyle with no smile." He took a gulp. "You gotta try this st-stuff. Maybe there's alcohol, but I c-can't taste it!"

"Sheesh Gabe, you're drunk." So much for his ride home.

Two girls on a nearby sofa were laughing about something else, and Carter was nowhere to be seen. Brock was at a table in the corner where several other guys were nursing longnecks and playing cards. He rose to meet them and nodded toward Gabe. "A little too much Everclear for your friend. Ready for that tour?"

Kyle shook his head and turned to Emma. "Can you drive me and Gabe?"

Brock spoke before she had a chance. "I've got a better idea. Let me take you home. Emma can drive Gabe." He pointed to the card game. "I'll get one of these guys to help me get his truck home later. His parents will never know the difference."

Emma gave Kyle a shrug as if to say it made sense to her. Gabe stared at the bottom of his cup, oblivious.

"Okay." Kyle turned to Emma. "Make sure he gets home okay. If he goes in the back door he can get to his room without passing his mom's." It might not even matter since she'd probably been passed out a couple of hours already.

———

Brock drove a brand-new, black Silverado, fully loaded. He cranked up the volume of his sound system before they hit the main road and joined in with the lyrics. The voice was authentically imperfect with a folksy, soulful ache to it. Brock turned the volume back down enough to be heard. "Heard this guy before?"

Kyle shook his head no.

"Tyler Childers. He's gonna be big. What you got on your playlist?"

"The usual country stuff, but I don't listen much," Kyle lied. Truth was, he immersed himself in it when he was drawing, usually acoustic blues. Dudes like Bukka White, John Hurt, and RL Burnside spoke to him in ways others didn't, with a sound springing from the Mississippi earth just like the wildlife he loved that teemed across it. As he drew, Kyle would imagine his fingers working across the page like those iconic guitarists, playing a different kind of music, but no less alive.

Brock turned down the volume. "So, what makes you click, Reynolds? If you don't like music, what is it?

Kyle measured his response. What he was hearing through the speakers actually wasn't half bad. Brock might like his music, too, but Kyle wasn't one to open up easily. "I'm just an outdoors guy. Anything outdoors."

"Football?"

Kyle tensed. Loaded question. Brock knew more about him than vice versa. "Not really that kind of outdoors. Hunting, fishing. Nature."

Brock laughed. "That's what Gabe told me. Not planning to follow in your old man's footsteps. I can respect that. My old man's a jerk." He patted the steering wheel. "But a rich jerk, so I'll keep him for now."

"Speaking of jerks—no offense to your dad—what's the deal with that Carter dude? Your friend?"

"We go back a ways, yeah. It's just been tough the past couple of days, with what happened to Ronny. Started to cancel the party but decided he'd want us to go on with it."

"Special occasion?"

Brock shrugged. "Just celebratin' a late start for school tomorrow. Gotta love them teacher enrichment meetings or whatever they call them. I can sleep late. And speaking of reason to celebrate, you gonna mark today on your calendar as the day you met the girl of your dreams?"

Kyle jerked his gaze away from the road ahead and frowned at Brock. "What you talking about?"

"I saw the way you was looking at Emma."

Kyle's face burned, and he wanted to roll down the window. Had he had some goofy look on his face? Brock must think he was a douche.

Brock gave him a back-handed slug on the shoulder. "Relax. Nobody would blame you on looks. Might be some stuff you don't know about her, though."

"Like what?"

"Like, she's got some baggage with Ronny's death too."

"Baggage?"

"Lena Cole is her sister."

The name didn't ring a bell. Kyle's face must have shown it.

"Stepsister, actually. Emma's dad married Lena's mom. Except they may not be together anymore. Anyway, doesn't matter. Lena was dating Devlin. And Ronny.

"Ohhh." Now Kyle remembered Gabe saying something about that, but he had only half listened. Gossip didn't interest him much. He would have paid more attention had he known he'd be getting assaulted for reasons connected to the thing, though. Still, he didn't get how Emma being related to Lena had anything to do with whether he would want to hang out with her or not. He hoped he'd have a chance to ask her more about it sometime.

Brock's cell buzzed, and he fished it out of his pocket. "Hello … Just taking a friend home." He glanced over at his passenger. "Kyle Reynolds. Yessir, you know him? … Yessir … Sure … Where?"

"What was that about?"

"A friend. We need to make a quick stop. Won't take long."

They rode in silence for a few minutes, and at the outskirts of town, Brock turned down a familiar road.

"Amberton Country Club?" Kyle asked.

"Sort of."

The road to the club wound along the ninth fairway and had no streetlights. There was no traffic, not surprising this late on a Sunday. The road circled the back side of the green and past the clubhouse, a single-story white building with columns and black shutters fronted by a circle drive. It was dark save a single streetlight, and instead of turning in there, Brock rolled on by. The road came to a dead end a couple hundred yards beyond the clubhouse at a tiny bungalow. A single dormer window was too low to be for anything but looks, and even in the inconsistent illumination of the headlights it was obvious the molded stucco needed a bleach spray-down.

"Come in, won't take a second," Brock said.

"Whose place is this?"

Brock ignored him and knocked on the door. It opened, but the single bulb mounted beside it did not flicker on.

Kyle was suddenly nervous, like a Little Leaguer finding himself in a Major League game. Or worse, since he didn't even know what sport he was playing. Maybe he himself was the game. He vowed retribution on Gabe for leaving him hanging.

Someone waved them in. Only when the door closed behind them did a light turn on. The walls were cloud gray with a couple of Ducks Unlimited prints hung on one wall and a whitetail buck mount on another. A couch, a recliner, two wooden chairs. Flatscreen on the opposite wall no less than fifty-five inches.

Kyle did not recognize the man who gave Brock an arm wrestler grip and chest bump and then turned to greet him. He had close-cropped blond hair and a square chin. The man's arms bulged out of his sleeveless T-shirt like balloons ready to pop, but their size was not the most impressive thing. The left shoulder and biceps sported an elaborate tattoo the likes of which Kyle had never seen, an intricate depiction of a fierce-looking eagle gripping an olive branch in one set of talons and releasing a missile from the other. "Buster Shane." The man reached out with a standard handshake. "You're Kyle."

Kyle nodded. "Shane?"

"Yes, you got it." There was hurt in his eyes. "Ronny was my brother."

"I was sorry to hear about that."

"Did you know him?"

Kyle shook his head and couldn't help staring at the tattoo.

"I'm easy to get along with if you're straight with me. But I'll blow you away if you're not."

Kyle blinked hard and met Buster's gaze. "Huh?"

"Nothing, dude, nothing. So you didn't know Ronny, huh?"

Kyle shook his head again.

"We don't have to talk about that," Brock said.

Buster nodded and waved Brock off with scalding frown. "I'll talk about Ronny all night if I want to. Get me?"

Brock's eyes widened. "Got you."

Buster turned back to Kyle but held the frown. "I understand your dad is working the case."

Kyle's heart flipped. He'd already been jumped once tonight about that. And he would fare much worse from these pythons if Buster decided to unleash them. At least it would be over quickly. "I'm, uh, not sure. Helping his friend Jack Masterson, I think."

Buster's expression softened. "The deputy. I've heard he's a good dude. I want them to get to the truth, though they'll be disappointed. That boy will get what's coming to him, one way or the other." Buster intertwined his fingers and flipped his hands in a way that made his forearms ripple like the ground over an earthquake. "Ronny and Devlin were friends, once. Jealousy is an evil emotion."

Kyle glanced at Brock. "Talking about Lena Cole? Emma's stepsister?"

Buster tensed. "I don't want to even hear that name spoken."

Kyle shifted his gaze toward the floor. *Stupid.* Shut up and keep the pythons quiet. Pit vipers have membranes that detect shapes from infrared radiation, but these guys had human eyes. And they were staring at him.

Buster tapped him on the chest and pointed to a chair. "Relax, kid. Take a seat. How'd you get hooked up with my man here?" He nodded at Brock and sat across from Kyle.

"Carter acted a fool and tried to hammer on him," Brock said. "Kyle here was brave but got caught by surprise."

Brock was either lying or closed his eyes during the fight, if one could even call it that. But if he wanted to tell it that way, it suited Kyle just fine.

"Good." Buster let that word hang while he gave Kyle a contemplative stare. "I hear you're quite the nature expert."

Kyle frowned. How did Buster know that? Brock had said nothing of the sort on the earlier phone call.

"Our friend Gabe brags on you," Buster continued. "Says you have a special gift."

"Gift? I don't know about that. I don't understand why I'm here. I don't, I don't know anything about Ronny."

Buster stood and walked to one of the two windows. He spread the blinds with two fingers and peeked out, then let them snap back into position and turned to Kyle. "What did you see when y'all drove in?"

"A golf course."

Buster nodded. "And do you know why I live in this house?"

Kyle shook his head.

"Because somebody has to keep the golf course looking good. Mowing, raking, trimming, et cetera. And as a special perk for being willing to take the tiny salary they pay me, I get to live in this mansion." He spread his arms wide and looked around the room, eyes wide.

Buster gave the impression of a man on edge, and it made Kyle even more nervous. His mind raced to connect the dots. How was anything the man was saying relevant to him?

"Are your parents in good health, Kyle?"

He nodded.

"Tell me about them."

"Mom is an attorney. Dad a football coach. That's about it."

"A lawyer. Impressive. I remember Coach Reynolds, yeah. Amberton beat us my junior year, but we got 'em back senior year." He flexed his shoulders in a football stance and smiled at Brock. "Fourteen tackles."

"That's, uhh, awesome."

Buster grabbed Kyle's shoulder and squeezed it. "What about you? Better hit the weight room if you're gonna play."

Kyle shook his head. "Not my thing."

"Interesting." Buster stroked the stubble on his square chin. "What's your dad think about that?"

"He doesn't say much about it one way or the other."

Buster stood and turned away, as if Kyle's words had stabbed him like a thorn. "That's gotta be tough. So I guess he hangs out with you a lot. Doing your nature stuff."

Nature stuff? Kyle wasn't sure if that was meant to be derogatory or was just inadequate vocabulary. "He's busy doing his coaching thing mostly. But we hunt and fish sometimes."

Buster nodded. "Glad to hear it. You're lucky about your parents. My daddy is long gone, and Momma is on a chemotherapy drug that costs five thousand a month and makes her sick as a gut-shot dog."

Kyle grimaced. "That's terrible." He was even more confused

than before about where this was headed.

"She's in awful shape," Brock chimed in. "She's such a sweetheart. Hard to see her like this."

Buster resumed his position sitting across from Kyle. "You would like her. So let me ask you this. What do you know about cannabis?"

"Like marijuana? I, uh, don't smoke it, if that's what you're asking."

Buster laughed. "Of course you don't. I'm asking about the health benefits."

Kyle shrugged. He had heard some argue over whether people with certain health conditions might benefit, but he'd never put much thought into it. He'd certainly never tried it. He had a difficult enough time thinking clearly sometimes—especially in the classroom—and had no interest in making it worse, in the classroom or anywhere else. "Not much."

"Well, let me tell you. It's a miracle drug. Certain strains of it will take cancer pain and chemotherapy sickness and wipe them out." He snapped his fingers. "Make life worth living again."

"Has your, uh, mom, uh, tried it?" Kyle waved a hand in a deferential gesture. "No offense."

Buster smiled. "No offense taken. And yes, it has changed her life. But here's the thing. We've tried several different strains, and only one seems to help her. And guess what?"

"What?"

"It's one of the most expensive ones." He spread his arms wide again. "And Momma don't have a job, so I have to help her pay those bills. Now I've got all this going on with Ronny's death."

"Five thousand a month?"

Buster nodded. "And that's just the medicine for the cancer.

Then there's all her other treatments."

"And the marijuana." Kyle was filling in some of the blanks but didn't like the shape the puzzle solution was taking.

"Exactly."

"She can't afford to buy the one she needs, and I can't either. Plus, it's hard to find."

"And illegal." Kyle clenched his jaw and watched the pythons as he said it, but they didn't uncoil.

"And illegal *here*," Buster said. "I know. Truthfully, it won't be long before it's legal in Mississippi like most others." He shifted his gaze toward the floor. "But that will be too late for Mom. And to watch her suffer even more now that Ronny is gone…"

"There's got to be something you can do." Kyle had never really known anyone with cancer, but he'd heard about it. Vomiting with a stomach virus for two or three days was next to death; he couldn't imagine having that kind of misery day in, day out.

"I'm sorry, Kyle." Buster motioned for Kyle and Brock to stand. "I didn't mean to dump my problems on you. Unless I grow the stuff myself, I don't know how to help her. Money don't grow on trees, and special weed don't grow itself." He pointed toward the door. "I know you've got to get on home. Thanks for stopping by. Gabe and Brock's friends are my friends."

"Tell your mom I hope she feels better." Brock moved toward the door.

Kyle hesitated. "Why don't you grow it yourself?" Buster had said it would soon be legal, so who would care? Especially for a suffering cancer patient. "You must be good at growing stuff if you keep the golf course going."

Buster cocked his head and looked up as if he'd spotted something in the corner of the ceiling. Then he looked at Brock. "Wish I could, huh?"

Brock shook his head. "If you got caught—"

Buster turned to Kyle. "Long story, but when I was young and stupid, I got in some trouble. A dude pulled a knife on me, I roughed him up with a two-by-four. They said I'd been drinking—one beer—but guess who got the blame anyway? Probation now."

Kyle wasn't exactly sure how probation worked, but he understood the gist of it. No second chances if Buster messed up again.

Buster sighed. "I'm almost desperate enough to try it, to tell the truth. But she'll be long past needing it before spring gets here."

TWENTY-ONE

Monday, October 29, 2018

KYLE found a scrap of paper in the kitchen desk drawer, scribbled a note—*fishing with Gabe, back B4 school*—and left it on the counter. His mother would text him later with some snarky comment about how it would have been nice to know he was leaving early instead of her finding his bed and room empty. But she wouldn't ask questions about fishing and wouldn't be mad, just glad he was involved with something.

Dad was more likely to push for details, but fortunately, he had left even earlier. Odd, since he had come home at who-knows-what time last night.

Kyle eased the door closed and held his breath as he opened the garage door, hoping the noise wouldn't bring a female questioning. The morning cool washed over him and captured his breaths in white puffs as he slipped along the edge of his neighbor's backyard into the trees. His tennis shoes were wet from the dew on the grass, and he wished he had worn boots. He picked his way through a copse of trees and found the trail used by two generations of kids taking shortcuts between neighborhoods. This early, especially on a day with a late start at school, he had it to himself.

He knew exactly which house Proffit had been talking about. The Dunbar house had once been a focal point of suspicion and speculation among the neighborhood kids, with the untrimmed shrubs and sagging shutters and the old man seldom seen. Kyle had once suggested that a Boo Radley might be hidden within the walls but had been met only with blank stares, so he had dropped it. Then a year or so back, Old Man Dunbar had died, a fact supposedly discovered only after a foul odor wafted all the way out to the street where two grandmothers were on their morning walk. Abandoned ever since, with no word on who it was left to or what its fate might be, the house had become an afterthought.

Until the night before, when Proffit had sent word by text from Gabe shortly after he got home.

Proff wants you to come to thw Dunbar place. Six-thitu.

In the morning?

Yep

For what?

How I sposed to know? He don't give detals and don't like questions. Says it's a job

Why the Dunbar place?

Oowns it.

Is this about that job he mentioned yesterday?

Tol u I don't ask questns. Just be there if you want find out. He says no word to no one either

And so now here he was. Kyle checked the time on his phone as he paused at the edge of the tree line directly behind the house. Six-twenty-three. He had never really looked at the house from this angle before, but there was nothing special. It was a brick ranch style with green shutters, most of them now sagging just enough to be off square, with a patch of repaired shingles one shade darker than the original. A wooden swing with a rusted chain hung in the corner of a brick patio relinquishing its mortar to decay and weeds. An assortment of plastic pots and buckets lined the periphery, each spiked with stakes and the barren remnants of some garden plant from two summers before.

A sound like the screech of a rusty gate off to Kyle's left caught his attention, and he turned to locate it. Gabe had almost jumped out of his shoes once at the same sound when they were exploring an abandoned barn near Gabe's neighborhood, and Kyle smiled at the memory. A flash of blue fifteen feet away caught his eye, and he held his position in hopes of getting a better look.

"He must not see you, or he wouldn't be this close. Very intelligent creatures."

Kyle jumped at the sound to his right, much like Gabe had under similar circumstances. Only this time, the source was an unexpected visitor of the human kind. "Lord, have mercy, you scared me."

Proffit smiled and followed the flight of the blue jay across Dunbar's yard and over the house. He wore dark jeans with a crease, brown boots, and a waxed cotton coat as before. "What's to be afraid of? Just a bird."

Kyle shook his head. He knew it was just a bird. That wasn't the point. But fine, if the man wanted to play that game. "It's a corvid, same family as crows and ravens, which is why they're so smart. Fun fact: The blue isn't a pigment, just the structural reflection of light within the feathers themselves." He smiled and cocked his head at the sound of another jay, higher up, this one calling with a harsher jeer.

Proffit studied Kyle with an expressionless gaze. "Saw one behead a sparrow one time. Nature can be both noble and nasty."

What was that supposed to mean? Kyle waited to see where

this was going, his heart quickening. Part of him wanted to sneak back home and crawl into bed, but mostly he felt exhilaration. Why was this man interested in him? The fact that a man who exuded such a confident strength might need Kyle for something sent an empowered charge surging to his very core. He lifted his chin and met Proffit's stare. "You said you had a job for me?"

Proffit blinked and tilted his head back. "You a churchgoer, Kyle?"

Kyle nodded. Every Sunday, whether he wanted to go or not.

"What do you know about David?"

That was easy. "He was the king who wrote Psalms."

Proffit smiled. "Something like that. You ever heard the story of David and the showbread?"

Kyle frowned. It was ringing a bell, but only a distant one. "Seems like it."

"It's in the first book of Samuel. David was on the run from Saul, the king who wanted to kill him. David was hungry and lied to the priest to get the holy bread to eat, which was illegal."

Kyle had no idea where this was going. Proffit hadn't struck him as the preacher type, and this line of dialogue seemed as out of place as a peacock flying over Dunbar's house. "Okay."

"And hundreds of years later Jesus came along and said it was okay."

The bell was still ringing only faintly at best, and even then, something didn't sound quite right about it. A peacock might appear any moment.

Proffit smiled. "The point is the laws aren't made for every situation. Sometimes a man has to do what a man has to do, legal or not."

Now they were getting back on track, at least in terms of making sense. The implication of illegal activities was both disconcerting and invigorating. "Did you have something particular in mind, sir?"

Proffit nodded, slow and deliberate as if a long-held question had been answered without the ask. "You met my great friend Buster last night, correct?"

TWENTY-TWO

"ALL rise."

Jack eyed the white-haired bailiff and sized him up while he complied with the instructions along with the others in the courtroom. The old codger's reflexes couldn't be that good. A surprise charge, tackle to the ground, toss of the keys to Devlin only feet away, and they both could escape. Useless thoughts but perhaps instinctual. That's what they would do in the movies. Tear off across the countryside until they could prove Devlin's innocence and come home to a parade.

"McKinley County Justice Court is now in session. The Honorable Judge Faith Anne Foster presiding."

Faith Anne Foster marched in and took her seat. She was not tall, but her broad shoulders and confident demeanor commanded the room. Her black hair was drawn up in a bun, and the roundness of it matched her face, with cheeks flushed like she was angry or cold or both. Wrinkles at the corners of her eyes indicated she might be accustomed to smiling, but the downturn at the corners of her mouth suggested otherwise.

"Be seated," the old bailiff said.

Faith Anne Foster was one of two hundred judges in the state, give or take, elected to four-year terms. Jack remembered her from high school. A year older than him, she came from money, maybe a grandfather who owned a trucking company or mobile home business or something. She had been a trombone player in the band. As a rule, he had never known who played what, since he didn't know a C note from a hundred-dollar bill, but he remembered her as the only girl trombone player. A girl he had been dating at the time had commented that Faith Anne looked like a tuba, and Faith Anne had promptly put her in a headlock and blackened both eyes.

As for her personal life, the judge had never been married but supposedly had a "close friend" of some sort, with much debate on what gender the mystery person was. Jack recalled she had a heavy crush on Case back in high school that was never reciprocated, and he wondered if Abi ever knew about it. Such a thing could make the courtroom dynamics even more interesting, which might be the last thing Devlin needed.

On the other hand, what if she held a grudge against Abi after all these years? Might that work in Devlin's favor? That's ridiculous. The judge may be prickly, but surely she was fair and professional.

In terms of her career, Jack knew only what Egg had shared with him about what happened to the judge between high school and taking the bench. After college, she had tried her hand in education as the Amberton High School Assistant Band Director for a few years, then as city clerk over in Haughton before going to law school. Just a few months earlier, she had been chosen as Justice Court Judge in a special election after the prior judge dropped dead right in the middle of the eighteenth green of Amberton Country Club. Now, Jack couldn't help picturing Faith Anne holding Devlin in a headlock. He wondered if the winds of change had blown the wrong way for the kid that day on the golf course.

Judge Foster nodded to her left at the woman seated across the aisle from Devlin and his attorney, Egg Eggleston.

The woman returned the nod and held the judge's gaze confidently. "County Attorney Abi Reynolds for the state, Your Honor."

For Jack, the room temperature went up ten degrees in an instant. Two of the people he cared most about in the world were on different sides of the aisle, and the stakes couldn't be higher. He had hoped Abi would recuse herself under the circumstances, but she said there was no need for the preliminary hearing. She would turn it over to the district attorney's office for the grand jury, if the case held together long enough for it to get to that. And the way things were going, he wasn't optimistic.

Jack glanced three rows behind Abi at the hulking figure with a scowl on his face and arms folded over his chest. It unnerved him to see Abi Reynolds and Buster Shane on the same team. Ronny didn't deserve to die, but Jack had a strong suspicion he had brought some trouble on himself.

And maybe his brother Buster deserved some of the blame. The former high school football star had a reputation for being wrapped up in drug movement in the area. He had gone to jail a couple years back for some type of assault—drug related, almost certainly. Now he was out, and the rumors had been swirling. Even Abi had mentioned his name as a person of interest in the drug war, if not an investigational target yet. And now his brother was dead. Did he have something to do with it? Jack vowed to find out.

Buster broke his stare at Devlin and glanced at Jack. Neither looked away.

The judge's voice intervened. "Would the defendant please step to the podium?"

Devlin glanced backward over his shoulder as he stood, and Jack gave him a supportive head tilt. Tammy grabbed Jack's hand. Her palm was sweaty and cool, and Jack squeezed it in an attempt to reassure her. Lena Cole made an indistinguishable sound behind them. Jack wished Case could be there but understood why he wasn't. Case had to sleep beside Abi.

"As you have heard, my name is Judge Faith Anne Foster. Please state your full name and date of birth for the court."

"Devlin Jason James. October 18, 2000."

Judge Foster peered at some papers before her for a few seconds. "And that makes you eighteen years of age, correct?"

"Yes, ma'am."

"Your Honor will do fine."

"Yes, ma'am. I mean, Your Honor. Sorry."

"The time to be sorry may or may not come, but it is not now. Now is the time to be certain." The judge watched Devlin through narrowed eyes for a moment then flattened the down-turned curve of her lips into what may have been her version of a smile. "Now. Mr. James, I see that you have obtained legal representation with Mr. Eggleston. Is that correct?"

"Yes, Your Honor."

"Good. And I assume he has informed you of all your rights, as did the arresting officers?"

"Yes, Your Honor."

"And you understand that this is not a trial? Today my goal is to learn the basis of the case against you, gain understanding of your particular circumstances, and set bail accordingly."

Devlin nodded and told her he understood.

Judge Foster gave the half smile again and turned to Abi. "Ms. Reynolds?"

"Thank you, Your Honor." Abi stood and clasped both hands before her. She wore a classic, dark-navy suit, and her long, black curls were gathered at the nape of her neck by a barrette, with a few strands flowing independently at the edges. Jack couldn't see her eyes from his angle, but he knew they would be blue enough to make the suit's color seem one shade lighter than it was. She glanced at Jack for a split second with pursed lips. Jack knew what the look meant. *This is difficult for all of us, but I'm going to do my job.* She cleared her throat and began.

"Two days ago, on the morning of Saturday, October 27, 2018, Ronny Shane was found dead at the bottom of Logan's Bluff, along the Timtullah River near the Amberton Lock and Dam. The state believes, based on the evidence available, that he was pushed to his death sometime during the night before. The defendant, Devlin James, was heard threatening to kill Mr. Shane the night before after an altercation during a football game. In addition, we have video showing Mr. James driving to Logan's Bluff near the time Mr. Shane was killed. We have tire tracks matching those of Mr. James's truck at the scene of the crime, and we recovered an envelope with Ronny Shane's initials containing two hundred and fifty dollars from Mr. James's truck. Based on information we have obtained, the two of them were in an ongoing dispute over a young woman. We believe Mr. James owed Ronny Shane that sum of money for drugs and decided to kill him rather than pay it. Not to mention the fact that killing Mr. Shane would eliminate him from the love triangle."

Lena's gasp was one of many in the courtroom.

"Order!" Judge Foster banged her gavel, and her cheeks burned red. "This is not the place for dramatic outbursts. We are gathering information about the state's case. If you aren't certain you can handle it, please leave now. Because I am quite certain I can handle you."

So that explained the money in the envelope. Jack wanted to reach two rows up and smack Devlin on the back of the head. One, for not telling him—why was he holding out, anyway? Two, for being so stupid over a girl. Was he stupid enough over her to kill Ronny Shane? Surely not. And three, drug money?

"Objection, Your Honor." Eggleston had his hand raised while the judge quieted everyone down. "That was inflammatory."

The judge frowned as if the attorney had blurted out he liked green eggs and ham. "Um…Mr. Eggleston, there is no jury here, remember? I'm smart enough to see through any rhetoric either of you throw at me. But if it will make you feel better, let's try again. Ms. Reynolds, would you care to rephrase that last part?"

Abi gave a cooperative nod. "It is our *belief*, Your Honor, that Devlin James's intent was to pay the victim what he owed him but had a change of heart and decided to instead eliminate him due to greed or love or both."

Money, love, jealousy, anger, hate. She had latched onto all the top choices. *Good grief, Abi. Why do you have to be so thorough on this one?* Jack hoped Egg would come through. Otherwise, Devlin was in trouble.

"And is it the state's belief that this crime was premeditated?"

"It is, Your Honor. Murder in the first degree."

Judge Foster nodded at Abi and turned her attention back to Eggleston, who again had his hand raised.

"May we approach, Your Honor?"

The judge frowned and gestured for the attorneys to approach the bench. "This better be good."

"What's going on?" Tammy whispered to Jack. Devlin looked back at them again with a puzzled upturn of one eyebrow.

Jack shook his head and put an index finger to his lips. The last thing he wanted was for Judge Faith Anne Foster to get her feathers ruffled. No headlocks, please, metaphorical or otherwise. Metaphorical. That's a word Jet or Case might use. They would be impressed he thought it. Too bad neither of them was here. This could get interesting.

Jack locked his eyes on the meeting at the front of the courtroom, waiting.

And then all three sets of eyes turned to look straight at him. Egg pointed at him and spoke in an animated manner. Jack didn't know whether to shrink in his seat or stand. Then Judge Foster pointed at him, and for a split second he hoped it was because Tammy had been talking. But he knew that wasn't the reason.

"Mr. Masterson," the judge said. "I need you to report to my chambers. Now, please." She banged the gavel. "Fifteen-minute recess. Bailiff, stay with the defendant. Take him to the holding cell if I'm not back in five."

TWENTY-THREE

JUDGE Faith Anne Foster pivoted around her desk with surprising grace for someone with a linebacker physique. In one seamless motion, she settled into her leather chair, adjusted her robe, and gestured for Egg and Abi to sit in the two chairs across from her. Jack looked for another chair but didn't see one. "You can stand, Deputy," the judge said. "This won't take long. Do you have something to say?"

Jack swallowed hard. He should not have sent Egg that text the night before, but he was upset. It was only because he and Case had found more evidence in one day than Egg could find in three lifetimes. He had no actual intention of knocking Egg's big nose through the back of his skull, then or any time, even if he did lose the case due to negligence. But would the judge believe that?

Jack gulped again. Could he go to jail for this? He would do community service if it would keep him out. He had done it before. Maybe if he showed adequate remorse, he would only get a reprimand. "I'm sorry, Your Honor. We've all been under a lot of stress. I kinda just lost my head. Devlin is a good kid, and we're very close, and—"

"Mr. Eggleston, please get Mr. Masterson in the same zip code as us. Heck, I'll take the same area code."

Egg cleared his throat. "Jack, this about what happened at your house Saturday night. With Lily."

"Jack, are you okay?"

He ignored Abi's question, trying to pivot to what Egg had said and make a note to buy him dinner for what he had not.

"Mr. Masterson, if you have something to tell me, please spit it out."

"Uh, yes. Yes, your Honor. I think someone else killed Ronny, and they don't like me trying to prove otherwise."

"Prove otherwise? I thought as a deputy you would try to prove the truth."

"I do, Your Honor. I just don't think saying Devlin James committed a murder is the truth."

She arched an eyebrow. "You were saying?"

Jack nodded and fought the urge to move from his position. He always thought better when he was pacing. "Saturday night, when I came home, I had my great-niece Lily with me. I saw someone lurking in my garage, and I jumped out to chase him. When I came back to my truck, Lily had been moved."

"Wait." Abi whirled in her chair, eyes wide in alarm. "Lily? Was she hurt?"

"No, no. She's fine. He moved her from her car seat to the front."

"Moved?" the judge asked. "And how do you know it was a man?"

"She's only four. Someone moved her from her car seat." He explained how she was unable to unbuckle herself and had told Jack "that man" had moved her.

The judge scribbled on a notepad. "And how do you know this wasn't just a silly prank? One of the defendant's friends, perhaps?"

"Like it or not, Jack, that is a valid consideration," Abi said. "Devlin James has had some shady friends. And Tammy hasn't always been rock solid, either. How do we know she didn't put someone up to it?"

Jack glared at Abi. Why did she have to go there? Sure, Tammy had a history of some addiction problems, but that was in the past and all related to her depression before it was properly treated. Did Abi throw that jab because she was mad at Case, disapproved of Tammy as Jack's romantic interest, or was she just doing her job? He knew her well enough to know it had to the be latter. Still, this whole situation was so…confounding. Too many connections across the aisle of justice.

Jack took his phone from his pocket and pulled up a photo. "This doesn't look like a prank or distraction. I found this stuck in her waistband." He passed his phone to the judge.

She scowled as she examined the image and read the message. *Stay out of it and let justice be served. Next time I won't give her back.*

Judge Foster passed the phone to Abi. "You submitted this for analysis, I presume?"

"I did," Jack said. "Nothing back yet. But clearly this is a kidnapping threat."

Abi returned Jack's phone to him. "You have Lily somewhere safe?"

"Yes." That reminded him. He needed to call and check on Janie and Lily as soon as he got out of there. He had promised to let them sleep late, so he hadn't talked to them yet. Janie was off and holing up at her friend Meg's, so they should be fine. But still…

"And you think it means what?"

"It has to be referring to mine and Devlin's relationship. He and I have grown close. And it's no secret I'd like to prove he's innocent. If that is the truth, of course."

"Sounds to me like this person is saying he's guilty. I'm not sure how this helps the defendant at all."

"Or they want him to be found guilty. Which, if incorrect, is more likely if I'm not on the case to prove it."

Judge Foster pursed her lips in a smirk. "Ms. Reynolds, it sounds like he fears your people will prosecute erroneously."

Abi waved a backhand toward Jack. "That's just Jack being Jack. Sheriff Rappaport and his team have accumulated plenty of damning evidence, and Jack—Mr. Masterson—is just having a difficult time being objective. But that's fine. The truth is the truth. My hang-up with all this is the immense waste of the court's time. This evidence can all be presented at trial."

Egg raised a hand and spoke up for the first time. "Your Honor, I wanted you to hear this in chambers because for one, I believe the investigation is best served by keeping what happened at Mr. Masterson's house private for now. More than that, though, I believe it merits a dismissal. There is as much evidence—a kidnapping threat, in fact—suggesting a perpetrator other than my client, as there is to the contrary."

Abi snorted. "I'm just getting started out there. Deputy Nash will testify he found a pawn ticket where Devlin pawned his grandfather's shotgun for two hundred and fifty dollars. Oh, and not surprisingly, his drug screen was positive too."

Jack felt sick. Devlin's grandfather, who grew up poor and never got far from it as an adult, had passed down perhaps his most prized possession shortly before his death. He used it for everything from hunting to personal protection. Always worried about Tammy, the old man had stared hard onto Devlin's eyes and told him, who knows, he may need it to protect his momma one day. What kind of kid pawns something like that?

And a positive drug screen? Jack had always hoped Tammy's predisposition, if one believed in such things, had not been passed to her son. Now he was beginning to wonder if he knew Devlin at all.

The judge adjusted her reading glasses while she studied her notes. "I'm not sure I agree with your estimate of the importance of a scribbled note attached to a toddler's clothes, Mr. Eggleston, but I'll take it under advisement. I do agree, however, the details of encounter are not to be shared for public consumption at this juncture."

"But Your Honor—"

Judge Foster stopped Egg with a raised palm and looked at Abi. "Ms. Reynolds, do you have anything else to add?"

"No, Your Honor, I do not."

Judge Foster nodded. "Good. And regardless of your personal feelings, may I suggest you go easy on the personal attacks, Ms. Reynolds? You know what they say about specks in the eyes."

"Excuse me, Judge?" Abi's face turned red, and her eyes blazed. "My husband's name was cleared a long time ago."

The judge gave a patronizing smile. "So you say. I've noticed sometimes, Abi, that you tend to get lost in the weeds at times. Ironic, under the circumstances." She paused and brought her hands together atop her desk. "We will reconvene in fifteen minutes."

TWENTY-FOUR

"THAT'S about as close to a girl as you'll ever get. What's your imaginary friend's name gonna be?"

Kyle slammed his notebook closed and glared up at Donnie Ronald standing beside his desk, peering over his shoulder. He was more irritated at the interruption than the insult. His pencil sketch of Emma Harlow was just getting started, but he was stuck on the eyes. There was a tiny curve at the corners that he hadn't quite captured yet. And if he didn't get the eyes right, he might as well trash the whole thing.

"Are you gonna sit there through the next class too?" Donnie said it loudly enough for others filing out of the classroom to hear, and a few chuckles erupted.

"Mind your own business." Kyle rushed to stand, cramming his pencil and notebook into his backpack. The bell had sounded, and he hadn't even heard it. He had to hurry, or he would miss his opportunity.

He pushed past Donnie, who fired off another empty insult, and hurried down the hallway, weaving between other students who mostly ignored him. Emma's text had said she would wait for him after period outside the door to the school library. Did she have something important to tell him, or did she just want to see him? Kyle hadn't asked, and he didn't care. Both options were equally splendid.

He rounded the corner and stopped short. There she was, as promised. But she was talking to one of the senior baseball players. He leaned in while he talked, his hand on the cinder block wall over her head as if he hoped she might climb in the jacket with him.

Emma glanced in Kyle's direction, and he almost turned and walked away to avoid seeing her ignore him. But she never gave him a chance.

"Kyle!" Emma ducked under the jock's arm and met Kyle with a smile. "Took you long enough."

"I was, uh, finishing up some homework." He hoped his face wasn't as pink as it felt. He followed as she turned and moved ahead toward the glass door leading to the courtyard where students spent their ten-minute breaks gathered in groups, usually griping about teachers, replaying events from the weekend, or gossiping about those in other cliques. Her group was always much larger than his, and Kyle wondered where they would go now.

Emma stopped just outside the door and sat on a brick retaining wall surrounding monkey grass, nandina, and a crepe myrtle. She crossed her legs and patted the brick beside her. Kyle obliged and sat beside her, hoping Gabe didn't come over and say something to embarrass him.

"How's the jaw?" Emma asked. "It's not as bruised as I thought it would be."

"It's nothing." Kyle resisted the urge to touch the sore spot. "No biggie."

"I been thinking," Emma said, "about something I said last night. You deserve more than what I gave you."

"Deserve?"

"I said something about being pretty sure Devlin is guilty. Since Coach Reynolds is involved, and now since you got hit for it, you should know what I know."

Kyle nodded. "Okay."

Emma leaned forward and craned her neck to look Kyle in the eye. Her eyes were different now, serious and wide without the little curl at the edges. "But you got to swear not to tell a soul. Not one, single, solitary soul in the world."

Kyle looked around instinctively to make sure Donnie Ronald or some other yahoo hadn't sneaked up on them, listening. Was Emma about to share actual evidence about a murder case? Surely she just had some gossip or juicy rumor. "I promise," he said.

Emma didn't flinch.

"I swear."

She nodded, satisfied now. "Devlin's motive went way deeper than just a fight on the football field."

Was that all she had? "Yeah," Kyle said. "Ronny was messing with his girlfriend." Everybody had heard that.

Emma shook her head. "They grew up best friends. Then Ronny started messing with drugs and stuff, and they stopped hanging out. But two, maybe three weeks ago, Ronny had sex with Lena, on the bus, on a school field trip."

Kyle couldn't believe it. "On the school bus?"

"Yep. So everybody at Haughton knows about it. Supposedly they ragged Devlin about it the whole game Friday night. Then to make it even more embarrassing, Ronny jumped him in front of everybody in the county."

Ouch. "That's got to sting. His former best friend too." Kyle didn't have a ton of friends and hated to think what it would feel like if Gabe did him that way. "But enough to kill somebody over?"

Emma shrugged. "Ronny wouldn't leave Lena alone, even though she said she loved Devlin. Called her every day almost."

"How do you know all this?"

Emma sighed. "Inside sources."

"What do you mean, 'inside'? Devlin?"

Emma huffed. "Heavens, no. I mean, I'm friends with Devlin, I guess, but he doesn't tell me anything. Believe it or not, Lena's mom and my dad were married for a while. So we were stepsisters. Divorced, now. But we talk."

"And Lena told you all this? Seems like she'd want it to be a secret."

"She would. And maybe it will stay that way. But I know you, Kyle Reynolds, even if we just met. So I know that if it comes out, it won't be from you."

The dramatic flair with which she said his name made Kyle's heart skip a beat. Alluring as Emma was, though, maybe that's all this conversation was too: a lot of drama and no real substance. Kyle was no attorney, but he'd heard his mom talk enough to know that what Emma had shared was nothing more than circumstantial evidence. "Still," he said, "that's not exactly a smoking gun."

Emma sighed. "Maybe not, but there's something else."

Kyle's heart skipped a beat again despite his doubts.

"Friday night, after they left the hospital, Devlin told Lena that he was going to take care of it."

"Take care of it?"

Emma nodded. "He said Ronny would never mess with her again."

"You're serious? He told Lena that?"

"To be specific, the words were something like, 'I'm getting rid of Ronny tonight once and for all.'"

Kyle gulped. And someone had taken a video of him heading straight to the crime scene too.

The bell sounded, and students began filing back into the building. Emma put her index finger to Kyle's sore jaw and then to her lips. She gave a subtle smile before turning and merging into the crowd.

TWENTY-FIVE

"EXCUSE me, I've got to take this." I pushed away from my desk and winced apologetically at the mother sitting across from me. She already blamed me for her son's failing English grade, and my exiting mid-tirade probably wouldn't help. But then again, it was likely that nothing would.

I stepped out into the hall and tapped my cell phone as I closed the door. "Tell me."

"Case, you're not gonna believe it." Jack was breathless, like he'd just run a 5K or wrestled a gator, the latter much more likely for my friend than the former. "She might as well have pronounced him guilty."

"The judge didn't throw it out?"

"Not only didn't she throw it out, she set bail at a half mil."

That couldn't be. Five hundred thousand dollars for an eighteen-year-old with no prior record? That meant someone had to come up with fifty thousand to pay the bail bond to get him out. "How is that possible?"

"She said he was a flight risk. Said there was, quote, a potential for interference that required extra incentive for him to show up in court. Looked right at me as she said it."

"I don't understand."

"Egg said she's pissed that I've been helping on the case. That I can't be objective and might know ways to help him run off. Stupidest nonsense I've ever heard." Jack paused, and his voice changed from indignant to solemn. "Rap said he should take me off the case for getting his department insulted, but it looks like I've helped keep Devlin in jail, so just keep doing what I'm doing."

"Don't blame yourself, Jack. That's baloney. Something else is going on. Hold on a second." I peeked back in on my angry parent who met my gaze with a hard glare. I held up one finger, gave a look that was more smirk than apology this time, and closed the door. "Okay, I'm back. Can Tammy come up with the money?"

"She doesn't have that kind of cash, and I don't either. Maybe we can get a loan, but it'll take some time."

"I can't help you, Jack. Not with Abi involved like she is."

"I know, bud, I know. We'll figure something out."

"So where you headed now?"

"Supposed to meet Jet for lunch. Can you come? We need to make a plan."

Jack and his plans. "I'm at school today."

"And you have to eat just like I do. Twelve-thirty at Dundee's."

———

Dundee's Grill had been an Amberton staple for blue plate specials and greasy burgers for two generations. My dad loved to tell of the days when carhops in cheerleader uniforms brought the food to you, and when I was a teenager, the canopy out front from the drive-in days was still hanging on, albeit a bit leaky in wet weather. Those days were long gone, but the restaurant's satisfying impact on the palate and the belly of the customers who came had never wavered.

Jack and Jet were both working on hefty helpings of

chicken and dumplings from opposite sides of a booth when I arrived. A television dangling from the wall above them was hosting a weather update from the local news, though the sound was largely drowned by the buzz of patrons catching up on news of their own. I stood at the end of the table and waited for one of them to slide over and make room for me to sit, but neither did. "Thanks for waiting, guys."

Jet wiped his mouth with a napkin. "People come from every corner of the county to get these on Mondays. They run out sometimes."

"I'm so sure that was the reason." I sat down beside Jack and elbowed him.

He slid over after a second elbowing. "Plus, you might've ditched us," he said.

A young waitress with a spray-tan complexion and a generous smile appeared at our table. "Hey, Coach. What can I get you?"

Suzie Delmore had graduated one or two years before, I couldn't remember. She had never been in any of my classes but had dated one of my players somewhere along the way. "Hello, Suzie. I'll have what they're having."

She put a hand to her mouth. "Sorry, Coach Reynolds. We just ran out of the dumplings."

I ignored Jet's spoon clattering to his plate and him leaning back with arms folded over his chest. "Cheeseburger then, all the way. Spicy fries and sweet tea."

Suzie nodded, spun on one heel, and flitted away.

I pointed at Jet. "Not a word about dumplings." I looked down at the table, as if I could see through it to his lower half. "How's the leg? Barometer's been up and down."

Jet grimaced. "Don't have to tell me when it's gonna rain. Eight out of ten right before it hits. Clockwork." He shrugged.

"It is what it is. Could be worse."

"Yeah, could be six feet under like VJ," Jack said.

"This is true," Jet said. "I wouldn't trade with him, or Lane, either."

It was difficult not to shudder at the names of those two best friend lunatics. The former who tried to kill Jet, and the latter who tried to kill all of us—and succeeded in killing Jet's brother Adam. None of us were ever convinced that VJ MacIntosh didn't have a bigger part in Adam's death than what Lane Buckley gave him credit for before he died. Fortunately or unfortunately, depending on how one viewed it, we would never know.

"I still have my letter," Jack said.

I scowled at him. "Say what?" I knew what he was talking about; I just couldn't believe what he was telling us. VJ had sent all three of us a letter with the exact same message before he went to juvie after running over Jet. What was it, 1986? Maybe 1987.

I WILL GET YOU ONE DAY. ONE DAY...

I hadn't thought of that letter, of those eight words, in so, so long. Its memory had lurked in the shadows through the latter years of high school and then college before fading away into a distant speck after finding out VJ had died of a drug overdose.

Jet laughed. "You're such a weirdo. That was what, thirty years ago?"

"Thirty-one years, three months, eighteen days, and..." Jack winked and looked at his watch. "Eight minutes, twenty seconds."

It was my turn to laugh. "Jet's right. You're a freak. Why in the world would you save such a thing all these years? He's been dead forever."

"Just a reminder. The world is out to get you, if you let it. He and Lane both got what they deserved, but there's plenty of evil where that came from. The depths of hell itself, I say."

I waved my hand as if clearing the air of smoke. Jack clutched grudges like raptors do rodents, except he never let go—even after they're dead. "Yes, VJ was a monster, and so was Lane. Sorry I brought it up."

"I'm just thinking there's something like that about this Buster Shane guy. I watched him in court today. He's hiding something. Reminds me of Lane. That guy would have killed his brother if it gave him an advantage. Maybe Buster did."

Jack had good instincts. I knew better than to dismiss his idea. I looked at Jet. "Tell me what you think."

Jet shook his head. "I don't know him, but sounds like he needs to be watched. As for Devlin, I think that bond was set too high." He shifted his gaze to me. "Maybe because the prosecutor is superbly prepared and remarkably convincing."

"Ha. Don't mention that, either. I'm in enough trouble at home already."

Jet wrinkled his nose. "She mad?"

"Something like that. Let's just say she's glad to be handing the case over to the DA's office." I didn't know if mad was the word as much as frustrated. Frustrated that my loyalty to my friends obligated me to help on a case opposite her, even if unofficially. Frustrated that she had no choice but to work a case against a boy so close to Jack, one of her best friends too. Frustrated that a good kid like Devlin had felt so desperate to commit such an awful crime and ruin his promising life.

Jack wadded his napkin up and dropped it onto his empty plate. "Jet, you're smarter than every DA in America. What do we need to do now?"

He shook his head. "Diagnosing idiopathic cardiac amyloidosis and solving a crime are not the same thing. But tell me again what you have so far and let me think through it. Start with what Devlin has said."

"That's a big zero," Jack said. "He confessed when we picked him up, but nobody except us at this table knows that. And I don't believe him."

"Why don't you believe him?"

"I can see it in his eyes. He's hiding something."

Jet raised his eyebrows and looked at Jack as if he'd just announced that snakes slither. "Murder will make you do that."

Jack brought his fist down on the table. "No. Not that."

"Okay," I said. "And I know you told him not to tell the sheriff or Egg. But why won't he tell you what happened?"

Jack shrugged. "Maybe he doesn't know."

"Or maybe he's protecting someone," I said.

"My money's on that girl," Jet said.

Jack nodded. "Lena Cole. Case, you know much about her? You're there at school."

I shook my head. "It's all hush around me right now. Kids know I'm connected, more ways than one. Besides, she's a Haughton girl. But she does have family at our school. Emma Harlow. Cousin, I think."

"Nope," Jet said. "Half sister. Wait, no. Stepsister. Wait, wrong again. Ex-stepsister. I've treated some of the family."

"Emma Harlow?" Jack's voice had a new edge to it. "Hang on." He pulled his cell from a pocket and tapped it a few times. "Nash texted me earlier, said they tracked down the source of the video that showed Devlin driving up to Logan's. Name didn't ring a bell. Yep, it was Emma Harlow."

What did that mean? Lena Cole's stepsister, or something

like that, was providing evidence implicating Devlin? I didn't know much about her. A sophomore, maybe a junior, maybe new this year? I couldn't even recall whom I'd seen her talking to at school. Either way, the fact she had shot the video and made it public supported what Jet had postulated. "There you go, Jet. Maybe Devlin and this Harlow girl are both trying to protect Lena Cole in different ways."

"Okay." Jet drummed the table with both index fingers, thinking. "Let's go with that a second. What would her motive be?"

"She wanted to be with Devlin, but Ronny wouldn't leave her alone," Jack said.

"Okay, that's worth asking some questions. Have y'all talked to Lena?"

Jack shook his head. "Nope. Nash says she told him Devlin threatened to take care of Ronny for good, whatever that means."

"That doesn't sound good, but that could mean anything. You need to talk to her."

Jack nodded in agreement. "No doubt, but Nash said she's off limits. Her father works for the news station. Made some veiled threats about how the news coverage might cast the sheriff in a bad light if he tried to drag other kids into this. So Rap hasn't been too keen on pushing that just yet."

"Especially if it seems obvious he has his man already," I said.

"Especially."

Jet stopped tapping and pointed both fingers at no one in particular. "Maybe Ronny was abusing her."

I thought back to how she looked in the emergency department with Devlin after the game, hours before Ronny died.

"Jack, she didn't have any bruises that I could see. You?"

"No, but I guess it's still possible." He grunted in frustration. "This whole idea doesn't make sense. The Harlow girl knew her former stepsister was going to kill Ronny at Logan's Bluff, so she took a video of Devlin, who just happened to be going there, too, to frame him?"

Seemed highly improbable to me. "It's a stretch for sure."

"Devlin could have told Lena he was going to meet Ronny," Jet said.

"Let me ask you this," Jet said. "Does Lena look like a gun-totin' killer to either of you?"

Jack chuckled. "Jet, I think you're missing some details here. Nobody was killed with a gun."

Jet tapped the table with his finger. "Because if she had planned ahead to kill Ronny, how else would she think she could do it? I mean, what are the odds that she would predict with any reliability that she could, on demand, talk him into getting close enough to the edge of that bluff for her ninety pounds to push his two hundred over?"

Jet was right, and Lena Cole as the killer didn't make sense for more reasons than that. We knew that Ronny had done Logan's Leap before, so one could postulate that she planned to trip him there or something. But that seemed like a long shot to rely on for the same reasons, and besides, he wasn't found below that end of the bluff. And if she had intended on using a gun, how would she have planned to frame Devlin?

Also, it would be one thing to plan to kill Ronny but another entirely to frame the boyfriend she supposedly wanted to be with instead. This whole line of thinking was a giant leap to nowhere cogent.

I was suddenly distracted by a commercial on the television

above us, perhaps because it corresponded to my next thought, perhaps because it was so obnoxious. A fat man in a white suit was jumping up and down on an overturned tire and shouting. "Come on down to Tire Town! Buy one set of rounds, get another fifty percent down!"

I'd seen the commercial before. It seemed silly to me. First off, the man looked ridiculous. Second, the "fifty percent down" rhyme made it sound like you had to make a down payment instead of getting them at half price. And who buys two sets of tires at once, anyway? "Jack, what kind of car does Lena drive?"

"A white Kia. Optima, I think." Jack was staring at the television, too, his mouth open as if the fat man had looked him in the eye and cursed him by name. "You've got to be kidding me." He elbowed me in the ribs, much harder than I had done him earlier. "Let me out."

I stood to let him slide out of the booth. "What is it?"

His expression had changed. Now he looked like he might be sick. "Gotta go." He turned and headed out the door without saying another word.

"What was that?" Jet craned his neck to better see the television, but a commercial about a magical carpet cleaner was on now.

"No earthly idea. Forgot to rotate his tires last oil change."

Jet smiled and shook his head. "Some master plan hit him, I guess."

"Any other ideas? I've got to get back to school."

"Any DNA evidence processed yet from the scene?"

"Not that I've heard."

Jet chuckled. "Whole case might've broken wide open with that cigarette you almost plunged to your death for."

"Let's not talk about it."

He laughed and shook his head. "Okay. I know you need to go. But I keep going back to the guy floating down on the kitchen table. Coincidence that he appears to have been at the bottom of the bluff just a short walk below the crime scene?"

I shrugged. My head was spinning with so many possibilities, none of which made more sense than that Devlin James killed Ronny Shane for all the reasons Jack said Abi had pointed out in court that morning and more.

"What about his name? Think that has any significance?"

"Peregrine?"

"Yeah. Know what that means?"

"Sure. It's a kind of falcon. One of the fastest animals, if I'm not mistaken."

Jet tilted his head side to side. I wasn't wrong, but that wasn't what he was going for. "You're right. It's actually the fastest member of the animal kingdom. But do you know why it's called the peregrine falcon?"

"No, but I know you're going to tell me."

"Because unlike many falcon species, they migrate across a broad range, sometimes entire continents."

"Great. Thanks for the biology lesson." Jet was full of what many would call useless information. Often interesting, often useless. I liked to give him a hard time, but I knew whatever he was about to say would not fit that category.

"The scientific name, *Falco peregrinus*, means wandering falcon. Peregrine means wanderer." Jet cinched his lips around the last word and nodded slowly.

It took me a moment to wrap my head around the idea he was suggesting, then I lost my breath for a quick second. "No way."

Jet shrugged. "It's worth considering. There's a hint of

homology there, too, if you think about it."

I jumped up from the table. "Keep your phone handy. I'm going to need you to send me some calculations."

"What?"

"Be ready!" I whirled and nearly bumped into our waitress. "Sorry, Suzie." I pointed to Jet. "My cardiologist friend there is picking up the tab. Smart man, very smart. Should be able to calculate a thirty percent tip with no trouble."

And I raced out the door.

TWENTY-SIX

THE more things change, the more they stay the same. Back in my college days as an English major, I had been able to quote Jean-Baptiste Alphonse Karr's famous aphorism in its original French. I couldn't recall why I had learned it or what the context of the writing was, but the expression now rose up and rammed into me like a rolling ocean wave as I left Dundee's restaurant.

Peregrine. Wanderer. Was it possible that I knew exactly who the strange man on the table raft was? Surely not. Thirty-three years was a long time. Was there a comparably pithy quote about coincidences somewhere in my mind's dusty files? I couldn't think of one. But I had learned, often the hard way, that coincidences seldom are.

My plan was a long shot but worth a try. I called my principal and told her I had to go out of town for a personal emergency. She told me it was no problem and to be careful, but her voice suggested she was none too pleased when I declined to give any details. I didn't care. Personal was personal, and I had put in enough time and extra hours over the years that I deserved some slack.

A web search on my phone found the US Army Corps of Engineers site quickly enough, and a few clicks later I found the information about the Amberton Lock and Dam. For would-be river travelers, there were three ways to notify the lock personnel you wanted to pass through: by pulling a rope at the end of the lock wall, by using a radio, or—there it was—calling the tower. I scrolled on down and found the phone number. A deep voice with a sandpaper finish to each word answered. "Amberton Lock."

"Hi, I'm looking for Greely Grantham. Is he by chance working today?"

"You locking through? I don't see you."

"No. I'm, uh, with the sheriff's department."

"This about that murder up on Logan's?"

"Not exactly. Can I speak to Mr. Grantham, please?"

"This is Poe. Boyd Poe. Maybe I can help you."

"That's nice, but I need Mr. Grantham."

Poe grunted and mumbled something, and a higher pitched, less confident voice answered. "This is, uh, Greely."

I wondered if I should have stuck with Poe. "Mr. Grantham, you spoke with my friend Jack Masterson the day before yesterday, yes?"

"Yeah. Who is this?"

It occurred to me that he might follow Amberton football. "C.R. Reynolds." It wasn't a lie.

"Ah, okay. Used to be sheriff."

I decided to go with it. "That's the name."

"Hey, what ever happened to your deputy Turnip? We was friends back in the day."

Turnip Green, my father's hapless deputy. That was back in the day, indeed. I couldn't even recall the guy's real first name. "Got out of law enforcement and went to work at the steel plant, I think. But listen, I'm just checking back with you about what you told Jack on Saturday. About the man who locked through earlier that day, before they found the Shane kid. The one on the table?"

"The falcon guy. Weird."

"That's him. Peregrine, wasn't it?"

"You got it. Did you know those birds dive like five hundred miles an hour?"

"Seems like I've heard that, yes. I'll get to the point so you can get back to work. First, did he say anything about where he was going? Anything at all? Think hard."

"Nope. Just that he was trying to stay ahead of the frost." He grunted. "Kinda like a bird going south for the winter. Get it? Falcons are birds."

"Very clever. Can you tell me what he looked like, about how old he was?"

"Hmm, I ain't no good judge of such, but if I's to bet, I'd say sixties. Hard to tell much else with the shaggy beard and all."

"Okay, one last thing. Exactly what time did he come through? I'm sure you have a record."

"Hang on." There was a clattering like the phone was dropped, a background mumble saying something about Saturday morning, some keyboard clicks, and then he was back. "Yessir, we keep up with it real meticulous." He stretched out the last word like he wanted congratulations for using it.

"And? You've got the time."

"Yeah. Yeah. It was eight twenty-two in the morning."

"Thanks. Take care. We'll let you know if we have any more questions."

As far as I knew, no one else had made much of the river man on the table. First of all, linking river travelers to activities way up on a bluff off the main channel and around the bend from a vine-choked uninhabited peninsula like Hog Island wasn't a natural jump. Yes, Ronny was found at the edge of the water, but to all except those intimately familiar with the area, the lock and dam and the top of the bluff where the crime was committed might as well be a county apart. The crime scene investigators must not have examined the entire shoreline like Jack and Jet and I had, however, or surely I wouldn't be the only one now chasing down this man named Peregrine.

I considered calling Jack to find out what had stirred him up so suddenly at Dundee's and learn what he was up to. Because he was surely up to something. Jack was many things, but short on action wasn't one of them. I decided to leave it alone, though. I had enough puzzle pieces of my own to sort through without tossing Jack's ingredients into the mélange of my thoughts.

I drove south for thirty minutes to give Jet plenty of time, then called him. "Eight twenty-two Saturday morning."

"You know this is inexact, right?"

"Since when are you inexact?"

"Since I'm a cardiologist, not a civil engineer."

"Thought you had an engineering degree?"

"Yes, biomedical engineering, which is in a different stratosphere."

I sighed and smiled. Jet could be exhausting sometimes, but he probably thought the same about me. "Do you have the information or not? I'm driving and need to know where I'm going."

"Yeah, hang on. For the record, I called the Corps of Engineers office, but no one could tell me anything other than some ranges and hypotheticals. I think they were looking at the same websites I tried." He mumbled some incoherent mental calculations in the phone. "Lucky for you I didn't have clinic this afternoon and had a break at the hospital."

"So you could make some calls?"

"No. So my nurse and I could go to the river. I spray-painted a stick of firewood white, tossed it into the channel at Merganser Point, and set my timer. Got her on the phone so I could mark the exact time when it passed under her on the bridge. A few measurements via Google Earth, and voilà, distance over time equals velocity."

"Wait, you had her stand on top of the river bridge and wait?" The Amberton River Bridge was a four-lane concrete behemoth with three hundred feet of horizontal clearance and seventy vertical to the water below but only a narrow space—I shuddered to even guess how sparse—between the white fog lines at the edge of traffic and the protective railing.

"She thought it was exhilarating. Do you want to know what I got or not?"

"Yes. Absolutely."

"Where are you now?"

"Going south on Highway 45. Hitting Aberdeen in a sec."

"Okay. So the internet says about one-point-two miles per hour. But we've had some heavy rain north of here too. It's a lot faster right now than that, Case. Take a guess."

Just tell me, please, Jet. "No earthly idea."

"It's rolling almost exactly two-point-oh at the moment."

That didn't sound good. Peregrine was getting away from us faster than expected. "And?"

"And, we have eleven hours and forty-five minutes of daylight this time of year, with sunrise about six forty-five. And if we say he needs an hour in the morning and evening, give or take, to unpack, pack up, tend to his fire, et cetera, that puts him floating about ten hours per day. And if he's not paddling, which is what that lock operator told Jack that he said, then he's going about twenty miles per day. Which means, if he left a bit after eight Saturday morning, maybe went only nine hours that day, ten on Sunday, and going ten today, guess where that puts him this evening?"

"The only thing I know is that my head is spinning."

"Pickensville, Alabama. If I'm right, he'll be locking through there right about the time you arrive. If you hurry."

"That won't be a problem. Thanks, Jet."

"Be careful."

I put my phone away, punched the accelerator, and prayed a highway patrolman wouldn't slow me down.

TWENTY-SEVEN

JANIE answered the phone quickly, like she always did.

The "Hello" wasn't as upbeat and chipper as usual, but Jack was relieved to hear her voice. "Janie, are y'all okay?" He would prefer to see her in person, but that would have to wait for now. Whoever had stalked Lily at their house two nights earlier could be anywhere. Under no circumstances would he lead him straight to his girls.

"Hey, Dad. We're fine. You?"

Jack had mixed emotions the first time Janie had called him Dad, only a couple of months after he had taken her in. He knew that, at five years old and parentless, she would need a father much more than an uncle. But he didn't want to disrespect her father Ron or for her to forget him. It was bad enough to have no memory of her mother.

Ultimately, Janie decided for herself. She called him Dad regardless of his reservations, and so she forevermore had two fathers. One present in this life, and the other she planned to see again in the next.

"I'm fine," Jack said. "Of course. How is Lily?"

"Great. Stop worrying. We're safe."

"So Meg is okay with you staying a few days? She understands the situation?"

"Meg is cool. We all are. Stop worrying."

Considering that her father's girlfriend's son had been accused of murder, and meanwhile some other monster had threatened them and actually put his hands on her daughter, Janie was handling it surprisingly well. Jack decided she was just putting on a front for his sake. "I know it doesn't make sense. I'm working on it. I'll figure it out. I promise."

Janie sighed. "I know you will."

"Give me one more day, okay? Got a good lead today. Maybe the break we're looking for." The truth was, Jack had no earthly idea what the threat with Lily had to do with anything and doubted if his new lead would shed light on that situation. In fact, if anything, it made it even more confusing. "I'll call you tomorrow afternoon, okay?"

"Okay, Dad. Be careful. Someone else wants to speak."

"Papa Jack?" The voice was tiny yet boisterous.

Jack's face broke into an automatic grin. "Lily Girl!

"I miss you, Papa Jack. When can we come home?"

"Soon, Lily Girl. Soon. You be sweet, okay?"

"Sweet like sugar."

"Like sugar."

The conversation left Jack both warmed and aching deep in his gut. Hearing their voices was medicinal but also rammed home something that had been weighing him down. He had always believed that there was no such thing as luck, that people forged their own paths and created their own destinies. But it was difficult not to question whether his destiny, and that of those around him, was somehow corrupted by factors outside his control.

The death of his father in Vietnam. The series of events that led to the tragic death of his stepfather, Stone. The cancer that killed his sister and Janie's mother, Michelle. The wreck that killed Janie's father, Ron. His own two failed marriages to seemingly normal women who became a gambling addict and a Blues Traveler groupie. His latest, downward-spiraling relationship with a woman whose troubled past did not seem as far behind her as Jack once thought.

Perhaps the curse, or whatever it was, lived on even with Lily. She was fatherless much like Jack had been a large portion of his life. If Janie knew who Lily's father was, she wasn't telling. From fragments of conversations, the best Jack had come up with was that whoever he was, he had moved on and out of Janie's life. Whether the man knew Lily existed was a mystery, and Jack wasn't asking. Wherever the loser was, he didn't deserve her. Jack might not deserve her either, but at least he was doing his best to earn it.

And now, as if that wasn't enough, there was Devlin. Fatherless himself, for all intents and purposes, for if the man knew his son was in trouble, he hadn't shown up to support him. It didn't take a mental giant to understand why Jack was drawn to the boy. He knew many were questioning his objectivity about the murder of Ronny Shane, but he also knew, deep down in his soul, that Devlin was innocent. The kid had to be. Or was he as oblivious to the truth in front of him as a fish is to the fact he is in water?

Jack was about to find out. The revelation had fallen onto him as abruptly as if the television in Dundee's had opened and spilled its parts onto his lap. A quick drive home to check his video recorder had confirmed that he was on the right track. Now the question was, did he have the guts to see it through? Part of him wanted to drive west into the sun, find a warm spot, and sleep until morning, cold night be damned. Maybe someone else would have the case solved by then. Someone, anyone.

Anyone but him.

But he had no choice other than to see it through.

———

Jack took a breath and stared through his windshield at the red bricks and mortar of the single-level apartment complex he had just left. How many times in his life had he left a place without knowing he would never return? He sensed this would not be one of those occasions. He picked up the papers he had located within the building's walls and studied them once more before folding and sliding them into the glove box as he backed out of his parking spot.

This should be fun.

Tammy's boss at Frisco Body Shop where she worked was a jerk, but Jack didn't care. He needed her. He called when he was two minutes away. "Hey baby. I'm coming to pick you up. Tell George you have to get off a few minutes to help me with something. Tell him I'll send two steaks next time I grill."

"What? Why? He's not gonna want me to leave."

"Don't care. Tell him you're leaving, or he and I are gonna have a discussion about aftermarket parts being sold as new."

Tammy sighed. "Where are we going?"

"I'm getting close to some answers, but I've got to go over a few things, make sure I've got them right."

"Go over things? What do I know?"

Jack exhaled into the phone to make his frustration obvious. "Just do it, okay? Meet me out front. I'm pulling in."

Tammy emerged from the front door of the corrugated-metal building with a perplexed look on her face. She shrugged at Jack with both palms upturned when she was halfway to him and then climbed into the passenger's seat. "What's going on, Jack?"

He avoided her gaze. "Nothing. Let's ride a minute."

"I'm not kidding. Is something wrong with Devlin?" Her

lip began to quiver. "Tell me."

The fireball who had burst into the sheriff's office two days prior was fizzling. Jack could see it, even if others could not. He had suspected it was just a matter of time. The reality of Devlin being locked up combined with Jack being absent in search of answers was proving more than she could stand. Tammy required nothing if not emotional support, now more than ever. And not only were her two rocks not there to lean on right now, but one of them was on the verge of being sunk.

What would happen now when Jack told her of his discovery? Maybe, just maybe there was some other answer. Maybe Tammy could help him find it.

Jack shook his head. "Nothing with Devlin. We're going up to Logan's, but I need to go over a few things on the way."

"Logan's?" There was alarm in her voice. "Why? It's just gonna get me upset."

"Why?"

"It's a bad place. Ronny Shane was Devlin's friend for a long time. Like one of my own for a time. And now there's no chance of them fixing that. And whatever happened up there is trying to ruin Devlin's life, as if Ronny's wasn't a high enough price."

Jack could not dispute either point. The place was a reminder of lost friendship and lost life. Maybe two lives before it was over. "I get it. But this is important. Help me with the timeline Friday night. You left my house at what time?"

"I told you. About midnight."

"About midnight? Or midnight exactly?"

"How am I supposed to know? Didn't know at the time it would matter."

"You live eighteen minutes from me. Was Devlin home when you got there?"

"Yes. He was in the bed."

"Are you willing to testify to those facts if it comes to it?"

Tammy jerked her head around. Jack didn't look at her but sensed her glare might just cut him down. "You listen to me right now, Jack Masterson. I'll testify to anything I have to to get my son off. You…you hear me?" Her voice crumbled, and she struggled to finish. "Anything."

Jack spun the steering wheel through a turn with his left hand and held his right out to her like a school crossing guard demanding a stop. "I get it, Tammy. But that don't mean a lawyer won't trap you in a lie. What you say ain't true, and I need to know what is. If you left my house at midnight or any time after and found Devlin in the bed, there's no way he could have been turning into Logan's at twelve thirty-two like that video shows. Logan's is easily twenty-five minutes from your house."

"C'mon Jack, that was just an estimation. Obviously, I left earlier."

"But you always watch *Friday Night Football Fever*. Doesn't go off until a couple minutes before midnight.

"Seems like I left before it was over this time."

Jack's stomach lurched. "You know what's odd about that? I remember us watching the highlights from Starkville versus Warren Central. Remember, you said you were surprised by the lopsided score?"

"Okay, so that must have been earlier in the show."

Jack shook his head. "Tammy, we didn't get home from the hospital until eleven thirty. Funny thing is, I recorded it like I usually do, in case Devlin makes the highlights. And guess where I just came from?" He dared a look in her direction.

Tammy's eyes were narrow like a partial eclipse. "How am I supposed to know?"

"My house. Where I found out that highlight ended at eleven forty-nine. So if somehow I fell asleep immediately, and you were in your car two minutes later—which ain't possible, by the way—you couldn't have been home before twelve oh nine. Meaning, if you went inside and saw Devlin and he left, say, two minutes later—which ain't possible, by the way—he couldn't have been turning onto Logan's until twelve thirty-six."

"Jack, what are you doing?"

"I'm asking the questions that are going to be asked sooner or later. And hoping you have other answers besides the lies."

Tammy's eyes widened at the sight of the Amberton Lock and Dam sign looming in her window as Jack turned onto Waterway Road. "I don't want to do this."

"Well, I'm doing it. So either jump out or be quiet." Jack was angry now. He punched the door lock in case she got some crazy idea to take him literally. She flinched but didn't say anything.

They rumbled up the overgrown access road to Logan's in silence, Jack's third trip in as many days, each with a different member of his inner circle: Case, Jet, Tammy. Two of them had been there for all the past years that mattered in his life. The third was a person he had at one time hoped might become someone he wanted there for all the years in the future. But lately he was not so sure.

Her mood and demeanor had been like one of those bell curves Jet liked to talk about, the ones shaped like an upside-down U, with the up and down axis— he couldn't remember which letter that was—representing sad at the bottom versus happy at the top. When they had first met, she had been timid and difficult to talk to. But he had detected something else aching to emerge and had indeed seen it blossom as they had begun spending time together. When she was happy, he was happy. At times it hadn't mattered what they did, as long as it was together—riding ATVs, watching movies, bowling, or just sharing funny YouTube videos—it didn't matter.

In the past several months, though, the joy had regressed, emerging less and less frequently, like an animal preparing to hibernate through an indefinite winter. Nothing he did seemed to help. He made sure she was taking her medications. He went with her to counseling sessions and collaborated to follow every instruction they were given. He set up dates with all the things they used to enjoy together. Despite his best efforts, the curve trended relentlessly downward toward the Tammy he had first met years ago.

He had empathy for her. He did. And he had vowed to help her, whether they stayed together or not. But some things crossed the line. And lying was one of them. If for no other reason than he had learned that the little ones usually hid much larger, deeper, and darker secrets.

Jack stopped at the end of the access road where he had before, just as it emerged into the clearing at the top of the bluff. He shifted into park and sat in silence for several seconds, hoping in vain that Tammy would offer something. "Did you come up with an explanation?"

"I'm not on trial."

"Maybe not, but your son is. And his life is at stake."

A single tear rolled down her cheek, and she wiped it away. "It's terrible, Jack. I know he didn't do it."

"Why don't you tell me who did?"

She turned away from him to look out the window, toward the edge of the bluff, silent.

Jack pointed to the clearing before them. "I couldn't

figure out why, if Devlin didn't kill Ronny, there were no tire tracks other than Ronny's and Devlin's up here. And two sets of Devlin's at that." He tapped the steering wheel like a backspace on a keyboard. "Correction: other than Ronny's and another set *like Devlin's* up here. His tires aren't exactly rare, you know. But you have to admit, it's suspicious when we have video showing him turning up here at the same time. But whoever it was, whether Devlin or somebody else with that type of tires, why did they leave and come back? Any ideas?"

Tammy shook her head but didn't answer and didn't turn away from the passenger window.

"Then today I realized we've been looking at it wrong." He snapped his fingers. "It didn't have to be the same person. It could have been two different people with the same kinds of tires. Now, I know in forensics, they can sometimes identify not just the brand of tire, but also how much wear there is on the treads. Sometimes they can even narrow it down to one tire on one vehicle if there are identifying marks. Not usually on new tires, though. And Devlin's are pretty new. Remember when he bought them?"

"Stop, Jack."

"No, hear me out, Tammy. I did know Devlin had gotten new tires. But it just so happens, I know about someone else getting new tires about a month ago. And it just so happens, there's a local tire store with a special going where you buy one set of tires and get another identical set fifty percent off. Which is crazy, because who needs two sets of the same tires, right?"

He paused for a response but didn't get one, so he handed her the sales receipt he had found in her apartment. "I'll tell you who. A mother and son who drive a 2008 Nissan Xterra and a 2014 Toyota Tacoma. It just so happens those vehicles accept the exact same tire, P265 65R17. Slightly different speed ratings are preferred, but I'll bet Tire Town Tony isn't too picky with little details like that." Jack let out a long whistle. "What an amazing coincidence."

Tammy's tears were flowing freely now. She didn't attempt to wipe them away this time.

Jack didn't know what happened on Logan's, but he was certain of one thing: It was much more complicated than anyone knew. Anyone except perhaps Devlin and Tammy. He stared hard at her, monitoring her reaction to what he said next. "Not only was Devlin up here Friday night, but you were, too, weren't you? This is only five minutes from my place, so no problem for you to get here by the time Devlin did. You never went home. Tell me what happened."

Tammy turned to Jack and held his gaze for a split second before withering and planting her face in both hands. "Yes, Jack. I did it. I'm a horrible person. I killed Ronny."

TWENTY-EIGHT

ET thought I needed to get to Pickensville, Alabama, by five o'clock, and I beat it by ten minutes. I hoped it wasn't all for naught. The table rider could have been pulling Greely and Poe's legs and, instead of planning to float all the way down to Mobile, was just on a five-mile joy ride. For all I knew, the man had exited the waterway around the bend from Logan's Bluff and was kicked back in a ratty recliner in some back corner of the county. But my gut told me that wasn't the case. The question now was, could I find him?

I turned off of Highway 14 onto Lock and Dam Road. This stretch of road just across the state line, with its gray asphalt, faded line markers, and dense foliage just off each shoulder could have been dropped in a thousand places in Mississippi and not been out of place. I passed the Tom Bevill Visitor Center and turned right into the parking area at the lock. My heart rate accelerated with anticipation as I slid out of my truck and moved over to the railing where I could see into the lock below.

It was empty. Six hundred feet long, one hundred ten feet wide, and nothing but two vertical concrete walls, gates on each end, and water in between, hazel brown like weak coffee with islands of foam like puffy flotsam. I shook my head at the ridiculousness of my expectation, as if Jet's rough calculation had been so precise to allow me to be there at the exact moment the man and his table locked through. From my limited vantage point, he could be upriver or down, and I wouldn't see him. Fortunately, I had an option other than sitting and waiting and hoping.

A quick search on my phone found the number.

"Bevill Lock and Dam."

I was surprised to hear a female, if for no other reason than the only two lock and dam operators I had ever known were male. "Hi, my name is Case Reynolds. I'm down here at the lock, hoping to track down an old friend. He doesn't have a radio, so I'm wondering if he's already locked through."

"We run twenty-four seven, don't always get the names, so who knows? What's his boat look like?"

I chuckled. "Please don't think I'm crazy when I tell you."

"The table?"

My pulse quickened. "That's it."

The woman laughed. "I don't know if you're crazy or he's crazy or all of us are, but yeah. Came through about two hours ago."

So much for Jet and his calculations. I would enjoy mocking his math deficiencies later, but now it meant I had missed my chance. The next lock south was forty miles away by river, which was two days. If I wanted to catch him tomorrow, my best chance was to find a boat and hit the river. Which meant heading home tonight and taking a personal day to come back.

I could borrow Jack's boat, maybe talk him into coming with me. Except I had no idea what mission he had set himself on when he left Dundee's, and he wasn't answering his phone. I needed a backup plan. "Yep, that's him. Always trying some offbeat self-challenge. I'll catch up with him tomorrow. Listen, ma'am—I'm sorry, I didn't get your name."

"Wilson. Shonda Wilson."

"Ms. Wilson, great. Do you by chance know anywhere around here I can rent a boat?"

"Hmm … there's a small boat ramp just below us near Ringo Bluff, but I don't think they do rentals. It's just past the restaurant."

Ms. Wilson was a genius, and I was anything but. A man has to eat, mission accomplished or not. Plus, I had another idea. "How far downriver is that?"

"About two miles, give or take."

I looked at my watch. "Great, thanks. And how do non-table riders get there?"

She laughed. "Go back out to the highway. South about a mile, then take 78. You'll find it."

———

There was no sign of the table or its rider at the boat ramp, which consisted of nothing more than a slope of concrete beside a patch of gravel for parking and one dilapidated picnic table. This wasn't the type of place the man I was chasing would normally go, but a ramp just south of the lock had seemed as likely a spot as any for him to stop before dark.

My belly rumbled to remind me it didn't care whether I had found him or not. The white mobile home a quarter mile back up the road with the neon sign and the smoke emanating from the back of it was suddenly calling my name. I aimed my truck in that direction, hoping The Hole Cut was as good as Ms. Shonda Wilson said it was.

The smell of hickory smoke and rendered pork fat hit me before I even parked the truck, and I followed it up a wooden ramp to the front door, which squeaked when I opened it. The place was larger inside than I had anticipated, with tables to my right and several booths to the left. A room had been added off the back for the kitchen and whatever else was needed. It glowed in fluorescent contrast to the darker amber lighting of the eating areas.

"You sit where you like," a young waitress with straight black hair and remarkably round eyes called out as she glided out of the kitchen with two loaded plates. She nodded toward a counter holding a cash register and a stack of laminated papers. "Grab a menu. I'll get ya in a sec."

I chose a booth and guessed what the menu would offer before I even looked. Pulled pork. Ribs. Burgers. Chicken strip basket. Fish basket. Fries, baked potato, or slaw, et cetera. It all sounded good to me; I just needed it to be quick. I had left Abi a voicemail while I drove but knew she sometimes missed those. She would be wondering about me. I pulled out my phone to text her but had no service. Metal roof.

"What ya havin'?" My round-eyed waitress was quick, as hoped. "Sweet tea to drink?"

I nodded. "That'll be fine. Pulled pork sandwich. Fries. Slaw on the side."

The door squeaked, and a young man in black boots, greasy jeans, olive-green T-shirt and a backward trucker hat stepped in. Unlike me, he knew where he was and what he was looking for. His gaze set on my waitress, and he spun ninety degrees to march toward her.

"Not now, Ray. You know I'm working."

"Yes, now. We gotta talk." Ray's forearms sported a menagerie of grotesque creature tattoos: teeth and bulging eyes and blood and tongues everywhere. The artwork was exquisite, even if the subject matter was bizarre.

"Go home. I mean it."

The waitress tried to walk past Ray, but he grabbed her arm and held fast. "No, Serena. You can't just walk out like that." She pulled back, but he jerked her toward him and leaned in face to face with a scowl. "I'm not leaving 'til I get answers."

"Stop it! You're hurting me!"

I shuffled in my seat and coughed. Ray glanced in my direction and let go of her arm as one might release a bumblebee. He turned and put his fist in Serena's back, pushing her toward the door. "Outside, now, if you know what's good for you."

I sighed. I'd coached dozens of Rays over the years. They'd show up for two days of practice and prance with their chests puffed like jake turkeys until they learned there were toms tougher, meaner, and more disciplined than them who were more than happy to embarrass them and make them pretend to like it. And the Rays would magically disappear before the first week was over to go back to their big talk, big trucks, and bigger gaps between ego and endowment. Was it too much to ask not to have to deal with one of them here? After a wasted trip, was it too much to ask to limp home quietly with a full belly?

The door squeaked as it closed behind the couple, and I caught it by the knob before the latch hit the strike plate.

Ray looked back at me over his shoulder from the bottom of the ramp. "I saw you watching us, old man. This ain't none of your business."

"Just getting some fresh air is all."

"Plenty of fresh air back inside. I suggest you go breathe it."

"Did I mention I'm hungry? Need my waitress to take my order."

"It's okay, mister." Serena's cheeks were bunched in a worried grimace, whether for herself or me or both I knew not. "Me and Ray'll talk a minute, and I'll be right in."

Ray turned his attention back to her. He curled his top lip and snickered. "Think you get off that easy for what you did? You're done working tonight." He grabbed Serena's arm again and began marching her across the parking lot. "Maybe for a lot of nights," he mumbled.

Serena turned and made eye contact with me, but her expression had evolved from worry to something else. Was it fear for herself or just a warning for me?

A sinking weight settled in my gut. It was likely that Ray and Serena had repeated this very scenario innumerable times. Surely she had passed up countless opportunities to leave his sorry butt but had chosen to stay. So why was it my problem? What if I wasn't there? But whether I liked it or not, I was there. And I would never forgive myself if Abi later showed me a news story about a poor girl down in Pickens County, Alabama, who was last seen leaving a restaurant with the loser boyfriend who always had a temper but who no one thought was capable of *that*.

I caught up to the Dodge Ram just as Ray threw the girl into the back seat on the passenger side and slammed the door. "Look, Ray," I said. "I don't want any trouble, I don't know you, and you don't know me. But would you consider just letting her come back inside? You're pretty worked up, and I don't want you to do something you'll regret later. Cool down a little."

Ray threw his chest out and brushed up against me, but he looked at my chin rather than my eyes. He smiled. "What is it, old man? Think you gotta chance with my girl? You thinking, 'Ray is a mean SOB, and I'm a nice guy with a pension, why don't she come take a ride with me?' That it?"

I'd been insulted many times before but never been told

I looked old enough for a pension. Maybe he thought I had been in the military, got the early retirement. Yeah, that would explain it. I smiled back, except mine actually contained an element of amusement. "No, I'm happily married, thanks. I'm just trying to help."

Ray grinned, took a half step back, and tilted his head and shoulders downward to his left. It was meant to feign an "Aw shucks, you're right," but I knew better. I'd used the same move before myself, back in my teenage fighting days. His left hook came hard but wide and wild, and I stepped back out of its reach.

"Whoa, whoa! No trouble here. Let's calm down!" My regret for leaving my booth inside the Hole Cut was growing exponentially now. This guy was nuts.

Ray wasn't interested in talking. He charged at me, swinging wildly again with both fists. I dodged another swing, took a glancing blow to my cheek, and deflected another roundhouse as I slid past him, chopping down on the junction of his neck and shoulder with the side of my hand. He folded as I grabbed the back of his neck. Instead of putting him out by slamming his forehead into my knee, I pushed him hard onto the gravel face first.

"Stay down there a second and calm down. Remember, son, you started this."

"And I'm going to finish it."

The sound of a hammer cocking behind me was as unmistakable as the feel of a gun barrel suddenly being pressed between my shoulder blades.

TWENTY-NINE

JACK stared at Tammy. The evidence had mounted toward what she was telling him, but he had been holding out hope there was a different explanation than that she murdered Ronny. Jack had considered the possibility that the matching tires and her lies about timing and whereabouts that night were mere coincidences. But if that was the case, it almost surely meant that Rappaport was right and Devlin was the culprit. Which was worse?

"It was an accident." Her voice quaked, barely able to form the words. "Horrible accident."

"Tell me."

"You know I love you, don't you, Jack?"

"That's irrelevant. Tell me what happened."

Tammy didn't look up. She reached into her purse for tissue and wiped her eyes and nose. "It's not irrelevant. Me and Devlin, we both need you. And I knew if I told you, that would be the end of us. You gotta believe me."

"Believe you? I'm not even sure you're telling the truth now. What kind of mother lets her son sit in jail for a crime she committed? You just said you would say anything to get him off the hook. Maybe that's what this is. Why were you up there on Logan's? Did you see it? Did Devlin do it?"

Tammy flitted her hands before her as if clearing a swarm of gnats. "No, no! I did it. And I thought you would get him out in a day or two. Prove somehow he was innocent."

The revelation hit Jack hard. "And in the process miss the fact that you were guilty—or overlook it—and we all live happily ever after. Is that it?"

Tammy's voice dropped to a near whisper. "I hoped."

Jack felt sick. The emotions of the moment, the realization of the depths to which she had fallen and the betrayal born there in the dark that had risen and enveloped him, twisted his gut like a dishrag needing to be cleansed of its filth. Whatever truth was soon to be revealed, Tammy had betrayed his trust, his loyalty, and his principles all at once. He reached across and clenched her forearm, not hard enough to hurt but to leave no room for waver. "Tell it to me, now, Tammy. Every detail."

Tammy pulled her arm away and nodded. "I was clean. You know I was. But then last year Devlin started talking about going away to play ball. Maybe join the Navy. You were working out of town a lot. I was so lonely before, and I knew it was coming again. My nerves couldn't handle it."

Jack knew what that meant. "So you started using again. Pills?"

She nodded. "Not using. Prescription. Not hard stuff at all. Benzos, Xanax mostly. That clinic in Point City helped me at first. But then the feds shut it down."

Jack resisted the urge to break into a lecture about the futility of her semantics. Using was using. But that would be equally futile now. "And?"

"And I couldn't stop just cold turkey. Plus, I needed them."

How had he been so blind? She had seemed more frazzled and on edge for many months, but Jack had attributed it to normal relationship struggles against a backdrop of emotional fragility and transition during "med adjustment" by her doctor. He had begun to question his feelings for her and their future together but always felt guilty for it. Now, other things were beginning to come into focus, too. "So you started buying from Ronny Shane."

Tammy blinked hard, apparently surprised he made that jump so quickly. "I heard things about him. Had his number, so I texted him. Turned out, what people said was true."

"That he was dealing? For his brother?"

She shrugged. "I guess. He never mentioned Buster, and I didn't ask."

"So just like that, you start buying drugs from a kid you used to make peanut butter and jelly sandwiches for."

Tammy frowned. "He is not—was not—that kid anymore. Ronny had gone bad."

Jack huffed. "That makes it all better and says nothing about you, I guess."

"I'm guilty, Jack. Not gonna make excuses now."

"So how does you buying pills from Ronny become him dead at the bottom of the Bluff?"

"He was always asking about Devlin. Acted mad when I told him what Devlin was doing. Next thing I know, Devlin is acting strange for no reason, moping around."

"Moping around? No, he wasn't."

"Not around you, Jack. Devlin would never show you that side. He thinks you're made of steel. Doesn't want you to see him as weak."

A wave of panic washed over Jack. Had he contributed to what happened, somehow? He had always considered it his responsibility to instill toughness—mental and physical— into Devlin, primarily as a prerequisite for success in an often-cruel world, but also, admittedly, as a counter measure to his mother's vulnerabilities. Still, Jack was determined not to let her off the hook. He hardened his glare. "Okay, so why was Devlin acting strange?"

"Because Ronny was messing with Lena, and not because he loved her. He made comments, like he was doing it for spite or something. Then, next thing I know, he's wanting more money."

"What you mean, more money?"

"More than the price of the pills. To keep quiet."

"He was blackmailing you? Not to tell who? Devlin?"

She nodded.

Jack's first thought was that Ronny had been bluffing, but then maybe not. Ronny knew addiction well enough to know Tammy was unlikely to refuse, and he knew Devlin well enough to know he would protect his mother's secret if it came to that. Jack wanted to put his fist through the windshield. If only she had told him! He might have put his fist in Ronny's face, but the kid would still be alive. And Tammy wouldn't be a murderer. There were more common motives for murder than blackmail, but not many. "So you killed him for that?"

Tammy's eyes widened. "No, no! It wasn't like that! I hated myself for it. I cried myself to sleep when you were gone and hid it when you were home. But no, that's not what happened."

Jack felt his temperature rising. If blackmail wasn't the motive, what was? Something even darker? Jack touched her arm, gently this time. "Did he hurt you?"

"No." She shook her head and buried her face in her hands. "When I saw what happened at the football game, I lost it. I vowed to die before I bought another pill from Ronny Shane. I texted him from the ER and told him we had to meet."

"Why meet? You couldn't just tell him you were done with him?" Tammy hesitated, and Jack answered his own question in that instant. There was no way Tammy premeditated to kill Ronny. There could only be one reason. "To pay him off."

"He said to meet him at midnight at—"

"Logan's Bluff."

She nodded. "I asked him what it would take to make him go away. That's when he told me about the two hundred fifty Devlin owed him. Said he was meeting him at twelve thirty to settle up. If I agreed to match it, he would go away for good. Otherwise, he tells everything."

That $250 was the amount Devlin got for the pawned shotgun. But no one had been able to explain what it was for, and Devlin wasn't saying. Jack dreaded the answer to the question he now had to ask, especially since Abi had revealed in court that Devlin's drug screen was positive. "Drugs? Was that why Devlin owed Ronny?"

Tammy shifted in her seat, turning toward Jack for the first time. "It was for the fight."

For the fight? What was she talking about? How could Devlin owe Ronny for that? "I don't understand."

"Devlin paid Ronny to go away, to leave Lena alone. The fight was part of it. Added incentive for Lena to be glad Ronny was gone."

Jack had come close enough a time or two to understand how love can make a man lose his mind, but he couldn't help feeling like he had failed Devlin somewhere along the way. How could the boy's self-esteem be so low that he would do something like that? Jack stared across the meadow atop of Logan's Bluff. He had brought Tammy to the spot to help spur her to tell the truth about why she was there Friday night, about what had happened.

Now that a collision with the secrets he sought was

imminent, his dread of the impact was stifling. The damage to the future would be severe enough, but how deep would the cuts into the past prove to be? Jack rolled down his window, welcoming a deep breath of cool, fresh air. "Tell me the rest, Tammy."

"Ronny walked to the edge, pointing down to Beaker Bottom across the river, rambling on about how he grew up with nothing his whole life. Every man for himself, do what you have to do to survive, no such thing as friends, stuff like that. It was so dark I could barely see my hand in front of my face."

Jack felt a rush of hope. Maybe for once the darkness would prove to be the light. "Did he slip? If he slipped in the dark, that's not your fault."

Tammy inhaled quickly and shook her head like an animal might do to rid itself of a biting fly. "I guess I could say that. But they won't believe me. Not with what he told me."

"What did he tell you? What happened, Tammy? Spit it out."

"He told me Lena might not go away, payoff or not."

"Why not?"

"Because she is carrying his baby. That's when I pushed him over."

THIRTY

"MISTER, I don't know who you are, but you about to eat a load of lead through a different hole than the ones God gave you."

The man's voice was a few thousand cigarettes rougher than Ray's. I raised my hands slowly, deliberately. "Easy, now, fella. Ray here attacked me, and I defended myself. Just trying to keep him from doing something that he's gonna regret later."

I heard the truck door open and Serena begin to say something, but based on the crash and slam the man with the gun must have kicked the door closed behind him. The gun scarcely shifted its position against my back.

"If my brother attacked you, he had good reason. Ray, get up and get them zip ties in my toolbox. Driver's side. Our new friend here wants to take a ride."

Ray was in the process of trying to stand upright again. He shot me a triumphant smirk and shook his right arm as if to sling paint from paintbrush. "Yeah, I'll get 'em."

"Can I at least turn around, or is this one of those deals like in the Middle East where you don't have the guts to show your face and blindfold me while you wait on the ransom?" I looked left and right as far as I dared, hoping to detect some customers coming or going or perhaps someone from Hole Cut looking for their waitress. Anyone would do, but from what I could see we might as well have been in the Dakota Badlands.

Keep talking, buy time. "If you go that ransom route, only problem is you'll have to take a pic of my face. You know, proof of life? But I might peek. Then that's a really tough decision. Kill me, lose the ransom. Let me live, got a witness. Might could use some tape over my eyes. Scotch tape is clear, so it wouldn't distort my facial features. Serena might have some in her purse. Serena!"

The man jabbed the gun in my back hard enough to leave a mark. "Shut up! Ray, who is this dude? Middle East? I ain't no Arab. Who said anything about ransom?"

"I don't know, Roy. He just showed up. Me and Serena were talking."

"Roy? Nice name. Is that short for Royalty? I've always wondered. Are you royalty?" I didn't feel the gun barrel in my back, so I turned around slowly while I was talking. If I was going to get shot, I wanted it to be where I could see it coming. And if I was to have a chance to make a move, I wanted to know it, not guess it. "That doesn't add up though because that would make Ray from ray-al-ty and as far as I know that's not a word. Right?"

I made my turn and saw Roy was distracted by his brother's search in the truck toolbox on the other side, but he turned his attention back to me before I could make a move for the gun. He was shorter than Ray but a ten-year-older spitting image otherwise. Triangular face, narrow eyes, cleft chin with a sparse goatee. The handsome train had pulled out of the station long before either of them arrived in this world.

He tilted what I could now tell was an M&P Shield back and forth to remind me of its presence. "Who said you could turn around?"

Before I could answer, Ray grunted and disappeared. There was the sound of feet in gravel, a loud thud, and a puff of dust visible above the truck bed. Roy heard the ruckus and grabbed me by the shoulder, careful to ram the gun into my ribs where I could not reach it easily. He rotated to my back again and shoved me closer to the truck. "Ray? Where you at? Ray?"

Serena, eyes bulging wide, tried to open the door but Roy once again kicked it closed.

I had no idea what had happened. "You'd best check on him."

"Shut up and move! Around the truck." He prodded me forward with the gun.

I thought the smart move was to keep the gun on me and peek under the truck. Light was fading, but we were a long way from dark. But Roy thought otherwise, so I complied, hopeful that enough distraction awaited for me to make a move. Maybe Ray had a seizure. Maybe a wild animal had him, in which case I hoped Roy was a better shot than he looked.

I spotted Ray lying next to the truck, face down in the dust and gravel, with his hands bound behind him by a zip tie. He was either out cold as a wedge or dead.

Roy saw it almost as soon as I did. "What in the—"

Before he could get the inevitable expletive out, a crash to our left near a looming American elm at the edge of the parking diverted our attention. Roy swung the gun around to shoot the perpetrator, and I heard Serena, out of the truck now, yell something behind us.

In the chaos, I saw my chance. In one sweeping motion upward, I brought both hands together in a fist to crash into the butt of the pistol, expecting it to career away. Roy's grip was stronger than I had hoped, though, and even though his arms flailed wildly back over his head, he held on. The force of the blow caused me to lose my balance, but before I could recover and lunge into Roy for the fight, I faltered at what I saw.

Someone else was upon us, and it was not Serena.

In a flash of fists, the gun flew out of Roy's hand, and a punch to the gut doubled him over. Before I could understand what happened, Roy was on the ground with a foot in his back, crying out in pain, his arm twisted awkwardly behind him in the grip of our new arrival.

The man was several inches shorter than me, thin as a cedar post and similarly bronzed, with a striking contrast of white hair pulled back in a ponytail. He wore a pair of worn hiking shoes, faded jeans, and a red fleece shirt. He gave me a Shaka sign, with his middle three fingers curled between raised thumb and pinkie. "Hello, stranger."

I had suspected that I knew who Peregrine was, but to see him here in the flesh, coming out of nowhere and pinning my adversary down like a schoolboy, was a shock. "What? How did you—? Where did you come from?"

Roy protested and demanded to be let go but only received a painful arm twist in return. His subduer told him to hush and reached down and cinched his hands together with a zip tie in one motion, then nodded toward The Hole Cut. "A wandering man has to eat too."

Wandering man, indeed. The person I once knew only by a nickname my friends and I had assigned had gone out of my life over thirty years prior. Back then he was seen as a harmless curiosity, known to wander the countryside, bathe in rivers, and occasionally wear clothing that covered less skin than would traditionally be thought of as culturally appropriate. We eventually learned he was much more than all of that, an intellectual free spirit with a tragic history, a kind heart, and a real name. Shortly after helping fourteen-year-old Jack and me avoid being falsely accused of a murder, he had disappeared forever. Or so I had thought.

"So the legend of The Vagabond grows."

Brendan Perry smiled and backed away from Roy wriggling on the gravel. "Haven't heard that name in a long time." He opened his mouth to say something else but stopped short and stared at something behind me.

Serena.

"That's right." Roy smiled. "Get 'em girl. Shoot 'em both!"

My heart turned cold, and I cringed, almost expecting the rip of a bullet in my back, hoping I had a chance to feel it, which would mean I had a chance.

Perry raised his hand. "Put that down, miss."

I began to pivot to face Serena, but she walked past me before I could fully turn. Instead of having Roy's pistol aimed at me or Perry, she was locked in on Ray a few feet beyond us. He was coming to life, shaking his head to get his bearings. His eyes flared like wide-angle camera lenses at the gun in her hands. He rolled and wormed to get away, trying to find refuge under the truck. "Wait now, Serena!" His voice went into the shriek octave. "Don't go looney on me now! Put that down!"

Tears flowed down her cheeks as she moved closer. The gun quivered in her hand like a leaf hanging on in the winter wind. "You ain't gonna do this to me no more."

"I was only messin' around," Ray said. "You know I'd never hurt you, baby." He was crying now.

"Whore like you ain't got the guts to shoot him," Roy growled.

Serena whirled, and Perry ducked to avoid being down range of the erratic sweep of the weapon. She moved toward Roy, pumping the gun up and down as if fighting herself over whether to pull the trigger or not. "It's your fault. You made him this way!"

I inched to my right and closer to Serena, hoping to stay outside the tunnel of her focus.

"I'll kill you both!" She was sobbing now.

Just then the shrill cry of a siren cut through the air. Serena looked toward the road for a split second, and that was all I needed. I lunged and grabbed the weapon. It separated from her hands much more easily than it had from Roy's. She dropped to her knees and crumpled, bawling with heaving breaths.

Perry reached for the gun and nodded when I questioned him with a look. He grabbed it and wiped it down with his shirt then pulled his sleeve down over his fingers so as to not touch it again. Then he crammed the grip into Roy's hands, still cinched behind him, before tossing it a few feet away.

"You can't do that," Roy said.

I chuckled. "Pretty sure he just did. Looks to me like he just showed up in the nick of time and subdued both of you yahoos who were threatening to kill me and Serena both. That what happened, stranger?"

"No doubt about it."

Serena was sitting on her haunches now, wiping her eyes. "Exactly right."

The source of the siren was upon us, now. The white Pickens County Sheriff's Department sedan turned in to the parking lot, paused, and pulled over to where we were. A man and woman in brown uniforms stepped out. They looked at each other and shared an amused expression. "Our favorite dynamic duo," the woman said. "Ray and Roy. Or is it Roy and Ray?"

The male deputy chuckled. "R squared."

The woman looked from Perry to me and then to Serena.

"Serena, honey, you okay?" She spotted the gun and moved to pick it up.

Serena nodded. "They can tell you."

I held up my hand like a school kid and immediately felt silly for it. "I am, uh, Case Reynolds. Actually here in town on business of the McKinley County Sheriff's Department. I witnessed this Ray fellow here trying to kidnap, uh, Serena. Came over to help and got a gun pulled on me by Roy for my trouble." I pointed at Perry. "Fortunately, this stranger here saw it all and took out these guys before they could kill us both."

The male deputy was examining the zip ties on the brothers. "I'd say so." He looked at Perry. "You special forces or some-thing? What's your name?"

"Harold Swanson. And no, just know a bit of martial arts. Wrong place, right time." He nodded at Ray. "You'll find a revolver in his front belt, by the way. One can't shoot with hands tied behind one's back, though."

"We're gonna need to ask you a few questions," the deputy said.

Perry—AKA Swanson, AKA Peregrine, AKA who-knew-what-else—nodded. "I'll answer your questions if you answer just one for me."

The deputy sighed and raised both eyebrows with a head tilt. *Spit it out.*

Perry nodded toward the restaurant. "What's the best thing on the menu? I'm famished."

THIRTY-ONE

THE owner of the Hole Cut was a clean-cut man with wire-rimmed glasses, khakis, and a Crimson Tide polo shirt. He gestured to a table by itself in the corner. "For my special guests," he said. "I knew when that moron pushed Serena out the door it was trouble. Woulda come out there and stopped it myself, but I had to cook. Knew them deputies would be here quick." He placed a menu before Perry and me. "What happened out there?"

Perry smiled. "Deputies got there just in time. Maybe we stalled them a little."

"Well, they'll be out of commission for a long while. The law don't take kindly to felons possessing guns over here in Alabama." He looked at a clock on the wall. "We close at eight, but I'll make sure we get you fed. Took awhile to get you in here."

I nodded. "At least they were nice enough to take our statements here instead of at the sheriff's office. I guess we looked hungry, and they felt sorry for us."

The owner looked Perry up and down and nodded. "I guess so. What y'all having?"

I repeated my order from earlier, and Perry said he'd take the same. We studied each other for a time, sizing up the moment. Where we had been, where this was headed. I broke the silence. "You've come a long way from the man I took down on that farm when I was fourteen. Doubt I could do it now with those moves you've got."

He laughed and shrugged. "It's a tough world out there. Had to pick up a trick or two."

"How old are you? Seventy?"

"Older than I've ever been and younger than I'll ever be."

"Not as good as you once was, but as good once as you ever was."

He smiled and held up two fingers. "R-squared."

I burst out laughing. "Toby Keith would be proud." It was good to see the strange fellow again after all these years. I hated it wasn't just a random encounter during a leisurely day on the river or backwoods trail. "You never came back to Amberton."

He shook his head. "Figured I'd worn out my welcome."

"And then you're back, all these years later."

He shrugged. "I was just trying to pass through."

"On a kitchen table."

He shrugged. "Found it in a junkyard not far from the river. A few nails, some rubber sealant, and voilà."

"But why?"

"Why not? Couldn't think of anything better to do. Plus, a fellow my age has to have a purpose, a reason to get up every day. It's one proven key to longevity. In Okinawa, it's called *ikigai*. Mine varies, but right now my ikigai is to battle the river on a table." He held up a hand. "Before you ask what I know you're gonna ask, what about you? Married?"

I smiled. "Same girl. Abi. Two kids."

He nodded in approval. "And your friends?"

"Jack and Jet?"

"Yeah. One of them got hurt pretty bad by that MacIntosh kid, didn't he? Family owned the farm?"

"Jet, yeah. That whole family is dead, farm gone. But Jet does fine. He's a cardiologist. We're all three still tight as ever.

Jack owns his own business, part-time deputy sheriff."

He nodded again, slower this time, looking across the room as one might stare into a sunset. "Some days the man, some days the dog—"

"But always a friend. That's the truth that lies between."

He chuckled and wrinkled his nose as one might do to fight back a tear. "You remember."

I might forget many things, but a mysterious wandering surfer's lecture about friendship to three boys around a campfire would never be one of them. "I do remember. And that friendship is why I'm here. For Jack."

"Figured that would come up sooner or later."

"I guess it's sooner, huh?"

Perry cocked his head. "Thirty plus years isn't sooner to many people."

It was clear that he and I were on different pages somehow. "I'm talking about what happened Friday. What are you talking about?" I slapped the table lightly as it dawned on me. He assumed I wanted answers about what had happened right before he disappeared all those years ago. A skeleton vanished, and Perry with it. Now he had dared show his face near Amberton again, and he figured the long-overdue reckoning was here.

He shook his head, puzzled. "What happened Friday? What are you talking about?"

Mr. Crimson Tide shirt stepped to the table and delayed my response. "Two pulled pork plates. Best in the county."

Perry grabbed his sandwich while the plate was still vibrating on the table and Pac Manned a huge bite. He gave a big thumbs up as our host turned to step away.

I made sure the man was beyond earshot before I spoke.

"I'm talking about what happened at Logan's Bluff."

Perry chuckled as he chewed. "Ahh, okay. I was afraid it would freak him out. Just a joke, though." He pointed at his beans. "Reckon these are better than beanie weenies?"

The man had a memory like a hard drive. I had watched him scarf down a can over a campfire the first time we had met. "Logan's Bluff. Tell me what happened."

Perry frowned. "Is this about him being left behind? It wasn't that far a walk, and I couldn't exactly help him."

This was getting more confusing by the second. "Who's walking? What freaked who out?"

"Who's on first? What's on second? I don't know is on third." He laughed. "Sorry. Loved Abbott and Costello back in the day. Anyway, I'm talking about the kid. That was a weird deal."

"You're talking about Ronny Shane? The kid who was killed?"

The color left Perry's face. He dropped a forkful of beans back on his plate. "Killed?"

I realized this might have been the first time Perry had been indoors since Friday night. He wasn't exactly catching the nightly news from his recliner, and none of the local papers had run since then. Despite having once been a telecommunications mogul, he probably didn't even own a smart phone.

"Found dead at the bottom of the bluff Saturday morning."

Perry shook his head. "You gotta believe me. I didn't know. Accident?"

"That's a good question. Some don't think so."

"Who is this Ronny Shane?"

"High school senior. Supposedly tied up with some drug dealings, but I don't know. Tragic either way."

Perry nodded and looked toward the ceiling as if doing a math calculation. Then his eyebrows arced, and he looked at me hard. "Wait, you said this was about Jack."

I hesitated but decided there was no need to hide what could be discovered in a two-minute library internet search. "His girlfriend's son has been accused. I know you were in the area. Tell me what you saw."

Perry took a deep breath and exhaled with ballooned cheeks like Louis Armstrong on a trumpet. "Not that, I'll tell you. But I'll tell you what I did see." He took another huge bite and chewed slowly while he stared over my shoulder at the wall. "You spend much time doing what I do, you learn that voices carry well over water. But sometimes it surprises even me."

I hoped Perry could get through the story before The Hole Cut closed for the night. "Okay."

"I was out cold in my two-man tent on Hog Island when I heard her."

"She? Who is she?"

Perry shrugged. "You tell me. Took me a minute, but I figured out she was up there on the bluff. On top of me, in a way. Did you know sound waves travel faster through air at higher altitudes than lower? It's because gravity makes the air denser at lower altitudes, slows down the sound waves traveling through it. But the difference between a hundred feet is negligible. Still, it was almost like the sound ran downhill right on top of me. Freaked me out a little."

I sighed. At this rate, if the story ever did get told, I was going to need Jet to interpret it. "Help me out, Perry. There's a kid in jail for something we don't think he did, and the clock is ticking. Can you get to the point?"

Perry smiled as if he had achieved the response he sought.

"Absolutely. So I thought she was in danger at first, but then I realized she was calling for someone. I couldn't make out the name. First instinct was to mind my own business, but that didn't last long. For one, I'm a curious type. And two, I was afraid she or whomever she was calling for might just walk off the bluff. And it's a long way down, in case you haven't noticed."

"I've noticed. So you went up there?"

He nodded. "Rowed my little boat across and slipped up the hillside. There's a trail there, to the top. Hard to see in the dark, but I managed."

I decided to keep it to myself that we had discovered the trail. "What did you find?"

"About halfway up I realized she was calling out a name, but I still couldn't make it out for sure." He leaned across the table and whispered. "Now that you say it, I'm pretty sure the name was Ronny."

"Did you call back to her?"

Perry frowned. "You kidding? I don't mind helping folks, but conspicuous assistance has never been my thing. I learned a long time ago people can behave like injured dogs, equally apt to bite rescuer and captor."

"Go on."

He wiped his mouth and took a sip of his drink. "She stopped calling out, then I heard a vehicle leave the scene, so I figured the lovers got reunited and split. But you know me, condemned to honor the curse of curiosity. Why not just ease on up to the top for a look around?

"Wait. Could you tell what kind of vehicle it was?"

"Nope. Nor the next one."

"Next one?"

Perry nodded. "Shortly after the first vehicle left, another came in, stopped for a minute or so on the bluff, and left."

"You didn't hear a male voice cry for help. Something hit the water?"

"I did not."

"So that's it?"

Perry rolled his eyes. "Coach, you should know better. Never assume a thing is all there is until you know that is all there is. And even then, you're probably wrong. I did not hear the things you asked about, but I heard laughter."

"Laughter?" I couldn't believe what Perry was telling me.

"Behind me, coming up the hill. It was eerie. Gave me chills."

"And?"

Perry shrugged. "And I became a tree. The guy walked right past me in the dark, mumbling something about couldn't wait to see the looks on their faces."

"Never saw you?"

He shook his head. "I'd bet my life on it."

I studied the paint on the wall for a moment, as if some answers might suddenly scroll across it. "I'm guessing the woman left and then came back. Forgot something, maybe?"

Perry smiled and shook his head. "Nope, didn't happen."

"Huh?"

"Wasn't the same person."

"But you said you couldn't see the vehicles."

"I couldn't, but I've spent enough time out on the road to be able to distinguish one type of engine from another. Couldn't see them, but I could hear. Different vehicles."

Interesting. I had an idea. "Could the second have been a truck?"

Perry pursed his lips and nodded. "Sure. Six cylinder, probably." He took a bite of his sandwich and flagged down a waitress passing by. "Can you get our check please?"

The waitress was about my age, average build, too much makeup, hair with dark roots and frosted tips. She smiled. "Mick said it's on the house. With you helping Serena and all."

"That's very kind," Perry said. "Hey, do you have a pen I can borrow? Need to write down a number for my friend."

The waitress gave Perry a thumbs up and dropped a pen on the table. "I'll get it later." She winked at me and moved along.

I nodded toward the napkin. "Number?"

"I'll give you an address where I check in sometimes. But I can see by the look on your face you have more questions." He gulped down a huge mound of beans.

"Well, yeah, I do. Most important question of all. What did the guy look like?"

Perry frowned and raised one eyebrow.

"Too dark?"

"Now you're getting the picture. I'd guess he was a teenager, but that's about it. Maybe twenty."

Was it Ronny, or the person who killed him? And who was the female? Lena? "Anything else you noticed?"

Perry shook his head. "He looked like someone not accustomed to being in the woods with no flashlight. But he sounded like someone having the time of his life. You're the writer, but I'd say giddy might be the word for it." Perry reached for his sandwich and disappeared a bite large enough to rival the beans before. He wiped a droplet of barbecue sauce form the corner of his mouth.

"So then what happened?"

"He went up ahead, and I headed back down."

My heart sank. "That's it? You didn't see what happened to him?"

"None whatsoever. Figured he either waited for someone to come pick him up or had a car of his own. Either way, I figured he was at least as safe as I was at that point."

"Hey, do you know what time it was?"

Perry held up both hands and pushed his sleeves up one at a time. "Do I look like a man with a watch?"

This was terrible. Perry's testimony was worthless. Maybe it was Ronny, maybe someone else. We didn't know who the woman was. Or the person who drove the second vehicle. And whomever they were—even if the second was Devlin—it did nothing to disprove that Devlin had come along later and pushed Ronny off the bluff at a different spot. The defense could possibly argue that Ronny had some weird death wish and did to Devlin what he had done to the woman, only this time it ended badly.

But why would he do that in a spot he presumably would have known would injure him? And if that was the case, why wouldn't Devlin have said so? I supposed one option would be to have Perry point out exactly where the moon was in relation to the trees at that time, which would allow one to nail down the exact time. Maybe it was well after Devlin was thought to have been there, not before. But Egg was no Perry Mason, and Judge Foster didn't seem the type to allow theatrics. Plus, for all I knew, the moon was covered in clouds that night.

"I'm sorry I'm not much help." Perry could sense my angst. "Glad we got to catch up a bit, though."

I sighed. "No, it's helpful. Just not completely illuminating."

Perry reached for his belly and wrinkled his nose. "Old gut isn't used to this kind of food. I'm gonna need to hit the can before we leave. Be right back." He nodded to my plate as he slid out of the booth. "You've got work to do."

I realized I had not taken a bite. Where there had been an ache of hunger before was now an ache of unfulfilled optimism and sidetracked hopes. From confident as I left Amberton to fearful for my life as Roy pointed a gun at me to certain I would save Devlin the moment my old surfer friend flashed the Shaka sign to utterly deflated now, my psyche had been stretched and kneaded like overworked pizza dough. And now my appetite was as thin as my flattened psyche.

I looked at my watch. Abi was going to have more questions than I had answers I was willing to share. How long was Perry going to take in the bathroom, anyway? I was ready for him to get back and write down that address so I could be on my way. I was sure Abi or Egg or someone would want to corroborate my version of our conversation. I glanced at his plate and admired the havoc he had wreaked while I was too enthralled to eat. He sure was taking a long time. Must have been the beans.

And then I noticed the pen was gone.

I sprang from my seat and called to the waitress who had been by earlier. "Bathroom?"

She pointed past a row of booths. "Around that corner."

I chose the bathroom labeled Boars rather than Sows and pushed the wooden door open. There was a urinal and single stall to the left, but I didn't have to look in the stall to know it was empty. A single frosted window on the back wall was unlatched and open.

Perry was gone, and any hope I had of gleaning more information had vanished right out the window with him.

I acknowledged the obligatory goodbye from a waitress as I exited the Hole Cut and trudged to my truck, kicking rocks as I went like a schoolkid walking home after losing his best friend. Nearly got myself killed, might have become embroiled in two felony gun possession cases for which I could have to return to testify, and had nothing to show for any of it. I had even failed to eat the free meal. I unlocked my truck and reached for my phone to call Abi as I stepped up and settled into my seat.

But the call would have to wait.

There was a note on my windshield, pinned beneath a wiper blade.

Scribbled on brown bathroom paper towel by the pen from our waitress, was a message:

> *The wise stop and think*
> *atop the boulder brink*
> *For Alethia resides*
> *where internuncios hide*
> *and millstones float*
> *when ghosts peregrinate the moat.*

The message had a signature, but not in the usual sense. It was a rudimentary drawing of a hand, with the thumb and little finger extended and the three middle fingers curled down to the palm. A Shaka sign.

PART THREE

It was growing late, and though one might stand
on the brink of a deep chasm of disaster,
one was still obliged to dress for dinner.
—Georgette Heyer

THIRTY-TWO

Tuesday, October 30, 2018

"IT really was him? On a tabletop?"

I looked at Jack as if he had asked if I thought Michael Jordan was a good basketball player. After telling him all about Ronny and the mystery woman at Logan's Bluff, my near kidnapping at The Hole Cut, and my struggle understanding the napkin message Perry had left me, Jack chose to circle back and ask me if the river traveler really was our old friend once called The Vagabond. "No, on second thought, it might have been Old Man Schlossnagle down at the bait shop."

Jack smiled and took a bite of his ham-and-omelet biscuit, the morning special at the 24-Hour Power convenience store. Its divine, made-from-scratch-with-real-lard biscuits were renowned in Amberton. The place had only three tables at the back, but fortunately most everyone took theirs to go. "It's just so hard to believe. After all these years."

He had a point. I wondered if I had seen Brendan Perry for the last time. Whether he had launched his table downriver again or abandoned it for more traditional means of travel, I did not know. And pursuing him struck me as not only pointless but sacrilegious somehow, even if I still had no idea what his cryptic message meant. I pulled the napkin from my pocket and laid it on the table between our coffee cups. "I thought you'd never ask. Here's the riddle. Mean anything to you?"

Jack's eyes widened then narrowed with a furrow of his brow as he read it through. "You know creative writing wasn't my best subject. What in the shiitakes is an inter-nun-see-yo?"

I shook my head at the juxtaposition of his creative expletive and labored pronunciation. "Internuncio. I had to look it up. It means a go-between. Messenger."

"And the rest of it?"

"I have no idea. It's gotta be important, though."

"Have you talked to Alethia yet?"

"Negative." I shook my head and cringed, much the way I had done when I read her name on the paper there in the bathroom. I couldn't imagine what Alethia Abbot had to do with this case, nor how Perry, who loved anonymity almost as much as he hated media types who would uncover it, had come to the knowledge that she was involved.

The *Amberton Advocate's* fire-breathing reporter and I had clashed a few times over the years, most monumentally early in my coaching career when she had penned her idea of an exposé about local high school football coaches' abuse of players. It was part fabrication, part hearsay. Her primary source was a single disgruntled player who had quit the team after refusing to complete the conditioning drills required of all players at the end of practice, but she printed other details—skewed and distorted as they were—that only someone on staff would have known.

I had never been able to figure out who it was and had been ready to file a lawsuit for slander until Abi decided a better plan might be for her to meet her toe-to-toe on her front lawn and work it out that way. The thought of my attorney wife being so angry as to prefer combat to the courtroom in defense of my honor became so endearing that I didn't want to ruin it. So I had left the situation alone, to waft to and fro like a breeze across hot coals and to savor her smolder while it lasted. Eventually, the scandal had died down and disappeared, and I moved on. Abi took it harder than I did.

"Maybe let Abi talk to her."

"We could sell tickets."

Jack chuckled. "And what about boulder brink? Millstones, ghosts, and moats? This is crazy talk. You sure ol' Perry hasn't spilt even more of his marbles than before?"

I turned up the last sip of my coffee. "I'm not sure of anything. Now tell me what you found out. Your text said you have astounding new information."

"Earth shattering."

"Okay. Earth-shattering new information."

Jack nodded slowly, as if confirming something in his mind. "It explains a lot of what you just told me." He held up the napkin. "But not this. And not what needs explaining the most."

"Just tell me."

Jack paused long enough to be sure he tested my patience. "Doesn't explain who killed Ronny Shane."

I spoke through gritted teeth. "If you don't tell me right now, I'm leaving, and you're on your own."

Jack held up both hands. "Okay, okay. I'm just trying to process how all this fits together." He paused and took a breath. "Tammy pushed Ronny over the edge of the bluff."

That made absolutely no sense. But then again, maybe it did. My thoughts jumped back to the frenzied momma barging into the sheriff's department shortly after Devlin's arrest. She had the look of someone who would do anything to protect her son, even confessing to something she didn't do out of desperation. "Think about that, Jack. Would she wait two days to confess if that was true? She would have come clean the moment

Devlin got arrested. She's lying to protect him."

Jack shook his head. "I believe she would lie to protect him, but that's not it. She's in a bad place, not thinking too clearly, and she believed that I—we— would have him proven innocent and out of jail before the weekend was up."

"If true, that's really messed up. You sure?"

"I have no doubt."

"That she killed Ronny Shane."

Jack grimaced. "I didn't say that. She pushed him over, but she didn't kill him."

Now who was talking crazy? "Didn't kill him? I don't understand."

Jack tilted his head forward and gave me an under-the-eyebrow look I'd seen many times before. *Think about it, Case.*

Then it hit me. "Logan's Leap."

Jack tapped the table with the palm of his hand. "Bingo. Tammy pushed him over, but he survived. She showed me the exact spot, give or take. Looks like he went over right about where you almost bought the farm chasing that stupid cigarette. Landed on the ledge, waited on her to leave, probably had that smoke, then walked back up to the top laughing at the whole thing just like Perry described."

"But why was she there in the first place?

My friend's expression soured, as if the paroxysmal pain from a cancer had allowed him a reprieve but was once again rearing its unrelenting head. "She's been using again, buying from Ronny. She was trying to put an end to it, put an end to Ronny messing with Devlin. They were arguing near the edge. She got angry, it was dark, one thing led to another."

I blew out a deep breath. "I'm sorry, man." I truly was. I had never thought Tammy a good fit for Jack, but I would much rather have him be happy than my concerns be validated. "She thought she killed him all this time?"

He nodded. "Yep. But she didn't." He sighed and dropped his gaze onto the table. "At least there's that."

"What does that mean for Devlin?"

Jack told me about the matching tires on Devlin's and Tammy's vehicles, corresponding to the two sets of tracks at the scene.

"That still doesn't clear Devlin," I said. "You've got a video of his truck at the scene, tire tracks to match, and now Perry hearing a second vehicle at the top."

Jack looked discouraged, and I hurt for him. Tammy was more lost than he could have imagined, and in some ways, Devlin looked as guilty than ever. "I'm hoping it at least muddies the waters enough to buy some time. He must be protecting her. Now that his momma has come clean, maybe he'll talk."

"Have you talked to Nash, Rappaport, anybody?"

Jack shook his head. "Autopsy is pending. Maybe forensics will find something on the body. Some fibers, something under his nails. Got my doubts, though."

I nodded. "We only have evidence for three vehicles: Ronny's, Tammy's, and Devlin's. If Devlin is innocent, there had to have been another person there. If so, where did they come from, and how did they leave? Did someone ride up with Ronny, hide when Tammy was there, and leave on foot later"?

"Seems far-fetched." Jack frowned. "You don't think Perry—"

"No way. I can't prove it right now, but the look on his face when I told him a kid had died was genuine. He was stunned."

Jack nodded. "Plus, it's likely that Ronny knew who pushed him and didn't suspect anything. I wouldn't stand near the edge of a hundred-foot drop with someone I didn't know, would you?"

"No, unless he was forced over, which Perry isn't physically able to do. Putting tae kwon do moves on a beer-bellied redneck is one thing. Dragging an athlete fifty years your junior to a cliff and throwing him over is something else entirely."

"Maybe they'll find something in the autopsy," Jack said, "but who knows how long that will take? Has Abi said anything?"

I laughed. "Not a chance, but she may open up when I tell her what all we found out. This case may not be a slam dunk like she thought." I dangled the napkin from The Hole Cut between us like a poster on display. "The answer must be here."

Jack nodded. "And speaking of napkins, they don't give you enough. These biscuits are greasy." He wiped his hands on his jeans and craned his neck to peer at Perry's writing more closely.

"I could call Jet, see what ideas he has," I said.

"Good luck with that. He and Gracie are over the Atlantic by now. Probably hard to get much out of him."

"Almost forgot. Annual mission trip."

Jack nodded and leaned back, thinking. He held up an index finger, presumably much less greasy now that he had transferred it to his pants. "But I have another idea. Perry found something out there in those woods around Logan's. And who is the best woodsman you know? Besides me, of course."

———

Two hours later, Kyle shuffled into my classroom with hands stuffed in pockets, studying his shoes as he walked. He stopped a few feet inside the door. "You needed to see me?"

Most people said Kyle looked like his mother and Kellen like me. He certainly had Abi's eyes. Brilliant blue and striking enough to cause a double take if one hadn't met him before. His hair was dark like hers but without the curl.

"I hear you were late to school this morning."

He shrugged and lifted his eyes to meet my gaze. "Yes sir. A little."

I rose from my chair and moved around to sit on the front corner of my desk. "Everything okay?"

Kyle cocked his head ever-so-slightly, like he was surprised by my response to his confession. "I'm fine. Just lost track of the time."

My son was a good kid. We had trouble connecting at times, odd since we enjoyed many of the same things: hunting, fishing, camping. Abi said he felt guilty that he didn't like sports, and I tried too hard to convince him it didn't matter.

I often wished he could experience the same type of childhood I had, with inseparable friends sharing untold adventures across the nether regions of the county. Kyle just didn't have friends like that for whatever reason. His new friendship with Gabe Liston showed promise, but it was new and therefore precarious, in my opinion. I hoped it would be lasting.

I glanced at the clock on the wall over the dry-erase board to the side. Two minutes until the morning break was over. "I lose track sometimes too. It happens."

"Is that what you needed, Dad?"

"Actually, no. I need your help."

"Help?"

"Yeah. It's the Ronny Shane case. I'm helping Jack. He doesn't think Devlin did it."

Kyle frowned. "Of course he did it. Fighting over a girl, all that stuff. There's a video, proves it."

"It may not be that simple."

He shrugged. "If you say so. But what do you need from me?"

"It's a long story, and I'll explain all of it I can. But I need you to help me with a puzzle. Come by here this afternoon. We're gonna ride out to Logan's Bluff."

Kyle smiled. "Like, go to the crime scene? Legit?"

"Legit. But you've got to swear to keep it to yourself."

He held up his left hand then quickly switched to his right. "I promise."

"One more thing." I reached for a sheet of paper lying on my desk behind me. "Take this. It's a poem. A riddle, actually. Brainstorm possible meanings. I'll tell you later where it came from, but I want to see what you come up with without context."

Kyle took the paper from my hand and set it back on the desk. He grabbed his phone from his back pocket and snapped a photo.

"What are you doing?"

"I'll just snap a pic. Paper's too hard to keep up with."

I sighed. "Maybe, but take it, please. I killed a tree to print that for you."

Kyle shook his head. "Whatever, Dad." He folded the paper and opened his backpack to put it in. A notepad slid out onto the floor, and I picked it up.

At first, I thought it was something for school, but then I recognized it as one of his sketch pads. The kid was always drawing something. Deer, turkeys, landscapes, occasionally a sketch of a friend. "What's the latest?"

Kyle reached for the pad. "Nothing."

"Aw, come on. You always show me." I flipped it open and turned to the last page. The image of an eagle jumped off the paper at me. It was striking in its intricate detail, but there was something else about it, a raw emotion captured in the bird's eyes, somehow simultaneously eyeing both me and its feet, where one was grasping what looked like a bomb, and the other was empty. "Wow."

Kyle successfully grabbed the pad from my hand this time. "It's nothing. Still working on it." The bell rang, and he turned to leave.

"Kyle."

The boy stopped near the door and looked back.

"You gonna look at the riddle for me?"

He nodded.

"Not a word to anyone. And don't send that to any of your friends. I mean it. Lives could be in danger."

Kyle nodded. "Not a word to anyone. I've heard that before. Sounds great."

THIRTY-THREE

ABI studied the passing scenery as I drove, seemingly intent on taking in each detail as if she hadn't seen this stretch of road a hundred times before. Her motivation for staring through the window had nothing to do with the sights, though, and everything to do with me.

"Mom, don't be like this." Kyle patted her on the shoulder from his seat behind her. "It's not a big deal."

Abi shot me a steely glare and shook her head. "I'm not mad at you, Kyle. But I wish your father hadn't dragged you into this mess."

"Nobody dragged me, Mom. Dad thinks I can help."

Abi sighed. "I sure hope so. And I hope it's worth it."

"He's camped up around the bluff before, Abi, so something in that message from Perry might ring a bell. And we need all the help we can get." Not to mention that it would be good for us, generally speaking. Kyle seemed to be struggling with his identity lately, at least as it pertained to his relationship with me. I didn't know if he could help us and really didn't care. I just wanted him to feel needed and to spend some time with him.

She shot me another glare. "We?"

"Yes, we need help. You, me, Jack. Devlin. Ronny Shane. To find the truth, whatever that turns out to be."

The truth. I had begun to wonder if there even was such a thing, or just hazy shades of reality converging like wax from a thousand melting candles. Devlin killed Ronny for reasons he wouldn't share, maybe because of drug money owed and the blinding rage of unrequited love. Admitted to it from the very start.

Wait—no—Tammy killed Ronny over drug secrets and his persecution of her son. On accident, of course. Or was it? Was she lying to protect Devlin, or vice versa?

Or was Luke Wiseman somehow involved, as once thought? After all, he had threatened Ronny the night before and later been at the scene of the crime, with a gun in hand, no less. No doubt we hadn't even scratched the surface of Ronny's acquaintances in the four days since the accident, so who knew how many motives lurked out there among his drug clientele, if that portion of his story was to be believed.

For that matter, what about the apex of the love triangle, Lena Cole herself? She was pregnant, according to Tammy, and whose baby was it? Could another suitor be angry enough to murder, or did rejection by the baby's father drive her to do it? How many thousands of murders had occurred over the eons for the same reason? Then if all that wasn't confusing enough, we had duplicate tire tracks, videos blurring the timelines, and discrepancies about where Ronny Shane went over the bluff's edge—and how many times, for that matter—all confusing enough on their own without river-tabling peripatetics wielding obfuscatory poem riddles.

Sorting it all out and gleaning the truth felt like trying to unravel an unginned cotton bale in search of a single thread of white silk.

So yes, we needed all the help we could get, and why not Kyle? I would make sure he didn't do anything to inadvertently interfere with evidence, if we found any. As for Abi, she was, regrettably but understandably, torn between her roles as mother and prosecutor. In my defense, her coming along on this particular adventure was never my intent. She just happened to call as Kyle and I were leaving the school. Ten minutes later, we picked her up, and my tongue lashing commenced.

"Dad, you okay?"

I blinked and realized I had stopped at the edge of the Logan's Bluff clearing.

"You know how he gets sidetracked by his thoughts sometimes," Abi said.

Kyle laughed. "Yeah, I've seen that look when he's designing a new football play in his head. Stares off into the sky like he's looking for Jesus to come back."

Abi spun in her seat and cocked her head with a raised eyebrow. *Watch it with the irreverence.*

Kyle shrugged and opened the door. "C'mon, Dad. Show me."

Abi grabbed her door handle but hesitated. "What you thinking, Case?"

I sighed. "Just trying to make sense of it. Not just what happened but how to handle it. My friend. My player. You. A lot of parts moving against each other."

Abi patted my arm. "I know you're trying to do the right thing. If it makes you feel any better, I discussed it with the DA, and we both agreed to recommend that the judge release Devlin. Not enough solid evidence to hold him right now."

"You think Foster will let him go?"

She nodded. "It's being processed as we speak. She's been acting weird, though. Made some snide comment at the initial hearing about you. I think it was a reference to that stuff Alethia printed way back. And then insulted me, saying I get off the path into the weeds too much."

I chuckled. "First of all, that's old news about me. I've done way worse than that since then. Second… well, I can't refute that part."

Abi punched me playfully. "Not funny."

"You still think Devlin did it?"

"I don't know. I just don't know." She opened the door and slid out of the truck. "Let's go see what we can find out." She pivoted and looked behind us, toward the sound of a vehicle approaching. "This should be interesting."

I glanced in my rearview mirror to confirm it was Jack's GMC pulling up, but it wasn't until I stepped out of the truck that I realized Abi was referring to more than the general Masterson flair that Jack brought to most any situation. He was not alone.

"Aunt Abi!" Lily's head protruded from the rear passenger window like a puppy on its first ride to the country, with a broad, toothy grin to match. "Aunt Abi!"

Jack stepped out and shrugged in response to my folded-arms stance as he went to the passenger side to help Lily down. "Janie had to work. What you want me to do?"

Lily squirmed from Jack's grasp and launched herself into a dead run toward Abi.

"Find a babysitter?" I murmured. "There's been enough trauma around here without worrying about a three-year-old running off a cliff."

"Four."

"What?"

"She happens to be four. And I won't let her out of my sight. Unless of course you want me to just go home."

"Do I have to answer that?"

"Wasn't a question. You heard anything from Rap? You know, any leads on the real killer?"

Jack spat on the ground. "He wouldn't know a lead if it was glued to his eyeballs. He can't see any possibilities other than Devlin. Gonna do his best to prove it was him even if he knows it wasn't."

"Maybe he's right."

"Nope." Jack punched me in the arm and headed out into the clearing. "C'mere, Kyle. Where's your sister?"

Kyle hustled to catch up. "Volunteering for some silly club she's in at school."

"Helping get ready for the Halloween festival," I added.

Jack winked at me and gave Kyle a fist bump. "C'mon. Let me show you where the accident happened. Your dad thinks you can help us."

I caught Abi's eye but lost it as she wavered between interacting with Lily, who was playing with her earrings, and watching Jack and Kyle move toward the edge of the bluff.

"Why do you have stars?" Lily tugged at one ear lobe, and Abi pulled her hand away to save it.

"Because you're a star, and it helps me remember."

Lily's eyes widened and her jaw dropped to form a round smile. "You 'member me a star?"

Abi laughed. "Absolutely. Let's go see what Papa Jack and Kyle are doing."

Jack was pointing down over the edge of the bluff, toward the spot where Ronny was found.

Abi thrust Lily toward me with a stern look. "Don't put her down." She turned and moved through the winter-dried grass toward the other two. "Jack, what are you telling him? He's only fourteen, for crying out loud."

I sighed and hugged Lily tight and followed quickly. "Lily girl, want to see something cool? I'll show you where you can see across the whole county."

She pooched her lips and frowned. "What's a county?"

I laughed. "The place where all the people you know live."

She arched her eyebrows like it was big news and instantly shrugged it off on second thought. Then she smiled. "I do want to see it."

"That's a long way to fall," Kyle was saying as we walked up.

I caught his eye and nodded at Lily. *Stop the talk about Ronny for a second.*

"Look, Lily. You can see forever here." The view was as spectacular as ever. It occurred to me that I hadn't even stopped to appreciate it with my recent trips. The raw power of the perch looming over the mighty river, the granular undulations of the bottomland treetops stretching toward the horizon, and the jagged shore below was at once majestic and ominous given recent circumstances.

Lily wasn't looking to the horizon. "It's way far down there. We should be careful."

Kyle stepped away from the edge and pivoted toward us. "You're so right. Falling off would be terrible." He gave his mother a smirk. "Have you guys figured out the riddle yet?"

Jack huffed. "Kyle, I've read over that thing a dozen times and can't make any more sense of it than the first time. Don't know what most of those words mean. Our old friend the Vagabond ain't wired up like normal folks."

"His vernacular is spectacular."

Jack shook his head at me and looked at Abi. "Your husband has spent way too much time with Jet."

Abi smiled. "If it makes you feel better, that's the opposite of the meaning of vernacular, so Case has a lot to learn."

"'Tacular 'nacular." Lily giggled.

We all laughed, and I tickled Lily's ribs to make her giggle more. "Now that's how you use those words the right way."

Jack reached over and gave her a playful pinch of her nose. "We needed that, Lily girl." His smile faded and he took a deep breath. "But I won't really feel better until we solve this."

"You're absolutely convinced it's not Devlin." Abi said.

Jack nodded. "But he and I have some talking to do tonight. I appreciate you helping him get released."

Abi held up a palm. "Just going by the evidence. Not enough to be sure he's the one. Not enough to be sure he's not, either."

"Fair enough. What do you think about Perry's riddle?"

Abi frowned. "There's a name in there I'm not excited about."

"Alethia Abbot," Jack said. "Case and I think you should be the one to interview her."

Her blue eyes flashed and jaw muscles tensed. "I'll be more than happy to go talk to that heifer."

I fought back a smile. "Maybe we'll go together. But what about the rest of it?"

"Can't make much of it, to be honest. There are two references to rocks—boulder and millstone. That may be important, but who knows what that's referring to?" She made a sweeping gesture. "This whole bluff is rocks and boulders. I had to go to my dictionary. Internuncio means messenger. Peregrinate, which means to travel, must be a reference to our so-called Mr. Peregrine himself. That's all I've got, but I'm sure there's more in there."

"What about the ghost part?" Jack asked. "Not my favorite subject, by a long shot."

Lily tapped me on the shoulder, but I ignored her.

Abi shook her head with a wry grin. "Ghost, oh, yeah, forgot that. I think that's our old pal Perry being smug and having a little fun. He ghosted us what, twenty-five, thirty years ago?"

Lily tapped me again, with more urgency this time. "What, baby?" I said.

"I don't like ghosts." Her eyes were wide and animated. "They are scary."

Abi chuckled. "Don't be scared, Lil'. Not that kind of ghost. This is the kind that just means somebody you don't see very often."

Lily gave a reassured nod. "Like Jesus."

Jack's mouth dropped open into an O shape, and we all laughed.

"Something like that." I gestured toward Kyle. "Read the whole thing out loud for us, son. Maybe hearing it here will trigger something."

He pulled his out his phone, tapped the screen a couple of times, and began to read. "The wise stop and think atop the boulder brink. For Alethia resides where internuncios hide and millstones float when ghosts peregrinate the moat." He chuckled. "That's a mouthful of nonsense right there."

"Come on, boy. You're supposed to be good at puzzles. It's why I brought you."

Kyle rolled his eyes and held up an index finger. "Okay, okay. For the record, I do happen to have one idea you'll find quite interesting."

"We're all ears," Abi said.

"And earrings." Lily pitched in. "To remember."

I gave her a squeeze. Kyle and Jack exchanged frowns. "Inside joke, guys," I said. "What's your idea?"

"A moat is like water around a castle, right?"

"Yep," Jack nodded. "With alligators and hot lava. To keep people out."

I didn't want to know whether he was joking or serious. "Water around a castle, go on."

"What if you look at Logan's Bluff like a castle? What would be around it?" Kyle shot a glance at Jack. "Minus the gators and lava."

Abi turned and looked out over the bluff edge to the river below. "Obviously there's water there. Think that's what Perry meant?"

"Maybe," Kyle said. "But a moat surrounds a castle. What's surrounding the bluff?"

I pivoted to look away from the river to the south, west, and north. "It's river on one side and woods on the other. Except for the overgrown access road that brought up here."

Kyle shook his head and went to his phone again. "Look at this app. It shows satellite images layered on a map." He tapped the screen and waved us closer. "Look beyond the woods around us. What do you see?"

The image showed a blue dot corresponding to the spot where we were standing. "I see the waterway there," Abi said.

"To the east," Jack pitched in.

Kyle traced his finger across the screen, drawing an approximation of a triangle around our location. "Logan's Bluff is surrounded. Yes, there's the waterway itself on one side, the blacktop road—Waterway Road—on one side, and look at this." He moved his fingers along a serpiginous line on the screen.

A creek. I knew immediately the name of it and wondered

why it hadn't hit me. Miller's Creek. It crossed Waterway Road about a half mile before the turnoff onto the logging road up to the bluff before meandering down to empty into the Timtullah River. Likely named for a long-forgotten man whose long-forgotten ancestor had held one of the world's oldest occupations.

And what did millers use to grind their grist? Millstones. "Maybe Perry is saying Ronny's killer traveled the creek to get here."

"But it sounds like he's saying he himself did," Jack said. "You know, ghost and peregrinate."

"Which doesn't make sense," I added, "because we know that's not the way he came up to the bluff."

Abi gestured with a finger pointing upward. "Or he's letting us know that way is possible, which means the killer could as well. Which would explain why only Devlin's and Tammy's tracks were found up here and the only sign of a boat was Perry's. The killer could have come downriver from who-knows-where, then up Miller's creek, then climbed up to the bluff from there. It's essentially untraceable."

"How would Perry have figured all that out?" I said.

Jack shrugged. "Who knows how that guy finds out anything?" He grabbed Kyle's hand to steady the phone for another examination of the map. "That's a long way through thick woods, up from Miller's Creek. Seems unlikely."

Kyle turned and began walking away.

"Where you going?" Abi asked.

"Come on. I'll show you." He waved at us to follow, moved about fifty yards to the other side of the clearing, and paused for us to catch up. He pointed down the hill, through the timber. "See that group of pine trees? There's an old walking trail. Nobody uses it now because it's overgrown up this way. But from there down to Miller's Creek it's pretty clear. Four, five hundred yards is all."

Abi folded her arms. "And you know this how?"

Kyle twisted his mouth in feigned disgust. "Mom, we camp not far from here sometimes. Besides, I know every patch of woods on this side of the county."

"Where all my people live." Lily kicked her legs and began to squirm. "I want down."

I let her slide down my trunk until her feet touched the ground, and she wriggled to pull her arms away from my grasp.

Jack gave Lily a stern glare. "Hold hands. Like we talked about."

She finished pulling away, pursed her lips and strutted toward Kyle with an outstretched hand. "Kylie will do it."

Kyle forced a grin and took Lily's hand.

"If your new job doesn't work out, maybe you can start up a babysitting service this summer," Abi said.

Lily frowned and stomped her foot. "I'm not a baby. I'm four."

Kyle tugged on her hand. "Come on, let's show them Miller's Creek."

"Hang on," Jack said. "Let's see what else is up here before we take off half a mile up and down hills and hollows. I'll be so gassed I can't think."

I was glad he admitted it first, but I had thought the same thing. "Let's go back and walk the edge of the bluff and see if we notice anything." I turned and took Abi's hand. As many times as I had done it over the years, I never failed to flash back to the very first time, as a tremulous, sweaty-palmed teenager on a porch swing by her pool. She squeezed my hand and moved with me.

Jack snickered. "Might see your belly marks on that boulder I rescued you from."

Abi jerked her hand away, and I flashed back again to the first time, when our old nemesis VJ MacIntosh, God rest his troubled soul, had spoiled the moment.

"Rescued? Excuse me?"

I didn't have to turn my head to know she was glaring at me. I shot Jack a laser look with a vindictive writhing of my lips. It wasn't the first time he'd seen it and would know what it meant. Payback would be forthcoming, like a thief in the night.

He just kept on grinning. "Yeah, Mr. CSI there decided a cigarette butt perched on a cliff below Logan's Leap would break the case wide open. Almost found himself broke wide open at the bottom."

"Case?"

"It was nothing, Abi. Only notable thing is that it didn't help our case."

"Whoa, Dad," Kyle said, "you did Logan's Leap? No way." He stepped past me, dragging Lily with him and craning his neck to read my face as if a split-second delay might allow me to hide the truth.

I ignored Abi's incredulous stare on my other side like Perseus would Medusa. "Not exactly, son."

Jack chuckled and winked at me. "Aw, now, Case. Don't sell yourself short. Shoulda seen him, Kyle. Amazing."

"Someone better tell me what y'all are talking about. And I mean right now." Abi's arms were now folded across her chest. I dared look and got exactly what I expected: Cerulean eyes blazing like a double-barreled blow torch. Beautifully terrifying.

"There's a ledge below the bluff that they say kids like to jump down to. A rite of passage or something." Jack's eyes flickered my direction. "They call it Logan's Leap. Me and Case went down there looking for evidence. His foot slipped, and I gave him grief about it. Wasn't no danger at all."

"Case told me about Logan's Leap. What I don't know is why it required you to save my husband."

Jack gave a dismissive wave and stepped over to give Abi a one-armed hug that nearly lifted her from the ground. "If you know anything about me, Counselor, I tend to overstate my case. I've been known to exaggerate a bit."

She pushed Jack away with two hands and succumbed to a burgeoning grin. "What is known is that when you two get together, trouble finds you way too often." She suddenly cocked her head and snapped her fingers. "That's it! Logan's Leap, boulder brink. The brink is the edge of the bluff, where they're jumping from. That's it. Show me this Logan's Leap."

"Be careful, Mom," Kyle said. "It's crazy."

"Crazy." Lily giggled.

"And how exactly do you know about it, mister?"

"Everybody knows about it. Ain't many people that've done it, but everyone knows who they are. TK Koening, Stan Vinson, Lyle Bertel, a few others. Even Delta Ostrovsky did it, so they say." He paused and looked at Jack with a grimace. "Devlin, too, I think."

"Ronny Shane," I added. "According to Perry."

Abi's stern look had returned, but this time it was Kyle getting blow torched. "What about you?"

My son's face turned white and crinkled like hip-pocket notebook paper.

Holy moly. What else didn't I know about Kyle? Sure, he spent a lot of time camping and roaming the woods, but that was supposed to be a good thing for a boy who didn't really like sports in the traditional sense and was not musically inclined. In Amberton, once you got past those things, there wasn't much else.

My grandfather had once told me that spending time in the hardwoods would harden you like wood. It was an awkward turn of phrase, but the point was valid: Woodsmanship had made—and saved—many a man through the millennia. How was I supposed to know Kyle was launching himself off cliffs like a blooming idiot?

Jack tousled Kyle's hair, gave him a light fist bump, and shrugged at Abi.

Abi pressed her lips thin as toothpicks. "Show me."

My face was on fire. "Yeah, son. Show us. Then maybe we'll show you something later. Like how you're not leaving the house for a month."

I expected Kyle to follow with a rude comeback, but he ignored me. "Come on, Lily." He pointed to the edge of the bluff, near where Jack had jumped to save me that day. "Let's go look at your county. But I have to hold you."

Lily nodded vigorously with a big grin.

Kyle swooped her into his arms and began to trot and skip across the clearing.

"He's good with her, huh?" Jack said. "Don't be too hard on him. Kids gonna be kids. And he's a good one."

I reached for Abi's hand again. She didn't pull away but squinted hard at me. I wasn't off the hook, yet.

Kyle was weaving side to side, jiggling Lily up and down as he did, pretending to stumble and almost fall with each step. Lily howled with laughter. She gave a high-pitched squeal when Kyle feigned a giant stagger as he neared the edge of the bluff.

Stop, Kyle, that's close enough.

"Kyle!" Abi called out.

Kyle steadied himself and stood upright, easing my angst. Abi elbowed me, and she didn't have to say a word. *That boy!*

Then Kyle pointed down toward the drop-off, and Lily nodded. He pulled her to him in a tight embrace.

And then he jumped off Logan's Bluff, with Lily in his arms.

THIRTY-FOUR

MY stomach plummeted through the soles of my shoes and glued them to the grass for a split second. Abi screamed. Jack blurted something unintelligible and exploded like a Preakness colt out of the gates.

Why? My question was asked and unanswered a thousand times in the five-second lifetime it took me to cover the ground between where we stood and the spot Kyle and Lily disappeared. Taking Logan's Leap would be terrible enough, but that wasn't where they had vanished over the edge. It was several feet further down the bluff, where the face was steep, and no ledge existed. In his haste to make whatever point his fourteen-year-old, undeveloped brain felt compelled to make, Kyle had missed the spot. I passed Jack and his football knees despite his head start, almost wishing I could get there last. Or not see it at all.

I almost fell on top of Kyle and Lily.

There was a drop where they had disappeared, alright. A whopping three-foot fall onto a flat, grassy spot with enough room for a family picnic between the tiny ledge and where the ground gave way to the precipitous drop to the river. Kyle and Lily were flattened on their bellies, smiling and side-eyeing the edge where they knew frantic grown-ups would soon appear.

I staggered and managed to stop short of tumbling onto them, even when Abi and Jack nearly ran up my back. Kyle rolled to his back and kicked his legs with glee. Lily jumped to her feet and began hopping in place at our feet, the bounces of her curls almost brushing our knees. "Fooled you, fooled you!"

Abi was not amused. "Kyle Reynolds! That was not funny!"

He sat up and crossed his arms across bent knees. "I think Lily would disagree."

Jack slapped me across the back as he struggled to catch his breath. "Case, they got us pretty good. Can't believe I fell for it. Should've remembered that little drop-off was there."

"Fooled you, fooled you!" Lily dodged Abi's attempt to pick her up and circled around the ledge where she could use the shallow slope to get up to us. She wedged herself between us and jumped again. "You thought we went down there!" She pointed to the edge of the bluff twenty feet away. "But we didn't, did we?"

Abi sat and dangled her legs over the edge of the mini drop. "Come here, Lily." This time Lily complied, and Abi swooped her up and onto her lap. "That scared us, okay? We did think you went over that other edge, which would have been very, very dangerous. So be careful and hold an adult's hand, okay?"

Lily nodded but then stopped, rolled her eyes, and cocked her little head. "Hello! I'm not a little kid. I know that."

I chuckled. "Hello, she says."

Jack hopped down, wincing as he landed. I still marveled at how he had made Logan's Leap to save me two days prior. He reached out and helped Kyle to his feet. "Son, I suggest you and I commence to examining this boulder brink before your momma whips you little-kid style for nearly causing her a heart attack."

"Sorry, Mom." Kyle blew her a kiss and turned to follow Jack.

"You're still in trouble."

Kyle looked back over his shoulder. "What if I solve the riddle?"

"We'll renegotiate." Abi slid off her mini perch and picked up Lily. "Let's go see what Papa Jack finds."

Jack and Kyle were standing shoulder to shoulder at the edge of the bluff when we caught up to them. They peered over it, eyeing the landing spot below. Jack toed a large, exposed rock. "Either this spot or where Ronny went over the last time has to be what Perry was talking about. But we don't see anything."

Abi stayed about three feet behind them. "That's Logan's Leap?"

Kyle turned and stepped toward her. "Not exactly. Leap is a verb. Not a place. It's something you do."

"Show me where you land. Then we'll go talk to Alethia."

I touched her arm and nodded toward the edge. "You don't want to go down there. Trust me, if you think where you're standing now is bad, that's worse. Just getting there is a booger."

"I want to see it. You and Kyle have been there, and I want to see it." Abi had always been an adventurous type at heart; it was one of the things that attracted me to her from the start. But that tendency had been tempered by motherhood and see-ing the results of stupid behavior too many times through her job. Plus, she hated heights.

Jack pivoted away from the edge and began moving parallel to it, toward the wood line where the trail up from the cove emerged. "We'll show you what we can, Abi. But Case, I've got a hundred bucks that says she don't go past that big rock where you have to climb up and over."

My jaw dropped, and Jack's eyes locked with mine in the same instant. *Boulder brink.* He broke into a jog, and I joined him, waving at Abi and Kyle to join us. "That's it! Come on!"

We paused at the edge of the meadow just past the point where the bluff's steep face softened and began to melt into the woods.

"What's it?" Abi called. "Hold up! Lily has short legs!"

Kyle caught up first, then Abi and Lily. Jack picked Lily up despite her protest. "I've got to hold you here. It's dangerous up ahead.

We moved into the shadows of the woods, and I tried to imagine Perry hunkered down against one of the trees as Ronny had come gloating up the path from below after taking Logan's Leap. Perry had seen something after that that he wanted us to see also. But what? And why couldn't the odd old wanderer have just told us? So frustrating. We meandered down the hillside, following the path that seemed intent on taking us away from the bluff and down to the cove. Jack paused, glanced to his left, and looked back at me.

I nodded. Yep, that's the trail.

We veered off our path and angled back up the hill.

"Where are we going?" Lily asked. "To the county? I'm cold."

"Something like that," Jack said. "We'll be done soon, and I'll get you hot chocolate on the way home."

"I still can't believe you guys know where this is," Kyle said.

Jack stopped and motioned for me to come around him. He wasn't getting any closer while holding Lily. "Here we are." There before us was the rocky outcropping where the trail ended and the hillside slipped away below us.

I pointed across the divide to the ledge and then to the arcing climb that required rock footholds and sapling handholds to make. "I think this is the boulder brink. I remember stopping and thinking long and hard about why the trail led here the other day. It wasn't until Luke pointed out the significance of the ledge and how to get to it that I understood. Logan's Leap will land you right over there, if you make it."

"And we do what here, exactly?"

"I don't know," I said. "It says the wise stop and think. He wants us to see something. Realize something. C'mon guys. Think."

"Maybe it's over there." Kyle pointed to the ledge. "I'll go look."

Abi slapped his hand down. "You most certainly will not."

Kyle huffed. "I've done it before."

"And you can do it again when you're twenty-one or so. But not today."

The wise stop and think atop the boulder brink. Alethia resides where internuncios hide. I replayed those words in my head, but nothing clicked. It had seemed so obvious moments before, but maybe we were in the wrong place altogether. We had yet to look at the spot where Ronny fell to his death, so maybe that was it. Maybe boulder brink wasn't even what we thought it was. Who knew with Perry?

"I'm cold."

"I know, I know. We're almost done." Jack hugged Lily tight to his chest and wrapped his jacket around her. "Okay, detectives. Any ideas?"

Kyle shrugged. "I don't see anything. What about the ledge?"

Jack shook his head. "Case and I have been there. I just don't see how that ledge could be what Perry was referring to. He never mentioned going out there. Plus, that dude is pretty nimble, but he ain't no spring chicken. Doubt he would have climbed up and over the gap to get there. No reason to."

I nodded. "I agree. Gotta be something else."

Abi had her phone out, pecking the screen. "Here's what I think. The key must be with Alethia somehow." She began snapping photos of our surroundings. "I say we take pics from this spot and the others, up top. I know y'all got some earlier, but you can't have too many. Then go talk to Alethia and see what she says. The riddle basically says she lives—resides—where messengers—internuncios—hide. She has some kind of message for us. I'm guessing Perry left something with her. Maybe because she's a media member, or maybe he knows her. Then, I'll bet when we go back and look—" she flipped her phone around to show a photo of the outcropping and the gap beyond it "—something will click."

Jack had his cheek pressed against Lily's. He nodded. "I don't have any better ideas."

I had some other ideas, but not better ones, other than me recusing myself from the whole investigation, or at the very least taking my foot off the gas. Jack had asked me to help prove Devlin innocent, and now that Abi was recommending he be released, we had some time. Letting Devlin go didn't mean he couldn't be arrested again, but the scales were tipping in his favor. Perhaps he would open up now about what he knew. I suspected he had been protecting his mother all along, something no longer necessary if we had evidence she wasn't actually the killer.

Aside from quizzing Devlin again, one thing Jack needed to do was talk to Buster Shane, Ronny's brother. So far, he had eluded Jack's efforts to corner him for a meaningful conversation, and Jack hadn't pushed it out of respect for a man grieving his brother. To hear Jack tell it, Rappaport and company had fared no better. But that time was rapidly approaching. The funeral, delayed for a sister stationed at an air base in Germany to arrive home, was scheduled for the next day. Once that was done, Buster would be on the hot seat. Whatever Ronny was involved in, Buster had been in the middle of it. Whether that was what had gotten him killed remained to be determined.

But as much as I wanted to step away, curiosity clung to me like a cocklebur. As a general rule, I wanted to interact with Alethia Abbott like I wanted a dislocated kneecap. And I knew Abi felt the same. But this time, learning what secret she hid held an allure akin to popping a kneecap back in place—painful but absolutely necessary. "We can call the newspaper tomorrow."

Abi frowned. "Bull. If I'm going to stand behind my recommendation Devlin be released, I need all the information I can get. And I just happen to have saved her number from the last time we spoke." She tapped her phone a few times and put it to her ear.

My eyes widened. I didn't know Abi had ever called her before. I vowed never to ask how it went. Jack made a clawing motion and hissed like a cat.

Abi pointed at Jack with a threatening look and then broke into a syrup-smooth Sunday school voice. "Alethia? This is Abi Reynolds ... No, honey, it's not about that. Water under the bridge ... If you don't mind, Jack and Case need to come ask you a couple of questions for a case I'm working on. Won't take but a second ... I'd rather not say on the phone, but that's a very good guess ... Yes, if there's information to be shared with the press, you get it first ... Okay, be there in fifteen."

Jack pretended to put a phone to his ear. "Hello, sweetie, is it okay if we pretend to be besties while we use each other? After this case is solved, we can have a sleepover and do each other's nails and stuff until we hate each other again."

Lily arched her head back away from Jack's face. "Why are

you talking like a girl? That sounds silly."

Abi reached for Lily, who reciprocated and fell into her arms. "Because he's intimidated by my ability to swim the moats that sink him."

Lily's eyes widened. "You're going swimming?"

Abi glanced toward the drop-off that led to the water. "No, but Jack might if he keeps it up."

Jack laughed and pointed up the hill. "Lead the way to the cars, Counselor. I'm gonna need you to get Lily some hot chocolate on the way home."

THIRTY-FIVE

SHILOH Park was a name I did not recognize at first. Abi had texted Alethia's address to us just before she, Kyle, and Lily left the bluff in my truck. The neighborhood sounded vaguely familiar, but I couldn't put it in any context. When Jack finally turned off the highway and I saw the sign, it hit me. Shiloh Park was the name of a motor home park. There was nothing wrong with that, but it defied my preconceived expectation of Alethia Abbott and her flowery, flowing blouses, cat-eye glasses, and flamboyant jewelry reading cozy upmarket fiction in a remodeled bungalow with a turquoise front door and white trim.

Jack read my mind. "Didn't pick her as being the camping type?"

I chuckled. "Nope."

"You know this whole thing is disappointing."

"How so?"

"If Abi is going to insist that we ruin our Tuesday night talking to this wench, the least she could do is come with and throw a sucker punch."

I smiled. He was not wrong. On the other hand, seeing my wife getting disbarred for slugging a witness did not sound like such a great idea. "Wonder why she lives here?"

Jack stopped the truck and shifted it into park. "Looks like you'll get the chance to ask her." He nodded to a window where a figure peering through parted curtains was silhouetted against the yellow glow of incandescent light.

"Lovely."

Allegro was painted in orange italic capital letters over a brown stripe that ran the length of the ivory-colored vehicle. I did not know much about motor homes but recognized the model as being manufactured a couple of counties over, up near Tishomingo. We had taken a school field trip to the factory there when I was a kid. From the looks of this particular motor home, it might have settled in its current location shortly thereafter, and it did not appear to be relocating anytime soon. Someone, presumably Alethia Abbott, had landscaped around it like one might a brick house in a suburban neighborhood: a row of boxwoods and azaleas across the front with junipers stationed at each corner. Precast concrete steps nestled up to the door completed the look of permanence.

Alethia opened the door before my foot hit the first step. "Case Reynolds. Number one hundred fifty-seven on my list of most likely suspects to darken my doorstep on this fine evening."

"Suspect, huh?"

"If the shoe fits." She was as snippy as ever, with a quickness of wit to match.

"It just might." I nodded toward Jack. "You remember—"

"Jack Masterson. Of course. Number seventy-eight on my list."

Jack slapped me on the shoulder. "Hear that? I beat you by, like, fifty or something."

"Seventy-nine," Alethia quipped. "And don't flatter yourself. Number four is Satan himself."

Jack chuckled and marched up the steps past me to stand nose to nose with Alethia. "May we come in? Won't take long. I think Abi called you."

She smiled and stepped back, making a sweeping gesture to invite us in. "Yes, you may, but not because Abi Reynolds called me. I'm curious."

Jack nodded and stepped in, and I followed. The place was impeccably clean, and I wondered if it was always that way or if she had done a lightning pickup just before our arrival. Jack settled onto a leather couch to our right, and I slid in beside him, saving the matching chair across from us for Alethia. "How many miles?" Jack asked.

"Thirty-two."

Jack let out a whistle. "Sweet."

Alethia eased into the chair and eyed both of us with a suspicious cock of her head. She was different than I remembered, with none of the garish jewelry and clothing I'd seen before. Just a green Delta State sweatshirt, jeans, and fleece-lined slippers. Her hair was straight and fine, parted in the middle, the color of honey. "I never was much of a traveler. But it makes for cheap rent. Important since small town news-papering doesn't exactly put one on the Forbes 500."

"Chevy 454?"

Alethia smiled. "I think that's what it was."

"Was?" I asked.

"Someone else wanted it more than I did."

"Thirty-two thousand miles it is, then," Jack said.

Alethia clapped her hands together and leaned forward, elbows on knees. "Let's get to the punch. Why are you two here? I don't know anything about that boy's death, and I doubt you're here to give me some scoop out of the goodness of your heart."

"Maybe we're here to get the scoop from you," I said.

"I doubt it. And like I said, wrong place if that's your plan."

"Ever heard of the kid who died? Ronny Shane? Or his brother, Buster?"

Alethia shrugged. "Buster, maybe. I mostly remember seeing his name in the sports section years back. Seems like his name's been mentioned in conversation about promising kids who got mixed up in the wrong crowd. There's a bunch in every county, I guess." She leaned back and folded her arms across her chest, eyes locked on Jack. "Now tell me why you're really here. I know it's not some random fishing expedition. Maybe I should be fishing in your watering hole, since I hear your kid Devlin James is on the hook."

Jack eyed her back without faltering. "Not for long. And his name wasn't mentioned by a man at the murder scene like yours was."

Alethia blinked hard and flinched. Was she caught off guard by the information itself or the fact that we had it? "Please explain."

"Did you read my first book?" I asked.

She frowned. "Excuse me?"

"My first book. Did you read it?"

She nodded slowly. "I did. Not bad, actually, for a novice."

"Remember Brendan Perry? The Vagabond?"

"Vaguely, but yes."

"He's back in town. And he was at Logan's Bluff the night of the accident."

Alethia shifted in her chair and looked past us as if an explanation might be projected on the wall. "Weird. And?"

Jack leaned in until her gaze met his. "And he didn't see what happened, but he saw Ronny Shane a few minutes before he fell to his death. And he gave Case here a clue. It includes your name."

"A clue? What kind of clue?"

Jack had sealed the napkin containing the original message in a plastic bag for preservation, but I had a photo of it on my phone. I debated whether to show it to her, but I couldn't see how that would jeopardize anything. If Alethia knew something, she was too smart to let withholding the information fool her, and if she didn't know anything, nothing was lost. I pulled out my phone and tapped the screen. "I'll show you on one condition. You can't publish until we give you the go ahead."

"Unless of course you're guilty in some way," Jack piped in, "in which case we won't have to worry about that, will we?"

She huffed and reached out, palm up, curling two fingers. "Let me see."

I held the phone for her to see the image but didn't hand it over. "It's a napkin. Perry wrote a message before he disappeared again. A riddle." I pulled the phone back and read aloud. "The wise stop and think atop the boulder brink. For Alethia resides where internuncios hide and millstones float when ghosts peregrinate the moat."

Alethia Abbott sat stone-faced for a moment. "Read it again," she finally said.

I complied, and her expression softened from granite to one more pensive and fluid.

"Spelled like my name?"

I nodded. "Yep. We think the millstone and moat references are to Miller's Creek, near the bluff. Not exactly sure on the ghost part. Boulder brink, we have some ideas. Internuncio means—"

"Messenger," she said.

My expression must have given away my surprise.

"English major," she said. "Words are my job, you know."

I chose not to tell her I was also an English major yet had never heard the word before. Of course, my job was to motivate, educate, and coach teenagers, many of whom couldn't care less about words longer than four letters. "Anyway, bottom line is that somehow Perry decided you are hiding something, unless you know of another Alethia around these parts. And I've learned not to question his information. It's like he's a fly on every wall."

She chuckled and rolled her eyes. "With a sense of humor, it would seem."

Jack frowned. "There's nothing funny about any of this. One person is dead, and another kid's life is at stake."

Alethia narrowed her gaze and nodded. "Tell Perry that." She turned to me. "You're missing something here."

"Please enlighten me."

"You've spent so much time on big words, you've overlooked an important three letter one. You said you think you know where the boulder brink is. If it's at Logan's, and I'm here, then you're missing something." She paused and leaned forward, elbows on her knees. "The word *for*, like so many in our English language, is polysemic, especially when used as a preposition. But when used as a conjunction, it essentially has only one meaning."

I nodded. *Because.*

Alethia stood and walked through the kitchen area toward her sleeping quarters. In seconds she returned to show us a five-by-seven black-and-white photo in a gold frame. The woman in the photo bore a striking resemblance to Alethia, only her hair was darker with coarse waves. "My mother passed away a week ago. Long bout with COPD. She reared me with no help from my no-good father, whom I never knew. Probably a good thing.

Mother always said he was a nice cheating liar when sober and a mean lying cheater when drunk."

Jack passed the photo back to Alethia. "Sorry about your mother. No disrespect, but I'm not sure I understand. And?"

She pointed at the photo, motionless for several seconds. "And… and Mother said she only ever wanted two things in life. One was a baby. The other was truth. Once she named me, she had them both." Alethia wiped a tear from her eye and smiled at me. "I never had one of them and am a living search for the other. Does that help?"

A wave of heat washed over me, and my pulse quickened. I stood up and looked hard into Alethia Abbott's eyes. "It does. You swear to me you don't know anything about this accident?"

She shook her head. "I do not."

"Come on, Jack." I moved toward the door. "Thank you, Alethia."

Jack stood. "Wait, I don't understand. She said she does not. Does that mean she doesn't know anything or doesn't swear that she doesn't know anything?"

Alethia laughed. "I always liked you, Jack. You are blessed with the rare ability to take things as they are. No more, no less." She tapped me on the shoulder. "You'll help him out, I'm sure. I'd like to go to bed now. It's been a long few weeks."

"We help each other more times than not," I said.

Jack shrugged and shook Alethia's hand as he moved past her. "Thanks, I think. Sorry again about your mother." He opened the door and headed down the steps.

Alethia grabbed my hand as I moved to leave, and I returned the handshake. "I had a source I thought I could trust," she said. "Back then. I was wrong." She held on for an extra second, and I understood.

Whether it was due to the passage of time, or her, or me, or her mother, we would move on. Which suited me just fine. I nodded and patted her hand, and she closed the door behind me without saying another word.

Jack was waiting at his post at the bottom of the steps. "Mind telling me what just happened there?"

"Just a little linguistics linkage between fellow English majors."

"I thought you were going to have some other type of linkage based on how she looked into your eyes there at the end."

I laughed so suddenly I coughed on my own saliva.

Jack smiled. "You're almost as much a nerd as Jet. Seriously, how about you explain in English?"

"Perry is having a little fun with us."

"Now I'm even more confused."

I pointed to the truck. "I'll explain on the way."

"I hope the way includes a stop for food. I'm starving."

I nodded. "Not a bad idea. Abi was picking up fast food on the way home. Said she'd try to get Lily to sleep early so she won't be ornery when you pick her up later. Where we going?"

"Where else? Dundee's. Tuesday special is brisket and garlic potatoes."

"Fine. Gotta feed the beasts. But then we've got work to do."

"I assume you'll tell me where we're going while we eat."

"Where else? Back to Logan's Bluff. Where the truth hides."

THIRTY-SIX

KYLE tiptoed down the hall, regretting not flipping the light off when he had passed by an hour before. Yes, his mom was likely asleep, with Lily curled up beside her and her book fallen haphazardly somewhere on the bed after trying but failing to stay awake until his dad got home. Still, darkness would have been more reassuring. He froze when an oak floorboard popped beneath his toes.

"Boo!"

Kyle jumped and the floorboard sounded again.

Muffled laughter seeped through the crack in a door to his right. He slipped through the crack and closed the door behind him. The walls were a pale Tiffany blue, a color shade he only knew the name of because his sister had mentioned it as her favorite color at least a thousand times. He put an index finger to his lips. "Be quiet, will you?"

Kellen laughed again, louder. Her sun-kissed auburn hair and freckles took on a spiteful glow against the background color of the walls. "Did my scary whisper make you pee your pants?"

Were all sisters this infuriating? "Shut up. You're going to wake Mom."

Kellen shook her head. "Abi's down for the count at this hour. What are you doing, anyway?"

Kyle hated how she called Mom by her first name behind her back. "Nothing. Just walking to the kitchen."

"Yeah, sure." She smirked. "You always look like SEAL Team Six when walking through your own house. That's stupid, but I'm not stupid. You're going somewhere."

Stupid, Kellen was certainly not. She was too smart for his own good sometimes. And technically, she was right. There was no reason to be in mission mode until he got out of the house. But Abi— er, Mom, had a tendency to stay awake if her sleep was ever disturbed. And then, to talk. He'd seen his dad sneak down the hall for the same reason on many occasions, whether coming exhausted in after a late game or intent on an uninterrupted, diet-breaking refrigerator raid. Kyle patted his stomach. "I need a late-night snack."

Kellen moved toward the door. "Let me double check whether Abi is asleep. She might want a snack too."

Kyle braced his foot against the door. "Don't, please."

"Then tell me where you're going, and I'm going too. I missed all the action today."

"That's what you get for being Little Miss Community Volunteer."

Kellen clenched her teeth and glared at him. "Tell me."

Kyle's mind spun to find a lie that would dissuade her. Why had he even acted like he cared if she woke Mom? Going back to the Dunbar house wasn't that important anyway, except for the fact he had promised Proffit, who might never know the difference. But then again, Gabe said he always knows, like he has eyes in every tree. Kyle sighed. It was too late now; Kellen knew he was up to something. "Gabe is picking me up."

Kellen raised an eyebrow. "Go on."

"That's it. Just gonna ride around."

Kellen frowned. "Y'all dating or something?"

Kyle wanted to smack her but decided to go a different,

more bold and brilliant direction. "Actually, I think we missed something today, so we're going back to Logan's."

Kellen blinked and twitched her head like the flick of a horse's tail. This was the part where she would admonish him for his idiocy, then he would pretend to be mad and to text Gabe never mind and then just go to bed. Instead, she gave an inquisitive cock of her head and raised one eyebrow. "You got an idea, or just going on a snipe hunt?"

"I got an idea. Just gotta go see." It was a response legitimate enough to be worth considering but vague enough to be dismissed when he refused to offer further details, since he didn't actually have any.

Instead, she smiled. "Let's do it. You can explain on the way."

Not the answer he had been expecting. "Huh?"

"Unless you're blowing smoke and are just planning to ride around with your boyfriend."

His face suddenly felt sunburned. He narrowed his eyes and glared at her. "I told you I have an idea. That should be good enough."

"Don't be so serious. I believe you. Sounds exciting. Let's go." Her eager expression suddenly reversed course. "But what about Dad?"

That question had already been asked and answered in his mind earlier, but things were different now. His original plan would have taken fifteen minutes or less, easy enough to explain away as just a walk around the block for fresh air. Now it mattered none, since he was planning on faking a call from Gabe saying he couldn't come.

Kyle puffed his chest out, all bravado. "Who knows? Who cares? You know how he gets sometimes, like a pit bull on a

T-bone. He may not come home tonight. Or he may be home in five minutes. But I gotta do what I gotta do."

Kellen pointed to the door without hesitation. "I'm in."

They exited through the kitchen door into the backyard. It was a longer path through the yard to get to the driveway, but it avoided the sound of the garage door opening. Kyle led the way, tiptoeing through the dew-moistened grass for a few steps before realizing his steps were quiet either way. He expected Kellen to gibe him and was glad when she didn't offer commentary.

He pivoted around the drooping branches of a Japanese maple at the corner of the house and was through the gate of their chain-link fence in a flash. He would get to the driveway, wait a few minutes, then fake the call. The blowing snort of a whitetail deer in the distance caught his attention, and he stopped to point it out to Kellen at the same moment she clutched his shoulder from behind.

"Look. I don't think that's Gabe."

Kyle froze and instantly did not like what he saw.

A truck was parked to their left, off the end of the driveway, on a patch of bare dirt where Dad had unhitched his trailer too many times for grass to survive. It wasn't unusual to see a vehicle in that particular spot when they had company over. But they didn't have company over, and this truck was backed in, like its occupant was watching the house.

Or prepared for a quick getaway.

They stood motionless for a time, afraid to move or talk. Finally, Kellen tugged at Kyle's shirt, and he followed her lead, retracing his footsteps backward, eyeing the truck with every step. Maybe the driver hadn't seen him. But who was it? The truck was a midsize, maybe foreign, but it was too dark to tell much else.

Before Kyle and Kellen could back through the gate, the driver's door opened, and a head popped up above the roof. "Hey, what y'all doing?" a male voice called from his perch standing on the nerf bar.

Kyle's first instinct was to run, and he stepped back hard, landing squarely on Kellen's foot.

Kellen pushed back even harder. "What are you doing, bro?" She stepped around Kyle and moved toward the truck. "Devlin? That you?"

The person hopped down and rounded the front of the truck. "It is, it is. Where you two kids heading? Ain't it past your bedtime?"

Kellen grunted. "We're almost fifteen. And don't you wish you knew." Kyle had heard that sharp edge in her voice many times and was glad it was directed at someone else.

Devlin James laughed. "I guess that depends on whether knowing might get me into more trouble or not."

Kyle felt foolish for wanting to run. He should have recognized the Tacoma crew cab as belonging to Devlin. Even if not recognizing it as a friend he should have stood his ground given the fact it was a strange vehicle on his property. With Dad not home, he was expected to be the protector. On the other hand, a kid not much older than him *had* been murdered only four days prior. And maybe he was a bit gun shy after running straight into that Carter kid's right hook at the party two nights earlier. He stepped forward to join Kellen. "Nothing to know. Kellen and I just coming out to talk for a minute."

Kellen's head swiveled. She was frowning, but this time it was at him. "If you thought of something, don't you think Devlin, of all people, should know? Not to mention, here's the ride we needed. Doesn't look like your friend is coming."

This is turning into a disaster. If there had been a chance Kellen would soon back off and not force Kyle to reveal his lie, it was likely gone now. If Devlin thought Kyle had an idea that would help exonerate him, he would surely push to see it through. What would he say if and when he realized it was an utter waste of time?

Devlin pounded a fist into the palm of his other hand. "Really? You thought of something? I came to get an update from Coach. I know he and Jack have been working hard, but I haven't heard from them. Jack said he'd give me an update tomorrow, but I can't wait. They're not answering their phones."

"Why not just wait on Jack to get home?" Kyle asked.

Devlin looked toward the ground. "Mom might be there. We ain't on the best of terms right now."

Understandable. From what Kyle had gathered from overheard conversations between his parents, Tammy James had thought all along that she was actually Ronny James's murderer. Whether she would have been willing to let Devlin take the ultimate fall for her or truly had confidence that Jack and others would quickly prove his innocence without discovering her role in it might never be known. Either way, the wounds it caused would not heal any time soon, if ever.

"Everybody thinks you're innocent, Devlin. That's what matters."

Devlin looked up and stared at Kyle long enough for Kyle to notice his own misty breaths puffing in the silence held by their gaze. Devlin stepped forward until the two boys were chest to chest. He wasn't much taller than Kyle, but his shoulders and chest showed the bulk of much more testosterone and hundreds of weight room presses. Devlin poked a finger in Kyle's chest, not hard enough to hurt but enough for Kyle to know he'd best listen to what came next. "Let's get something straight. What matters is once upon a time me and Ronny were friends. And he's dead. And I could still get arrested again. And even if that don't happen, unless somebody else is convicted of it, my name will forever be whispered when his story is told."

Kellen grabbed Devlin's hand and pushed it away. "Easy, Dev. He wasn't saying it doesn't matter. Besides, you should be nice to Kyle. He has an idea about how to help you."

Devlin pulled his hand away and stepped back. "Yeah, sorry. I'm just on edge. Three days in jail, among other things, has a way of doing that." He patted Kyle on the shoulder. "So you can help me? I'll owe you."

Kyle gulped. *Here we go again. Think. Think!* What to do now? Unless he fessed up, he would have half the people he knew mad at him before the sun rose again. Proffit, for not checking on their operation at the Dunbar house. Devlin and Kellen, for leading them on a wild goose chase. Mom and Dad, for being out too late and interfering with the investigation. Jack too. But what if he could come through? There *was* that one thought he had. Just a passing mirage of an idea when it hit him, not worth pursuing, or at least best left to others more officially in charge. It was farfetched. Wasn't it?

"Hey, Kyle."

The voice was coming from the truck, and Kyle recognized it instantly. His pulse quickened.

"Emma, I told you and Lena to shush and let me handle this." Devlin said.

"Well, you're taking forever." Lena Cole's voice this time. "And we can't tell that you're handling anything."

Devlin sighed.

Kellen shifted her weight and folded her arms.

Kyle strained his eyes to see if Emma Harlow was looking at him.

"Carter Strevel will get what's coming to him," Devlin said over his shoulder as he punched the accelerator. "I'll see to it after all this is done."

Emma shined her phone light onto the left side of Kyle's face and giggled. "Ooh. That may hit every color in the rainbow before it's gone."

Kyle touched the sore spot where he had been slugged two nights before. "At least I'm not eating through a straw."

Kellen elbowed Kyle from her seat by the door to his right. "You gonna tell us your plan or not?"

Kyle liked the "or not" option, except it couldn't be an option much longer. They were on their way to Logan's Bluff, with Devlin driving like they were in the NASCAR Truck Series.

Despite her initial enthusiasm, Kellen had first required Devlin to explain why he had two girls in the truck with him if he was so serious about finding out the truth. His explanation had been far short of eloquent, but the gist of Lena, the passionate girlfriend seeking vindication for her "true love," and Emma, the remorseful former stepsister seeking restitution for sharing the video that had implicated Devlin, had been convincing enough for Kellen to relent.

Part of Kyle had wanted Kellen to buck it and back away and save him from embarrassment. The other part of him wanted to be in that truck so bad he could hardly stand it, whatever the cost. He had doubts about Lena's true loyalty and motives, given what he'd heard about the love triangle with Ronny, but he needed no convincing about anything from Emma.

Kellen elbowed him again. "Well?"

Kyle's mind raced. Even if they found nothing, which he fully expected, the logic behind their crusade had to sound reasonable. He could sense that his dad knew they were missing something in the message from that Perry vagabond guy he had heard about all his life, but what? Kyle had wanted to show his parents and Jack how to get from Logan's Bluff down to Miller's Creek, where it seemed like Perry was suggesting the killer came in, but no one was interested. Maybe that was the play now. But what sense would it make to try to accomplish that in the dark? The odds of finding anything were nil in those conditions, and he knew what the girls would say if he led them down a hill a quarter mile through the woods in the black of night.

He had read the poetic message so many times he had it memorized. He had been the one to come up with an idea about the meaning of the last verse. But what about the first two? No one had any answers. They had stopped to think atop the boulder brink just like it said, but nothing happened.

And maybe his dad and Jack had found out something from the newspaper reporter Alethia about internuncios, whatever that meant, but for some reason Kyle doubted it. Something was eating at him about that name, Alethia. It sounded a lot like that goddess Athena he had learned about in the Greek mythology section in eighth grade, but he knew they weren't the same. Why did that keep popping in his head?

Kyle took out his phone and began a Google search.

"What are you doing?" Kellen asked. "Please tell me you have an actual idea and aren't scrambling to find one now."

Kyle nudged his sister hard with his shoulder and angled the phone so she couldn't see what he was typing. He felt

Emma's chin on his shoulder, looking. He didn't even have to scroll down before he had his answer. "Holy cow, that's it." He handed his phone to Kellen to peruse the screen.

"What?" Emma asked in his ear.

"The truth. Believe it or not, Perry pointed us straight to it."

THIRTY-SEVEN

"PLEASE explain," Devlin said. "Something tells me it can't be that easy."

Kellen gave the phone back to Kyle and elbowed him again. "Brother, that's good work. Now we just have to find it."

Lena clapped her hands like a kindergarten teacher getting her students' attention. "Would somebody please tell me what's going on?"

Kellen recited Perry's riddle and gave a brief overview of their progress deciphering it. "But Alethia isn't the newspaper woman. It's a synonym for truth. So the message basically says, 'the wise stop and think atop the boulder brink, for truth resides where messengers hide.'"

Kyle was impressed. She had evidently memorized the riddle too.

Lena huffed. "Still makes no sense."

Devlin rolled the steering wheel to the left and angled his Tacoma up the access road to Logan's Buff. "We're almost there. Hope somebody has a plan."

Kyle leaned forward, both to better see how Devlin was navigating the ascent along the dark two-track road and to make sure he was heard. "Basically, we already established where the boulder brink is, but we weren't sure what to do with the information. Now we know. There's another message of some sort hidden there. A message with the truth. I assume

Perry left it for us. Now we just have to find it."

———

"I don't like the dark." Lena hooked her arm in Devlin's and pulled herself to him as she eyed the trees looming before them at the edge of the clearing. "This place gives me the creeps."

"You're the one insisted on coming," Devlin said. "I told you I didn't know where I'd wind up."

"You said you were going to talk to your coach. You didn't say nothing about going back to where Ronny was killed."

Devlin ignored her and began picking his way down the hillside ahead of the others, using his phone light to find his steps and identify low-hanging limbs that needed brushing aside.

The dew had begun to freeze, exacerbating the crunch of the dry leaves beneath their feet. Kyle couldn't decide if the noise of the crunching in silence or of their voices when talking was more disconcerting. He would have much preferred more stealth, like when he was tracking a young doe just to see how close he could get before she detected him. Once he had been quiet enough, with the benefit of a breeze in his face strong enough to wiggle the foliage around them, to get within three feet, almost close enough to reach out and touch her. Tonight they sounded like sumo wrestlers wearing snowshoes in the woods. How did they know the killer wasn't watching their every move? Lena wasn't wrong about it being spooky.

Devlin marched on, and his cohort followed diligently. Kyle shined his light back and forth into the shadows but saw nothing. Finally, Devlin stopped and turned his light back toward them. "Be careful. I'm right here at the edge. Go over it, and God help us all."

Emma slid her hand under Kyle's arm and squeezed. His heart skipped. Was she cold, or nervous, or did that mean something else?

Kellen moved up to stand beside Devlin, craning her neck to see what lay before them without getting any closer. The rock outcropping shone like a gray ghost rising from a long serpentine ribbon of depthless black. "So that's the boulder brink. I must say, it's impressive in the dark."

Kyle took a deep breath and unhooked his arm from Emma's. He moved past Devlin and Kellen and stepped onto the boulder.

"Get back!" Lena cried out. "This is crazy!"

"The wise stop and think atop the boulder brink," Kellen said.

"And if I'm standing on top of something," Kyle said, "thinking about where to hide something else, where's the first place that comes to mind?"

"Underneath it!" Emma chimed in excitedly. "Look underneath it!"

Devlin was on his knees before she had finished repeating the words. "Lena, grab my belt from behind in case I slip."

"I'm not moving." Lena's feet might as well have been buried in cement, five feet back from the edge.

Kyle hopped off the rock and grabbed Devlin's belt, leaning back to brace himself. "Got you."

Devlin shined his phone light along the edge of the rock. "It's straight down right here. I can't see underneath it, can't reach it, and can't get any closer. Maybe that's not it."

"Over here," Kellen said. "There are two sides, you know."

"Careful!" Kyle hissed. He let go of Devlin, who was pushing back from the edge, and slid over to get behind Kellen. She didn't have a belt, so he took a fistful of her shirt instead.

"Thanks." Kellen shifted to get in a more upright position. "Guess what? There's a foothold right here at the base of the rock." She reached back for Kyle to grab her hand instead of her shirt and moved her right foot down the edge of the embankment while keeping one knee on the edge.

"Got you." He grasped her forearm while she reciprocated on his. He wished he had a belt to hold but vowed to go over with her before he let her slip away.

Lena gasped. "I can't take this."

"You better be hanging on to her tight, bro," Devlin said. "On second thought, Kellen, let me down there. I'm bigger, stronger, older. Plus, if you get hurt, Coach will kill me. Jack too."

Kellen ignored him and tossed her phone back up on the ledge to free up her right hand. "I can't lean out far enough to see anything. Got to assume Perry was by himself, so it can't require too many acrobatics to get to it. Let me just feel around."

The earth around the boulder brink and the crevasse it guarded fell silent while Kellen probed, and her spectators held their breaths. Suddenly her movement changed from slow and deliberate to short lunges. Kyle thought she might be slipping and squeezed tighter.

"I think I feel something!" Her labored breaths became rapid and shallow. She lunged again, and Kyle felt a slip of her hand along his arm.

"It's not worth it, Kel. We'll come back in the light."

"Just don't let go. There's a hole here. I can feel something at my fingertips at the back."

"Probably a rattlesnake," Lena said from her cemented location.

"Lena, don't say another word, or I'm gonna choke you out," Emma said.

Kyle smiled to himself, but it quickly evaporated when Kellen lunged again, and he felt another tiny slip of their grip. "Come on up here and let's rethink this. Let me do it. Or Devlin, like he said. His arms are longer." Kyle had never seen Perry, but if the description of him in his dad's first book was accurate, he was taller than Kellen. Which meant he had a longer reach. She was physically mature and tall for her age, but not enough, apparently. Unfortunately, he knew his sister's mindset. She wouldn't give up, especially not to be replaced by a boy.

"Like Emma said," Kellen hissed, "just be quiet and hold on."

Kyle considered talking a lot more in hopes Kellen would abandon her current position and try to choke him out, but he feared that would distract her. Instead, he said, "I got you. Just get it."

She leaned in again, her fingers clutching Kyle's arm. He couldn't see her very well from his sideways angle, but it seemed like she had her entire shoulder buried into the face of the ledge. Suddenly, she out a whoop. "Ha! Got it! You're not going to believe this!"

Before Kyle or anyone else could ask what she meant, Kellen shrieked. The sound itself was cutting enough, but the simultaneous realization that she was slipping was like a rip in his gut. "Hang on! Hang on!" he cried.

"The rock! My foot! It's gone!" Kellen writhed and kicked, scrambling to stabilize herself.

Kyle was pulled toward the edge as he strained to hold her with his left hand and flail for extra purchase on the rock behind him with his right. It wasn't enough, though. She was going to slip away, and he leaned in to stay with her, hoping one of them would find something more to hold onto before it was too late. It was no use; his balance began to tip toward the point of no return.

Suddenly the tension of her weight relaxed, and a micro-second of panic that their connection had torn away enveloped him. But she was still there, being lifted up over his left shoulder onto stable ground, as if he had acquired supernatural strength in the heat of the moment.

"We got you." It was Devlin's voice, above and behind him atop the boulder. He had Kellen by the right arm.

Kellen fell to the ground on her knees, and Kyle rolled onto his back beside her. The alternating cadence of their heaving breaths filled the air. "Thanks guys," she gasped. "Thought I was a goner."

"That was too close," Kyle huffed. "Too bad it was all for nothing,"

Kellen rolled onto her belly and brought her knees under her chest. "What you talking about?" She pushed herself up to a more upright position.

"You said it's gone. You lost whatever you had."

Kellen cuffed her brother on the top of his head and stood up. "No, silly. The rock I was standing on is gone. That's why I slipped. You don't seriously think I would drop this, do you?"

Kyle rolled over and launched himself into a standing position. "You got something? What is it?"

Kellen pulled her shoulders back triumphantly and held out her hand, palm up. "I present to you the internuncio where Alethia resides."

Devlin shined his light onto her hand like a spotlight on a Broadway star, and a collective gasp erupted all around.

"That's Ronny's," Lena said. "Ronny's extra phone."

THIRTY-EIGHT

"LITTLE brother, as always I was skeptical, but you proved me wrong." Kellen handed Kyle the phone. "Your prize, sir."

He ignored her double jab. He didn't count fifteen minutes older as meaningful, but she loved to point it out. As for the skeptical part, it was true but unfounded. But that was a discussion for another time. He took the phone and examined it. It was a flip phone, the cheap kind one used due to either financial constraints or, apparently in Ronny's case, as an extra. It was either broken, or the battery was dead. "Lena, you say this was Ronny's extra phone?"

"Yeah. I recognize that crack in the screen. Looks kinda like a tic tac toe."

Kyle squinted his eyes and rotated the phone. There were some semi-perpendicular cracks, but Kyle didn't see the pattern. "I guess it's like one of those inkblot things."

Kellen huffed. "Rorschach test." She turned the phone toward Lena without taking it out of Kyle's hand. "Doesn't matter. All that matters is whether she recognizes it. You sure, Lena?"

Lena nodded. "No doubt."

"I recognize it too," Emma said. "But I don't see a tic tac toe."

"It's heartwarming that you two know Ronny's belongings so well," Devlin said with a sarcastic edge, "but now what?"

Kyle pointed up the hill. "Now we get out of here. Get home, charge the phone, see what's on it." He looked at Devlin and hesitated, then turned to Lena. "Any chance you know the password?"

Devlin huffed, and she shook her head. "No, I don't. I'd see him open the phone sometimes, but he always hid what numbers he punched in."

Kyle stuffed the phone in his pocket and began trudging up the hill. "We'll cross that bridge when we come to it. Get the phone charged first."

"Give it to Jack first," Devlin corrected. "He's been given official permission to investigate this." He reached out and snapped his fingers. "In fact, why don't you give the phone to me, and I'll take care of it? I'm the one affected, anyway."

Kyle turned and retraced his steps. He held the phone out. "If you don't mind having the phone of the guy you were accused of murdering, I certainly don't. Not to mention the fingerprint thing."

"Kyle!" Kellen's voice was chastising. "Too soon!"

"I'm just saying. Like it or not, it should be considered."

Devlin blinked hard. "Fingerprints?"

"I'm assuming your fingerprints are currently not on Ronny's phone," Kyle said. "Am I wrong?"

Devlin gave a backhanded waving gesture. "You keep the phone. Just give it to Coach or Jack."

Kyle nodded and pocketed the phone again. "Can we please go now?"

Emma stepped beside him and nudged him with her shoulder. "Amen, Mr. CSI."

By the time the five emerged into the meadow at the top of Logan's Bluff, patches of clouds had moved in to obscure the meager light offered by the quarter moon. Devlin's truck was barely visible only fifty yards away.

"I hate this place," Devlin said.

"I'll bet," Kyle said. He couldn't think of anything else to say.

"Give me a sec." Devlin turned toward the tree line to their left. "Gotta drain the main."

Kyle actually felt sorry for Devlin and marveled at how well he appeared to be holding up. The emotional cement mixer he had been in over the past few weeks, and especially the last four days, was almost unimaginable. Betrayal by his former friend with his girlfriend, Lena. Staging of a fight in his last football game to preserve his honor and salvage a tenuous relationship. The murder of his friend, the suspicion that his mother had done it, and maintaining his silence to protect her amidst his own arrest. The realization of the depth of his mother's betrayal, from hiding her drug use to allowing him to take the fall for her. And now, a visit to the place where it all happened, knowing the murderer responsible for most of it—or could it be all of it? —was still on the loose. It really was unbelievable that he was doing as well as he was.

Devlin emerged from the shadows and headed toward his truck without saying a word. Whether it was collective respect for his somber sentiment or mental exhaustion from Kellen's near disaster, no one else spoke as they moved toward the truck.

Kyle contemplated where things might go from there. He hoped his father would let him help with the case since he had proven his worth by solving the riddle, although he doubted it. Case Reynolds—he might just start referring to his father by his proper name the way Kellen liked to do—had a way of underestimating his abilities, since he wasn't into sports and such. If

Dad didn't let him help, then so be it. Proffit's Project, as he liked to call it, could occupy his extra time. As for his father—er, Case—he would be none too pleased with that development. But what he didn't know wouldn't hurt him.

It was like Proffit said, though. Sometimes the greater good is more important than trivial legalities, laws made by people who don't understand the nuances of individual situations. Buster needed their help. To be more precise, his mother did. No, Devlin wasn't the only one around who was suffering. Buster had lost a brother and was about to lose a mother too. The least Kyle could do was help them both by doing what he does best. Whether his dad approved or not.

Speaking of Buster, where was he, anyway? Kyle had overhead his mother say he had raced out of the courtroom after Devlin's arraignment, and no one had been able to find him for questioning. They were hoping he would show up for the funeral tomorrow. Some even suspected he might have killed his brother. Rumors were that both were involved in illegal drug sales and that something might have gone bad between them. Deep down, Kyle had difficulty imagining either as being the case, though. People just didn't understand what they were trying to do. Who wouldn't help their mother, whatever it took? On the other hand, even the worst of the worst loved their mothers, didn't they?

Devlin unlocked the truck with his key fob, and they all climbed in simultaneously.

Emma broke the silence. "Good work there, Kyle. I knew you had it."

"Kellen too." Devlin smiled back over his shoulder. "Even though you almost got us both killed."

"First of all, I wasn't going to fall. Second of all, you looked pretty safe on that solid rock above me."

"I'm not talking about falling. I'm talking about what I said. Jack and Coach would have both killed me for letting it happen."

Kyle was glad to see Devlin's mood lifting, but it was time to go. He tapped Devlin's headrest. "Get us on home, now. They'll be wondering where we are soon." He pulled out his phone to confirm neither parent had texted him. With any luck, they would beat Dad home. It would be better to be handing over Ronny's phone at the moment they had to tell him they had sneaked out.

Devlin complied and pointed the Tacoma back down the access road. He adjusted the radio settings, and rhythmic, folksy rolls of an electric guitar filled the air. The voice that joined them was clear and edgy, like the guy next door who shocks you because you had no idea he could sing like that.

"Interesting," Emma said. "Your playlist?"

Devlin shrugged and began singing along, his voice subdued but right on pitch.

Kyle didn't know Devlin that well but thought they might have more in common than he had realized. "Who is that?"

"Aaron Burdett. It's called 'Wolves at the Door.'" Devlin resumed singing, his head bobbing with the anthemic beat.

"You should hear Dev play guitar too." Lena patted his shoulder.

The headlights revealed the blacktop of Waterway Road perpendicular to them ahead, and Devlin slowed to navigate some ruts at the edge. He began to turn the truck to the right, to take them away from the river and back toward town, and his voice rose with the steady arc of the truck, suddenly full of ache and soul like that of the artist lamenting the presence of untold evil preying upon his family and his burden of protecting them from it.

Blue lights and a siren blast exploded in front of them, causing Devlin to jerk the wheel violently to the left. All of them jumped, and more than one of them shouted expletives. Devlin kept going with the hard turn and pressed his right foot toward the floor, gunning the engine to escape the blue flashing monster. The truck teetered heavy onto two wheels causing Lena and Kellen to slam into their doors and the others into the unyielding tether of their seatbelts.

"What are you doing?" Lena screamed. "It's the cops! You gotta stop!"

"I don't know! I don't know!" Devlin yelled. He yanked the wheel to the right, and the overcorrection jolted them all again. "I can't go back to jail! I'm not!"

"Did you eat any more of those brownies I gave you the other day?" Lena's voice was full of panic.

"Brownies? Who cares about brownies? No! Just Friday after the game. I've been in jail, if you recall."

The siren had only pulsed one time to alert them initially, but it was back again now in full force, sounding the alarm as it bore down on them from behind, its waves arrhythmic to the rotation of the blinding blue rooftop lights.

Devlin gunned it again.

"They had some weed in them," Lena said. "You don't need to be high!"

"I'm not high!" Devlin said.

Kyle craned his neck to see what was happening behind them. Their acceleration gained some separation, but only briefly. The law vehicle, whatever it was, was on them again in seconds. "You've got to stop, Devlin!"

Devlin ignored them and settled into a cruising speed of about sixty, moving into the middle of the road.

"Devlin, please pull over," Kellen said with remarkable calm in her voice. "There's nowhere to go. This road ends at the Lock and Dam."

Devlin began pounded the steering wheel with his open palm. He rubbed his head in a gesture of distress, and his hand was shaking. Lena was crying.

"We don't even know what they want," Kyle said. "It's going to be okay." He didn't know if that was true or not, but there was no doubt what would happen if Devlin continued this madness.

"I can't go to jail," he repeated. "And they'll take Ronny's phone." There was a quiver in his voice.

"Who cares about the phone?" Lena said. "They'll shoot you if you don't stop!"

Kellen nudged Kyle. "Give me your phone."

"What? Why?"

She gave him a hard, wide-eyed look and showed him the screen on her phone. "Do you have anything on yours you might not want them to see?"

Did she know what he had been up to? How? And why would anyone search his phone? He was just a passenger; he couldn't make Devlin stop if he didn't want to. Then it dawned on him. He nodded and they made a swap without another word.

"Please, please stop," Lena sobbed.

Before Devlin had to make a decision, it was essentially made for him. The road ended at the base of the Lock and Dam tower in a small parking lot. Devlin swung the truck around, and for a brief moment Kyle feared the law vehicle might T-bone them. Instead, Devlin slammed on the brakes, and what could now be seen to be an Amberton Police patrol car slid in beside them at just the angle needed to block their exit. Two officers popped from the front seat and began screaming at them to come out of the vehicle slowly, with hands raised. It was too much of a blur and too dark to see for sure, but their body language made it clear their guns were raised and pointed at the occupants of one gray Tacoma, undoubtedly known by now to belong to Devlin James.

"Out of the vehicle now!" they yelled again. Kyle recognized their voices as Wayne Rappaport and Deputy Nash. "Hands above your heads!"

The girls opened their doors and complied. "Don't shoot! Please, God, don't shoot!" Lena screamed.

Kyle stumbled out behind Emma and stopped. Devlin's door wasn't open yet. He grabbed the driver's door and opened it, ignoring the yells of the officers. "Come on, Devlin. There's nothing good gonna happen if you stay in there."

Devlin nodded and slid out of his seat with hands in the air.

"On your knees, all of you!" the sheriff growled. "Keep those hands up!"

"Why, it's just them kids, Sheriff," Nash said in his low drawl. "That's Case's kids right there, them twins. What are y'all doing here?"

"Shush, Nash. I'll ask the questions."

Kyle shifted positions to get off a rock trying to bury itself in his kneecap, awaiting instructions to fall to the ground face first, but they never came. Instead, the sheriff approached them like a lion stalking its prey, low and slow, eyes narrowed. "I should arrest all of you right now. Mr. James, you didn't get enough of jail already? And I can't wait to tell Mr. Do-gooder crime fighter what his kids are up to."

"We didn't do anything," Kellen said. "Just riding around."

"Oh, is that why you almost ran off the road speeding away, evading an officer?"

"You startled us is all," Kyle said. That was at least half true.

"I'll startle you alright, when I slam the bars in your face."

Kellen raised her chin defiantly. "Kyle and I are only fourteen, the rest of us not much older. I'm pretty sure you don't slam bars in the face of juveniles for being passengers in a speeding vehicle. At least, that's what I've gathered from numerous conversations with the county attorney."

"I think she's talking about her momma," Nash said.

"I know what she's talking about," Rappaport said through gritted teeth, "and I don't care."

Kyle snickered. Kellen might get them all thrown in the river before the night was up, but she would do it in pure Reynolds style.

"To your feet, all of you," Rappaport said. "Empty your pockets."

"Pockets?" Devlin said. "You got no right!"

The sheriff laughed. "I have every right to search your pockets, your vehicle, and where you hide your toe jam if I want to. Now empty 'em."

They followed his orders to put everything on the ground at their feet. Kyle put a phone on the concrete along with a small pocketknife, his wallet, and a dried buckeye he kept for good luck. Other than their personal phones, no one else had anything of significance.

"Interesting, Mr. Reynolds. You think I'm stupid? What's that in your front pocket?" He nodded at Nash, who patted Kyle down and forced him to fish it out.

"Look what he's hiding, boss," Nash drawled.

Rappaport took the phone from Nash and examined it. He scowled at Kyle. "Two phones? Only people I know who do that are drug dealers. You a drug dealer? You or somebody better start talking. The better the info you give me, the better your chances are of not getting crammed into this patrol car like clown midgets."

Kyle had never seen clown midgets and had no idea what they would have to do with anything, but he got the gist of it. And if they were anything like that Stephen King clown, he wanted nothing to do with them. "Okay, okay. We went to Logan's Bluff. Trying to help figure out what happened to Ronny."

"Be quiet, Kyle," Devlin said. "They'll take me, but you haven't done anything."

"I knew it!" Rappaport shot Nash a goofy, crooked smile. "They think they're crime fighters too!" He turned his gaze to Kyle and Kellen. "And just like their daddy, all they'll do is screw everything up."

"Really?" Kellen said. "So you solved the riddle? You know, the poem from the witness?"

Kyle grimaced. No need to share that information, but Kellen couldn't stand it. Given the opportunity, she would load as many zingers as she could and fire them in rapid succession until the chamber was empty.

Rappaport frowned and glanced at Nash. "Riddle? What witness?"

"I knew it!" The voice off to their side startled them all. "I knew that guy had something to do with it!" Kyle squinted to try to see who it was, but he didn't recognize him. He was slender, like a scarecrow with a wisp of graying hair on top and a glowing cigarette between his index and middle fingers.

"Greely, now don't be sticking your nose in police business," Nash said.

Greely glanced up at the control tower. "Just coming down for a smoke is all. I get two breaks a shift." He looked at Kellen. "It's that man ridin' the river on that table, ain't it?"

Kyle liked how he used present tense, like Perry was riding a table at that very moment. Heck, maybe he was.

Rappaport's face told the tale. No one had shared that information with him, either. "Shut up with your nonsense, Greely. We don't care what weirdo stuff you've seen this week." He turned back to Kellen. "What are you talking about, riddles and witnesses?"

Kellen ignored the question. "I'm sure you knew about Ronny's extra phone, right?"

"Quiet, Kellen!" Devlin insisted again. "Sheriff, just take me on in. I freaked out, okay? Couldn't stand the idea of going to jail again, even if I didn't do anything. I can tell you, everybody else is innocent. They tried to stop me from running."

Rappaport grunted. He leaned in close to Kellen's face. "I can assure you, my investigation is going just fine. But if you or anyone else here is withholding evidence, there will be a steep price to pay." He smiled and moved back to confront Kyle. "Ronny's phone, huh? That sounds like a useful piece of information. And believe me, I will find out how you came up with it."

Kyle sighed and mouthed *Sorry* to Devlin.

"Head up, boy. No need to cry about it. It's in the hands of somebody who knows what to do with it now. Just pray you didn't come by this by some nefarious means."

"I know it was that dude on the table. Had to be," Greely chimed in.

Rappaport pointed to the control tower, flexed his elbow, and pointed hard again. Greely nodded and headed back to work. Rappaport moved behind Devlin and smiled as he removed handcuffs from his belt. "Now then. Devlin James, you're under arrest. Seems like I've heard those words very recently. For reckless driving and resisting arrest this time, though. Who knows? We may even work up a murder charge again before it's all said and done." He picked up the keys at Devin's feet and tossed them to his deputy as he guided Devlin toward the patrol car. "Nash, drive these other yahoos home. I've got this one."

THIRTY-NINE

JACK studied the dessert menu at Dundee's while I tapped my foot impatiently. Maybe he had a flexible schedule, but I had to be at school at 7:30 the next morning. And even though I suspected that Abi had dozed off since she hadn't texted me, that wouldn't last all night. She would awaken, and if I was out too late, she would give me grief about fighting other people's battles at my family's expense, not to mention my own. Abi was a believer in the positive health benefits of adequate sleep. The older I got, the more convinced I became that she was right.

Finally, I couldn't take it any longer. "Let's go, man. I'm telling you, I know where the clue is at Logan's, but we can't find it sitting here thinking about pecan pie. I'll buy you a Snickers on the way."

Jack held up a finger to tell me he hadn't yet made up his mind, but the staticky voice suddenly arising from the radio at his side averted the next in a long line of trivial arguments between us over the years. "Officers in pursuit of gray Toyota Tacoma, license 18DJ18. On Waterway Road, headed east, toward the lock."

I knew that number and those initials all too well. "Is that—?"

"Devlin." Jack slammed his napkin down on the table and fished two twenty-dollar bills from his wallet to lay beside it. "Dang it, Dev! I'm gonna kill him. Let's go. Don't know who's chasing him or what he did, but let's get there before something stupid happens."

My fears that Jack might get us killed before we got to the waterway were only heightened when he couldn't get Sheriff Rappaport or Nash to answer him on the radio or their phones. He sped through every turn and ran through every intersection. "This can't be good," he kept saying over and over.

"There!" I spotted the patrol vehicle marked Amberton Police Department up ahead in the small lot near the Lock and Dam control tower. "But where is Devlin's truck?"

"This can't be good," Jack repeated. "Can't be."

Maybe it was a false alarm. A misunderstanding of some sort. Maybe the relay of the truck and license plate information was erroneous, though that seemed highly unlikely. "We're about to find out," I said. "Hope Rap hasn't done something stupid."

Jack pulled up parallel to the other vehicle from the opposite direction, window down.

Sheriff Rappaport rolled down his window and rolled his eyes. "Figured you couldn't stay away long."

"That is protocol for backup in such situations, Sheriff," Jack said. "It would help if you would answer my calls."

"We've been busy."

"Did you call in a chase of a Tacoma?"

"Don't quiz me, Jack. I'll make you a crossing guard at the nursing home before you can say 'Old Timer's.'"

Jack's jaw clenched but he held a straight face. "Just seeing what help you might need."

I wanted to blurt out "Alzheimer's" but held my tongue. I couldn't care less whether Rap thought I was quizzing him or not, but I didn't want to fluster him into not answering our question.

"Where's Devlin, Sheriff? The call said you were chasing his truck. What happened?"

Rap sneered at me with a contemptuous grin. "I'll bet you of all people would love to know, huh?"

His facial expressions often made me want to punch him, but something in his eyes this time sent a chill rushing over me. "What are you talking about?"

Rap turned to Nash and spoke loudly enough to make sure I heard him. "They got here fast, but I wonder how fast ol' Hong Kong Phooey there would have made Jack drive if he'd known his kids were in that truck?"

The chill rushing over me turned fire hot, and I lost it. I was out of Jack's truck and around the front of it before even I knew it. I aimed for Rappaport's door, seeing red and intent on getting an answer, whatever it took. *Don't have that look in your weaselly eyes and mention my kids, I don't care who you are.*

The black bore of a forty caliber Glock stopped me short. Rappaport had it up and pointed at my head through the window with scarcely a flinch. "I'd stop right there, Mr. Reynolds. Nash, did you see him come at me in an aggressive, attacking manner? Would a pull of the trigger be justified?"

"Sheriff!" Jack said, out of his truck now.

"I think he's unarmed, Sheriff," Nash drawled. "Might not be justified."

"Ever seen that show, *Justified*, Mr. Reynolds? I think Raylan Givens might deem it necessary to pull the trigger under such a threatening situation."

I didn't know if this man had the cojones to shoot or not, but my estimation was that he was so incompetent it didn't matter. He might just pull the trigger on accident. "Easy, now Sheriff. I came over here to talk. You said something about my kids."

"Do you always rush upon people like a wounded Cape buffalo when you want to just talk? Because that could make it difficult to find new friends."

"Sheriff." Jack eased up to put himself between me and the sheriff. "He didn't mean anything. We're all just on edge."

I frowned at Jack and put my elbow out to stop him. "Let me just back away, Sheriff, and we'll talk like peaceful adults."

Rappaport shook his head and opened his car door without altering his weapon's aim. He gestured toward his back seat. "We're gonna be peaceful, alright. You're coming with me."

"I didn't do anything."

"Assaulting an officer of the law."

Nothing had made any sense for several days now, from the moment Devlin James and Ronny Shane tied up on the football field Friday night to the murder of Ronny hours later to Devlin's arrest to Devlin being chased to this moment where I was being arrested for walking too fast.

"There's no weapon and no contact," Jack said.

"He's right," Nash concurred.

"Shut up, both of you!"

Nothing made sense. Nothing at all. I was being arrested for next to nothing, but Devlin was nowhere around after evading arrest? And what did he say about my kids? "I didn't do anything, Sheriff," I said. "But I'll come with you without saying another word if you'll answer my question."

Rappaport glared at me and answered with only a wiggle of his gun.

"Where are Devlin and Kyle and Kellen? A high-speed chase is much more of a danger than what I did."

Rappaport holstered his pistol and chuckled with a smirk. "Things ain't always what they seem. Especially when you think you know more than you do." He turned and peered into the cruiser. "Show 'em what we got, Nash."

Deputy Nash held up a black cell phone and tilted it back and forth. "Jackpot."

"We supposed to know what that is?" Jack asked.

Rappaport shook his head and heaved a satisfied breath like he had just eaten his last bite at an all-you-can eat buffet. "Nope, I reckon not, but I'll tell you. Y'all's offspring—wait, I guess not yours, Jack—had sense enough to find Ronny Shane's phone somewhere up there." He nodded toward Logan's Bluff in the distance. "But not enough sense to hold on to it."

My heart sunk. Surely not. *The internuncio. The messenger. The truth!*

"No worries, though. I'll have all the info I need from it to solve this case by morning. My guess is young Mr. James was hoping to destroy this first chance he got. Phone conversations can be quite incriminating."

I turned to Jack, anxious and confused, hoping something he could say would clarify what was happening.

Jack was in no condition to clarify anything. He looked like the captain of a ship going down with his doomed vessel.

FORTY

KYLE answered on the first ring, and I kept my internal vow not to yell at him. With Kellen you could raise your voice if needed, but Kyle would withdraw like a turtle into its shell. I told him to wake his mother up, ask her to have Lily ready, and don't leave the house if he and his sister ever wanted to see the light of day again. Jack and I would be there shortly.

They were sitting at the kitchen bar when we walked in. Their elbows were on the granite, their expressions similar, as they often were, this time an interesting conflation of angst and eager anticipation. While they often shared mannerisms and even thoughts, it seemed, their personalities and appearances were strikingly different. The spotlight of the moment and the overhead LEDs highlighted both to me in that moment. Kyle, quiet and introspective, pale with a ruddier look when sun swept or stressed, with brown wavy hair and Abi's blue eyes. Kellen, more outgoing and commanding, with olive skin, jet-black hair like her mom but straight, with eyes brown as coffee beans.

"Where's your mother?" I asked.

Kellen held an index finger to her lips then hooked a thumb toward the wall behind her. "In the living room. But Lily's still asleep."

I glared at my two kids while Jack tiptoed into the adjacent room. He emerged a few seconds later with a pink backpack on one shoulder, Lily sprawled on the other, and Abi trailing behind. "I'll get her on home," he whispered. He stopped in the open door and winked at Kyle and Kellen. "Good luck."

Abi locked the door behind him and turned to me with a puzzled look. "Good luck? What's going on?"

"Oh, you're not going to believe this."

Abi tilted her head to read me and tucked a wayward curl of black hair behind her ear. I had learned long before not to try to hide things from her, but this time I was happy for my face to read like a billboard. Without a word, she moved around the counter and leaned in on the opposite side to face the kids, elbows propped and fingers intertwined near her chin like a judge hearing riveting testimony from unreliable witnesses. "Somebody better start talking."

"It's not what he thinks, Mom." Kyle turned to Kellen for affirmation.

"Yeah. Kyle had a great idea, and we wanted to help, so we did it."

Abi's eyes grew wide. "Oh no, you better not have—"

"Yes, yes they did." I rapped my fist on the countertop. "Devlin, Lena Cole, Emma Harlow, and these two. At Logan's Bluff mucking up evidence."

"It was a good idea, Dad." Kellen's voice rose. "And it worked too. Sort of." She folded her arms across her chest and lifted her chin in defiance. "Better idea than you or Jack or those idiots at the sheriff's department."

"Watch your tone, missy," Abi said, her voice and jaw both set stronger than her strong-willed daughter's. She held Kellen's gaze with eyes blazing until Kellen looked away, then turned to me. "Case, what is going on?"

I gestured to Kyle and leaned back against our refrigerator. "Let's let the man of great ideas tell it. I'm trembling with breathless anticipation."

Kyle took a deep breath. "So, I knew we must be missing something about the boulder brink. That name Alethia seemed out of place, like maybe it meant something else. We had studied Greek mythology in school. Anyway, I looked it up." He paused. "It means truth."

I think my jaw dropped. He had figured out the real meaning behind the word that sent me and Jack on a time-consuming diversion. "Go on."

"Kellen and I decided there had to be a message hidden at the boulder brink. So we went to find out."

"Snuck out of the house," Abi said. "Where did these other people come in?"

"Devlin happened to be outside, waiting on Dad. They were with him."

"Well, I hope you're happy," Abi said. "Out contaminating evidence while your Dad and Jack are doing real work to solve the case."

Both of the kids grinned, and I wanted to ground them for a year. Their idea and intent had undoubtedly been good, but the results were potentially disastrous. Rappaport now had Ronny's phone, and the number of ways that could go wrong were untold. He seemed intent on making the murder stick to Devlin, and I wouldn't put it past him to destroy evidence if it didn't fit his agenda.

"Wipe the grins off. Abi, believe it or not, they found Ronny's phone. Jack and I had figured out the same thing, but they beat us to it."

Abi poked her lips out in puzzlement and raised one eyebrow. "So you're mad that they beat you to it?"

I chuckled. Abi, the expert interrogator and ever the pragmatist, was turning on me. "Nooo, there's more. Son, why don't you tell her the rest of the story?"

Kyle focused on his mother and held his grin but turned it down a notch in deference to my tone. "Yes, we found the phone. But the sheriff and Deputy Nash stopped us when we were leaving."

"Chased them down, Abi," I interjected. "Called it in on the radio. Jack and I heard it."

Kellen raised her hands. "That was Devlin, not us. We told him to stop."

Abi shook her head. "Good grief. And then?"

"And—"

I held up my hand to interrupt Kyle. "And then Rap claimed the prize, which may ultimately doom Devlin. Or if not that, ruin our chances for finding the actual truth, given his incompetence. The thing is, Jack and I were one piece of pecan pie away from getting there in time to find it ourselves."

"Dad—"

"I don't want to hear any excuses, Kellen." My cheeks burned just considering all the implications. I turned and looked out the window as if something there might point me toward what to do or say next, but there was only black. "Maybe you were trying to do right, but that doesn't change the outcome."

"But Dad—"

"Hush and let me think!"

"Case."

The tone of Abi's voice saying my name stopped me short. There was a message there other than the one to calm down she had used a hundred times before.

I turned to see Kyle holding something up. He laid it on the counter. The grin was broader than before. "Dad, we got the phone."

I blinked hard. A black flip phone was lying on the counter. "Wait, what?"

"We outsmarted ol' Sheriff Rap and Deputy Dog," Kellen said. "Kyle and I traded phones, and he pretended to try to hide mine."

"He took the bait, hook, line, and sinker," Kyle said.

"Why your phone, Kellen?" Abi asked. "Won't he figure that out pretty quickly?"

"I have a generic wallpaper. Kyle has our family photo. And no, he won't, because A, he doesn't know my password, and B, I shut down my phone from my laptop as soon as I got home."

What did wallpaper have to do with phones? And how did one shut down a phone?

Abi appeared to know, because she was nodding. "Pretty slick," she said.

I reached for the phone. "Let me see that." It was nondescript, a brand I didn't recognize. I opened it, but the screen was black. I set it back down. "Battery's dead."

"Likely a burner phone," Abi said to me. "Everyone says Ronny had an iPhone, but it wasn't on his body. Most of us figure it's at the bottom of the river. No luck so far trying to get at his info on the cloud." She turned to the kids. "I'm curious. Dad said Devlin ran from the sheriff. How did he not get arrested?"

Kellen smiled. "Another interesting story. Thank Emma Harlow for that."

"Speaking of," I said, "please also explain how the person who got Devlin arrested to begin with is now hanging out with him."

"I got the scoop on the ride back. You know Lena is her stepsister," Kellen said. "Sort of. Lena's mom and Emma's dad were married for a couple years. Didn't work out. Anyway, Lena thought Devlin might be cheating on her. So she asked Emma to find out. Thus, the video."

"Yeah, it's messed up," Kyle added. "Lena was messing with Devlin and Ronny both but was spying on Devlin. Emma said the whole videoing thing wasn't her finest moment. But she thought Devlin was guilty."

"Plus," Kellen said, "Lena feels guilty for giving Devlin brownies with the weed in them that showed up on the drug test."

"Sounds like Lena Cole isn't having many fine moments at all." Abi's frown dripped with the kind of disapproval only a mother can have for another female.

"Back to Emma," I said. "How in the world did she keep Devlin from being arrested?"

Kellen giggled. "Apparently, our noble, married sheriff is messing around with Ms. Molkentine at school. As Devlin was getting handcuffed, Emma told him how disappointed in her former pupil Ms. Molkentine would be. Sheriff Rap got so flustered we all thought he might arrest Nash instead."

I broke into a laugh. Hilda Molkentine was an adequate math teacher, but she was as unattractive and unfriendly as her last name was unusual in Amberton. To think Sheriff Rappaport was that tangled up with her was delightful.

Abi wasn't as amused. "Emma better be careful. Rap can be vindictive, as we know."

Kellen shook her head. "Emma says he won't mess with her. Said something about her mother can make his life miserable with her job."

That was a puzzler. I thought Dana Harlow was an accountant. Did she work for the IRS or something? I certainly wouldn't put tax evasion past Rap.

Kyle caught my attention. He had gone silent, digging in a drawer. "Look." He dangled a black cord. "Found a charger that will fit it. Probably gonna need a password though."

"Buster should be at the funeral tomorrow," Kellen offered. "Maybe he'll know."

"Maybe, honey," Abi said, "but I'm not sure how you approach that. 'Buster, I know this is your brother's funeral, and I know you were dealing drugs with him. Do you mind telling us his phone password?'"

Kyle snickered. Kellen rolled her eyes.

I sighed. The reality of it was that we were no better off with Ronny's phone than Rap was with Kellen's.

FORTY-ONE

Wednesday, October 31, 2018

BUSTER was there in the receiving line with his sister, beside Ronny's coffin at the front of the church. A few out-of-town aunts, uncles, and cousins sat in the pews nearby, speaking to the few who recognized them or offered condolences out of obligation, but Ronny's siblings stood alone. It was a rueful sight, made worse by the knowledge their mother was on her death bed and their father had put himself in the ground by the bottle so many years before. "A man with unfulfilled promise," my father had once commented.

I sat on one of the middle rows with Abi since I didn't really know the Shanes, but Jack went through the line with Devlin who had, after all, been friends with Ronny for longer than they were enemies. Tammy was nowhere to be found. I watched Buster's reaction closely as Devlin approached, but it revealed very little. They eyed each other a second, then Buster leaned in and whispered something to Devlin. Devlin shook his head, and Jack bristled but said nothing. Then they exchanged cursory hugs, and Devlin and Jack moved along.

Rappaport, Nash, and another deputy watched the proceedings from the opposite side of the aisle. They had told Abi that out of respect they would wait until after the funeral to talk to Buster, but that was it.

He hadn't garnered any favorable will by making himself

scarce for the past few days. Word was that he had been around, but no one could seem to catch him at home or his usual hangouts, and he wasn't answering or returning calls. The only thing that had been accomplished was raising the suspicion he was involved, and that level was rising by the minute. Once Ronny was laid to rest, Buster would be in a spotlight until the case was resolved, and maybe beyond. Even if not guilty of the murder, he was guilty of something. Everybody knew it.

Janie joined us just before the funeral began. She was as pretty as usual, with a petite nose, round cheeks, and brown hair similar to Jack's, minus the gray. She wore a navy dress with a cream-colored floral pattern. She reminded me of her mother Michelle, Jack's sister, more and more with each passing year. I hadn't seen a photo of Michelle in a long time, but being in Janie's presence certainly took me back in time. She slid in beside Devlin and patted his knee. There were tears in her eyes, and the funeral hadn't even begun. Was she there for Jack and Devlin, or had she known Ronny? Probably all of the above. In a small town like Amberton, almost everyone knew everyone, and Janie had a tender heart.

The Haughton football team filed in wearing their jerseys and took up the rows at the front of the church to the right. Another high school kid from Haughton began the ceremony with an acoustic guitar rendition of Vince Gill's "Go Rest High on That Mountain." Abi whispered that the kid had received a call back after his audition for *American Idol*, and a lot of people thought he had a chance. I didn't doubt it. His voice moved me, and I didn't even know Ronny. Evidently he did, because he struggled mightily to finish.

The choir sang a couple of more songs while my mind wandered, then an ancient preacher with perfectly combed but incongruously black hair took to the pulpit. For the next twenty minutes he worked fervently to preach us all into heaven to one day join Ronny, while my mind wandered some more.

The service ended with a prayer and the usual procession to the cemetery out back of the church. I wanted to go ahead and leave, but Abi wouldn't let me. We lingered at the periphery as we had inside, while the family gathered into their designated chairs under the tent beside the casket. The preacher got everyone's attention with his booming baritone voice and set in again to saving those who weren't yet convinced.

Before my thoughts could wander again, movement on the front captured my attention. Buster was leaning to the side, close enough for his sister to whisper something up to him. He removed his navy jacket, which seemed poised to burst anyway, and placed it around her shoulders. He put his left arm around her and squeezed, and I could see his triceps ripple from where I was standing. Men's muscles didn't normally intrigue me, but his tattoo caught my eye. Some type of foliage and a missile or rocket or similar peeked out from beneath his short-sleeved shirt. The juxtaposition of them was both unusual and, for some reason, familiar.

I grabbed Abi's hand and turned to leave simultaneous with the "Amen" of the final prayer, a suitable compromise in my opinion. If I had to stay for the graveside service, I didn't have to stay and make small talk afterward. I nodded at Rappaport and his cronies, who appeared poised to corner Buster as promised.

Jack grabbed my shoulder and stopped me. "I'm gonna stay a minute." I didn't have to ask why. Based on the look on Jack's face when Buster had spoken to Devlin earlier, Jack planned to be right beside Rappaport when he questioned Buster.

Jack turned to Janie. "I think it's safe now for you and Lily to come home. Give Kellen a twenty when you pick her up. Tell Meg thanks for letting y'all stay."

Janie nodded. "Sounds good. But I want to speak to the family before I go."

Jack frowned but didn't ask why. "Okay… but make it quick. Other people are gonna want to talk to him."

Devlin nodded toward the parked vehicles. "Coach, I'll walk with y'all. No reason for me to stick around. I drove, anyway." We meandered through the maze of open ground between the tombstones for a moment before Devlin stopped where a cedar-lined gravel drive intersected our path. He pointed to our right. "My ride."

His gray Tacoma, made semi-famous locally by the Emma Harlow video and in my household by the incident at the waterway the night before, was parked facing away from us about fifty feet away. 18DJ18, the tag read. I remembered Rappaport's call of it when Devlin was racing away from him. Something about it struck me then, and it struck me now. Something more than the memory of number eighteen playing his heart out for me the past three football seasons.

"Hang in there, Dev." I patted him on the shoulder as he turned to move away. "Get all this behind you, okay?"

He stopped and hung his head for a second, toeing the gravel. "Gotta figure some stuff out."

Abi grimaced in empathy and wrapped him in a bear hug. "We're here for you if you need us, okay, hon?" She pushed back to arms' length to look him in the eye. "What about your mom?"

Devlin shrugged and looked away. "Haven't seen her. We were supposed to meet for lunch and talk today, but…"

"I'm sure she's fine." I reached out to shake his hand and

made sure he looked me in the eye. I spoke in my coach voice he had responded to so many times before. "You be tough enough, now, you hear?"

Devlin nodded and walked away.

"Bless his heart," Abi said. "Jack is gonna have to be a rock for him."

I told her I would check on Devlin later, too, but to hold on just a second. I reached into my jacket pocket and pulled out the phone Kyle and Kellen had found.

"What are you doing?" Abi rolled her eyes. "Here? Now?"

"Just got an idea." I turned it on and held my breath while I punched four numbers: 8282. If Devlin thought enough of his football number to put it on his license plate, might Ronny do the same for a phone? I had already tried his birthday and the date of his father's death with no luck.

Bingo.

The screen lit up a light blue color and waited on me to tell it what to do next.

"You got it?" Abi reached out to take the phone from me, but I was already turning it over to her. She was much more tech savvy than me. She tapped a few buttons, and her eyes grew wide, their blue as bright as the screen. "Oh my."

I moved beside her to see what she had found.

"Looks like Ronny deletes—deleted—his messages on this phone every day, so there's only messages from Friday and early Saturday. Either the battery died then, or everyone who would've messaged him heard that he was dead. Word did spread fast. Anyway, no names in the contacts here, just numbers. This one has to be Buster."

Bro, what's up today?

Business as usual call you later

G luck on game tonight. Come over after we need to talk
Thx.
Maybe. Got some meetings after. Gotta settle some scores
Where
LB
Ok but dont be stupid or I'll settle you
haha
Sorry bout the loss. Call me
Hey call me
You good?
Where u at

Seeing the messages between brothers in the hours just before and shortly after one of them was killed brought tears to my eyes. The last one was early Saturday morning. What a waste, what a waste.

"What you think, Counselor? Buster kinda threatened him there. Then either became alarmed when Ronny didn't answer later that night, or he texted him to cover his tracks."

Abi nodded. "Yep. The times on these would match either possibility." She brought up another text string with a few punches of her thumb. "Look at this one."

Ronny we need to meet. Now.
I ain't talkin about me and dev
but if you need stuff logans bluff midnight
I'll be there.
Be on time got somethin else at 1230

"That's gotta be Tammy," I said, "based on what she told Jack."

"Assuming that's the truth. Who knows?" Abi thumbed up another one and studied it for several seconds. "This one started as an outgoing message at 10:15 Friday night."

Did my part
Yes and I'll do mine like I said. 1230
be there
might sell you something else for a change
Not a chance. Finished with u after tonight. Not playing w u
u neither

"That's him and Devlin, huh?" I asked. "Faked the fight, agreed to meet up for Devlin to pay up."

"Doesn't sound like old friends, does it?"

"Contentious to say the least. That 'finished with you' part isn't a good look for Devlin if he remains a suspect."

Abi shook her head. "He isn't. At least, not right now."

The only other message there was a single, incoming, unanswered one, undoubtedly from Ronny's mother. I wondered if she normally used his other number but tried this one to make sure he got her message. It broke my heart.

Wish I could be there tonight. Just too sick but doesn't
mean I don't care. Love u all the way all day.

"That's tough to read," Abi said. "Terrible."

"I feel like we're violating his privacy."

"We're trying to solve his murder, which we both have a vested interest in doing. But your point is well taken. We need to turn this over to Rap." Abi smiled. "And get Kellen's phone back, I suppose. Oh, the look on his face will be worth videoing."

I chuckled. "Maybe we can get Emma Harlow to come along as a bonus." It was nice to share a laugh under the circumstances, but it was short lived. "Let's show Jack what we've got first. He is a deputy, after all. Maybe he's gotten some info from Buster by now."

Abi pivoted to head back to the tent where Jack and

the others were. "You know what we're not seeing, and it's frustrating?"

"Lately, a lot of things."

"No, seriously. There is nothing earth shattering here. Naturally, Perry must have thought that Ronny's phone would bare all, but we've struck out again."

Abi was right. The texts were only confirmation of what we had already gathered. I turned and followed her. "We will just have to find out some other way." I wanted to believe that the word *we* was out of place, that now I could just walk away and let others handle it. With Abi still peripherally involved, it was best if I was not. Plus, Jack had only asked me to help clear Devlin's name. Mission accomplished, right?

The question to myself was rhetorical, and I didn't like the answer. This would not be the first time I had pushed things too far in search of the truth. Perhaps it would be the last.

FORTY-TWO

AFTER the funeral I headed back to the school and told Abi I would meet her at the Halloween festival. She thought nothing of me going back to finish up my day's work since I had left early, but with football season being over, there was no rush on much of anything. I had all winter to clean up and prepare for the next season. I just needed to think.

The field house was dark and quiet inside as I expected. The uniforms and equipment had all been washed and cleaned, but the musty smell of sweat never totally disappeared. It was a comforting aroma. Whenever the world went crazy, that place, with its singularity of purpose, was always a haven. I unlocked my office and settled into my worn pleather chair, ignoring the photos and coaching books and memorabilia scattered on the walls and bookshelves. My computer desktop popped a colorful photo of a place I would never visit when I inadvertently tapped the mouse, but I didn't login.

Where did we go now? I truly wanted to walk away, but did I have an obligation to press on? Ronny Shane was just a number on a jersey before Saturday morning, but now we were connected. Despite my best efforts, many of my own players had wandered off the right path over the years, leaving me questioning what I could have done to better influence them. I didn't know Haughton's coach well but suspected he must feel similarly. The difference between us was that I was involved in the case in ways he wouldn't—couldn't—ever be. Under the circumstances as they had unfolded, did I have a responsibility to get justice for Ronny like I would if he was one of mine?

I wanted to talk to Jack again, but he was busy, having left the funeral in search of Tammy after I told him what Devlin had said about her standing him up for lunch. Jack's attitude toward Tammy seemed to be trending toward an end to their relationship, but he still felt a sense of obligation to her. We were kindred spirits in that way, loyal to a fault toward our goals and our friends alike, ever since we were kids. That ideology had almost cost us our lives on more than one occasion.

My buddy Jet Townsend, the greatest mind I had ever met, would be a good one to talk things over with as well, but he was even busier than Jack. He and Gracie had left the country the day before for Africa on a medical mission trip. Abi had already shown me a photo of them surrounded by snaggletoothed children with smiles as bright and broad as the midday sand on a Florida beach. Jet and Gracie had not been able to have children of their own, so fostering and missions had been their way of parenting.

My other option was my father. The former sheriff was a wealth of information and experience. But he would want to know the whole story—every detail—and would extract it, one way or the other. His ability to do that was uncanny. The problem was that would lead to one of several outcomes, none of them ideal.

First, his loathing for Wayne Rappaport, the man who had coerced his ouster as sheriff, would rile him so that he might burst into the sheriff's department itself and lecture Rap about his shortcomings and ineptitude in the case. His patience wasn't as long as it used to be.

Second, Dad would lecture me to no end about how I

needed to stick to coaching, stay out of Abi's business, and avoid bringing danger home with me.

Third, after tiring of his criticism, I might get so angry I would point out a similar case that occurred a couple of years after Abi and I moved back to Amberton. Dad, among others, had falsely accused an Amberton basketball player of killing a teacher, and that kid had to clear his own name— something Devlin had thus far not proven able to do. It was a rare misstep in Dad's career, with no long-term consequences once the truth came out. But it still haunted him, and I never spoke of it. But sometimes my temper got the best of me.

As I heard his booming voice in my head and imagined those things and their repercussions, my decision was made. I would leave former sheriff Rex Reynolds out of this. But then I heard his voice one more time, reciting one of a half dozen tenets he had repeated so many times at the dinner table to Mom when discussing cases. "It's the ones closest to them until it's not."

Buster.

Buster Shane was the key to it all. He knew something that would solve the mystery, and the fact that Rappaport and his team had not gleaned it from him meant nothing. It could not be a coincidence that he had been avoiding questioning ever since the murder. In fact, when Rap and Jack had tried to talk to him after the funeral earlier, he had disappeared again. They thought he likely climbed over the fence and disappeared into the trees on the back side of the cemetery. Someone surely picked him up on the gravel road a few hundred feet beyond.

I knew where Buster lived only because one of my assistant coaches had rented the place for a time. When I was helping him move out, Buster had popped in to do a walkthrough uninvited. It annoyed me, but my coach didn't seem to mind. "He wants to know whether to rent it or not, so why not?" he had said. Buster was about my height but evidently much more of a fixture in the weight room than I had ever been. I could see why he had been an All-State football player at Haughton.

Instead of driving up to Buster's front door and risk being seen by him or any number of deputies likely assigned to look for him, I pulled into the driveway of a home off the third fairway of Amberton Country Club. The two-story colonial dwarfed a three-car garage to the side that was as large as my house.

Roosevelt Pringle had made a small fortune developing commercial real estate in nearby Tupelo, his business bolstered by his constant support of Elvis Presley-themed events attracting hordes of fans to the city where the star had been born. But Pringle always called Amberton home, and all three of his boys played football there. He had given me permission years before to use his golf cart to play the course any time I wanted, and I took him up on it on occasion. I doubted he would approve of the use of his cart I had planned now; he might find it odd that I was playing so near twilight. Fortunately, the lights were off. No explanation needed. The Pringles weren't home.

I parked to the side and entered the punch code to open the door to the end bay of the garage. The key to the Club Car was in the ignition as usual. Moments later I was on the golf course moving down the cart path, headed toward Buster's house. The chilly punch of the evening breeze was magnified by the speed of the cart, and I wished I had added a jacket.

I didn't spot anyone else on the course, which meant I could not be inconspicuous in plain sight. Even the most die-hard golfers were off the course well before nightfall this time of year. Still, since there was only a single road in and out by automobile, my chances of evading someone if surprised were better by golf cart. There were dozens of points of egress from the course that way, to numerous streets ten minutes away from the club by car.

Buster's bungalow was situated in the perfect location for someone wanting to avoid attention. It was nestled in a copse of pine trees too far behind the clubhouse to be noticed from it and guarded on two sides by hedges of red tip photinia, which concealed it from golfers on the course. Basically, you had to be going there to get there and be there to see it there.

I parked the cart far enough off the path to be in the shadows and moved along a weathered split-rail fence toward the house, shielded by the red tips and listening for activity. Assuming Buster still didn't want to be found, he wasn't likely to be there. But given his purported side hustle and the events of recent days, who knew what other shady characters might show up? Not to mention Rappaport's crew. Any of them would surely be thrilled to interrogate me—or worse—to find out the reason for my presence.

Was I actually going to break in once I got there if no one was around? What, exactly, was my plan? I didn't have an answer. Suddenly my actions seemed silly, juvenile even. Rappaport loved to accuse me of playing cop. And here I was.

The gravel parking space in front of the house was empty. My watch showed just a few minutes after six. The shadows were lengthening, and the temperature was dropping. I cupped my hands and blew warm air into them while I stopped to think. I decided if I was going to play cop, I didn't need to pretend at spy games too. Stop skulking around. Just knock on the door, right in the wide open, up front and personal if someone answers or sees you. Then go from there.

I crossed the diminutive patch of grass that served as a front lawn and approached the door. The single bulb over the door was off, as was the one inside. The latter gave me pause, as I initially thought I had glimpsed a glow through the front window. I knocked but heard nothing. I knocked again. *Probably best to abort this so-called mission.* But I didn't. Just for kicks I palmed the doorknob and twisted.

To my surprise, the latch bolt gave, and the door swung open. The room was dark, as expected, but there was a glow coming from the back. Perhaps that was what I had seen before. Even in the limited light the front room screamed southern male bachelor—a deer mount, outdoor prints, sparse but functional furniture. I took a deep breath and stood in the doorway. "Anybody home? Buster? I don't mean any harm, just want to talk."

Nothing.

I remembered there was a back door and decided to use it for my exit after a quick search of the house. That also gave me a way to escape if someone came in the front, if needed. A short run to the golf cart, and I could speed away. Would it still be breaking and entering if the door was unlocked? Trespassing, at the very least. Was that a misdemeanor or a felony?

My stomach churned, and the thump of my heartbeat broke through the silence. This escapade could cost me my job, my career. In the world of teaching and coaching minors, it didn't take much in small town Mississippi to get fired and permanently tarnish one's reputation.

In no time I was through the front room and standing in the short hall. I looked back at the front door. The smart play was to back out and leave.

But I had come this far. What if there was an answer just around the corner?

Just walk through the house to the back door and get out. Go home. Never tell a soul.

I crept across the linoleum and noted a small kitchen to my left. A small oven and stove, microwave tucked in the corner of a Formica countertop, two-chair table beneath a window. The counter was bare, but might the drawers hold important information? *Move on. Get out.*

Intent now on getting to and out the back, I passed a tiny bathroom to my right. It emitted a yellow glow from a light over the shower, the only light in the house, which was getting darker by the second. A quick peak in revealed nothing interesting, so I moved on. The hallway opened into the last room of the house, the bedroom. Buster's bed was against the wall to my left, and I spotted the door I had seen from the outside to my right on the back wall. *Get on out.* But something caught my eye on the wall.

It was a small wooden desk, the darkness of its top punctuated by the rectangular paleness of some loose papers on it. Might that be something useful? I chanced turning on my phone light to thumb through them. Utility bills for the house, nothing more. No list of names, sticky notes with phone numbers, or suspicious receipts. A single drawer contained only pens, an old phone charger, some loose change.

Over the desk were two framed photos. One was a pretty young woman with a crooked smile and puffed hair with a part in the middle, I guessed 80s era. The other was a group of military men I didn't recognize. The one in the center looked vaguely familiar and was the only one smiling. His arms were crossed over his chest, and his biceps bulged out of a sleeveless shirt. His left arm had a tattoo I had seen before. It was identical to the one on Buster's arm, with the eagle and olive branch and missile. It still intrigued me, and I still didn't know why.

Hanging beside the photo was a framed handwritten document written in crude block letters with blue ink. It was titled Voices and dated May 26, 2003. Memorial Day? It was not signed. The words drew me in immediately, but I didn't have time to read them all. I snapped a photo. Maybe it contained a clue, but I couldn't imagine how.

I turned my attention back to the soldiers in the photo and snapped a pic to study later.

It was time to go. I clicked off my light and moved to the door and grabbed the knob, stopping to survey the room one last time. Was that all there was to find? I had skipped looking through the kitchen contents but wasn't going back. I had already pushed my luck much too long.

A rectangular black hole stared at me from the opposite wall.

The closet. Was there a more popular place to hide something? One quick look and I would be gone. Buster would never know.

I crossed the ten feet quickly, now interested in speed much more than stealth.

I clicked on my light just as I reached the threshold and thought the gates of hell had erupted.

An unholy shriek like a tortured demon accompanied a hard object pounding my ribs. I doubled over with a shriek of my own, grabbing at my right side with one hand and instinctively reaching out to block the next blow with the other. Another blow never came, but my feet were suddenly kicked from beneath me by the dark figure exploding from the closet. The first thing to hit the carpet was the back of my head. I thought of my pistol and heard a muddled echo of Jack's past admonishments about the uselessness of having a concealed carry permit if I wasn't going to carry.

Get to the door! I rolled to my stomach and tried to crawl away before a fatal blow of the bludgeon did me in for good. But the room was spinning, and I wasn't sure which way to go. My attacker was on me again and kicked me in the opposite ribs. They turned, whether to make another move on me or get away I knew not. Instinctively, I spun on the floor and returned the favor, kicking the legs from beneath them.

The light from my phone shined toward the ceiling a few feet away. I scrambled to the light and grabbed my phone, orienting myself toward the door as I struggled to my feet.

"Mr. Case?"

The voice stopped me in my tracks. My head ached, my lungs burned, and my ribs screamed. But I knew that voice.

My attacker flipped on the light and stood to face me.

It was Janie Cervelo.

"*Janie?*" My chin may have been touching my chest as I said it. "What are you doing? Do you know whose house this is?"

She dropped the Louisville Slugger bat and stepped toward me, reaching out toward my ribs but stopping short. "I'm so sorry. It was so dark, and you were sneaking, and I thought—" The floral dress and flats from the funeral had been replaced with jeans, a sweatshirt, and tennis shoes.

My mind was doing somersaults. "I thought you were going to kill me. What are you doing here?" Then it dawned on me. She was trying to help. And why wouldn't she? She'd heard Jack's and my stories for years and probably read the books. Plus, the old cliché about the apple falling close to the tree was as true as ever. "Janie, baby, you don't need to do this. It's admirable, but Jack and I are going to figure this out and clear

Devlin's name for good."

"Huh?" Janie frowned. "Figure what out? Devlin?"

"Figure out who really killed Ronny. What Buster has to do with it. He knows something, may even be the killer." I motioned toward the door and winced with the stabbing pain in my side. "We've got to get out of here. He could be home any minute."

Janie frowned and waved her hands in a dismissive gesture. "No, no. Buster's no killer. He loved Ronny."

"Maybe so, but I don't want to find out differently the hard way. Let's go." I touched her elbow and nudged her toward the door, but she withdrew and stepped back.

"You don't understand. I'm not here to help solve any crime. Hang on a sec." She took a deep breath and went into the closet. I stared blankly and waited until she emerged a few seconds later. She set a shoe box on the desk and opened it.

"What are you doing?"

Janie didn't say a word and methodically removed photos from the box, one at a time. Photos of her and Buster at a beach. Of Buster holding Lily when she was a baby. One of the three of them together that looked quite recent.

I couldn't believe what I was seeing. "Janie? What is this?"

She pursed her lips and raised both eyebrows. "What it looks like."

"You and Buster? Dating? What? How?"

She shook her head. "No. More than that. He's Lily's father."

FORTY-THREE

"JANIE, this is terrible. You can't do this."

She recoiled. "Can't do this? Mr. Case, I'm sorry, but that's ridiculous. It's done. Lily is here, and she is his."

My mind raced. The subject of Lily's parentage hadn't come up in a long time. When Janie had first become pregnant, Abi and I had asked Jack about it. But he didn't know who the father was, and Janie wouldn't tell. It had been such a point of contention between them that Janie moved out for a couple of weeks until Jack relented and promised he would never ask again. She could tell him when and if she got ready if she would just come home. And he had kept his promise. And he had loved Lily ferociously from the first moment he knew she existed.

Buster Shane? He had been in prison, hadn't he? How was this even possible? But the evidence was right there before me in vivid color. Buster had been around when Lily was born, and clearly he was in their lives again now. "You've been staying here, haven't you?"

Janie nodded toward a suitcase by the bed that I hadn't noticed before. "Dad doesn't know yet. About any of it."

"Lily staying here too? Meg?"

"Meg knows. Lily's been staying there some, while Buster and I work. My car is at her place. But that's it." She sighed. "Dad wants us to come home, thinks it's safe now. I'm going to get Lily from Kellen and go tell him tonight."

This was awful. Buster had wrecked the life of his brother and undoubtedly countless others. Now he was expanding the reach of his destruction to include my friends. If I couldn't stop him, Jack would go to the ends of the earth to do so, whatever it took. "Jack is gonna blow a fuse," I said. "You know how protective he is. And Buster is dangerous."

Janie huffed. "Dangerous, huh? Dad's idea of danger isn't always on target."

"What are you talking about? His instincts are quite good."

"So good that he sent me to stay with Meg to avoid the person who threatened us. Except that the person who threatened us was Buster."

My blood ran cold. It made sense. Buster had staged the threat against Lily at Jack's house four nights earlier and coerced Janie to convince Jack they needed to leave. The man was heartless, and poor Janie was brainwashed. "I'm not surprised it was Buster. But I am surprised that you ran right into the teeth of the lion."

Janie began returning the photos to the shoebox. "Don't you get it, Mr. Case? Buster did that for us. For his family."

I wanted to wrap her in my arms and get her out of that house, dragging her if I had to. But given the state of my ribs and the viciousness with which I had seen her fight, that was not an option. Jack had taught her well.

Janie looked up and wiped tears from her eyes. "He's been trying to get us together ever since he got out, if only for a little while, and this seemed like a good way to help it happen."

Ever since he got out. The thought of Lily's father being a convicted criminal made me sick. "Janie, let me ask you something. If Buster cares about you and Lily so much, why does he have your photos stuck in a shoebox in the closet?" Bless her. Alarm sirens were sounding, but she wasn't listening.

She shrugged. "Because he doesn't want some people to know."

Deaf *and* blind when it came to Buster. "Can't you see it? Of course he doesn't want anyone to know. You may be one of a half dozen women. Pulls a different shoebox out every time one comes over." It was brutal, but she needed to hear the obvious truth.

Her eyes flashed hurt and anger and brimmed with tears again. "No! He's *protecting* us. Working through some things so we can be together for good. But his mom is sick. Now this with Ronny."

I was getting nowhere and could see it wasn't going to change. Not in that moment. "Okay. Okay. But you have to tell Jack. If you don't, I will. He is owed that." I didn't look forward to that explosion.

Janie hung her head. "I know. Let me do it. Tonight, after the Halloween festival. I don't want to ruin it for Lily. She's been talking about it for a week."

———

I fingered the black ticket with white lettering in my pocket as I walked into my garage, considering ways I could get out of going to the Amberton Halloween Festival. It had been a tradition for at least thirty years, growing from a dozen or so people handing out candy from the trunks of their cars while kids ran wild through the city park the first year to a county-wide attraction now. A haunted house, pony rides, rock climbing, a dozen or so amusement rides, chili, cake, and costume contests, rows of decorated booths for trick or treating, and—of course—hundreds of kids scrambling around like a kiddie Times Square were the norm now. Kyle and Kellen had outgrown the trick or treating part, but being there together as a family was a tradition no one had yet shown any interest of abandoning.

For a thousand reasons, I was not in the mood to go, but I had no choice. Kellen was freshman president of the Amberton High Community Connection Club, aka C3, which was assigned to various festival functions, one of which was selling tickets. The festival committee had committed to donate a certain dollar amount for every hundred tickets sold by the club. If I didn't show up, Kellen would give me grief I had no interest in fending off.

I sighed and turned the knob to the kitchen door. *Let's get this over with.* It might be the last normal thing we did for a while, depending on what happened after Janie confessed to Jack.

I expected Abi to be sitting on go, pretending not to be impatient with me, but the house was quiet. No one was in the kitchen or living room. Then I remembered I had told Abi I would meet her there. I checked my phone and saw that she had texted me.

U coming? Jack and everyone are here.

I smiled. Been a little busy, but yes, dear, I'm coming. I responded that I wouldn't be long.

I did look forward to seeing Abi in her costume. This year she was Maleficent, and in my opinion, Angelina Jolie had nothing on her. To her chagrin, I refused to participate. I had enough trouble being myself without pretending to be something else, even for fun. She said it would improve rapport with the students who saw me and that I was a fuddy-duddy. I didn't disagree on either count. But I would be going in jeans, boots, and a brush jacket.

I heard a rustle from Kyle's room and was surprised to find him sitting at his desk, penciling something on his sketch pad as was often the case. "What's up?"

He looked up and smiled. "Waiting on you. Mom said you were stressed. Might need company."

Right again on all counts, as usual. "You bet. Let me take a leak and I'm ready. Where's your costume?"

Kyle rolled his eyes. "The girls would love that, but no."

I winked and pivoted to go to the bathroom. "Good call. Be right back." It would be good to go with Kyle, to share in a mutual conspiracy of too cool for costumes. Seeing his sketch pad made me remember the week after Halloween the year before. He had filled the pages with images of costumes seen and others imagined.

I washed my hands and splashed water on my face to freshen up, and it hit me just as I brought the towel to my face.

The sketch pad.

An eagle with an olive branch in one set of talons and a missile being released from the other.

I knew where I had seen it before, at school on Monday when I had told Kyle I needed his help.

Kyle knew Buster Shane.

The aura of father-son camaraderie disintegrated when I snatched Kyle's sketch pad from beneath his pencil and began flipping pages, but I did not care.

"What the heck, Dad?"

"Is this your only pad?" I flipped through it and found otters, whitetail bucks, bobwhite, a sketch of Lily on a swing, a portrait of a teenage girl I didn't recognize, and a lonely figure walking a dirt road by a rustic barn, but not what I was looking for. I tossed it back on his desk and looked around the room. Numerous other sketches and watercolor paintings were pinned to two different corkboards, and there was a shadowbox filled with Native American arrowheads, a bookshelf filled with adventure fiction and nonfiction nature books and a stack of notebooks. "Where's the one you had at school?"

"When? That's like asking which pair of socks I wore last month. Why?"

"Monday, Kyle! You had it Monday."

He shrugged and eyed me with a look of angst. He opened a drawer and pulled out an identical pad. He held it out and then pulled it back when I reached. "First, tell me why you want it."

My glare convinced him to hand it over without further explanation. I turned pages of sketches: wolves, ducks, fighter jets, and people, both realistic and caricature.

And an eagle.

I slapped the sketch down and patted it hard with my open hand. "What is this?"

He looked away. "Just a drawing."

"It's not just a drawing, son. Where did you see this?"

"It's just something I saw, okay, Dad?" He attempted to close the tablet, but I stopped him.

"You saw? Who? Where? You look me in the eye and tell me." I knew the who, of course but wanted him to say it.

"Buster Shane. He's a friend."

Hearing the drug dealer's name and the word *friend* off my son's lips in the same sentence made me sick. I felt for Jack, who would soon be having the same reaction to that name, and worse. Or would it be worse? I didn't even know yet. "Kyle, what have you gotten yourself into? The man is a criminal.

Maybe a murderer. Did Janie introduce you?"

Kyle blinked hard and frowned. "Janie? What?" He stood and gave his best attempt to look me in the eye. "Dad, he's not like that. It's his mother. She's sick and needs our help."

"Our help? You better get your explanation together before we get in the truck, because you're going to tell me everything. Then I'll decide what your mother needs to hear. For both our sakes." I turned to leave.

"Stop, Dad."

I paused but didn't turn around.

He sighed. "I need to show you something."

———

Our neighbor Nelson Dunbar had been something of a friend before he died, albeit an odd one. His wife died shortly after Abi and I had moved into the neighborhood, and I never remembered her name. He had been aloof when we brought him supper a week or so after her death, which we attributed to his personal grief mechanism, but that never changed with subsequent attempts to be friendly over the years. He just kept to himself and would return a cursory wave if we crossed paths going and coming.

Once I came home from summer vacation expecting our lawn to look like a jungle since I had run out of time to mow it in the week before our departure, but instead I found it cut and manicured. A couple of investigative calls revealed Dunbar had come over and cut it for us. When Abi baked him a plate of cookies, he took them, gave a tiny smile, and gently closed the door in her face. The plate was on our steps the next morning.

He had no children, only a couple of nephews who lived

on opposite ends of the country and never came around. After a lengthy probate period, the house and its belongings were sold at auction. Supposedly an "out-of-town investor" had purchased the house, but it had been sitting vacant for a year or more with no movement that I could see.

As Kyle and I approached the house through the woods, it occurred to me that I wouldn't really know if the house had activity or not unless I made it a point to go look. It sat off the road far enough that one couldn't really tell much about what was going on there unless you staked out the driveway.

"Tell me again why we're going this way?" The sensation of early evening cool against my cheeks was magnified by contrast to the angry hot flush that had set in at my encounter with Janie at Buster's. "You know I have a truck. We could have driven right up."

Kyle answered without breaking stride. He wanted to get this over with, whatever it was, as much as I did. "Trust me, Dad. This is better."

"Trust you?"

He stopped and mumbled something deferential about being sorry, but—

"Forget it," I said. "Just go."

I followed as Kyle plodded on, clicking his phone light on and off as he picked his steps, much like we did when sneaking in before daylight on a deer hunt. I tried not to conjecture why such stealth was required. It couldn't be good, especially if Buster Shane was involved. I remembered once again that I didn't have my sidearm and hoped I didn't regret it. There was nothing worse than bringing a knife to a gunfight. Then I remembered that Buster was Lily's father, which made things even more complicated. And unpredictable.

Kyle stopped at the edge of the back yard and glanced around, then was off again just as I caught up. We crossed an undulating brick patio and stopped at the back door. "It's in here," he said. "You're not gonna like it, but let me explain."

"This isn't your house. Somebody owns it. You can't just walk in."

Kyle shook his head. "I have permission." He held up a key.

"Give me that." I snatched it from his hand. "Where'd you get it?"

"Can we please just go in and let me show you *before* you blow a gasket? No point in doing it twice."

This was going to be bad.

"I'll decide how many times I want to blow up." It was a silly comeback, but I didn't care. Maybe he was right. The old lock was stubborn, but with some jiggling of the key it finally succumbed and let us in. We stepped into a dark room, as expected. I flipped the light switch by the door, but nothing happened. "No electricity."

"This way." Kyle crossed the frayed carpet of the vacant room and went through another door into an equally dark hallway. He closed the door behind us. He took a few steps, stopped, and grasped the handle to a door to the right. A thin ribbon of light shone along the bottom. "Here we go."

He opened the door, and the light was almost blinding until my pupils adjusted to the change. The walls were white and bare, and a single window was covered with black plastic. Six square LED panels hung from the ceiling. Beneath each one was a cluster of four potted plants sitting on a basin raised about six inches off the floor and equipped with a drain hose stretching to an adjacent room, presumably the bathroom. An acrid aroma like rotting fruit and sulfur permeated the space.

I don't think a shotgun blast to my gut would have felt any worse. "Marijuana?"

"Let me explain, Dad."

I grabbed a fistful of Kyle's shirt, and his eyes flared wide with alarm and uncertainty. "Explain is right. Do you know what you've done?"

"It's for Buster's momma. I think she's dying, but these are the kind that help her sickness. It's a rare hybrid indica strain. I didn't want to do it. I mean, I didn't start this. I'm just filling in, watching them for a few days until they get somebody else who has more time."

"They? Who is they?"

Kyle hesitated and looked over the room. "Buster is all. His mom."

I rubbed my face and then pounded my fist into my palm. I intended to pound Buster Shane if I could find him. I wanted to kick one of the pots through the wall and across the neighborhood. "Don't say another word. Get out. Right now. Get home. I'll figure out what to do." I pushed Kyle toward the door and hesitated, considering ripping all the lights down. But I had no intention of putting my fingerprints on anything in there before I called the authorities. Maybe I could come back and wipe down anything Kyle had touched. Would I call Jack or someone else? No chance did I want Wayne Rappaport anywhere near there. What would happen to Kyle? What would we tell his mother?

Kyle dropped his head and went into the dark hallway, shoulders slumping. I ached inside, searching a boy's lifetime in an instant for an explanation of where I had gone wrong. Could I have seen this coming? Had my son become that rebellious right under my nose—our nose—without us having the slightest suspicion? The events of the past twenty-four hours bore all the signs: sneaking out, subverting our investigation, running from the sheriff, blackmailing the sheriff into letting Devlin go. He and Kellen blamed the latter two on Devlin and Emma, but was that even true? Was Kellen involved in this too?

I should have taken up more time with him. So many hours spent away from home at the football field, which Kyle cared nothing about, no matter how difficult that was for me to understand. I had worked to find mutual interests such as hunting and fishing and other outdoor activities, but lately he would rather draw the wildlife he encountered than harvest it.

His talent in that regard was undeniable. It must have come from Abi's side of the family, because no one I knew in my family could draw a stick figure. That his interests differed from mine was fine with me; I just wanted him to be happy. But Abi had told me he felt like a disappointment. Had I failed to support him enough? Had I driven him to this moment?

I flipped the light off and turned on my phone to find my way out. I needed to catch up with Kyle. This was not the time to widen the chasm between us.

He was leaning against the wall in the dark hallway, looking down at his feet.

I stopped and dropped my phone to my side when the light shining on him seemed awkward.

"Ready, Dad?"

He had not followed my order to go home, but there was no rebellion in his posture or his voice. "Yeah, let's go. We'll figure something out at home." I patted him on the shoulder and pointed toward the way out. "Lead on."

Kyle opened the back door we had come in and stepped down onto the patio with me right behind him. I turned back to the door, debating whether to lock it or not. What did I care if someone came in and stole everything?

Suddenly, Kyle and I were enveloped in a blinding light.

I whirled to find the source of the light and my son to shield him from whatever was coming.

"Freeze! Hands up and turn around! FBI!"

FORTY-FOUR

THE spotlight upon us was from the convergence of two sources, each flashlight blinding us to who was behind them. Both were yelling the same orders, one male and one female. I didn't have to see to know their weapons were pointed at us.

"Stay calm, son. Do what they say."

Kyle was way ahead of me, hands high and turned away. "Dad?"

"Easy! Easy!" I said it loud enough to cut through the yelling from the agents. "I'm Case Reynolds. Football coach here at Amberton. This is my son. We live nearby."

"Be quiet. Keep your hands where I can see them," the male voice said from our right, stepping toward us. He had a pistol raised. "Any weapons?"

"Just a pocketknife."

"Put it on the ground."

The agents dropped the beam of their lights out of my eyes, and I removed my Case knife, the brand for which I had been named, from my pocket and showed it to the agents before setting it on the ground at my feet.

"Anything else? What about you, kid?"

Kyle shook his head vigorously. His breaths were short and rapid. "No, sir. No, ma'am."

The agent to our left moved closer and gestured for her partner to drop his weapon, which she did as well. "Go ahead and turn back around, kid." She held up a badge where her gun had been. "I'm agent Dana Harlow with the FBI. This is my partner, Ray Shumaker. What are you two doing here?"

Kyle turned to face the agents as instructed, wide-eyed. He began to speak, but I cut him off. "Kyle told me he's seen some suspicious activity here, and I came to see. I don't like suspicious activity in my neighborhood, as you can surely understand."

Kyle stayed wide-eyed, but I recognized it becoming a look of surprise more than alarm. I hoped it was the kind of subtle transition that only a father could recognize.

"Suspicious activity?" Shumaker shined his light in Kyle's eyes. "What kind of suspicious activity?"

My heart sank. What Kyle said next might set his fate. I wanted to kick myself for not talking it all through before we walked out of the house, but how could I have known this was waiting on us? I still wasn't exactly sure what was going on. Was he guilty, or was this something else? After all, Devlin James had willingly spent three nights in jail for a crime he had nothing to do with in order to protect someone else.

"It was, um, just some people going in and out." Kyle's voice was small and uncertain.

"Describe them to us."

Kyle toed the bricks beneath his feet. "Can't really. Just saw some people in and out through the back door the past few days. From a distance."

"And why were you back here?"

He looked up and met the officer's stare. "Why does any kid walk through the woods of their neighborhood?"

Shumaker snickered. "To find contraband?"

Harlow moved closer to face Kyle. "And Kyle, do you

always become suspicious when you see neighbors go in their back doors?"

He looked at me, and I nodded, knowing what he would say. "Mr. Dunbar died awhile back. Nobody s'posed to be here."

"So I told him to show me," I said.

"Out of the blue on a Wednesday?" Agent Shumaker cocked his head and said it with sarcasm, as a statement. "On Halloween? After dark?"

"If your kid told you there was something suspicious in your neighborhood, what day and time would you schedule to go look?"

"Easy there, Coach," Agent Harlow said. "It's a legitimate question. What were you doing inside?"

The way she called Kyle's name and now called me Coach seemed familiar in some way. *Dana Harlow.* Did I know her?

What I said next might help determine Kyle's fate as well as mine. If he was guilty, the time for justice, whatever that meant, would come. I was reminded of a particular article from the Armed Forces Code of Conduct instituted by President Eisenhower, one of many military examples I had used in my coaching career. *I will never surrender the members of my command while they still have the means to resist.* I didn't consider these officers of the law to be my enemies, but Kyle was under my command, and until proven to me that he was guilty, I would help him resist. To what end, I did not yet know.

I pointed to the house behind us. "Trying to see what was going on there. Nelson Dunbar was my friend. I thought I owed it to him to look."

"Mr. Dunbar doesn't own this house anymore," Shumaker said.

I shrugged. "No one sent me the memo. Who does?" That

was a question I wanted the answer to but knew it wouldn't come here.

"That's for us to know," Agent Harlow said.

"Then I suppose you know who is growing marijuana in there?"

Harlow and Shumaker exchanged looks. Harlow flipped off her flashlight, but Shumaker kept his pointed squarely upon us. "We received a tip," she said. "But I'm curious about one thing. How did you get in? I feel certain that if what you say is true inside, the doors would not be unlocked."

I dug the key out of my pocket and held it up. "Like I said, Mr. Dunbar was my friend."

———

Kyle and I rode mostly in silence to the McKinley County Fairgrounds where the festival was taking place. Or had been taking place. I wasn't sure we would even get there before it was over. Abi had already texted me again asking where we were, and I saw I had missed her call twenty minutes earlier during the FBI fiasco. I knew I should call her but didn't have my story straight yet.

Agent Harlow had given us her business card, told us to call if we saw anything else suspicious, and sworn both of us to silence. I got the distinct impression she believed our explanation, but it didn't take a criminal justice degree to know that if we spread the word about what we had found and been questioned about, the FBI's investigation, which I assumed was aimed at if not through Buster Shane to even bigger fish, would be crippled. I couldn't even bear to think about where their case would lead in the end and what that meant for my son.

Until then, I had every intention of ensuring we both kept our mouths shut. Even though they apparently didn't have evidence or the motivation to arrest Kyle or me for anything drug-related, that didn't mean they couldn't take us in for questioning and make things miserable for a time. Or worse, get Kyle to implicate himself unnecessarily.

What I could gather before I told Kyle I didn't want to talk about it anymore for the time being was that he had been coerced into believing he was helping Buster's mother, who was critically ill. If that, it was at best ill-advised and at worst straddling the moral gray area. I just hoped it was as simple as doing some plant maintenance like he said. Whatever the case, I told him that what the FBI would do paled in comparison to what punishment I would mete out if he so much as sniffed a word to anyone about what had happened, his mother and sister included. Abi would know when I decided she needed to know. I just needed time to think, a seemingly simple yet infinitely precious thing that had been in short supply the past few days.

For now, the only thing to do was hustle to the festival and pretend everything was normal to the extent possible based on the shared knowledge of the moment. To not show up would demand an explanation I did not have. It was going to be difficult enough to explain our delay.

My phone buzzed again. It was Abi. *Here we go.*

"Case, where are y'all? Kellen's been asking about you." She was irritated. "We're supposed to talk to Jet and Gracie. People are beginning to leave."

Jet and Gracie. I had almost forgotten. They loved Halloween and Amberton's Halloween festival more than Christmas, it seemed. Perhaps it was because they didn't have children of their own and, as opposed to Christmas Day when kids were often out of sight playing in their pajamas or sharing dinner with family, on Halloween they were out and about in full sight and full costume, full of smiles and laughter. Plus, Jet and Gracie loved to dress in costumes of their own. Luke and Leia, Shrek and Fiona, ham and eggs, they had done them all. Since they couldn't be there tonight, we were all supposed to FaceTime them together from the festival.

"Almost there, babe. Got some news about Janie I need to tell you." I paused and looked at Kyle, who was eyeing me from the truck seat beside me. "And we got delayed when Kyle and I thought there was a disturbance down the street. Tell me where you are, and we'll meet you."

"Meet at the pony rides. Lily is about to ride for the tenth time or so. Then we're going to meet at the fountain to call Jet."

I relayed the information to Kyle, who remained silent as I found a parking spot on a side street. When I shifted into park and said, "C'mon," he spoke.

"How did you know about the key?"

I frowned and hesitated to sort out what he was asking. "The key to Dunbar's?"

"Yessir. How do you know it wasn't locks that… they put on? The FBI will figure that out if they were."

"Because that lock's been on there a long time. Never knew anyone to replace antique locks with antiques, especially if they're trying to keep people out." Which was a point I had already considered. If someone was really trying to hide an illicit drug grow and didn't want to get caught, why wouldn't they at least protect their asset with new locks? And video cameras? The Dunbar house had neither. I wished I had pointed that out to Harlow and Shumaker earlier. Surely they would come to the same conclusion on their own.

Kyle nodded and got out of the truck. He headed toward

the traditional site of the pony rides at the edge of the fairgrounds, and I followed.

If people had already left like Abi said, I couldn't imagine what the scene had looked like earlier. Kids were running
everywhere, some with costumes intact but many more with
them hanging tattered and askew like they'd been through a
drive-thru car wash. The sugary-crisp smell of funnel cakes
piqued my appetite, and I wanted to snatch a turkey leg from a
woman walking by me, just for one bite. We passed a teenager
getting tossed from a mechanical bull to the delighted jeers of
his friends and another hitting the bell at the top of the rock
wall. Music from a carousel played in the distance, and game
booths of every sort lined the edge of the park.

A few kids and some former students called out to me as we
meandered through the crowd, some whose names I recognized
and others with too many graduations gone by since for me
to remember. Kyle was not spoken to that I could see, and he
treated the corner column of a castle-shaped bouncy house like
a boxer's punching bag as we passed by it. Was that frustration
at himself for the trouble he was in, at getting caught, or something else?

We spotted Abi, Jack, and Janie leaning on a temporary
split-rail fence surrounding a riding pen where two ponies were
trudging in a circle, each being led by a worker. Abi was decked
out in her horns and cape and heels, and Jack was in uniform.
The ground inside the pen was strewn with hay and sawdust
and bits of manure missed by the cleanups between rides.

Lily was riding a flaxen chestnut, its natural coloring contrasted by the turquoise of her costume of Elsa from *Frozen* and
the bright pink of her helmet. She smiled and waved at Kyle
with a jerk of one hand before grasping the horn again with a

look of laughing surprise, like she had risked bodily harm by letting go for that split second.

"Last ride, okay, Lily?" Janie was calling out. She caught my eye as we joined her at the fence but quickly looked away.

Abi turned and gave us a semi-smile. "There you are. You boys missed most everything."

Kyle was looking intently at his phone and didn't acknowledge Abi, and I wondered if he had even seen Lily wave at him. I hated to think about what he was looking at or who he was messaging. I wanted to slap it out of his hand and stomp it in the ground but resisted. *Later.*

I leaned down and touched the jack-o-lantern bag full of candy that Jack was holding. "Looks like somebody racked up. Did you let Lily get anything?"

"Nah, bad for her teeth," Jack said, smiling. His gaze darted toward Kyle, then he squinted at me. *I don't know what's going on, but it's something.*

He would know soon enough, and it would be terrible.

I looked over at Abi and sighed. "Sorry we're late. I'll explain later. What's next?"

She nodded toward Lily, who was listening intently to the worker helping her off the pony. "Gather her up, find Kellen, and call Jet and Gracie like we promised. Then go home."

"One more time, Mommy?" Lily bounded over to where we stood at the fence, ignoring the gate one of the workers had opened.

I reached and lifted her over the top rail and planted her on my hip.

She pointed to the parking lot behind us. "See that red trailer over there? The ponies have to get inside and go home. They're tired. I might can ride one more time, though."

I shook my head but chose to distract rather than disagree. I leaned over and grabbed her candy bag. "Why don't you show me what you got tonight trick-or-treating?"

Lily studied the trailer for a second more before turning her attention to the candy, with a high-cheeked grin. "They said I was a pretty Elsa and gave me lots and lots and lots of candy. I like the Reese's."

"Good choice." Kyle stepped in and pretended to peer down into her bag. "I think I'll take those."

Lily jerked the bag away and poked her lips out with a pouty frown. "No, you won't!" Then her expression brightened, and she removed a stuffed animal from the bag. It was a pink pony about the size of a gerbil. "Devlin won it for me. Hit that jug with a baseball. I'm gonna ride her when I get home."

We all laughed and followed Abi toward the center of the fairgrounds to meet up with Kellen. The crowd was thinning considerably now as everyone was either working to clean up or get home. I chuckled at the sight of a rather diminutive Kansas City Chiefs football player wearing number fifteen with shoulder pads, helmet, and all, standing in front of the fountain as we approached. The contrast of shadows and lights made it appear the pulsations of streaming water were coming out of the top of the red helmet.

"Tryouts aren't until March, but I'll take you," I said.

Kellen removed her helmet and smiled. "About time y'all showed up." Her smile faltered, and she looked from me to Kyle. "Everything okay?"

"All good," I said. "Record crowd tonight, maybe?"

Kellen's expression brightened. "I hope so."

Jack held up his phone. "Let's give ol' Jet a report. Weirdo loves Halloween like nothing I've ever seen."

Lily squirmed to get down, and she ran to Kyle, who picked her up and pretended to reach into her candy bag again.

"What time is it in Kenya, anyway?" Jack asked.

"They're eight hours ahead of us," Abi said.

"Which means he's even more a weirdo than I thought if he's awake at this ungodly hour." Jack touched the screen on his phone and waited while it made a characteristic ringing sound. "May take the signal awhile to get all the way over there."

Kellen's mouth opened, undoubtedly to correct him with some statistic about the speed of light, but I stopped her with a look.

Then I heard Jet's unmistakable voice come through the phone. "Hey guys! Happy Halloween!"

"Happy Halloween!" Gracie's voice chimed in.

"Except it's actually All Saints Day here!"

Jack held up the phone and moved it around to show all our faces. "Nobody's ever heard of that, Jet. But we got Maleficent, MVP Patrick Mahomes, and Elsa here."

"Elsa is even prettier than in the movie," Jet said, and Lily beamed.

"Don't forget Barney Fife holding the phone here," I said.

Kyle slipped a pale gray mask over his face and wagged his head in front of the screen. "And Voldemort."

"And I'm a Yellowstone cowboy who lost his hat," I said.

Jack snorted in protest. Abi took the phone from him and peered at the screen. "How is your trip? Successful?"

"Great," Jet answered. "I'm doing heart screens. A lot of pathology here. Gracie's getting this new primary care clinic up and running."

"I think we can do a lot of good here," Gracie said. "There's an orphanage nearby too. These kids are amazing." She rattled off a succession of descriptions of the kids, their interests, and projects she and Jet and the other workers were planning.

"Well, you kids have a great time," Abi said, laughing, when Gracie finally took a breath. "Do your thing and get home safely."

"Will do." It was Jet's voice now. "But I'm going to sleep for a week when I get back. Gracie is wearing me out." He paused. "Hey, Jack."

Abi gave the phone back to Jack.

"Glad to hear about Devlin being cleared. Is he there with y'all?"

Jack shook his head. "Not at the moment. Out and about with some friends."

"Any closer to finding the real killer?" Jet asked.

Jack shot me a look. "Not as close as we'd like. We may need your brain if we don't have it solved by the time you get back."

The image on the phone screen shifted, and Gracie's face appeared. "Negative. He's been retired from crime fighting since medical school. I'm confident you'll get it done. Let me speak to Elsa before we go. I promised her we would go for ice cream when I get back."

Jack turned to get Lily front and center but didn't see her.

My eyes darted from Janie to Abi to Kellen and back again, and a sudden wave of dread enveloped me.

Everyone in the group spun in place simultaneously, scanning our surroundings in vain as the same horrible realization set upon each of us.

Lily was gone.

FORTY-FIVE

"**S**HE was just here! Kyle, you had her!" Janie was panicked, and we felt it with her.

He was several feet away, looking at his phone. "She… she wanted down. I thought—"

"She can't have gone far," I said, glaring at him.

Gracie was calm and practical. "I'm going to hang up now. But it will be okay. Kids wander off all the time. Think about where she would go. Let us know when you find her, please. We love y'all!" And she and Jet were gone.

"Has anyone seen Devlin?" Jack asked. "Maybe Lily saw him or someone else she knew."

"Everyone spread out and search," I said. "Kyle, check the pony corral. Maybe you can get off your phone long enough to do that." I made a beeline toward the red trailer. What had Lily said? *I might can ride one more time.*

I spotted one of the men who had been working the ponies earlier and approached him. "Hey, buddy. Did you see a little girl over here?"

The man was wiry with patchy beard stubble and an Adam's apple bulging from a turkey neck. He wore a sweatshirt, jeans, and high-top canvas tennis shoes. He took a drag of his cigarette and snickered. "Seen an ocean of kids tonight, dude. Can you be more Pacific?"

"Do I look like I'm joking? A little girl, in a greenish-blue dress."

He held up a hand. "Didn't mean nothin' by it. You mean the girl riding at the end. Dressed like Elsa?"

I was taken aback that he knew of Elsa, but whatever. "Yes, yes! That's her."

"That other dude was talking to her. I thought he's kin to her or somethin'."

Other dude? Kin to her? A wave of relief hit me. It must have been Devlin. "What did the other dude look like? High school age?"

Turkey Neck shrugged. "The one that was working the ponies. Older fella."

Wait, what? Was this guy on drugs? "Working the ponies with you? What's his name?"

He shook his head. "Don't know. Other boy they hired with me, his name is Cupp, didn't show up tonight. This dude said he was his replacement." He shrugged again. "Don't matter to me 'long as I get my money."

My heart sunk. I desperately tried to recreate an image of the man who had been helping Lily on the pony but had nothing. I had little doubt who was behind it, though. "You know a guy named Buster? Buster Shane?"

Turkey Neck nodded and gave a sheepish grin. "Everybody knows Buster."

If I had wanted to hurt Buster before, it was now magnified tenfold. Of course it was him. Classic father abduction. We were hot on his heels for killing his brother. Maybe he had some money saved up, decided it was now or never. Paid one of his drug buddies to grab his child and hand her off, to disappear forever. Or so he thought. He didn't know Jack. Or me, for that matter.

I made a circle around the red trailer, which now contained

the two ponies. It was hitched to a late model GMC dually. "Your truck?"

Turkey Neck chuckled. "Naw, I can't afford that. Don't know whose that is."

I took a pic of the license plate and called Janie, and she answered before the first ring finished. "Find her?" She was breathing in gasps.

I covered the phone and moved away from listening ears attached to long necks. "It was Buster."

There were several seconds of silence and heavy breathing before she responded. "What?"

"I'm pretty sure it was Buster. This guy over here at the ponies said he saw Lily talking to another guy. Says he knows Buster. Is Jack with you? It's time."

Janie was no less panicked by the time she met me at the rock-climbing wall two minutes later. Her eyes brimmed with tears, and she was trembling. "We've got to send out an Amber Alert!"

"Where's Jack?" I asked.

Jack's breathless voice behind me answered before she could. "Anything? Abi's texting and calling everyone she knows. Facebook, everything. I called Devlin and told him to do the same. Where's Kyle and Kellen?" He put his hands on his knees, working to catch his breath.

"Amber Alert, Dad," Janie said. "What about that?"

Jack nodded. "I called 911. They are sending someone. Law enforcement has to determine if it's appropriate before they activate it."

"Law enforcement?" Janie's eyelids flared like she had touched an electric fence. "You're law enforcement! Call an Amber Alert!"

She wasn't wrong. Jack was a deputy, in uniform in fact. But I knew what this would boil down to.

Jack grabbed a footrest on the wall and yanked at it in frustration. "It doesn't work that way. There's a procedure." He looked hard at me. "We've got to find her. Can't wait on Rap."

I nodded and stepped over to Janie, who looked ready to collapse, and gave her a bear hug. I didn't know all the criteria, but one of them was that the child's life or safety had to be suspected to be in imminent danger. I didn't trust Buster Shane and had no idea where he would go with Lily, but surely he wouldn't hurt his own daughter. "I'm not sure this will qualify for an Amber Alert, Jack. The child has to be in danger."

"Of … of course it does!" Jack stumbled with his words, trying not to alarm Janie even more. "D-danger or not, Lily's been taken, and the clock is ticking."

On second thought, was I certain Buster wouldn't hurt her? How did I know Janie hadn't been so blinded by his spell over her that she was oblivious to the fact he was capable of something so heinous? After all, what kind of person would kill his own brother? I grasped Janie by both shoulders and looked her in the eye. "Tell him."

She shook off my grip and stepped back, wiping tears. "He … he wouldn't hurt her." She tapped her phone hard with both thumbs like she was mad at a video game controller. "He's gonna text me any minute. I think his phone is dead right now."

Jack lunged toward us and leaned down to face Janie. "He? Text you? What are you talking about?"

"Tell him," I said.

Janie shook her head no and turned away. She made a motion like she might throw her phone but stopped short and crammed it in her pocket.

I sighed. Now was no time for secrets. "Buster Shane. He is Lily's father."

Jack slumped like he'd been shot in the liver. "What? That's not funny." He grabbed Janie's shirt sleeve and spun her around. "Janie?"

Jane was sobbing now. "He won't hurt her. I don't know if it's him. He won't hurt her. He loves us."

Jack let go of Janie and turned to me, jaw dropped, speechless.

"That was Buster at your house Saturday. He orchestrated that whole thing to get Janie out of your house. She's been staying with him, not Meg."

"We broke up when he went to prison," Janie blurted, "right after I got pregnant. He's been trying to get me back. I didn't want to, but he's been really sweet."

"Sweet?" Jack said. "Buster Shane the drug dealer and murderer is sweet?"

His words stung me too. The thought that Kyle might be mentioned in the same sentence as Buster once word got out about his contribution to the local marijuana grow made me sick. Would it get out? Would my conscious require that I be the one to tell it?

"He's had problems, but he's trying to correct them!" Janie yelled. "And he's not a murderer!"

Jack was glaring at me. "You knew about this?"

I shrugged. "Not for long."

Jack looked at his watch. "Unless you found out about thirty seconds ago, you've had time to tell me."

"Jack, listen—"

"No, you listen. You knew this and didn't tell me? Look around!" He gestured wildly with his hands wide and stepped toward me. "Do you see Lily anywhere? Our little girl is missing, and it's your fault!"

I braced myself for him to push me, but Janie stepped between us. "Don't blame Case! It's my fault."

"That too," Jack's expression was wild and angry like I'd only seen a few times over the years. "Both of you!"

"Okay." I tried to sound calm but was fighting the inclination to become defensive and violent myself. "Take it up with me later, Jack. But right now, we've got to find Lily."

"Oh, don't worry." Jack wagged his head. "I've got a lot to take up with a lot of people when this is over." Just then his phone rang. He turned away without explanation as he answered. "Rap, listen here, got a situation…" He stepped away, talking rapidly.

My phone buzzed against my hip. It was Abi. "Anything?" I asked.

"Maybe. One of my friends thinks she saw her just a few minutes ago."

"Saw Lily? Where? Was it Buster Shane?"

Abi didn't respond for a moment. "Buster Shane? Why would you think that? No, not that at all. She said she saw Lily get in the car with a woman. A black SUV."

FORTY-SIX

KYLE gravitated toward his mother as the search at the fairgrounds died down and it became obvious Lily was really gone. He had first gone to the corral as ordered, then raced around the perimeter of the place, thinking if someone was sneaking away with her, he might be able to see them. Heck, if they slipped into the shadows to a vehicle parked nearby— like he had seen in movies— instead of just getting into a car parked alongside everyone else, he might even be able to track them. He kept an eye out for white vans, too, but saw none. After two circumferential treks with no luck, he saw his mother headed to her car and decided to ride with her. It was bad enough to have the stress of what had happened at the Dunbar house weighing on his mind—and now Lily was gone too—without having his father put a boot in his back and twist the heel. That would come, but tomorrow sounded better than today.

"This is terrible," Abi said, more to the windshield than to Kyle. "Terrible."

"I'm sorry. I thought she was beside me." He wanted to vomit.

"Your dad and Jack and Janie are still looking and I'm sure will want to be there when law enforcement arrives. I've got some connections checking the addresses for all the pedophiles in this area, especially any with a black SUV, because who knows how long it will take Rap to think of that." She paused for a second and cocked her head. "Although, it's unusual for a pedophile to be female. Anyway, in the meantime, I'm going to go by Jack's in case someone takes her home." Abi tossed her phone into Kyle's lap. "Let me know if I get any messages that help us. I've texted everyone I know."

Kyle texted Emma. *Hear about Lily?*

Moments later, he got the response. *Yes its awful. Any ideas?*

Nothing. Tell everyone to be looking.

I'll tell mom but Im sure she knows

Kyle mulled over the events of the past few minutes, wondering what or who they were really looking for. Something was going on with his dad. There was a look in his eye, something there even before the anger that came when Lily had disappeared. The kind he had at the dinner table when he needed to tell Mom something but had to wait until they were alone, often related to a scandal of some sort involving a player, teacher, or church member. Kellen and Kyle often knew what it was before their parents did, but this time Kyle had no idea. All he knew was that Lily was gone, it was at least partly his fault, and his father was acting strange.

What did Kellen know? He called her but got no answer. "Where's Kellen?" he asked his mother.

"With her C3 group. They're organizing some search teams."

Of course. *Kellen is out organizing the community, and I'm riding in the car with my mother.* The outcast, being her secretary or something. As if on cue, her phone rang in his lap. He recognized the name but didn't know the woman.

"Somebody named Patricia."

"Answer it."

Kyle ignored her and handed her the phone. No point in mixing up information and getting blamed for it. His over-achieving twin wouldn't mix it up. In fact, she would probably find Lily, maybe even win the Congressional Medal of Honor or something. A notch in her belt and a missing link in his, yet another shortcoming to haul around like a ball and chain.

He had drawn that once, a kid hauling a ball and chain behind him. *Ball and chain.* That reminded him of something he had just read at church Sunday while the preacher was chattering on with his boring sermon. Kyle loved to read in the book of Revelation, not because he understood it, but because he did not have to try. The language was colorful enough, with talk of jeweled cities and dragons with multiple heads and a rider on a white horse. And the verse he was suddenly thinking of— an angel throwing the wicked city of Babylon into the sea like a millstone, to never be found again.

Millstone. The word had jarred him even then. It took him of course to Perry's riddle, but hadn't they already fully sorted out what that meant? The word struck a chord in another way, now, though. Weren't there other Bible verses about that? Something else about being thrown into the sea?

Kyle pulled out his phone and searched the word in his Bible app, like he had been trying to do at the festival. He went back to where he had found it in the book of Luke. "It is better for him if a millstone is hung around his neck and he is thrown into the sea than that he may cause one of these little ones to sin."

Kyle swallowed hard, like he was gulping down a millstone of his own. Oh no. What had he done?

Jack was furious. "Bastard son of a bastard's whore." He kicked hard at something imaginary and looked at his phone as if he wanted to smash it on his forehead like a tin can.

"What is it?" Janie put her hand over her mouth in dismay.

Jack made a reassuring motion in Janie's direction. "Nothing bad about Lily. Pardon my language. But Rappaport won't issue the Amber Alert."

"Why?" I asked.

"Because he has no reason to believe that Buster would harm his daughter, so this doesn't meet the criteria. Unless we learn something different."

"It's not Buster." Janie's voice rose. "I've told y'all. Abi said it was a female in a black SUV. That's a start. We've got to go find her!"

Jack frowned. "A female? That doesn't make sense. Rap just told me it was a male with her. Young, maybe a teenager. Black SUV, like you said."

I turned to Janie. "Could it be your friend Meg? Could she be mistaken for a male? What does she drive?"

She shook her head. "No. Silver Taurus. I called her. She's searching too. She …"

"She what?" Jack said.

Janie dropped her head. "She thinks it's Buster too. She doesn't know him like I do."

And I had no doubt that Meg was absolutely correct, no matter what Janie thought or what was reported to Abi and Rappaport. "Think about how many little girls were dressed in Elsa costumes tonight. It could have been any one of them getting into the car with their mother or brother or both, for all we know."

Janie held up her phone with an expression like a child lost in the wilderness. "I'm sure he's going to text me back any minute. He just needs to charge his phone."

Jack shot me a glance and jerked his head toward the

parking lot. "I'm sure he will, Janie. Let's get over to Buster's to be sure, though. Rappaport is on his way here. He and Nash can flounder around without our help."

Janie refused to let us take her home. I didn't know if it was because she was convinced Lily was not with Buster or because she feared that he might actually have her. I wanted Jack to give her no choice, but she was a grown woman, and he had taught her to be tough and fend for herself. I had the bruised ribs to prove it.

Even though it was much darker now, Buster's tiny bungalow was less ominous from our approach in the front than it had been for me before. Perhaps it was the routine feel of driving past the Amberton County Club clubhouse and pulling up to a small house with a single streetlight, as one might do delivering Christmas cookies. Perhaps it was because this time I was not alone and sneaking in the back. Or perhaps it was because, even though I sensed that danger was in the air, Janie exuded a sadness that threatened to overwhelm all other emotions. I empathized with the sorrow she faced with the realization of deceit and false dreams, but if she was bleak about Lily, I refused to share that feeling. We would find her, whatever it took. There were no other options.

I parked my truck behind Jack and got out.

"His truck's not here," Jack said as he slammed his truck door. He had put his magnetic emergency beacon on his roof but had not turned it on. No point in attempting to be discreet. If Buster was there and wanted trouble, Jack would give it to him.

"Let's go in. See if he's been here since Janie and I left," I said. "Where was he supposed to be earlier?"

Janie gave a half-hearted shrug. "Said he had things to take care of. That's all I know."

Taking care of making a criminal out of my son. Or planning to kidnap his daughter. Or both. *And before this is over, I'll take care of him.* But Lily's safety came first. Justice for his other sins could come later. "Let's go."

Janie was in the front door first. She turned on the light and called out. "Buster? Buster?"

The door opened into the living room, and I watched Jack take it in as I had earlier. A whitetail buck mount on the wall. A sectional sofa and a flat screen television.

I pointed to a few kid's toys gathered in a corner. I had not noticed that before.

"That's been here," Janie said.

What else had I missed?

"Take a look around, Janie," Jack said. "See if you notice anything different." He did not wait on her and began moving down the hallway.

A quick search through the house to the back confirmed Buster was nowhere to be found, and Janie reported seeing no sign that Lily had been back there, either. Janie's suitcase was still in its spot on the floor beside the bed. Jack eyed it but didn't comment.

"What now?" Janie said. "My baby."

"Think, Janie," Jack said. "Where might he have taken her? Were y'all thinking of running away? Did you ever talk of going to a particular place? Meeting up? Does he have family out of town?"

Janie sat on the bed and brought her hands to her head. "No, I'm telling you." She slapped the bed. "He didn't take Lily! He's not going anywhere. At least not while his mother is still alive and—"

Jack moved to her and squatted down. "Janie? And what?"

"She's real sick, on hospice."

"I've heard she was ill, Janie. That's terrible. But is there something else?"

"And he sees justice done for Ronny's killer."

Jack's eyes widened, and he stood and looked at me. "Devlin."

Janie grabbed his arm. "No, Dad. He doesn't think Devlin did it."

Who would Buster be after if not Devlin? Tammy? If that was the case, she wouldn't be difficult to find. Jack had said she had gone to stay awhile with her sister down in Natchez. Or was that talk from Buster all just a ruse to fool Janie and keep her around?

"Who, then? Who is he after? Or does he even know?"

I was suddenly locked in on Buster's desk. Not on the papers lying on it, but what was framed and hanging above it. There was the photo of the soldiers with the eagle tattoos like Buster's, and then, propped on the back of the desk and leaning against the wall was the handwritten poem I had seen before. "Janie, this poem. It was hanging on the wall before." I leaned in and confirmed the presence of a nail still embedded in the wall.

She was up now, pacing and typing in her phone. "He won't answer."

"What's your point, Case?" Jack said. "You sure?"

I shook my head. "I don't know, on both counts." Then I remembered. "Wait a sec." I pulled out my phone and brought up the pic I had snapped earlier, planning to read the poem later when I had more time.

There it was, hanging on the wall. Less than two hours before. I handed Jack the phone to see the photo and ushered Janie over to the desk. "Janie, he was here. He took this off the wall for a reason. What does it mean?"

She pointed at the photo of the soldiers and tapped the image of the man in the middle. That was his father. He was smart. An engineer, from down around Noxubee. Buster says he grieved himself to death over something that happened in the war."

"The war?" I asked.

"Maybe not a war. A battle. In Africa, I think? 1993, maybe."

"Bet it was Mogadishu," Jack said. "A lot went wrong with that one."

"He never forgave himself," Janie said. "He came home, but his buddies didn't. Buster says his father thought of himself as a coward until the day he died. Drank to forget until he forgot forever." She grabbed the frame and stared at the words. "Wrote this ten years after it happened."

Jack peered over her shoulder and read through the words as I did. "God help him," he whispered.

I patted him on the shoulder, wondering what his thoughts and emotions were. Jack could empathize with such a thing like few others. His father had died in Vietnam before he ever knew him, and his stepfather had been an abusive alcoholic with demons of his own.

"What are you thinking?" Janie said.

"Buster knows who has Lily," I said. "And he's going after them, no matter the cost."

The question was, who? And where?

VOICES

The voices, they carried
Aired messages of freedom,
Of a price to be paid
And the ones who would need him.

Of lands never seen
Or envisaged import,
But called there he was
To a faraway port.

The voices, they carried
Allegiant salutations
To spangled emblems of blue
And the force of a nation.

They urged him to train
Sunrise to deepest night
Through rain, sand, and snow
To be a master of fight.

The voices, they carried
Him in, proud and strong,
Son, be brave and battle
But find a way home.

Your father will love you
Without commendation,
Trinkets silver or bronze
Need not be taken.

The voices, they carried
Him through hell and rest,
You need not give life
To give them your best.

Have courage you will
But grant me this favor,
Remember one truth
Mother's love never waivers.

The voices, they carried
Echoes deep to his soul
From the holder of his heart
Who made him feel whole.

I don't pray for a hero
But the father of my son,
Hold close these five words,
It is okay to run.

The voices, they carried
Comrades hard and hot,
Spouting shouts of "Hooah"
For cowards they were not.

Billowing dust, lead, and fire
Charged the smoldering air,
Press on, o'er the brink,
Let 'em hold if they dare!

The voices, they carried
'cross the field there that day,
Tides of fortune had turned
There deep in the fray.

The enemy awoken
Straits suddenly too dire
To hope for salvation
No matter the desire.

The voices, they carried
Echoes deep to his soul,
Home, life, and his love
Should be his true goals.

He turned away for a moment,
But 'twas not to run,
No, his brothers were calling,
So the boy picked up his gun.

FORTY-SEVEN

KYLE decided he had to get out of the house or he might burst.

His mother looked up from checking phone messages and frowned when he opened the door. "Where are you going?"

"Just need some fresh air."

He closed the door behind him and indeed took in a chest full of cool night air. The words of the Peregrine table-riding fellow's riddle continued to haunt him. He had been so confident, elated even, when he had figured out the reference to Miller's Creek, where the killer likely came up to the bluff. It hadn't led to any evidentiary discoveries, apparently, but at least they didn't have to wonder what it meant any more. Or so they thought.

Now he began to wonder if it had a much deeper meaning than that.

The guilt over what he had become involved with two days prior was eating at him like a cancer. He had been proud to be invited—based on his personal skills at all things nature, no less—to help ease Buster's mother's suffering. So what if growing marijuana, even if for medicinal purposes, was a bit illegal? It wouldn't be for long, and what was more important than easing someone's suffering? Surely there were allowances for that in the legal system. Proffit had suggested so himself.

And what was Proffit's connection to Buster, anyway? The mysterious man didn't fit the stereotype of drug lord or anything like that. Was he kin to Buster somehow? Surely there was a good reason he had become involved in helping Buster with his mother's problem. Whether or not to mention Proffit to his father was a question hovering over Kyle's head. He had elected to leave it out thus far. It was easier to defend helping a son help his dying mother than to answer questions about someone whose full name he didn't even know.

As for Buster, what about his true motives? Yes, he had a reputation for being involved in illicit drugs and dragging Ronny into it. But was that even true? What if it was all a misunderstanding and was related to his mother's cancer problems all along? Even if that were it, it was now apparent that not only was Buster on shaky ground in that regard, but he was a potential suspect in both Ronny's death and the disappearance of Lily. Buster's daughter Lily! A fact which neither Jack nor Dad nor Mom even knew about when the day began.

And then there was the text earlier in the day, from a number Kyle didn't recognize, telling him not to go back to the Dunbar house. Who had sent that? Proffit or Buster or someone else? He now wished he had heeded the warning. It was a miracle that he and his father both had not been arrested by the FBI. It remained to be seen what would come of that. Of some degree of guilt, his father seemed certain, but thankfully he had reserved final judgment until he had time to get more information.

This was all so crazy! Was Kyle now reading too much into it to think that the millstone reference was about him, about Buster's—or was it Proffit's—corruption of a young man? If it was about him, what did that have to do with Ronny's death, and how did the Peregrine fellow know about it on Friday night when Kyle hadn't met with Proffit until Monday morning? It made no sense. It couldn't be about him. No way. It had to be about Miller's Creek.

Kyle remembered that poem by Edgar Allen Poe about a man who had a dead man buried under his floor, and his guilt raged so hot that he imagined the man's heart beating so loud everyone could hear it. That's all this was. The telltale millstone.

Had his guilt become his own millstone? Hanging onto him, dragging him down. Wait, maybe that was it. Maybe that *was* an actual clue about the killer himself—or herself, for that matter—other than a location reference. Could the key be hidden somewhere in Ronny's past that no one had yet looked? Something dragging him down from behind that finally rolled upon him? Or was it someone else's past?

Kyle peeked into the house to make sure his mother was otherwise occupied. Seeing her scrolling through her phone on the couch, he quietly opened the storage room door and got his father's working coat off a nail. What he needed to do wouldn't take long, but no point in being cold for no reason.

He took out his phone and texted his father.

Can you come home? We really need to talk.

I looked at the message from Kyle and ached inside. The kid was hurting. He was in trouble. I was hurting, too, but for different reasons. And we might both be in trouble, before it was all over, depending on what Agent Dana Harlow decided. Had she pretended that we weren't suspects only as a ruse to see what we would do? Or did she believe my story? Time would tell.

Right now, though, my son was absolutely correct. We needed to talk, whatever the consequences. I looked at Janie. What would she give right now to be able to talk to Lily? What would Jack do for that chance?

"Jack, I'm going home. See what Abi has heard. You should

get Janie home in case someone calls or comes by."

Jack nodded and looked at Janie, who didn't protest. "I'll do that and get down to the station. Get Rap to change his mind about the Amber Alert or else. I'll call the governor if I have to."

Kyle was waiting in the kitchen when I got home, sitting at the bar and spinning a quarter on the counter, over and over. He was wearing my work jacket, about three sizes too big.

"Where's your mother?"

"Went to pick up Kellen, then check on Janie. So she wouldn't be alone."

"I can't imagine what she's feeling right now. Jack will make sure somebody pays, though."

Kyle kept spinning the quarter, watching it flicker and whir on the polished granite.

"You tell her?"

He shook his head. "Not yet."

I sat on the stool beside him and flattened the quarter beneath my palm. "I'm trying to wrap my head around it, son. Growing marijuana?"

"I think I'm connected to Ronny's death, Dad. Maybe Lily too."

His words hit me like an SEC linebacker. I paused and sucked in a breath. How was that possible? "What are you talking about?"

"Hear me out. It's about that riddle that Perry wrote. We thought millstone was a referral to Miller's Creek. Maybe it was. But what if it's about me? What if it's a message to you about me? You know, what the Bible says about adults causing kids to sin, that they should be sunk in the sea with a millstone?"

Bless him. Guilt was eating him up. "When did you first go to the Dunbar house?"

"Monday. Day before yesterday."

I patted him on the shoulder. "Ronny died Friday. Not connected."

He nodded. "Maybe. But there's something else."

I spun the quarter on the counter. "Tell me."

"You remember on Saturday when I told you I might have a new job?"

I had completely forgotten about that conversation. What was the name of the guy he had mentioned? Something about the pizza place? "I do. What about it?"

"His name is Proffit. He knows Buster. He's the one who got me to do it."

That was it. Proffit's Pizza but not kin. "You met him with Gabe?"

Kyle nodded. "When we were camping. He knew I was good at growing things."

"And how does Buster know him?"

Kyle stood and moved around the counter, pacing. It reminded me of Jack when he got worked up. "I'm not sure, Dad. I should've asked more questions."

"First name? Where he works? Where he lives?"

Kyle shook his head. "Don't know."

"I'll find out tomorrow who owns the Dunbar house now."

"Wait. I can tell you right now. Remember, I have that land app." Kyle took out his phone and tapped it. He frowned. "Odd."

"What?"

"It's not Buster, and it's not Proffit. It's a company called EVM Holdings."

"Never heard of it. So you don't know anything else about this Proffit?"

Kyle shook his head. "No, and I don't think anybody else does, either. Except maybe Buster. Gabe says he just shows up when you don't expect him. Doesn't use a phone."

"Call Gabe."

"I did. He didn't answer."

I felt my temperature rising. How stupid could Kyle be, agreeing to help a weed grow for people he didn't even know? I slapped the counter. "What's the matter with you? If a stranger shows up and asks you to rob a bank, what you gonna say? 'Sounds great, when do I start? Need me to kill anyone while I'm at it?'"

Kyle withered, and I regretted my words. Not the sentiment behind them, but the presentation of it.

"I'm sorry," I said. "I know you meant well, but dang, son. Not your best judgment. I just hope it doesn't ruin you in the end. Maybe not. You just went there once?"

He nodded. "Yeah, I got a text yesterday. Warned me not to go back."

"A text? From who?"

"Didn't recognize the number."

"Give me your phone." I reached out, intent on checking the number against the ones from Ronny's burner phone, but I remembered Jack had it. I waved it off. "Never mind."

"One more thing." Kyle reached into his pocket and pulled out a small rectangular object.

It was an SD card. "What's that from?"

Kyle smiled. Despite the seriousness of the situation, that was still good to see. "Remember I told you I've seen some deer in the neighborhood? A good buck last year?"

I returned his smile. "Your trail camera?"

Kyle reached for his laptop computer at the end of the bar

and flipped open the screen. "I've had the camera set up back there for a few weeks. Almost forgot, just pulled the card a few minutes ago. No big buck on here, but I do have one interesting pic." He inserted a card reader into a USB port and held the SD card up before plugging it in. "Haven't downloaded it yet. Hard drives are, uh… more difficult to get rid of than SD cards."

I didn't know whether to be impressed or worried that he had thought to avoid downloading the photo data. Why couldn't he have used that wisdom on Monday when approached about the Dunbar grow?

He made a few clicks and then grinned triumphantly. "There are a couple of shadowy pics, but this is the one you can see his face." He spun the computer around for me to see the screen.

For a split second, the blood in my veins ran so cold I'm certain it came to a standstill.

FORTY-EIGHT

I JUMPED up so fast my stool fell over and crashed onto the tile floor.

"What is it, Dad?"

A giant vacuum had just sucked the air from the room. I was suddenly nauseated. This was impossible. No possible way. No way!

My phone rang, and I jumped at the vibration in my pocket. I walked outside as I answered, welcoming the cold fresh air.

"Case, I got something."

"Jack, you're not gonna believe—"

"I know where Buster went. I'm pulling into your driveway."

The luminance of his headlights swept across my neighbors' yard and into my eyes before he had finished the sentence.

The truck had scarcely stopped rolling before Jack was out of it. "Buster must have charged his phone. Janie found him on that location app."

I was about to burst with what I now knew, but Jack was bouncing like a pogo on a trampoline. Finding Buster, and in turn Lily, was all-consuming. And for good reason. He didn't need any distractions, so my news would have to wait. If I could catch my breath. "Where is he?"

"You coming with me? I'll tell you if you're coming."

"You call it in? Seems like it would be good to have backup."

"Are you kidding me? Rap and his merry men? I want to save Lily, not get her disappeared for good. Or hurt. Plus, Rap already told me he's not buying the Buster thing, especially not that he would hurt Lily. And what evidence do we have that Buster is going after the person who did it? A photo moved from its spot on the wall? I'll take my chances with the two of us taking a look-see first. You coming or not?"

"You wouldn't be here if you thought there was a chance I wouldn't."

"I'm coming too." Kyle's voice surprised me. I hadn't heard him come outside.

"No way," I said. "You're not going anywhere."

"Yeah," Jack added. "Your dad might be right. No telling what we could get into."

Then I thought about what I had learned. About who knew Kyle and where he lived, and what his motives were. And what he might be capable of. What if we called and told Rappaport that information? He would laugh and hang up. "Actually, Kyle, yes. You can come. But I'm taking my truck too, and you're staying in it."

Kyle replaced my jacket with his and was headed toward my truck before I even finished.

Jack patted me on the shoulder. "You remember what we were doing when we were his age? You think either of us would have sat around at home?"

He had a point and didn't even realize the irony of it. "No, I don't think we would. We had crimes to solve."

"Wanna know where we're headed?"

"I'm afraid to ask."

"Here's a clue. His cell signal disappeared just off of Waterway Road."

Of course. Of course it was. Buster was headed to Logan's Bluff.

Kyle waited several minutes in silence before asking me about my reaction to the photo he had shown me.

"We'll talk about it later. Right now, we need to find Lily."

Kyle nodded and looked out his window.

"Whatever happens up here, you stay in the truck. If something goes haywire, you call 911 and drive straight to the sheriff's department. You know how. I'll give you the keys."

He nodded but didn't say anything.

"You hear me?" I spoke as sternly as I knew how. "I mean it."

"Yessir. Got it."

I turned off of Waterway Road behind Jack and half-heartedly counted how many times I had made that turn in the past five days. Was this the third? Fourth? How many others had been doing similarly, trying to get to the bottom of all this mess? Why would Buster be bringing her here, of all places? There was nothing but trees and a meadow and—

"You think we'll find her here?" Kyle said. "I don't want her to be hurt."

"I don't know. Me either. But I don't know what to expect anymore."

My heart hurt for him. He was being forced to grow up too fast, too suddenly. I could empathize, and Jack even more. I liked to think that all of our troubles beginning when we were Kyle's age had forged and hardened us in ways that proved to be assets later on. But was that true, or was that take merely justification by denial of the consequences? And did Kyle have the fortitude to withstand the fire the way we thought we had?

The silver paint of a parked truck flashed in Jack's headlights ahead of us. "That's Buster's," I said. Jack coasted to a stop beside Buster's Ford, and I stopped behind him with enough room for both of us to maneuver out separately if needed. I left my truck running and told Kyle to get behind the wheel.

"You really that worried, Dad?"

"No," I lied. "But let's just be smart."

I stepped out and closed the door quietly, like I did when parking for a morning deer hunt. Jack did the same. He made a circle around Buster's truck, feeling the hood, peering in, checking the doors, which were locked. "Truck's still warm. Nothing else." He stepped around to the front of his truck and stood tall, with a wide stance and hands in his pockets. "What now?"

I stood beside my friend and didn't answer for a time, listening. The night sounds were subdued, like the critters were listening too. A brisk breeze weaved through the few remaining clusters of dried leaves in the treetops around the edge of the clearing, circling us, dropping cold upon us like arctic waves. I remembered the forecast calling for temperatures below freezing by midnight. Each cloud of my breath was instantly swept away. I shivered, but it was as much from nerves as the cold. "I guess we make a circle, see what we find. Did Janie try to call him?"

He nodded. "Yep. No answer. Just saw his phone was here. About had to tie her down to keep her at home."

"Don't tell her Kyle came."

"Nope."

I began walking toward the edge of the clearing, and Jack joined me. I was puzzled by what was happening. It hadn't really occurred to me that Buster might be difficult to find. I had envisioned him standing here talking to someone just like Jack and I had been doing, or maybe sitting in a vehicle. I'm not sure why that made any more sense than what we were now facing, since that wasn't exactly the norm for an encounter between an abductor and the father of the abductee. Or was it? What was even normal anymore? Were we absolutely sure that Janie was right, that Buster was innocent? If not, what had led Buster here in the first place? Why here? There wasn't really any other reason to be here than to meet in the clearing. Unless—

I stopped abruptly and pointed at the edge of the bluff. "Do you think?"

"Surely not." Jack trotted toward the brink and began working the edge, peering over, hissing Buster's name. I joined him in the search, first at the spot where Ronny had fallen to his death, then to the site of Logan's Leap, then to the trail head leading to where we had found Ronny's phone. Nothing.

"I don't get it," I said. "Unless he left with someone." I wanted to call Janie to see if his signal had popped up again, but a quick look at my phone confirmed what I already knew. No cell service. It was not unusual to find pockets like that throughout the county, but it seemed odd for that to happen at a high vantage point like this. On the other hand, nothing about Logan's Bluff was normal.

My thoughts jolted back to my conversation with Kyle earlier. Jack didn't even know about the Dunbar house incident, much less what I had found out from Kyle's game camera. To add the shock of what I had learned to the overwhelming worry about Lily would be hard to bear, but Jack needed to know it all. Besides, I saw a growing cloud of dark dread that every single one of the past five days was connected. And that prospect was growing more terrifying by the minute. "Jack, I need to tell you something."

A blast behind us shook me to the core.

Jack and I whirled and ducked, on instinct. "Your truck!" he said.

"Kyle!"

The horn blasted again. And again.

Something was wrong. But why wasn't Kyle peeling out and roaring away like I had told him to do?

"Come on!" I ran without looking to see whether Jack was with me. The horn sounded again. I pulled my SIG Sauer 9mm and checked the safety. I had come prepared for anything.

The fifty yards between us could have been a mile. The horn honked twice more, both short and urgent. I expected the truck to begin moving at any second, or for Kyle to shout out the driver's window on the other side. Why wasn't he doing something?

Then I saw it.

Someone was at the driver's side window. The shadow loomed large and threatening, barely visible over the roof of the truck. It was pounding on the window but not saying a word, like a voiceless phantom.

"Get away from there! Now, or I'll shoot!"

"I'm going left!" Jack said.

I circled to the right, around the front of the truck, drawn down on the attacker, ready to shoot at the first sign of threat to me, to Jack. To Kyle. If that truck door opened…

"Get away! Now!" Jack was shouting too.

No shot rang out, but the figure went to his knees beside the truck. He turned toward me, and in the scant glow from the yellow parking lights the eyes of the man looked hollow and vacant.

Then he collapsed in a motionless heap.

I was on him in less than a second, gun leading, and Jack was there too.

Kyle opened the truck door and leaped out of the truck, a safe distance away from his attacker.

"Light! Light!" Jack said.

Kyle had his phone ready, and the light fell upon the man's face and torso.

His eyes were closed, and his sweatshirt was covered in blood.

It was Buster Shane. And if he wasn't dead yet, I was certain he would be soon.

FORTY-NINE

"IS he breathing?" Jack shook Buster, disregarding the blood that soaked his hand. "Buster! Buster!"

I felt for and found a faint pulse. "He's still alive. Kyle? What happened?"

Kyle was wide eyed and frozen with his light fixed on Buster. "I was just sitting there looking at my phone and all of a sudden there he was. Beating on my window. He didn't say anything. Just hitting my window. I was afraid to open the door. Should I have opened it?" His voice was quivering.

"No, you did the right thing."

Buster moaned again, and Jack shook him, harder this time. "Who did this? Hang with us!"

I lifted the sweatshirt to search for the source of the blood. It was difficult to see the exact nature of the injury in the dim light with blood pouring, but it looked like he had two or three linear wounds in his chest and abdomen. "He's been stabbed."

Buster opened his eyes wide like a wild animal, then narrowed them into tiny slits. "Help," he whispered.

"We are, Buster, we are," Jack said. "Who did this? Tell me!"

"I told him I knew," Buster gasped. "Lily and Ronny."

"Knew what, Buster?" Jack's voice was desperate, and he shook Buster again. "Who?"

Buster's eyes were closed again.

I grabbed Jack's arm to get his attention. "We've got to get him out of here. He's gonna die if we don't."

Jack blinked hard and nodded. He reached for his radio. "This is Masterson. I've got a stabbing victim. Logan's Bluff. I'm en route with him to the hospital. Suspect is still at large. I need a unit here now. No, I need all units." He stood and looked at me and Kyle. "Help me get him in the truck."

I hooked one of Buster's arms around my neck on one side, and Jack did so on the other. "Get his feet," I said to Kyle.

We strained to lift him and hurried to Jack's truck. Jack opened a back door and ordered Kyle to climb in while we repositioned. "You pull, and we'll lift." It's odd how things pop into one's head at inappropriate times, but as we laid Buster down, I thought how it was a good thing Jack had leather seats.

"You go," Jack said to me, bending Buster's knees slightly so he could close the door. "Kyle can go with you and help you watch the road. You need to fly."

I shook my head. "You gotta drive, Jack. You can blue light it. I can't. And you're a better driver than me. It's his best chance."

"No, I gotta find Lily."

I gave him a hard, quick hug and pushed away. "I'll find her. And she's gonna need a father."

Kyle slammed the door on the other side and hurried around the back of the truck.

Jack nodded and opened the driver's door. "You're with me, kid. Gotta hurry."

Kyle frowned at me. "You're staying?"

"Someone needs to explain what happened when the law gets here."

"You're going after him, aren't you?"

I didn't answer.

"It was Proffit," Kyle blurted, pointing at Jack's truck behind him. "Buster just told me."

And there it was. My stomach churned in a battle between disbelief and absolute certainty. "Are you sure?"

"Hundred percent."

"Proffit?" Jack asked. "Do we know him?"

"Don't think so," I lied. "Y'all get out of here." I pushed Kyle toward the truck.

Jack held out his balled fist for an air bump. "Find her, Case." He climbed in behind the wheel and urged Kyle to come on.

"Dad?" Kyle hesitated. He pulled out his phone again, tapped the screen twice, and held it out toward me. "Remember what I told you about the Dunbar house, the name I found on the app of who owned the property now?"

"I do. I don't know the name. Y'all have to go, Kyle. Get him out of here."

He tossed me his phone and told me his password. "Look at the photo. I screenshotted it and circled something. There's a piece of land down there, across Miller's Creek. I wonder if it's the same." He raced around the truck to get in just as Jack shifted it in gear.

Jack hit the blue light and made a hasty loop to get turned around. I waved him down as they passed and motioned for Kyle to roll down the window. "Show Jack that trail camera photo of Proffit when you get to the hospital, but not before."

Kyle nodded and called out as the truck sped away. "Love you, Dad."

"I love you too, son." But he didn't hear me. They were gone.

The quiet became deafening as the roar of Jack's engine died in the distance along with the remnants of the pulsating light atop his truck. What now? I massaged the grip of my 9mm, comforted by its feel. Yes, the chest wounds on Buster were grisly, but if Proffit wanted to bring a knife to a gunfight, that would be fine by me. I would do whatever it took to save Lily.

I studied the photo on Kyle's phone. It took me a moment to become oriented to what I was seeing. It was the app he had used earlier, when he had figured out that the "moat" in Perry's riddle was likely referring to Miller's Creek and when he had identified the current owner of the Dunbar house. The map outlined each parcel of land and gave the name of the owner in the center of it. Since it belonged to the US Corps of Engineers, the parcel where I was standing, on Logan's Bluff, was labeled United States of America. It extended to the river, out to Waterway Road, and down to Miller's Creek. Lined along the opposite side of Miller's Creek were parcels with names I didn't recognize, but Kyle had used his photo app to circle one name on the screenshot: Elijah Mack.

What was the name of the Dunbar house owner? I had barely even made a mental note at the time, expecting to explore it later. Then I remembered. EVM Holdings. That could be Elijah V. Mack. But how was that tied to Proffit and who I knew him to be?

Then it hit me like a wave off a winter Northeaster, washing over and through and into my soul with a sudden, bone-chilling comprehension of what I was dealing with.

I WILL GET YOU. ONE DAY. ONE DAY…

I could see the letter just like I was holding it in my hand. The letter Jet and I had laughed at Jack for keeping, originally sent to all three of us back when we were teenagers by a teenage psychopath.

It was a prophecy of sorts.

From someone who thus undoubtedly fancied himself a prophet. Or a Proffit.

A prophet, just like the famous one of biblical fame, Elijah.

Elijah Mack, of EVM Holdings.

Elijah Vance MacIntosh, Jr.

VJ MacIntosh.

FIFTY

JUST as suddenly, I understood the riddle from Brendan Perry in a way none of us had before.

Millstones float when ghosts peregrinate the moat

It pointed straight to VJ MacIntosh all along. How could I not have seen that?

Yes, the millstone clue likely pointed us toward Miller's Creek. And yes, perhaps it was metaphorical for the deserved punishment for an adult corrupting a youngster, not a direct reference to Kyle because of the timing of it but possibly the other young men VJ had been influencing, like Ronny, Gabe, and more. But it was undoubtedly much more than that. It was a metaphor for a heavy burden, difficult to carry and impossible to leave behind. And clearly, VJ MacIntosh, who was supposed to have been buried on the remnants of his grandfather's farm after an overdose sometime around 1999, was both a burden—a *millstone*—that neither Jack nor I could discharge and a dead man walking—a *ghost*.

His face on Kyle's trail camera had been as clear to me as if I were seeing my own in the mirror. The beard and silvery, long hair were different, but the high cheekbones, sharp nose, and narrow eyes with the venom burning in them like two serpent's lenses formed a visage that I could never, ever forget.

I knew when I saw the trail camera photo that he was alive and was a menace to me and my family, but it was only now that I could make other ominous connections with certainty.

He had killed Ronny.

He had stabbed and likely killed Buster.

And he had Lily. Precious Lily.

And he was nearby.

A rage ignited within me like the core of the sun itself. It was one thing to take the life of an innocent adult—and innocence was relative, for I had done my share of wrong too. But it was another thing entirely to harm a young child. A baby. Something told me that she was alive, though.

I didn't understand how all the events of recent days had come to pass, how these things had fit into VJ's plan. But I understood one thing clearly or thought I did. He was willing and had already schemed to harm us indirectly, through those we cared about, but I would bet my life he would prefer the opportunity to do harm up front and in person. He had bet on Jack or me, or both, coming for him if he took Lily.

Buster had done so and paid the price, and I suspected Lily herself must have been the chink in the armor for Buster. VJ was keeping her alive, for in doing so he maintained an advantage in leverage. Otherwise, Jack would allow justice to come swarming down in a hailstorm of SWAT teams and armored fury.

But then again, what if I was wrong? I thought VJ had been dead for almost twenty years. Nothing was certain with that maniac. Maybe his intention was to take her and disappear, to torture those who loved her for the remainder of their lives. I had to go find her, before VJ disappeared like an apparition again. I took another look at the screenshot Kyle had given me, oriented myself, and took off across the clearing atop Logan's Bluff. Down the back side of it was a slope to Miller's Creek. And down the edge of that was a property belonging to a man calling himself Elijah Mack.

Kyle turned in the seat of Jack's truck to take a look at Buster. The man wasn't moving. He wasn't saying anything. He wasn't even moaning now. His body shifted just a bit when they turned out of the meadow at the top of the bluff and hit a set of ruts hard on the trail going down, but he was too heavy for it to bounce him off the seat.

"You know this Proffit guy?" Jack asked.

"Not really. Met him through a friend. Didn't know he was bad like this."

"Your dad know him?"

"I'm not sure," Kyle lied. His father's face had left no doubt. Kyle just didn't know how he knew him. But it was a look he had rarely seen before: fear.

Jack nodded. "Don't worry about him. He'll just wait and talk to Rappaport or whoever else shows up."

"You know that's not true. He's going after Lily." Kyle wasn't naïve enough to think Jack had brought him along because he needed help watching the road.

Jack kept his eyes forward, focusing. Branches protruding over the primitive roadway scratched the truck as it sped downward, lurching from side to side as it hit the ruts too hard, and he fought to keep it centered. "He'll be okay," he said.

The road flattened out slightly near the bottom of the hill before its final descent to the point where it ended at Waterway Road, and the foliage along the road thinned and opened into a small clearing on Kyle's side.

Kyle slapped his window. "Stop! There he is!"

Jack hit the brakes but didn't stop. "What? Who?"

"Stop! Stop!" Kyle yelled.

Jack slammed the brakes harder this time, coming to a

complete stop, and Kyle reached back to make sure Buster didn't roll off the seat. "What are you talking about?" Jack said.

Kyle hit the unlock button and opened his door. "Sorry, Jack. You can take it from here." He jumped out of the truck, ran through the tall grass in the clearing, and disappeared into the woods.

I remembered the spot where Kyle had pointed out an old, overgrown trail leading away from Logan's Bluff down to Miller's Creek, and I set my sights on that as my best option. The small Maglite I held wasn't very bright, but its beam extended much further than my phone light could. I aimed for a group of pine trees based on what Kyle had said, hoping the trail from there would be more obvious.

The cold of the pistol's polymer grip in my hand felt reassuring, but my confidence in the safety of my mission was small. VJ could be anywhere. Behind any tree, hiding in any clump of bushes, crouched over the next tiny rise. Could I get on him before he stabbed me like he had Buster? For all I knew he had a gun, too, and would pick me off from a distance before I even knew he was there. I stopped every few feet to listen. Each rustle of leaves and night animal sound made me flinch and my heart pound harder.

I took another look at the photo on Kyle's phone. I was going in the right direction. The main thing was to get to the bottom of the hill, to the creek. Getting across it would be the next step. I would swim it if I had to. If VJ was headed to his property, he would have used a boat. I would have no such luxury.

I pushed through snagging limbs and vines and even had to

crawl on hands and knees in one spot to get through a thicket. If a trail still existed, I had missed it. Suddenly, much before I expected it, I popped out of a tangle of briars and saw the white of sand at my feet. I was at the creek bank. I realized there was a murmur in the air so soft it had sneaked into the air without me recognizing it: running water.

Where are you, VJ?

This was a wild goose chase. What was I thinking? Did I really think I could find VJ in the dark? Wouldn't it have been better to have an expert analyze the crime scene, possibly even track the man from there? I could hear Rappaport now. "We're up here working the crime scene, needing someone to tell us what happened and show us where, and you're playing in the weeds down on the creek bank? Messing up the scent trail? Thinking you're a Navy SEAL sneaking up on a man as dead as Lee Harvey Oswald?" He would have a field day with it. And what if my impetuousness led to VJ getting away? To Lily never being rescued?

It was time to go back. I had little confidence in our sheriff and his crew, but at least they would be properly equipped. Was there someone else we could call? Wasn't there a better way to get to the property owned by "Elijah Mack?" I angled down the creek bank, tiptoeing along the edge where the less-than-usual rainfall had revealed a sandy shore typically obscured by water, looking for a better egress from the edge than the one I had crawled out of to get to it.

And just as I turned to hop up through a break in the foliage and forge back uphill, I saw it.

A ten- or twelve-foot aluminum johnboat, about twenty yards downstream. It was tied to a river birch leaning out over the water.

Was that VJ's? If so, what did that mean? Was VJ still on

the Logan's Bluff side of the creek? If he was, taking the boat to cross and go find and search his property might save Lily and also strand him, helping ensure he was apprehended.

If it was not VJ's boat, whose was it and why was it there? Regardless of the answer to those questions, there was no question what I needed to do next.

The rope was barely secured by a loose slip knot, and I had my gun holstered and was pushing off in the boat within seconds. Fortunately, a paddle was lying in the floor. I debated whether to go straight across or drift downstream first and chose the latter. If I was where I thought I was, VJ's land was less than a quarter mile away—not much by boat but a long way to navigate through the woods on foot, at night, over unfamiliar terrain.

The risk was overshooting my mark, though. Even with the paddle I didn't think I could work my way back upstream. Which, as I thought about it, also answered my original question. I didn't know whose it was, but this couldn't be the boat VJ used to cross from his land to Logan's. It had no motor.

My thoughts turned back to my safety. I had seen far too many movies where the enemy lurked in the brush alongside a waterway, ambushing unsuspecting soldiers or travelers, giving them no chance. I was a sitting duck.

I hunkered low in the boat, peeking over the bow and sides, hoping for a sign telling me where to stop, making myself a small target for fear of a bullet in my skull. The creek was only about thirty feet wide, and its edges were bisected with pieces of wood, some still connected to their trunks, some fallen and rotting. The clanging of limbs against the side and hull as I drifted made me nervous; I might as well be ringing a bell to announce my arrival.

Once again, just as soon as I questioned my decision, it was made for me.

I came upon another boat, on the port side. Elijah Mack's side.

Similarly, it was tied to a tree, with no dock or other permanent structure. It was different, though, as its bow was slid up onto a clear patch of sand. It had rested there many times before. And this boat had a twenty-five horsepower Mercury outboard.

This was it.

Moments later I was standing on the opposite shore of Miller's Creek from where I had begun. My Maglite revealed a well-worn trail meandering away from the creek between black tupelo, willow oak, sweetbay, and pools of murky water in the low spots.

Up the trail, in the distance, past the point where the gray-green of the night woods darkened to black at the end of my light's reach, I saw something flicker. I took a step to my right for a better look and confirmed what I was seeing.

There was a light.

Lily will be there.

I froze and listened for sounds out of place but heard only the hum of the water behind me and the flow of my rapid breaths in my throat. I pulled the pistol from its holster at my waist and moved toward the trail but only made it two steps.

A tree before me seemed to split, and a figure in a long coat was suddenly standing before me, twenty feet away in the center of the trail.

The ghost was very much alive, and he was smiling.

FIFTY-ONE

"IT'S been a long time, Case." VJ's voice was much deeper than I remembered it. It was odd, seeing the older version of the teenager I had known yet being surprised when his voice had aged too. He leaned back onto the tree he had been hiding behind and folded his arms across his chest. He wore a dark trench coat and Stetson, both of which blended with the darkness and contrasted with his silver hair flowing down near his shoulders.

"Where is Lily? Up there?" I motioned in the direction of the light I had seen.

"Ahh. The child. That seems a likely location. My humble home."

I leveled my pistol at him.

"If you pull the trigger, you'll never find her alive. And if you don't, I'll never comply with your wishes. Quite the conundrum, yes?"

I contemplated shooting him in the leg. Don't kill; just incapacitate. But I wasn't the shot with a pistol that I was with a rifle, and what if I accidentally killed him? Or worse, missed and he cut me in half with a shotgun he had hidden under that coat?

He looked at his watch. "You're just in time, but I was beginning to wonder. Did you like the boat I left for you?"

"You can't get away, VJ. Jack has already called it in. The entire sheriff's department, the FBI, game wardens, and who-knows-who-else will be here any minute."

He spread his arms wide. "Be here? Where is here? I'll be long gone by the time they get here. That creek leads to a river with a thousand places one can catch another ride. Besides, all of those organizations are currently much more interested in preventing the destruction of a vinyl chloride plant on the other side of the county."

"What are you talking about?"

"Continental Chemicals. Haven't you heard? Some madman called in a highly credible-sounding threat to blast their storage tanks wide open. You know how many people would be killed in that neighborhood just across the fence? Then there's the creek nearby that runs through the wildlife refuge. Those poor animals. Vinyl chloride is highly toxic, you know.

"Speaking of Jack, I hate that he didn't make the trip. It would have been a delightful reunion." He made a clicking sound with his tongue. "And too bad Jet is in Africa. The timing of recent events was not of my choosing."

"What do you want, VJ?" I fired the gun into the air, prepared to dive for cover if he pulled a weapon of his own.

But he didn't flinch. Instead, he stood up straight and moved toward me. "I want to fulfill my promise to you."

"Stop right there!"

"You for the child." He stopped. "Put the gun down, Case. How would it look if you shot me? Vigilante, out in the woods, chasing down and shooting an unarmed man for whom he has a long-held and well-publicized grudge. You would go to jail for that one. Even in Mississippi. Speaking of public grudges, your books were quite entertaining. I didn't like the light in which they portrayed me, but I can understand your unwillingness to see things the way they really were."

This man was truly insane. What was he even prattling on about? "You said me for the child. What do you mean?"

"I mean, you come with me, and I will let you tell her good-bye before you release her to return to her family."

"You said I would never find her if I shot you. Now you're saying she's right up there? Which is it, VJ?"

He smirked. "You always thought you were so smart. I didn't say where she was. You have merely assumed." He opened the palm of his hand to reveal what appeared to be a small remote control. "But to your credit, you assumed correctly. The problem is, one tap of this will send the poor child into a million pieces. It would be tragic." He gestured up the trail. "So if you want to find her alive, we must go this way. I do insist that you lead, however."

What was I to do? I had already determined that shooting him posed too great a risk to Lily's safety and possibly mine. And that was *before* I knew he had a bomb ready for Lily, if he was telling the truth. If I agreed to go with him, might that buy some time for others to show up?

I was not foolish enough to believe he would fulfill his end of the bargain, though. He had evidently bought himself some time with a bomb threat—false or real—on the chemical plant, but if he was planning on escaping by boat, leading me the wrong direction could only mean one thing: I wasn't coming back.

I had no choice, though. If I could lay eyes on Lily, maybe I could see a way out. I nodded. "Okay."

"I'll have to insist that you rid yourself of the weapon. For Lily's sake. I would hate for you to flinch and pull the trigger. It would almost certainly cause me to do the same." VJ was smiling again, just like he had been when he stepped out into the trail moments before. Just like he had as a teenager whenever he thought he sounded clever. I wanted to throw my gun down, shove my fist through his teeth, and stomp his head into the sand. But I couldn't do that. I would have to go with him.

"Throw it into the weeds."

I tossed my handgun into the bushes and made a mental note of where to find it, not entirely confident that I could. In the darkness most of the foliage looked the same.

"I hate guns. So boring and impersonal."

Then I saw it.

A shadow behind VJ. Stalking. Creeping. Utterly silent.

Jack. But how? Had Buster died, and Jack turned around and come back? How had he gotten across the creek?

Then I realized I was wrong, and it made me sick.

The shadow was feet away from VJ, now, and I did not know whether to attack or yell out. Before I could do either, Kyle sprang like a bobcat upon VJ's back and clamped his forearm around VJ's neck from behind. "Get him, Dad!"

"It's a bomb, Kyle! No!"

No explosion occurred, though, and I bolted into action, aiming straight at VJ and the son desperately trying to save his father. Before I could get to them, VJ lunged backward and slammed Kyle into the trunk of an oak. Kyle made a sickening grunt, and VJ whirled and punched him. Kyle collapsed in a heap at the base of the tree.

I was on VJ now, though, raging to inflict the justice he had evaded for so long, down to his last breath or mine. I had whipped him into cowardly submission with one punch when we were kids. I would beat him into oblivion this time.

Then I saw the glint of silver, and I knew I was in trouble. Buster's injuries flashed in my mind as I rammed into VJ, and a searing pain split my chest with a warm wetness against my skin.

VJ spun, and we hurtled to the ground with him upon me. The back of my head hit hard against a tree root at the same instant a shock of cold took my breath. I was underwater, straining to find air, to block another stabbing from his knife, to gain an advantage, knowing I would die if I failed any of them.

I twisted just enough to slide away from VJ's knee in my chest, and I pushed myself away and upward. On my feet now somehow, I staggered back, feeling my strength draining quickly. Too quickly. I went to one knee, too weak to stand. VJ stood and smiled, wiping water from his face with a vile, crooked smile full of satisfaction to match the sadism glowing in his narrow eyes. He bent down and then stood, once again brandishing the knife that had been knocked away in the struggle.

I couldn't win. Not now. Adrenalin was keeping me alive for the moment, but I needed more than that. My clothes were soaking wet. Blood and water? The trees were dancing. Were they happy, or was it a dirge? Surely they were on my side, weren't they?

A fire glowed beneath me. Was that the fire of hell, or something else? Hell was VJ's fire, not mine. Right? What is that fire? It's not fire. My Maglite. It's not hot like fire. Grab it. Don't quit. *One more play.* Who said that? *One more play.* Wait, that's me talking. *One more play.* Just like on Friday nights.

I grabbed the Maglite and threw it as hard as I could.

It hit VJ MacIntosh right between the eyes.

He staggered backward two steps, smiled again, and was swallowed by the earth.

FIFTY-TWO

Thursday, November 1, 2018

"COACH Reynolds! I need you to take a deep breath and exhale. Mr. Reynolds? Can you hear me?"

I nodded, gagging on the tube in my throat. It must have been the size of a water hose. Where was I? Who was this talking to me?

"Take a deep breath and then breathe out."

I blinked hard, trying to focus. I took a breath and pushed it out, and the water hose was pulled out, possibly along with one of my lungs. I gagged and coughed and heaved.

A beeping noise above me and bubbling sound beside me blended with the words of the person talking to me while she listened to my lungs. "Ninety-eight percent oxygen sats," she said. "Great job."

I coughed again and surveyed the room, hoping to orient myself. It was bright, sterile, square. A curtain was drawn across the front.

The woman at my side smiled, and a man joined her from behind me. "I'm Adrian, your respiratory therapist," she said. "And I hear you know your nurse, Curtis. Congratulations, you've just been successfully extubated."

I nodded and tried to sit up, but a pain shot through my chest, and my head was on the brink of exploding. I grimaced and moaned.

"Easy, there, Coach." Curtis smiled and grabbed my forearm, examining the IV tubing attached to it. "There'll be time for that soon enough. Rest a minute. I'll let your family in shortly." He leaned down closer and lowered his voice. "Supposed to be only one visitor at a time, but I'll make an exception for my old ball coach."

After an eternity, the curtain parted, and a black-haired, blue-eyed beauty with a worried smile walked in.

"Abi."

She grabbed my hand and squeezed. "You don't remember me doing this last night, do you?"

I shook my head. The last thing I remembered before the water hose affair was VJ MacIntosh gloating about killing me, then disappearing. "What…what happened?"

Abi leaned down and kissed me on the forehead. She inadvertently leaned on my chest, and I grunted in pain. She popped back upright and put her hand over her mouth. "Oh! I'm sorry. Your chest tube."

"Chest tube?"

Abi held up a finger. She pulled out her phone and touched the screen. It beeped several times, and Abi smiled. "He's ready," she said. She handed me the phone.

Jet was staring back at me with a huge smile. "Hey, Case! Good to see your ugly mug."

"I knew you wouldn't believe anything the doctors said without Jet agreeing," Abi said, "so I got him here all the way from Africa before you could insist."

"You had a triple whammy," Jet said. "Pneumothorax, a coup contracoup injury, and early hypothermia. Fortunately, no vascular structures large enough to cause exsanguination were compromised."

"Stop it." Gracie popped into the screen. "Collapsed lung, concussion, too cold. They almost lost you last night, but you're going to be fine."

Jet was back again, smiling. "Sorry, had to do that. Basically, you'll have the chest tube a few days until the air bubbling stops, some headaches, some time to get your strength back. But you'll be back in no time. One hundred percent recovery."

That answered some of my questions, but I had a thousand more.

"We have to go," Gracie said. "Abi gave us a two-minute ultimatum. Plus, the orphanage here never sleeps. Greatest thing I've ever done. We love you and are glad you're okay."

"Hang in there, buddy," Jet said. "See you soon."

Jet and Gracie waved and disappeared.

I gave the phone back to Abi and asked the question I dreaded. "What about Kyle?"

Abi smiled. "He's fine."

"Lily?"

Abi patted my arm and shook her head. "Not so far. Not a trace. We're still looking."

My heart sank. With every passing minute the odds of finding her plummeted.

The curtain quivered and parted, and three welcomed faces appeared. Jack, Kellen, and Kyle stepped in. Curtis poked his head through and made a "shh" sign behind them before disappearing.

"Hey guys!" My eyes welled with tears, and Abi patted me again. "I'm so glad to see you!"

Jack tried to smile, but his struggle was obvious. "Hey, bud. About time you woke up."

"I'm sorry about Lily," I said. "I'll get out of here soon. We'll find her."

Jack waved me off. "You get better. Plenty folks looking."

Kellen stepped over and gave me a hug. She was crying. "We've tried, Dad. I thought we could find her. I've been so worried. You, her, Kyle, it's terrible."

I brought her hand to my lips and kissed it. "You're a rock-star, babe. I'm fine. They'll find her."

Kyle was standing back, beside Abi.

I gestured with a curl of two fingers. Come here, son. What happened?"

"I'll tell you," Jack said. "He saved your butt. Sneaky joker bailed out of my truck, circled back."

My boy. "How did you get across the creek?"

Kyle smiled. "There's a tree fallen across the creek just upstream. Just gotta know where it is and have good balance. Sorry you got stabbed. I thought I had him."

I touched the deep purple bruise around his left eye. "You did great. Don't be sorry. But I thought you were going to trigger the bomb he had."

Kyle shook his head, and I thought I saw him puff his chest just a bit. "I went up to the cabin first. Lily wasn't there. So I knew he was bluffing. Plus I kicked it out of his hand when I jumped him."

"How did you get me out, though? Did you use VJ's boat?"

Kyle looked at Jack, who spoke up. "Kyle had the bleeding stopped and a fire going to warm you up when help arrived."

Kyle smiled. "Flint and steel, baby."

I smiled back, but I was confused. "Help?"

Jack pulled a business card from his pocket. "Found this on the seat of my truck. Dana Harlow, FBI. And as a bonus, someone we know wrote the GPS coordinates on the back for a property on Miller's Creek owned by one Elijah Mack."

Kyle shrugged. "The coordinates are on the app. And that shot you fired helped too. Those game warden boats can fly down that river."

"Let's just say that Kyle lit the fire, and Agent Harlow poured gasoline on it," Jack said. "She's somethin' else." I thought I detected a twinkle in his eye, one I had seen too many times before. But it disappeared quickly. He clenched his jaw and frowned. "Now I need her to find Lily."

I wanted to reassure him that would happen but couldn't. I barely knew anything. "Tell me. What about VJ?"

Abi grimaced, and Kyle turned away. "He's gone for good," Jack said.

"He disappeared after he stabbed me."

"You could say that," Jack said. "Remember when we were kids, Case? We tried to make that mini Burmese tiger pit for that armadillo Papa Mac said was rutting up his fields? Made the sharp stakes in the bottom out of hickory sticks? Well, VJ had a full-sized one built for you. Or me, I guess, depending on who showed up."

Now I understood why VJ had insisted I lead the way up the trail toward the light. He had intended on watching me die, impaled in a pit beneath his feet. Kyle's attack and mine had evidently disoriented him in the dark, and he'd fallen into his own trap when I hit him with the flashlight. I shuddered to think how close I'd come. Or, God forbid, Kyle. But I still had questions. "I still don't understand what VJ was doing. Why did he come back? Just to get at us?"

"Kids, why don't you go on out to the waiting room?" Abi said. "Adults need to talk for a bit." Both of them began to mount protests, but a sharp glare and lift of the chin from their mother ended that.

"C'mere and give me a hug," I said. "Love you guys."

Kellen leaned in and rested her head on my chest for a moment. I would have let her stay there all day, but Kyle pulled her away playfully. "Love you, Dad," she said. "Glad you're okay."

Kyle hesitated and reached out to give me a fist bump, but I grabbed his hand and pulled him closer, trying not to wince.

He smiled. "Next time you bring a gun to a knife fight, hang on to the gun."

I laughed and groaned at the pain in my head suddenly equaling that in my chest. I held on to his hand and looked him in the eye. "Thank you. You saved my life."

He shrugged and smiled. "Never know. You might've had one more play in you even if I didn't show up." He leaned in and hugged me hard, and I didn't mind the pain.

After Kyle and Kellen left, Jack pulled up a chair and leaned forward, elbows on his knees. Abi sat beside me on the bed. I noticed for the first time she had a book with her but didn't ask what it was.

"News that bad, huh?"

"Naw," Jack said. "I'm just exhausted. Not everyone got an eight-hour stress-free nap last night."

I knew he must have been scouring the county and beyond looking for Lily. "My night wasn't exactly stress free," I said, "but I wouldn't trade with you. I'm really sorry."

Abi looked as tired as Jack. I realized she had probably been up all night too. "You should go get some rest. No court today, I guess?"

"Fortunately, I didn't have to cancel. Judge Foster did it for me. But to answer your question about VJ, we've learned a lot but may have questions for years. Jack and I may have been told more than we should know by our contacts, so just keep this to yourself."

I suspected Abi's contact was the district attorney, possibly the judge, but I wondered about Jack's. Somehow I doubted Rappaport knew or would tell him much of anything. I had a hunch it was a five-foot-seven spitfire of an FBI agent. Either way, I didn't care. I just wanted to know what they knew. "Tell me, Abi."

"Buster Shane was working with the FBI."

Buster. "Oh no. So he was innocent? What a waste of a life."

Jack and Abi shared a look I didn't understand. "He's alive," Abi said. "Jack got him here just in time. He's two rooms down. On life support but hanging on."

"Wow." I fought back tears that came from a place I couldn't identify. *God, let him live.* There had been too much lost already. Whatever Buster had done before, good needed a chance now. "That's great," I stammered.

Abi rubbed my arm and nodded for Jack to go on.

"I'll get back to Buster, but VJ disappeared off the map back in '95 or so. Had some money from his father's estate, just disappeared. Who knows why Lane Buckley told us he had died and been buried out in the woods? We'll never know. I remember now they looked for his remains for a bit, but it was half-hearted. Nobody doubted he was dead. It wasn't like he was DB Cooper or something. Nobody cared. Anyway, he got a new identity. According to what Buster told the FBI, a man named John Proffit met Judith Shane online several months back and moved into her life soon after."

"A widow living off her husband's pension," I said.

"Exactly. And we suspect he's done it before," Abi said. "Won't be surprised if he's been doing it for years. Bilk a woman under an alias for all she's worth and then disappear."

"This time, though, it brought him close to home," Jack said.

"Funny thing is, she started getting sick shortly after he came into the picture," Abi said. "According to Buster, VJ began providing her with some "special" marijuana to alleviate her symptoms. Buster didn't mind at first, you know, especially since he'd been involved in some suspicious stuff of his own for years before he went to jail. He was up for whatever it took to help his dying mother. But then he found out Ronny was selling. First some weed, then pills. And he had one customer in particular."

Jack shook his head, and I understood. "Tammy."

"Yeah," Jack said, sounding dejected. "We think VJ singled her out to get at me. She was an easy target. Folks around here knew her history."

"Probably knew about her from Ronny," Abi said, "who had been Devlin's best friend when they were younger."

"I don't understand where the FBI comes in."

Abi nudged me. "Patience, babe. About that time, Buster got busted—no pun intended—for possession of marijuana, which he said was for his mother. Given his criminal record, that was a big deal. He was about to go back to jail for a long time. But because of the uptick in drug activity in the county, the narcotics folks were looking for confidential informants. Buster was happy to tell them that he had connections to a local drug kingpin—even though he knew it wasn't technically true—and he would deliver him to their feet. What he really wanted though, was to prove his theory that VJ was poisoning his mother and had done it to others before. Not to mention, avoid going back to prison just as he was getting back into his daughter's life."

"Somehow," Jack said, "VJ must have gotten wind of someone being a rat. He thought it was Ronny and planned to kill him."

It was convoluted, but it was beginning to make sense to me. "I'll bet Ronny told him about plans to meet Devlin and Tammy at Logan's Bluff, and he saw an opportunity."

"Yep," Abi said. "Not just to eliminate Ronny but to implicate Devlin and/or Tammy. What better way to really get at Jack? He may have even convinced Ronny to have them meet at that location because he knew he could get in and out undetected."

"What about Kyle?" I asked. "I guess you know all about that."

"Evidently, VJ had that set up as a parting shot to get at you, Case," Abi said. "Or us, actually. He had cleared out Judith's bank account and was ready to leave town."

"But Buster got to him first."

Jack leaned forward in his chair. "He told Dana, er, Agent Foster, that he initially thought Devlin had killed Ronny. That threw him off for a bit. But when Devlin got off and Buster saw some of the bank transactions, he knew. Plus, Janie had been keeping him updated on the case while he was laying low."

"Where does Lily come into this?" I hated to bring it up for the pain it caused but needed to know. Plus, I had learned from past mysteries that talking it out sometimes leads to a breakthrough.

Jack shook his head and clenched his fists. "No idea. There's no evidence that VJ ever had her. Not a trace at that cabin in the woods, in his boat, at the Dunbar house he had bought. His truck was at Judith's house, and nothing there, either. They're running forensics but so far nothing."

"But Lily was the reason I went after him," I said.

Jack nodded. "I know. Buster, too, sort of. He wanted vengeance for Ronny also."

"And he had the trap set for me. I remember now, he said he didn't know if it would be me or you. But he was ready."

"If he didn't have anything to do with Lily, maybe he just used it as an opportunity," Abi said. "Evil has a way of exploiting other evil."

That seemed reasonable. "He did tell me he was about to give up on me. Like he wasn't sure we would come and was about to leave. Something about speeding away in his boat before anyone even knew he was there." But wait, that didn't make sense either. "No way he could have dug that pit in such a short time."

Jack shrugged and shot Abi another look like before, but this time it was lighter. He broke into a smile. "You won't believe this."

"You're probably right."

He pulled out his phone. "Look at this. He wasn't going very far."

It was a photo of the inside of a boat. It took me a second to orient myself, then I recognized it as VJ's boat, the one I had come upon in my little johnboat. It was full of water, like the plug had been removed. And drawn in mud on the white of the gunwale was a hand, with three fingers flexed and the thumb and pinky extended. A Shaka sign.

I smiled and vowed to hug and punch Brendan Perry if I ever saw him again. I would decide when the time came which would be first, but one would be for trying to stop VJ in his own peculiar way, and the other would be for almost letting me get impaled. The Vagabond was one of a kind.

FIFTY-THREE

JACK stood and moved to put his phone in his pocket, but it buzzed. He studied the text a moment, frowned, and cursed.

"What is it?" I asked.

"Can't be." He shook his head. "One of the other deputies tells me they're searching a kid's house about Lily. Says they've found something."

"A kid?" Abi asked. "What about Lily?"

Jack looked pale. "She's not there. 'Evidence' is all he says." He put the phone to his ear for a time and cursed again as he dropped it to look at his message again. "Not answering. Sorry for the language, Abi."

She gave a dismissive wave. "Who is it?"

"Teenager. Gabe Liston is his name." Jack blinked hard and cut his eyes to me. "Isn't that Kyle's friend?"

My breath left me. What was happening? There was no part of me that believed Kyle was involved, but his friend? Was it possible? I feared for Kyle's reputation if so. And I feared for Lily infinitely more. I remembered reading about a seemingly normal teenager who had raped and killed a young child over around Tuscaloosa a few months back. It was sickening.

"It is," Abi said, "but I don't think—"

"Do you know him?" Jack's eyes were wide with alarm.

Before either of us could answer, the curtain to the room parted again. Curtis stepped in and let the curtain settle behind him. "Coach, there's someone here says he needs to see you right now."

"Who is it?"

Curtis winced. "It's the sheriff."

"Tell him to get in here," Jack said, standing.

Curtis looked to me, and I nodded. He waved Wayne Rappaport to the door but stopped him with his forearm. "He's had too many visitors already. So be quick."

"Yeah, yeah." Rap marched in and stood at the foot of my bed. He folded his thick arms over his chest and eyed the monitor above me like he knew what he was looking at. He pursed his lips and frowned, bringing his bushy gray eyebrows and mustache closer together. "Guess you heard about the Liston boy." He wasn't looking at anyone in particular.

"We didn't hear much. Tell me, Rap," Jack said. He gripped the side rails on the bed, and his knuckles were white.

"Got a tip. Found this in his car." He showed Jack a pic on his phone.

Jack closed his eyes and brought his fist to his mouth. "That's Lily's." He grabbed the phone and turned it for Abi and me to see.

It was the pony Devlin had won for her at the festival the night before.

"What kind of car?" Abi said.

"Black SUV. Jeep Compass. Nothing else so far at the house. Going through his phone now. We'll find something there." Rappaport frowned again and took a deep breath that made his broad chest rise, pause, and fall with a slump of his shoulders. He focused on me for a moment then turned to Abi. "There's something else."

"Spit it out," Abi said.

"I'm not supposed to do this, but I think you've earned the courtesy. Got a warrant to search your house too. On the way there now."

"My house? I'll make you think my house." I lurched to try to sit up and yelped with the pain. "My house?" I didn't know what would happen if I ripped the chest tube out, but I was ready to try.

Abi put a firm hand on my chest. "Stop." She gave me a stern look like she often did with our children. "Sheriff, you better have the best reason you've ever had."

He showed his palms in a defensive gesture. "I know we won't find anything, but this type of thing isn't always my decision. And we know this Liston kid and your son are good friends. And your son and the Cervelo girl are close—"

"We are *all* close to her," Abi said, slow and emphatically. "She is our *family*."

"Lily," Jack said. "Her name is Lily. And his name is Kyle. And you better get one thing straight. I'm not the smartest guy in the world. There are a lot of things I don't know. But what I *do* know…" He poked his finger in Rappaport's chest. "What I *do* know is that Kyle Reynolds didn't have anything to do with this. I'll bet my life and my career on it." Jack's face was blood red, and the vein in his temple bulged like a rope. He pushed his finger in hard and pulled back and started walking toward the entrance, glaring back at Rappaport. "So if you want to say otherwise, I'll end my career right now, and we can go settle your doubts outside."

Abi stepped into the space between Jack and Rappaport and gestured for Jack to stop while looking at Rap. "Tensions are high, and we don't need the situation to get worse. Sheriff, you implicated this wasn't your decision. Whose was it?"

Rappaport was eyeing Jack like a man locked in the room with a tiger. "I, uh, didn't say that exactly. But some things are, uh, classified."

Abi rolled her eyes. "Classified? Yeah, okay, whatever."

"What about Gabe?" I said. "I guess you're going to tell us that how you got the tip on him is classified, also?"

Rappaport finally took his eyes off Jack and looked at Abi, then me. "Gabe? Oh, the Liston kid. Uh, yes. That is also confidential pending the outcome of our, uh, investigation."

Jack snorted and fidgeted, like the tiger Rappaport feared.

Abi gestured for him to calm down. "One more question," she said, like a prosecutor interrogating a witness on the stand. "Who issued the warrants?"

Rappaport coughed. "That's irrelevant."

"It's not irrelevant," Abi said. "I want to know the names of every single person in our justice system, besides you and your cronies of course, who is sidetracked on this nonsense while the real kidnapper is getting away." She stepped up to Rappaport and glared at him. "Tell me right now."

Rappaport frowned again, and I thought his eyebrows and mustache might touch this time. "It was Judge Foster."

Abi nodded. "Okay."

Rappaport gave a patronizing smile. "Now if you'll excuse me, I have an investigation to run." He stepped back and turned toward the entrance.

Jack blocked his path for a moment before stepping aside, glaring at him all the while.

Curtis stepped in as Rappaport left. "I'm sorry, folks, but it's gonna be my hide if I don't clear this room. Too many visitors, too long."

Abi gave me a kiss on the forehead. "You rest. I'll take care of things. Let me go talk to Kyle."

Jack gave me a fist bump. "Sorry you got dragged into this, buddy. I've got some work to do myself."

I nodded at both of them, too stunned to speak. I needed one more play but didn't have one in me at the moment. I didn't know whether to scream or cry, but either was a better alternative to the nothing I was capable of at that instant.

FIFTY-FOUR

ABI led Jack to the ICU waiting room where Kellen and Kyle were and stopped at the entrance. "I need you to do something for me."

"I'll take the twins with me," Jack said. "You go to your house."

Abi shook her head. "No. I need you to go there and sub for Case. I've got something else I need to do. The twins can go with me. I need to keep Kyle away right now anyway."

Jack frowned. "I don't understand. I…I need to be looking for Lily, but I don't know where to go." His voice cracked and he paused, his eyes full of anger and anguish. "But I'll help you guys if you insist. Where are you going?"

"You've got to trust me on this. Just make an appearance. Let them know there'll be hell to pay if they go too far." Abi patted him on the shoulder. "Just like Case would if he could."

———

Kellen called "shotgun" and got the front seat without protest from Kyle, and Abi wondered if he knew about Gabe yet. Rappaport said they had taken Gabe's phone, but word travels fast in a small town. Kyle was quiet, and she left it that way. There would be plenty of time to talk later. Or at least, there should be.

Kellen asked where they were going, but Abi's reply was curt. "You'll know when you know." Her mind was racing. Was she way off base? Should she be at home hovering while they searched her house, trying to explain to Kyle why he wasn't really a suspect?

"I can't believe all this," Kellen said. "Do you think Lily is still okay?"

"I hope so," Abi said. "I sure hope so."

Kellen opened the book in her lap. "This VJ guy looked like a killer even then. How did Kyle not see that?"

"Shut up, Kellen!" Kyle snapped from the back seat.

Abi had thought it less-than-ideal but not necessarily inappropriate when Kellen had brought her dad's old yearbook to the hospital. Ever curious, she wanted to see what VJ had looked like in high school; she just couldn't imagine someone being that vengeful for that long.

Kyle had folded his arms and kept to himself, which was fine. He had a lot more to reconcile in his mind than Kellen. It was only when Jack had become emotional that Abi had taken it away and closed it for good.

Abi pointed at the ever-present phone in Kellen's lap. "Look up the number for the Sunset Shores Marina." Kellen gave a questioning look, but Abi wasn't having it. "Don't ask. Just do," she said.

"662–"

"Call it and give me the phone."

Kellen complied and handed Abi the phone as she spun the steering wheel, turning onto a narrow road off the highway.

"Sunset," a man's voice said.

"Sir, this is Abi Reynolds. I'm the county attorney. Are you the owner or manager?"

"Both."

"Fine. What's your name?"

"Hakeem."

"Hakeem, this is very important. I don't know if you've heard or not, but a little girl is missing. And I'm trying to find her."

"Yes, police came by this morning. Wanted to know if we have a camera."

"Do you?"

"No. It stop working a few months ago. Expensive to replace."

"What did the officer look like?"

"It was two men. Tall man. Short man, bushy mustache."

Nash and Rappaport. Of course. "Did they tell you that the man who kidnapped the little girl might be parking his boat at your marina?"

"No. They only asked for list of names who dock here but that is all. I told them get a warrant. They got mad and left."

Abi didn't know if Hakeem was being difficult or prudent. "Can't blame you there. Listen, Hakeem, I'm not going to ask anything specific like that. I just have one question. If you tell me, I'll leave you alone. If you don't, I'll have some officers by there tomorrow with that warrant. Fair enough?"

"What?" Hakeem said flatly.

"I'm sure you've figured out by now who the person is that they're talking about. He was killed last night, but we still haven't found the girl. I have a feeling he's been coming there quite awhile. Can you tell me, when he's not in his truck, who usually drops him off?"

"I do not know person's name."

"Can you tell me what they look like?"

"No. Windows are heavy tinted."

So he has seen the vehicle. "Hakeem, this is so important. What does the vehicle look like?"

"Black," Hakeem said. "One of those, what you call it? SUV?"

Abi turned her Chevy Tahoe off the county road and onto an asphalt driveway angling uphill into a wooded area. The underbrush had been cleared away, and the ground beneath the canopy was covered in a layer of dried leaves. The house wasn't visible from the road but jumped into view immediately once on the driveway. It was a cottage-style with dormer windows, a screened porch, and cedar-shake siding. The driveway ran all the way up to the front door where it circled back, but Abi didn't go that far. Instead, she stopped about a hundred feet short of it, did a three-point turn between two trees, and turned the car to face away from the house.

"What are you doing?" Kellen asked.

"Whose house is this?" Kyle piped in from the back seat, breaking his silence.

"Don't' worry about that," Abi said. "Kyle, when I get out, you get up here in the driver's seat. Leave the car running."

"Kyle?" Kellen protested. "He hasn't even been paying attention."

Abi gave her a shut-it-down glare. "You called shotgun. You got shotgun. Now, your jobs—both of you—is to pay attention. That's it. If you see anything suspicious at all, drive away from here as fast as you can."

"Mom?" Kellen's eyes were wide. "What's going on?"

Abi looked at Kyle in the rearview mirror. He looked almost as alarmed but didn't say anything. "I just need to check on something. But these are crazy times. And crazy things can happen. So be ready."

Without another word, Abi got out of the car. She didn't look behind her but heard Kyle open one door and close the other. *They'll be fine.* She wished she had somewhere else to send them. Somewhere other than home, where their rooms and private belongings were getting turned inside out, and here, where the next ten minutes were as unpredictable as the ocean waves. There was a strong chance she was about to lose her job. Or worse. But if she didn't go, she might lose her mind. Or worse.

The garage doors were closed. Abi considered checking the side door but decided against it. She might lose the element of surprise if seen. Instead, she went straight for the front door. A row of azaleas six months past their blooms lined the front of the house and led to the screened porch. The door there swung open easily and sprung back closed.

Abi paused, wondering if someone would open the door to the house, but no one did. There was no doorbell, only a bronzed brass door knocker. She banged it three times, wondering how often visitors ever actually came.

It sounded like some type of music was playing, but it stopped abruptly. Someone fiddled with the knob on the other side, and finally the door opened wide. "Hello, Abi. What a surprise!"

"Good morning, Judge. Just wanted to come by and check on you."

"Check on me? Why, whatever for?"

Abi looked past Judge Foster but saw nothing out of the ordinary. A living room with hardwood floor, couch and loveseat, bookshelves flanking a fireplace on the far wall. "They said you cancelled court."

Judge Foster lowered her eyebrows in a puzzled frown. "I knew with, you know, considering, what happened to your husband, that you wouldn't be up for it."

Abi nodded. "I appreciate your consideration. But they said you decided to cancel next week too. That made me think you must be sick. Or having surgery or something."

The judge scoffed. "No, no. Just a vacation I've needed for some time. Thought it might be a good time to work it in while the dust settles here." She smiled. "You seem to have something on your mind, Abi. Would you like to come in for a cup of coffee?"

Abi blinked. This was unexpected. But okay, why not play along? "Sure, Judge. I'd love to. I drink it black."

Music was playing toward the back of the house as the judge led Abi through the pristine living room and into a small kitchen. A square wooden table sat between two chairs in front of a window with a view of the front yard, and Abi took a seat. The judge filled two coffee cups and sat down across from Abi. "I see you parked oddly."

Abi forced a chuckle. "Silly me. Wasn't paying attention." She peeked toward her Tahoe but saw no movement there. *Kids on their phone, not paying any attention.* Maybe it wasn't smart to bring them. If she needed their help, she was in way too much trouble already.

This was a stupid idea.

"What do you have there?" Judge Foster nodded at Abi's hand.

Abi shrugged. Too late to turn back now. She set the yearbook on the table. "My kids were looking at it at the hospital."

"Ahh, 1987. I should be in there somewhere." The judge opened it and searched the glossary for a moment before flipping back to the middle of the book. She blinked and fidgeted in her seat ever so slightly before closing the yearbook. "That was a long time ago."

Abi stared at the judge, measuring her next words carefully. She took a deep breath. "Interesting photo on page sixty-three, isn't it?"

"Page, uh, page sixty-three?"

"I saw it too, Judge. Didn't remember that."

"What?"

Abi was all in now. "Says right there in black-and-white. You and Alethia Abbott were the best of friends. You certainly look the part, all happy and hugging."

"I know Alethia, yes. We were close once."

"Were you still close in 2006? Twelve years ago, when her article series nearly cost Case his job? Don't I remember you were working in the school music department then?"

"It's possible, yes. I'm not sure of the dates. You should watch yourself, Counselor."

"It just made me wonder, you know? If I've learned anything in the past week, it's that revenge is often served cold. And I do believe you had a thing for my husband in high school, am I right? And Alethia recently told Case she was sorry about what happened, that she just had a bad source. A source which we have known for years had to have been someone in the high school system. But that's all water under the bridge, eh? What concerns me now is something you said on Monday at Devlin James's arraignment."

"What are you talking about?" Judge Foster stood and waved her hand as if to delete the prior sentence. "On second thought, I think it's time for you to go."

Abi stood and faced her. "I'll tell you what I'm talking about. You told me to go easy on the personal attacks and cautioned me about criticizing the speck in someone's eye. I know the reference. It's from the Bible. Don't notice the speck in another's eye when you have a beam in yours. I thought you were referring to what happened with Case all those years back. Of course, I know now that you were behind Alethia's story all along. But then you said something else. You said it was ironic that I get lost in the weeds sometimes. I didn't understand why that was ironic at the time, but I do now. You were talking about Kyle."

Judge Foster's jovial countenance had shifted to mirth. "It is unfortunate that he decided to become a weed farmer, you must admit."

"Yes, yes it was, although his motives were pure. But here's the problem, Judge. On Monday morning, no one but VJ, Buster, Kyle, and whoever they might have told knew about that plan. How did you know?"

The judge blinked hard, and her jaw dropped, and Abi knew she had her. She had seen that look too many times in interrogation rooms and on witness stands. "VJ told you, didn't he? I'm curious, did he call himself Proffit or Elijah or something else with you?"

"We are done here," Judge Foster said. "You are finished. I'll... I'll have you disbarred. I suggest you go home and reconsider your career plans."

"Oh, you want me to go home? Well, guess what, my home is being ransacked right now, at your direction."

"Who says?"

"Sheriff Wayne Rappaport says. And it wasn't his idea to get my house searched; it was yours. You recommended it. You issued the warrants. He as much as said so himself."

"Get out."

"That's a nice distraction, isn't it, Judge? Where is Lily?"

Judge Faith Anne Foster reached for her phone. "I'm calling 911."

"Good. I'll ask them to search the house while they're here. By the way, how is your black BMW X3 driving these days? I hear black SUVs are popular around Amberton. Gabe Liston has one. You have one. The person who's been dropping VJ off at the marina to get his boat has one. That was a nice touch, by the way, planting Lily's pony in Gabe's car.

"But I suppose you heard, word on the street is that Buster was souring on his mom's suave new boyfriend because he was becoming more and more scarce as her bank account did, too. Buster was certain that Proffit had another middle-aged female in his sights. Had Proffit—VJ— promised you y'all were going to move away and live happily ever after together?"

"Shut your mouth!" The judge was crying now.

"How does it feel to be a pawn, Judge? To know you're going to prison for a long time?" Abi inched toward the living room. Lily was in the house. She knew it. Music had been playing in the living room but moved to the back before the front door was opened. It had taken Abi a minute to place it, but she recognized the song. It was from the animated movie *Frozen*. Her little Elsa was here. And Abi would get her out at whatever the cost.

"Get out!" Judge Foster reached and jerked a kitchen knife from a wooden block. "Get out!"

Abi darted out of the kitchen but didn't go through the front door. Instead, she headed down the hall, flinging open one door after another. "Lily! Lily! Lily" Nothing. Nothing. Nothing. At the last door she stopped and grasped the knob.

"Let it go, let it go!" The voice of Elsa belting out the words resonated through the door.

Abi sensed the judge closing in and looked back.

Judge Foster stood at the entrance to the hall, blocking any exit. She gripped the knife at her chest, nostrils flaring, blood in her eyes. "I'll do what I have to do," she said.

Abi pulled her S&W Ladysmith .38 Special revolver from her coat and leveled it at Faith Anne Foster's chest. "So will I." She flung the door open as she had the others, expecting Lily to jump up and come to her. And possibly to have to shoot to save them both.

The room was empty.

A small television perched on a dresser was on, playing the animated hit just as expected. The bed was made without so much as a dimple in the bedspread. Everything else was in order. A tiny closet was open and completely empty.

Abi pivoted back to face Judge Foster. "I don't understand." She held her aim. "Where is Lily?

Foster dropped the knife to her side and backed away. Tears streamed down her face. She gestured toward the front door. "Get out, please."

Abi holstered her pistol and trudged toward the door, suddenly overwhelmed with doubt and utter regret. She eyed the judge to make sure she didn't attack her from behind. Abi wondered if a stabbing might be a welcome relief from the misery she felt, but Faith Anne Foster wasn't studying her. Instead, she went out the back door.

Abi moved across and out the screened porch and made her way toward her vehicle. How could she be that stupid? What did it take, five minutes—ten, tops—to utterly ruin her career? Not just that, but she would likely spend some time in jail for this. Her mind was too jumbled to even construct what charges applied, but there would be plenty to choose from.

What would Case say? How much would them investigating her actions distract from the search for Lily? What if it was already too late for her? Would she even get to the highway before they showed up to arrest her? A patrol car might be in the immediate vicinity.

Abi reached for her phone to call Case but decided against it. He had enough on his plate right now. She would call Jack instead, but only after telling Kyle and Kellen what was about to happen. She didn't want to be on the phone when the blue lights descended upon her. They deserved to know first.

Just as she reached the vehicle, Kyle jumped out and moved to the back seat. Abi opened the driver's side door and fell back into the seat, defeated.

Kellen giggled, and Abi felt something moving against her seat from the back. "Stop, Kyle," she said. "I've got bad news."

Kyle made a snickering sound.

"Stop!"

Then Abi heard a giggle behind her. But this time it wasn't Kyle's.

She turned to look behind her, over the console.

Lily was staring her in the face, smiling.

"Surprise!" Kellen and Kyle said at once.

"Lily? Lily!" Abi reached back and brought the child's face to hers, clutching her.

"You said watch for anything unusual," Kellen said. "We thought Lily peeking through the curtains was unusual, so we sneaked in and got her while y'all were talking."

Lily nodded. "Yes, yes they did. Ms. Faith said to sit criss-cross on the floor and don't move and I would get hurt and be in big, big trouble if I left the room, but Kyle and Kellen said it was okay. Am I in trouble?"

Abi burst into tears. "No, baby, you're not in trouble. You're perfect."

Lily's smile was as warm as sunshine. "Can I go home now?"

433

EPILOGUE

Spring 2023

DEVLIN James laughed and pretended to try to dodge the square of cake that Jessica Johnson James, his new bride, crammed into his face. She made no such attempt and opened wide for the oversized bite he fed her. The crowd around them laughed and clapped.

Abi hooked her arm into mine. "They make a beautiful couple, don't they?"

"No doubt about it." Jessica reminded me of Abi, with a strong will, even features, and black hair, though she didn't have my wife's knockout blue eyes. She was an infinite improvement from Lena Cole, from whom Devlin had finally moved on after seeing the light at the end of a tumultuous two-year relationship. "I think they'll be very happy."

Someone rammed a shoulder into me from behind. "What a day! What a day!" Jack laughed as I pitched forward and braced myself for him to ram me again. "A little light in the britches there, bud."

I stood upright and patted my midsection. "Abi has me on a diet. Getting me ready for retirement in a couple years."

"Not exactly," Abi said. "Maybe retire from coaching, but you'll have to find something else to do or you really will get fat."

"Can't retire from coaching any time soon," Jack said. "Gotta get ol' Devlin up and going."

I watched Devlin celebrating and thought about how easily his life could have taken a different path. Jack had stuck with him even after his relationship with Tammy had ended abruptly and especially after she had moved away to Oklahoma with the trucker she met online. Now, largely thanks to Jack's support, Devlin was a month away from graduating from college and beginning his new job on the Amberton High School football staff.

"I'm proud of him. I know you are." I nodded toward the woman standing behind Jack, watching the newlyweds. "How was your anniversary trip?"

Jack shook his head and reached back to coax her into our conversation. "Case wants to know how we liked Martha's Vineyard."

Dana Masterson wore a champagne dress that highlighted her slim waistline and sleek, muscular shoulders. Other than her wedding day, it was the only time I had seen the FBI agent in anything other than pants, and she carried it perfectly. She smiled. "I thought it was marvelous. Nantucket was great too."

"Too bougie for me," Jack said.

Abi laughed. "Bougie? Where'd you learn that word?"

"From Emma, of course."

Dana patted Jack on the back. "You didn't seem to complain when you were stuffing your face with all the lobster rolls."

"True that," Jack said. "On second thought, maybe we should go back next year for anniversary number three."

"Maybe we'll come too, huh, babe?" Abi said.

I shuddered at the thought. The lobster rolls sounded good, and a getaway with Abi even better, but my life wasn't getting any less expensive. Kyle, a wildlife management major at Mississippi State, and Kellen, a kinesiology pre-med major at

Ole Miss, seemed to find creative ways each and every month to drain my bank account with some new school expense. "Let's talk about it if you get the DA job."

Jack winked at me. "I know you're proud of them."

"Speaking of proud," Abi said, "when's the due date?"

Jack gave Dana a blank expression, and she rolled her eyes. "September first," she said. She looked past me, and her expression brightened. "Speaking of… there she is. Janie!"

Janie stepped into our circle and hugged Jack then Dana. "Hey, Mr. Case, Ms. Abi."

The bulge in her abdomen had grown since the last time I saw her. "Jack was telling us your due date," I said.

"Bull." Janie gave Jack a playful backhanded punch on the arm. "He never can remember. It's September first."

Dana elbowed Jack from the other side, and he winked at me again. He liked the attention from his girls. No way was he forgetting that date.

"Is Buster excited?" Abi asked.

Janie beamed and craned her neck, looking around the room. "He is beyond excited. He was hoping to get off work and get here, but I don't see him." She looked down and patted her belly. "And you can't imagine how excited Ms. Judith is."

She didn't have to explain. Nothing could replace the loss of a child, but a new baby boy in the family would help soften Judith Shane's loss. To hear Jack tell it, she still struggled on a daily basis with Ronny's death, almost five years later.

Being in a near-death state when Ronny was killed had made the blow even more harsh. Fortunately, Gracie and Jet had made it their personal mission after returning from Africa to make Judith comfortable in her last days, only to find out she didn't have cancer after all.

VJ had been poisoning her and fabricating discussions with doctors all along, to the point there was "nothing else that could be done." Physically, she was fine now. Mentally, she still had a ways to go. Maybe baby Shane would help.

Not so fortunate was VJ's other local victim. Faith Anne Foster had died quietly and alone while in prison serving her sentence for kidnapping Lily. Abi said the official death certificate had listed cardiac arrest as the cause of death. Jet had said that only meant that her heart stopped, which meant very little since everyone's heart stopped when they died. He suspected she had broken heart syndrome, a legitimate cardiac diagnosis with an official name I couldn't pronounce. We would never know for sure.

My thoughts turned to happier things. "What about Lily? Is she ready for a brother?"

Janie laughed. "What do you think? She's making lists of things she plans to teach him."

"Where is she, anyway?" Abi asked.

"Probably warming up a microphone," Jack said.

That child had discovered a love for music, and she could fill a room with a voice like an angel. I followed Janie's gaze and spotted her laughing and talking rapid fire while looking at a phone screen, flanked by two other children whose smiles were as broad as hers. Her porcelain skin tone contrasted with the ebony of theirs, but their smiles matched perfectly.

"Wonder what they're talking about?"

I turned to see Jet beside me. "I don't know, but I think they're having more fun than we are."

"No doubt about it. I'm sure Colleen and Cathy will be begging for Lily to spend the night before this event is over."

"And you and Gracie will say yes."

"Yep," he said, chuckling. "I guess that's the least we can do."

"Yeah, sure," I said. "It's about time y'all stepped up and did something for them." I was joking, of course. The girls might not fully appreciate it yet, but one day they would. The two sisters had hit the jackpot in the world lottery when Jet and Gracie had shown up to volunteer at their orphanage. Little had they known, they would soon be on an airplane to America as children of two of the best parents the country had to offer.

Abi nudged me. "The band is starting."

"And?"

"And come on." She grabbed my hand and led me to the edge of the dance floor, where Devlin and his new bride were dancing to Restless Road's "Growing Old With You."

After a few minutes, Dana stepped in to dance with Devlin in his mother's absence, and Jessica's father took her hand. He kissed her on the cheek and whispered something in her ear that made her wipe a tear away.

"Remember when that was us?" Abi hooked her arm in mine like she so often did and nestled close against me. "We've come a long way, haven't we?"

I nodded. "And a long way to go, I hope."

The band closed the song and then transitioned into some background guitar picking for a moment.

Jack took the microphone and got everyone's attention. "What a great day! I'm so happy to have all of our friends here to share in this. Now is the time when everyone gets to dance together to honor the new couple, and we have a very special guest to lead us. Let's all give a big hand to welcome the one and only, Lily Shane!"

Lily stepped up, grinning broadly. Jack gave her the

microphone and motioned for everyone to gather around.

Lily smiled and waved toward the back of the room. "Hi, Daddy."

I spotted Buster there, his smile as big as his biceps. He waved back.

The band began playing, and Abi pulled me to the center of the dance floor. Jack and Dana joined us, as did Jet and Gracie. The tune was more whimsical and upbeat than I expected, but it was perfect.

Lily took it from there, belting out the iconic theme from *Toy Story*—"You've Got a Friend"— in perfect tune and timing while we danced.

Indeed.

THE END

ABOUT THE AUTHOR

W. D. "Dwight" McComb earned a chemical engineering degree before deciding that a career in medicine was his true calling. He is board certified in internal medicine and specializes in wound healing and hyperbaric medicine, currently serving as the medical director of wound care services for the largest non-metropolitan hospital in America.

His books have garnered numerous awards, but with every keystroke of *The Truth that Lies Between*, *Anatomy of the Truth*, and *Truth on the Brink*, his goal has been to create and share astonishing stories drawing readers into the adventures of characters they will never forget.

He is the proud father of three children and lives in northeast Mississippi with his wife and whichever of the children happen to be home at the moment.